The Montanari Marriages

Wedding bells ring for the Montanari family...

by Mills & Boon Romance bestselling author
Rebecca Winters!

Brother and sister Valentina and Rinieri
Montanari have never had time for love—in
the Montanari family, work comes before
everything else.

Yet when romance blossoms unexpectedly,
will they both find themselves saying "I do"?

A hospital mix-up brings single mom
Valentina a whole new family in
The Billionaire's Baby Swap

Alessandra has always been overlooked in favor
of her more glamorous twin. Dare she hope
billionaire Rinieri is different? Find out in
The Billionaire Who Saw Her Beauty

Let Rebecca Winters enchant you with this
heartwarming and emotional duet!

THE BILLIONAIRE WHO SAW HER BEAUTY

BY
REBECCA WINTERS

First Published in Great Britain 2016
By Mills & Boon, an imprint of HarperCollins*Publishers*
1 London Bridge Street, London, SE1 9GF

© 2016 Rebecca Winters

ISBN: 978-0-263-91983-7

23-0516

Rebecca Winters lives in Salt Lake City, Utah. With canyons and high alpine meadows full of wild-flowers, she never runs out of places to explore. They, plus her favourite holiday spots in Europe, often end up as backgrounds for her romance novels, because writing is her passion, along with her family and church. Rebecca loves to hear from readers. If you wish to email her, please visit her website at www.cleanromances.com.

This is for my super marvelous father,
Dr John Z. Brown, Jr., who was adored
by his many thousands of patients during
his long career. I've praised him before in
other books because he was the best!

CHAPTER ONE

"SIGNOR MONTANARI?"

Rini was just getting in the limo. He looked around in the direction of one of the reporters who'd followed him outside the doors of the fourteenth-century Palazzo Colonna in Rome. Dozens of them had assembled to cover the European Congress of Businessmen.

"A moment of your time, *per favore*—one piece of news I can use for my lead story in *La Repubblica*?"

Why not?

"Since Italy imports almost all of its hydrocarbon demand, a doubling of domestic production would help the country reduce its energy bill. I'm planning to find them in Italy."

"Where?"

"That's my secret for now."

The reporter beamed for having been given a partial scoop. "*Mille grazie, signor.*"

He nodded and closed the door before his driver took him to the heliport for the flight to his mountaintop villa in Positano, on the Amalfi Coast. Now that the two-day September conference covering the economic problems facing Europe was over, Rini was eager to explore his latest project. On Monday he'd be leaving for the coast of Southern Italy, but tonight he had other plans.

Once the helicopter landed on the pad behind his villa, he jumped down and found his housekeeper, Bianca, out by the pool watering the tubs of flowers. She looked up when she saw him.

"Welcome back."

"It's good to be home."

"How's your father?"

"Well as can be expected." Rini had flown to Naples after yesterday's session and spent the night with his *papà*, who seemed to be handling the loss of Rini's mother a little better these days. She'd been the heart of their home and Rini would always miss her happy, optimistic spirit.

"Was the conference beneficial?"

"I'm not sure *beneficial* is the right word. *Chilling* would be more accurate. Europe is in trouble economically, but I'd rather not think about that tonight."

"Do you want dinner?"

"I'd love one of your meals, but I'm meeting Guido tonight. It's his birthday." His best friend from childhood, the son of Leonides Rossano, who owned Rossano shipping lines, had texted him earlier in the day:

The parents are throwing a party for me on the yacht. Please say you can make it. I know you're at a conference, but I need your advice about something serious. By the time you arrive it will be breaking up so we can talk in private.

The message sounded serious, even for Guido, who clearly wasn't in a celebratory mood. He obviously had no plans for the weekend with a woman. His friend was as bad as Rini, who had no plans in that department, either. The two of them made quite a pair, but for entirely different reasons.

Guido was still looking for the right woman who hadn't come along yet. Rini didn't have the same problem. The right woman wasn't out there for him because she wouldn't want him when he had to tell her he was infertile. An old soccer injury he'd suffered in his youth had made it impossible for him to give any woman a child.

The pain of that realization had grown worse with every passing year, increasing his dissatisfaction with his own personal life. Whenever he did meet a woman he cared about, he held back, not allowing the relationship to develop into something deeper. It always came down to his fear she would reject him if she knew the truth.

He'd been denying his deep-seated needs for such a long time, he'd forgotten what real fulfillment was like. Since his sister Valentina—the mother of two children and now ecstatically married—had recently moved out of his villa, his unhappiness had deepened.

She'd lived with him through her whole pregnancy. He'd helped her with the baby when she'd first come home from the hospital. He'd loved every minute of it, but he'd carried a secret pain in his heart because he knew *he'd* never be able to be a birth father. When she'd married Giovanni and moved out, Rini felt the emptiness of the villa. It echoed the emptiness in his soul for what could never be.

Valentina's happiness, not to mention that of his younger brother, Carlo, who enjoyed a wonderful marriage and had a little girl, heightened his awareness that the key element in his life was missing. He envied his brother for being able to give his wife a child. Rini's doctor had told him he was a fool to let that prevent him from falling in love. "The right woman will be able to handle it," he'd reminded him.

Rini didn't believe it as he walked through the villa to his suite and stripped for a shower to get ready. After slipping into his black tuxedo, he reached for the wrapped gift he'd bought for the occasion. Once he'd said goodbye to Bianca, he left for the helicopter. The new hand-tied fishing fly he'd purchased for Guido was reputed to bring results. They often fished the mountain streams for trout. He thought his friend would be pleased.

Twenty minutes later he landed on board the Rossano luxury superyacht moored in the Bay of Naples, reminding him that not everyone was feeling the economic crunch. The yacht boasted seventeen staterooms and all the amenities of a five-star hotel, including a swimming pool and dance floor.

Twilight had descended, lending magic to the spectacular surroundings of one of the most beautiful and photographed bays in the world, with Mount Vesuvius in the background. He told his pilot to come back later and jumped down as Guido strode over to him.

"I've been waiting for you. Saw you on the evening

news. Impressive stuff. I was afraid you wouldn't be able to make it. Thanks for coming."

"As if I'd miss your birthday." He pulled the small package out of his jacket and handed it to him. *"Buon compleanno."*

They gave each other a hug, then walked into the salon-cum-bar for a drink. He opened his present and held up the lure. "Just what I need."

"Good. Let's go fishing next weekend. I'll clear my schedule for next Saturday." Rini had been working himself into the ground and needed a break.

"Perfect." With a smile of satisfaction he put the present in his pocket. With dark blond hair, good-looking Guido could have his pick of any woman. The money behind his family name made him sought after and somewhat cynical, as he feared no woman saw him for himself. Guido was the best friend Rini could ever have had. He hoped the only son of Leonides Rossano would end up one day with a woman worthy enough to win his heart.

Rini's name and wealth made him a target, too. Women came on to him, causing him to question if any of them loved him for himself. Coupled with his problem of infertility, Rini imagined it was possible he'd end up a bachelor for good.

"Was it a nice party?"

"Different. One of the big fashion houses asked Father for permission to film a show on the yacht. You missed the whole thing."

"Sorry about that. The meeting in Rome went longer than anticipated."

Rini followed him down the steps to the deck, where he greeted his friend's parents and family, who made up some of Naples's most elite socialites and were beautifully dressed. Rini was well acquainted with many of them. An orchestra played music and the drinks were flowing.

They moved over to the area where a smorgasbord had been set up. By now he was hungry. After filling his plate, he joined his friend at one of the tables away from the others, where they could eat and talk alone.

"Your text said you wanted advice. What's going on with you?"

Guido started to say something when his father broke in on them. Two attractive women with long hair he hadn't seen before were with him. Rini exchanged a glance with his friend, who looked annoyed at the interruption. They both got to their feet.

"Dea Loti and Daphne Butelli, may I present my son Guido and his best friend, Rinieri Montanari."

"How do you do," Rini said, eyeing both of them.

"You missed their show, Rini," the older man interjected.

"As I indicated earlier, I was unavoidably detained on business."

"Well, you're here now. They have to leave on the tender in a few minutes. Maybe you could give them a dance before they go?"

Guido's father never stopped hoping his son would meet the woman he couldn't live without. Rini knew his friend was upset at being railroaded, but agreed to the request. "It would be our pleasure."

He gravitated toward the woman closest to him, who was dressed in purple. After walking her over to the dance floor, he drew her in his arms. "I've never been to a fashion show before. I'm sorry I missed it."

"I doubt it's the kind of thing the CEO of Montanari's generally does on the weekend." By now Guido was dancing with the other model.

"I understand it's hard work. Did you have a chance to eat yet? We don't have to dance if you're hungry."

"Thank you, but no. I don't want anything. I have to watch my figure."

"Well, your discipline definitely shows."

She flashed him a beguiling smile. "Do you live in Naples?"

"No, but I work here."

It surprised him when her hands slid up his chest and around his neck. "Daphne and I are going to be in Naples one more night because of an afternoon show at the Grand Hotel Parker's, then we have another show in Rome. Perhaps we could get together tomorrow evening for dinner after the show?"

Her eyes stared up at him in unmistakable invitation.

"I'm afraid my plans are indefinite at the moment, but I've certainly enjoyed this dance with you."

She held her smile. "Well, if you straighten them out, call me around seven at the Grand Hotel Vesuvio, where I'm staying, and ask for Signorina Loti." In the next breath she planted a hungry kiss on his lips he hadn't been prepared for. Then she darted away.

Rini went back to the table to wait for Guido. In a few minutes his friend joined him. "Sorry my father did that to us." One eyebrow lifted. "After the kiss she gave you just now, are you going to see her again?"

"No." Her pushy style had put him off. "What about you?"

"Not interested. You know damn well Papà told her you're the most eligible bachelor in Italy, next to me, of course." He said it without mirth.

Rini shook his head.

Guido studied him. "Maybe she decided to try the direct approach to get beneath your armor."

"I'm afraid it didn't work."

An exasperated sigh escaped. "Papà doesn't know when to give up. In fact it's because of him I need to talk to you. I've made a decision to take a year off from the family business to invest in something I really want to do. He won't like it, but I want your opinion. Come on. Let's get a drink in the bar."

Rini followed him, wondering what was on his friend's mind.

After a dive with colleagues that produced no new finds, twenty-eight-year-old Alessandra Caracciolo returned home late Monday afternoon. Bruno Tozzi had left his scuba gear in the cruiser with hers and would come by for it in a day or two. Instinct told her he'd done it on purpose so he'd have an excuse to see her again.

Since their last dive, when Bruno had buddied her, he'd made it no secret that he wanted to be with her all the time, but she didn't have romantic feelings for him. Though she dove with him and their friends for their work, that had to be the extent of their relationship. The next time they were together, she would make it clear she wasn't interested and never could be.

She tied the boat to the dock of her family's private pier. Garbed in flip-flops and a man's long-sleeved shirt that she'd thrown over her blue-and-white polka-dotted bikini, she headed for the Land Rover with her duffel bag.

Once in the car, she drove on sand past the helipad and around to the front of the castle. When she reached it, she would take a shower and wash her hair. Alessandra wore it neck-length because she spent so much time in the water. It dried fast and the natural curl made it easy to take care of.

As she pulled up near the main entrance, she saw a limo parked in the courtyard, making her curious. All vehicles came across the causeway from the mainland at Metaponto, a port town of Basilicata, Italy. But after five o'clock, any visitors were escorted out by staff.

Their family's castle on the tiny island of Posso off the Ionian coast dated back to Queen Joanna of Naples, who ruled in 1343. Besides tourists from Bari and Taranto, who were allowed visits to the castle four hours a day on Tuesdays and Wednesdays with a guide, dignitaries from the world over called on her father, Count Onorato Caracciolo, asking favors because of his influence in the region.

Alessandra got out of the car and hurried inside past the tapestry of the queen hanging on the wall in the huge front foyer. She headed for the grand staircase, eager to make herself scarce until she'd cleaned up.

The moment she reached the first step, a deep male voice called to her. *"Signorina?"*

She whirled around to see a tall, incredibly gorgeous dark-haired man in a charcoal-colored business suit walking toward her, his dark brows furrowed. Still holding the duffel bag in one hand, Alessandra clutched the railing with the other.

He stared at her so strangely. "I thought I was hallucinating, but it *is* you. Since Saturday night you've cut your hair. I don't understand. How did you know I was coming here today? On the yacht you told me you had another show to do in Rome," he murmured.

The way his piercing black-brown eyes played over her face and figure, she knew he had a history with her identical twin, Dea. He was the most striking male Alessandra had ever seen in her life. She found herself envying her beautiful sister for having met him first and couldn't fault her taste. Men had never been able to resist her.

Alessandra cleared her throat. "I'm sorry, *signor*, but I'm not Dea."

Embarrassed to be caught looking so messy and disheveled after her diving trip, she ran up the steps without looking back. Her sister would never allow herself to be seen like this. All the way to the next floor she felt the man's penetrating eyes on her retreating back and bare legs, causing her to tremble.

Had her sister finally met the one she'd been looking for? Dea had always kept their family identity private. Because she was a model, she called herself Dea Loti so no one would know she was the daughter of Count

Caracciolo. For her to divulge her secret to this man meant their relationship must have turned serious, otherwise he wouldn't have known where she lived.

No doubt she'd invited him to come. Did she want the family to meet him? But his scrutiny of Alessandra led her to believe he hadn't looked pleased to see her here. Maybe Dea hadn't told him she had a twin. Alessandra didn't know what to think.

If only she hadn't arrived back from her dive trip until tomorrow, this wouldn't have happened and she wouldn't be haunted by that man's image engraved on her mind. It shocked her to realize that at long last there might be an important man in her sister's life. Alessandra knew her sister's quest had been to find the perfect man while she made the most of her modeling career. Their parents would be overjoyed.

Six years ago she and Dea had gone through a terrible experience involving a man, one Alessandra had hoped to marry. But when he met Dea, he fell for her and followed her to Rome. Their relationship didn't last, but the pain of betrayal had cut Alessandra like a knife and it had taken a long time to recover. Since the falling out with her sister, no man of importance had come into either of their lives.

In the last two years she'd tried to put the past behind her and get back the friendship they'd once shared. Dea came and went from home according to her hectic schedule and their family had enjoyed some good times. Evidently this past summer Dea had found romance after she'd gone back to Rome. Love on a yacht, no less… If that gorgeous man owned it, then he could keep her in the lifestyle she desired.

But for some reason Alessandra had been oddly upset by the encounter in the foyer, unable to understand why. *Except that she really could…* These days her own love life was nonexistent.

Once inside the bedroom, Alessandra plopped the duffel bag on the floor and got out of her clothes. Her mind was still on Dea, whom she hadn't seen for six weeks. Her sister had developed an interest in fashion and modeling at an early age and that hadn't changed.

Alessandra led a different life altogether. She couldn't remember when she didn't have an interest in the archaeology of this region of Italy. The island castle itself was built on an ancient archaeological site. Since college she'd been involved in several multidisciplinary studies in the field of archaeology within a Mediterranean perspective, with particular emphasis on Southern Italy.

Without being able to scuba dive, she could never have achieved her dream to do the necessary underwater work with friends she'd made among the archaeological staff at the University of Catania. Scuba diving wasn't for everyone. Dea couldn't understand her passion for it, but it didn't matter because their parents approved and supported both her and Dea in their individual endeavors.

After a shower and shampoo, she blow-dried her hair, then dressed in pleated tan pants and an ivory-colored linen blouse. With an application of coral frost lipstick, she left the room on khaki wedges and went in search of her parents. They'd married for love and were very close. Unlike many couples, they did everything together whether it was for business or pleasure. Though Alessandra had never discussed it with Dea, their parents' happy marriage had been the ultimate role model for both sisters.

On the way to their apartment she saw Liona, the wiry housekeeper who'd come to work for them at eighteen and had been with them ever since. She was like another member of the family and ran the large staff with precision.

"If you're looking for your *mamma,* she left for Taranto two days ago to help your aunt, who fell and broke her hip."

"Oh, no! Poor Fulvia."

"She'll be all right, but your mother will probably be gone for a few more days."

"I need to call them."

They started down the staircase together. "I'm glad you're back. You know how your father worries."

Liona was the one who worried about Alessandra. She thought scuba diving was dangerous. Alessandra gave her a hug. "It's good to see you. How's Alfredo?" Liona's cat had been sick.

"The vet says he's getting old and shouldn't go up and down stairs."

"I'll help carry him for you."

"Bless you. Did you have any luck on this last diving trip?"

"I wish."

"Oh, well. Another time. Are you hungry? I'll tell the cook."

"Please don't bother her. I'll find something to eat later. Thanks, Liona."

She hurried toward her father's office, wondering if the male visitor was still with him, then scoffed with impatience because the man was on her mind at all.

"Ciao, Papà."

"Alessandra!" Her grayish blond father stood up from his desk and hugged her. "You were gone too long this time."

"It was only a week."

"We always miss you. Did you have a good time?"

"Yes, even if we didn't find anything of significance." She walked around to sit in one of the leather chairs facing his desk. "I'd much rather know about you and mom. Liona told me Zia Fulvia broke her hip and Mom went to Taranto to help her."

He nodded. "Your aunt will make a full recovery. Your mother could be back tomorrow."

"Oh, good. So tell me what else has been happening while I've been away."

His brows lifted. "Something unexpected. I'm glad you're back so we can talk. More than anyone else I want your input because you have a fine mind."

"I got it from you and Mamma." Her comment produced a chuckle. So maybe her assumption had been right. "It wouldn't have anything to do with the man I saw in the foyer earlier this evening, would it?"

He cocked his head. "Actually it would. When did you see him?"

"I'd just come in the castle when he spoke to me."

"Did he introduce himself to you?"

"No. It wasn't like that. On my way up the staircase he mistook me for Dea before he headed for your office, that's all."

Her father nodded. "I guess I shouldn't be surprised. Her face is everywhere."

"Papà—" She smiled at him. "Are you pretending with me?"

"About what?"

"Was he here because of her?"

The count blinked. "Not that I know of."

"Oh." She needed to keep her thoughts to herself. "Who is he?"

He smiled. "If you didn't live in your world of books and ancient underwater artifacts, you would have recognized him as the CEO of Italy's most powerful engineering dynasty, Rinieri Montanari."

She stirred in the chair. "Of course I recognize the Montanari name. Who wouldn't?" It explained the man's aura of authority.

Her father sat back and touched the tips of his fingers together. "His family has accumulated great wealth. He's the brilliant one driving the company to new heights. A week ago he made an appointment to come and see me about a business proposition."

"That sounds interesting."

"I'll give you a little background. Night before last he was on the news following the European Congress of Businessmen held in Rome. I saw the gleam in his eyes. He said he had secret plans to grow the economy.

Today we talked and arranged for him to come back tomorrow to get into the details."

He'd aroused her curiosity. "What is he after?"

"He'd like to drill for oil on our property."

Alessandra shifted in the chair. "He and dozens of others who've wanted the same thing for the last half century," she muttered. "Since he knows it's not for sale, why is he coming back?"

"This man is different from all the others. He wants to lease the land."

Lease? "Are you considering letting him?"

"I'm thinking about it."

"Wow."

Her father eyed her curiously. "Why do you say that?"

"I thought our property was inviolate."

"Leasing isn't the same thing as selling."

"You're right."

"Alessandra, something's on your mind. Why did you ask if he was here because of Dea? Has your sister confided in you about him?"

"No, Papà. In fact I haven't spoken to her for almost two months."

"Hmm. If he'd met her before, he didn't mention anything about meeting her to me."

"Why would he if he didn't know anything about our family?"

"But what if he does know? It makes me wonder what came first, the chicken or the egg?"

"What do you mean?"

"He might have met Dea before he ever called me."

Alessandra was trying to understand what her father was getting at. "Why is this troubling you so much?"

"I'm your loving *papà*. My daughters were born princesses of the Houses of Taranto and Caracciolo. Because of our family history, you know I've always wanted to protect you from unscrupulous men."

His explanation surprised her. "That sounds like medieval thinking. Papà, you don't honestly think the CEO of Montanari Engineering fits in that category?" *That gorgeous man? The one she'd envied Dea for meeting first?* Alessandra didn't want to believe it. Something about him had impressed her deeply.

"Though we don't use the titles anymore, there are some men who try to calculate the monetary worth of our family. There's nothing they would like more than to acquire your bank accounts and assets more than your love."

Alessandra frowned. "The man comes from his own family dynasty and doesn't need more."

"One would assume as much, but for some men one dynasty isn't enough." His gaze swerved to hers. "I don't want to think it. But if he has targeted Dea to marry her and eventually gain possession of our property, I don't like the thought of it."

She didn't like it, either. Not at all. "Personally I don't believe it." Alessandra didn't want to believe it. Not about that man. Whatever history her sister and Signor Montanari might have together, she didn't want to think about it. To be with a man like him...

Alessandra got to her feet. "Don't let it bother you, Papà. Have you had dinner yet?"

"No."

"I'll bring you something."

"*Grazie*, but I'm not hungry."

"I'm afraid I am. I haven't eaten since I got back. Excuse me while I grab a sandwich. If you want me, I'll be in the library."

Alessandra left the office and headed for the kitchen to find something to eat. Afterward she walked to the castle library on the main floor, the repository of their family history where she could be alone. Years earlier she'd turned one corner of it into her own office, complete with file cabinets and a state-of-the-art computer and printer, plus a large-screen television for viewing the many videos she'd compiled. This had been her inner sanctum for years.

She sat down at the desk and got back to work on the book she was writing about Queen Joanna. Just as she'd settled down to get busy, the phone rang. It was her father.

"Papà?"

"I just wanted to let you know I've got business in Metaponto. The pilot is flying me in a few minutes."

"Do you want company? I'll go with you."

"Not tonight, *piccola*." Her father's endearment for her. When Alessandra was born, she was the younger twin by three minutes and the name *little one* stuck. "I'm sure you're tired after your scuba-diving trip, so you get some sleep and we'll talk in the morning. I could be gone a couple of hours and will probably get back late tonight."

"All right."

While she got back to work she heard her father's helicopter fly away. She kept busy for another hour, then went upstairs to get ready for bed. But when she slid under the covers, she didn't fall asleep right away. Memories of the past with her sister filtered through her mind.

Though their personalities were entirely different, she and Dea had been as close as any two sisters until college, when Francesco had come into Alessandra's life. She'd fallen in love and they talked about getting married. But before they got engaged he met Dea, who was more confident than Alessandra and had already started her modeling career.

Her sister had a beauty and lovability that had drawn guys to her from her teens. By contrast, Alessandra felt rather dull and unexciting. Certainly she wasn't as attractive. But she'd always accepted those truths and never let them affect their friendship. Not until Francesco had laid eyes on Dea. From that moment everything changed. Alessandra felt herself lose him and there wasn't anything she could do about it.

He followed her sister to Rome and she never saw him again. Francesco sent Alessandra a letter explaining he couldn't help falling in love with Dea and hoped she wouldn't hate him too badly. As for Dea, Alessandra didn't see her for two months. When her sister came home, she told Alessandra she was sorry for what had happened. She explained that Francesco had done all the running, and she'd soon found out he was a loser. Alessandra was lucky to be out of the relationship.

The trauma of being betrayed by Francesco and her

sister had completely floored her. It had taken a long time to work past the pain. Though they'd shared sisterly love in the past, from that time on they'd had a troubled relationship and two truths emerged. Alessandra didn't know if she could trust a man again and Dea would always be the beautiful one who usually got the best of Alessandra. People seemed to love her the most.

Alessandra had to live with the knowledge that she was known as the clever one, a scholar with a sense of adventure. She'd thought that by the age of twenty-eight she would have finally gotten past her jealousy of Dea's ability to attract men. But it wasn't true. Otherwise meeting Signor Montanari, who'd met Dea first, wouldn't have disturbed Alessandra so much.

If her father was right, what a sad irony that this man might be using Dea to get what he really wanted, making both sisters appear as poor judges of character. First the chef Alessandra had fallen for who couldn't remain faithful once he'd laid eyes on Dea. Now Signor Montanari, who looked like the embodiment of a woman's dreams. But what if her father learned this man had a secret agenda? The troubling thought kept her tossing and turning all night.

CHAPTER TWO

ON TUESDAY MORNING Alessandra awakened and headed to the bathroom for a quick shower. She dressed in jeans and a blouse. After brushing her hair and applying lipstick, she walked down the hall past the stairs to her parents' apartment wearing her sandals.

She knocked on the door with no result, so she opened it and called out, "Papà?" He was probably in the sitting room drinking coffee while he read his newspapers, but the room was empty. Frowning, she retraced her steps to the staircase and hurried downstairs to the small dining room where the family ate breakfast. Maybe she'd find her father there.

The second she opened the doors, she received a shock. Her sister stood at the antique huntboard pouring herself a cup of coffee.

"Dea! What a surprise! It's good to see you!" She looked beautiful as usual in a stunning blue dress and high heels. Alessandra rushed over to hug her. "Where's Papà?"

"In the office."

"I didn't know you were coming home." She reached for a glass of juice and a roll.

"Neither did I until I got a phone call from him last night."

"You did?" That was news to Alessandra. He must have called her on his way to Metaponto.

Dea's eyes darted to her without warmth. "He told me Rinieri Montanari had come to the castle to do business with him and wanted to know if I had been dating him. He seemed concerned enough that I decided to make a quick trip home to talk to him about it."

"He's always trying to protect us, you know that."

They both sat down at the banquet-size table. "What I'm curious about is how *you* know Rinieri Montanari." The tone of her sister's point-blank question had an edge. There had to be another reason her sister had made a sudden flight home. Alessandra didn't begin to understand what was going on.

"I don't! Didn't Papà tell you? Signor Montanari was in the foyer when I came in from my scuba-diving trip yesterday. As I started up the staircase he called out to me. I had no idea who he was. He thought I was you."

"Did he say anything else?"

"Only that he acted surprised you were here at the castle and commented that you'd cut your hair since he'd been with you on the yacht. He said you'd told him you had another show to do in Rome. I took it that's why he seemed shocked to find you here. I told him I wasn't you, then I went up the staircase. That's it."

Dea sipped her coffee slowly. "So he mentioned the yacht."

"Yes."

She could hear her sister's mind working. "Is that *all* he told you?"

Dea sounded so worried, Alessandra was perplexed. "I swear it."

Her sister's mouth tightened.

"Have you worked this out with Papà?"

She put down her empty cup. "Not yet, but I will when we fly back to Metaponto in a few minutes."

"But you just got here last night!"

"I have to return to Rome for another show. As soon as Papà finishes up business with Signor Montanari, he's flying me to the airport." She checked her watch. "They've been together for the last half hour."

With nothing more forthcoming, Alessandra knew she'd been dismissed and rose to her feet, feeling chilled. "Then I'll say goodbye to you now." She leaned over to kiss her cheek.

Until Alessandra could talk to her father alone, she would have to wait to know what had gone on. Dea was going back to Rome without clarifying anything about her relationship with Rinieri Montanari. In fact she hadn't been this cold to Alessandra in a long time.

She left the dining room without saying anything and rushed down the hallway to the library, where she could get to work.

When her phone rang two hours later, she saw that it was her father and clicked on. "Papà? Where are you?"

"At the airport in Metaponto, waiting for your mother. She's flying in from Taranto."

Thank goodness. Alessandra needed to talk to her. "Has Dea gone back to Rome?"

"After our talk this morning I put her on the plane."

"You sound more calmed down. Is everything okay?"

"There was a misunderstanding that was all my fault, but I've spoken with Signor Montanari and it's been cleared up."

Except that Alessandra still knew next to nothing. She gripped her phone tighter. "I'm relieved for that. How did Dea seem? She was chilly with me."

"That's because I upset her. After I apologized for minding her business, I explained it was my way of being protective to prevent her from being hurt in case Signor Montanari wasn't being sincere. You did absolutely nothing wrong, so don't worry about it. Now the main reason for my call. Do you have plans for the rest of the day?"

"I'm working on my book."

"Would you have time to do me a favor?"

"Of course."

"Signor Montanari is going to be our guest for the next few days."

What? Alessandra almost fell out of her chair. The change in his attitude toward the other man was astounding.

"He needs someone knowledgeable to show him around today. Since I don't know how long I'm going to be gone, you're the only one I trust to drive him and answer his questions. Your work with the institute has given you vital insight into the importance of any changes or disturbances to the environment here in the south. Will you do it?"

His compliment warmed her heart, but it was already getting a workout because it meant she would be spending time with a man whose name was renowned throughout Italy. Her father had yet to explain what he'd found out about Dea's relationship with Signor Montanari.

"Yes." But Alessandra was so attracted to him, she would have to be careful it didn't show. No way would she give her sister a reason to suspect her of coming on to him when she'd met him first.

"Get him back in time, *piccola*. I've asked him to join us for dinner. Liona has put him in the guest apartment on the third floor. He's probably eating lunch right now. Your mother's plane is arriving so I have to get off the phone. *A piu tarde, figlia mia.*"

Rini had just finished a second cup of coffee when the beautiful woman he'd seen yesterday on the stairs walked in the dining room. He should have realized right away that she wasn't quite as slender as Dea, but he preferred her curves. "Signor Montanari? I'm sorry if I've kept you waiting. I'm Alessandra." She sounded slightly out of breath and looked flushed.

Earlier in the morning, after the count had asked him about his relationship with Dea, he'd left the castle for the airport. Rini thought it odd to be questioned about her, but he let it go.

At that point the count said that while he was gone, his daughter Alessandra would give him a tour of the property. According to him, she understood the impact of drilling on the environment better than anyone else and he would be in the best of hands. If she was an engineer, Rini had yet to find out.

He got up from the table. "We meet again. I've never met identical twins before."

"Dea's the older sister by three minutes."

"Which accounts for the difference," he teased. "I can see that." He smiled and walked toward her. "Call me Rini."

After a slight hesitation she shook the hand he extended. "*Benvenuto a Posso*, Rini. Papà told me you'd be our guest for a few days and asked me to show you around today."

"That's very kind of you, but I don't want to inconvenience you." He couldn't read her thoughts.

"It's all right. Papà said this was important."

She'd dressed in a simple short-sleeved peach top and jeans. Her tanned olive skin indicated she spent a lot of time in the sun. His gaze traveled from her cognac-brown eyes to her neck-length slightly tousled brown hair rippled through with golden highlights.

As she pulled her hand away, he noticed she didn't wear nail polish. The reason she looked so natural was her lack of makeup. Except that she did wear lipstick, a coral color that blended with the golden tone of her skin and drew his attention to her voluptuous mouth.

He remembered Dea's mouth being sculpted the same way before she'd kissed him. How remarkable that identical twins could look so much alike, yet on closer inspection were so different.

"Your father said you're the one who knows everything."

"Oh, dear. I hope he really didn't say it like that."

Rini got the idea he'd embarrassed her. "He meant it as a compliment."

"I'm his daughter so he has to say it," she commented in a self-deprecating manner. "If you're ready, we can go now."

"Please lead the way."

He followed her ultrafeminine figure out of the castle to a Land Rover parked near the main doors. Rini had done his homework. Her island home was renowned as an Italian treasure. What a coincidence the castle was home to both women!

Before Rini could credit it, she climbed in the driver's seat. "You'll need to move the seat back all the way to accommodate your legs," she said after he opened the passenger door.

One corner of his mouth lifted as he did her bidding and climbed in. They attached their seat belts and she took off across the causeway to the mainland. She drove with expertise, as if she could do it blindfolded. After leaving the small town of Metaponto, they headed for verdant hills that were covered in ancient olive groves.

"My father explained why you're here. Now that we're on Caracciolo property, tell me why the CEO of Montanari Engineering wants to lease this particular piece of property in order to drill. A lease means taking on a lot of controls." She didn't mince words and was all business.

"Your land may not be for sale, but a lease means compromise that benefits both parties and could be lucrative." Rini looked out over the mountainous, sparsely populated province of Basilicata. "Hidden in the arch of Italy's agricultural boot is the home to Europe's biggest on-shore oil field."

"That's what I've heard."

"Italy produces one hundred and twelve thousand barrels a day, one tenth the North Sea's level. My goal is to double Italian oil production within the next five years. If not on your land, then I'll find others because as you know, the south is underdeveloped."

"Your goals are very ambitious."

"Agreed, but the potential of this particular untapped oil field is huge. We're hoping to drill for the billion-plus barrels of crude oil that lie beneath it. Your father and I are hammering out ideas to preserve the existing environment while drilling for oil to boost the suffering Italian economy."

"You sound like a politician."

"Everyone should be concerned over our country's unemployment problems. I'm particularly anxious for us to bring down the country's twelve-percent jobless rate through new employment. The goal will be to obtain oil, yet maintain sustainable development of agriculture that will offer real career paths for the future."

"I have to admit you make a good case." She kept driving to the top of a ridge that overlooked the huge valley. Onorato Caracciolo was a clever man to send Rini out with his daughter first. Rini had a hunch it would be a smart idea to win her over to his idea since her father appeared to place great trust in her knowledge and intelligence. But after the misunderstanding involving his other daughter, he needed to walk carefully.

"If you wouldn't mind stopping, I'd like to get out and look around."

She pulled off the road and turned off the engine. While he walked a ways, she climbed down and rested one curving hip against the front fender to wait for him. When he returned she said, "I know you see oil beneath the property. But what I see is a fertile field that has been here for centuries. Your plan would create giant, unsightly scabs."

His eyes narrowed on the features of her beautiful oval bone structure. "If you're imagining dozens of derricks, you'd be wrong. My gut instinct is to build several right here in the shadow of the mountain out of sight. The existing road to the south travels straight to the sea, where the oil would be transported to tankers. One would barely be aware of the activity."

"And if you find it, does that mean more derricks?"

"We'll make that decision later."

Her softly rounded chin lifted. "What if you don't discover any?"

"Preliminary reports from this part of Italy indicate vast reserves. We'll find it, but we'll proceed slowly with your father having the final say in how long we are allowed to drill. Let me ask you a question."

"Go ahead."

"If I were to appeal to Queen Joanna herself and explain the benefits, what do you propose she would say? Forget how long ago she ruled. Your father tells me you're a historian writing a biography on her. Your research means you know her better than any other living person today. Was she a risk taker?"

He could hear her mind working.

"She backed Antipope Clement VII against the unpopular Urban VI. For that she was given this papally owned land eventually bequeathed to our family. So yes, I'd say she was a risk taker."

Rini's lips twitched—he was fascinated by the knowledge inside her brain. "You think she would have granted me an audience?"

She stared at him. "I have no idea."

"Humor me and put yourself in Joanna's place."

A smile broke the corners of her mouth he found more and more enticing. "It was a man's world. I wouldn't have trusted any of them. You, particularly, wouldn't have been given a second audience."

"Why single me out?"

"Because you're handsome as the devil, increasing the odds of Joanna being tricked. Give me a little more time to think about your ideas that have persuaded my father to give you a hearing."

"You mean you're not tossing me out on my ear just yet?"

She opened the driver's door. "Of course not. That's for Papà to do." On that note she climbed in and started the engine.

He went around to the other side, glad to hear she wasn't shutting him down yet. "In that case, let's take the road that leads to the sea. En route you can tell me more about the subject of your future best seller."

"I'd rather you gave me more reasons why you think this project of yours outweighs the many negatives. My father will want a report to run by my mother and her sister, Fulvia. The property comes through my father's line, but he always leans heavily on the opinions of his wife and sister-in-law."

"Who makes the ultimate decisions?"

"When it comes to business, the three of them go back and forth until there's a consensus."

"He's a man surrounded by women."

She smiled. "As my Aunt Fulvia says, behind every successful man *is* a more successful woman."

Food for thought. "Do your parents love each other?"

"Very much."

"That's nice. Before my mother died, my parents had the same kind of relationship."

"I'm sorry for your loss. It sounds like you've been lucky to have great parents too," she murmured on a sincere note as they started down into the valley. "What does *your* father think of this latest idea of yours?"

"Though he and I are always in consultation over business, this is one time when he doesn't know where I am, or why." He angled his head toward her lovely profile. "I've taken this time to do reconnaissance work on my own. I told no one where I was going, not even my best friend. That's why I was so surprised when I thought you were Dea. I couldn't figure out how you could have known my destination."

She darted him a questioning glance. "So it really was pure coincidence that you had business with our father?"

"I was introduced to her as Dea Loti. But the misunderstanding has been cleared up. The simple fact is, I thought you were she. But I shouldn't have called out to you before I'd met with your father for an explanation, then none of this would have happened. To be honest, I wasn't ready for you to disappear on me the way you did."

Her pulse sped up. *Did he just say what she thought he said?*

"I was a mess and hoped no one would see me sneak in the castle."

"Not from where I was standing."

She swallowed hard and appeared to grip the wheel tighter. "When Dea and I were younger, we got taken for each other a lot. Not so much now that she's become a top fashion model. She's the true beauty. I've always believed I looked different even though we're identical. But I'm aware other people can't always tell the difference. Under the circumstances I understand why my shorter hair gave you a shock."

Not just her hair. As he was coming to learn, many things about her were different from her sister and other women. She was so genuine and charming, it knocked him sideways. "Your hair is attractive and suits you."

"Thank you."

"I can see why your father wants to protect you." Rini decided not to argue the point further when her physical beauty was self-evident. But Alessandra Caracciolo had been born a twin and he'd heard it could be a blessing and a curse, so he left it alone.

They'd reached a crossroads that would take them back to Metaponto and the causeway, but Rini wasn't ready to go home yet. To his surprise he found he wanted to get to know her better. *Much better.* Besides her intelligence, she spoke her mind and was like a breath of fresh air. "Do you have time to drive us along the coast? I want to inspect the shipping access."

"We could do that, but if you want to get a real feel, you should view everything by boat."

That idea sounded much better. "When we reach Metaponto, let's find a marina where I can charter one for tomorrow."

"You don't need to do that. I'm sure my father will want to take you out on our cruiser so you can talk business."

"Then let me buy you dinner in town in order to repay you for driving me around today."

"Thank you, but that's not necessary. My parents are expecting you to eat with them and I have plans after we get back."

He had no right to be disappointed that she'd just turned him down. She was probably involved in a relationship right now. Why not? She was a stunning woman. He imagined that men flocked to her.

After having shown him around the property for her father, she'd done her duty and had other things to do. Though it was none of his business, for some odd reason the possibility of her being interested in another man didn't sit well with him.

Wednesday morning Alessandra was just getting out of the shower when her phone rang. She reached for her cell and checked the caller ID. "Mamma?"

"*Buongiorno*, darling."

"I'm so glad you're back home. How's Zia Fulvia?"

"I thought she was better. That's why I came home yesterday. But after your father and I finished having dinner with Signor Montanari last evening, we got a call from her. She's having a bad reaction to her new pain medication and it has frightened her. I told her we'd fly to see her this morning. Your father and I are on our way to the airport and will stay with her for another night to watch over her."

"I can't believe you've already gone," Alessandra said in surprise. "I haven't even seen you yet." She needed to talk to her.

"I know. Where did you disappear to last evening? I expected you to join us for dinner."

"I'm behind on my book. After I brought Signor Montanari back to the castle, I went straight to the library to work."

Before Signor Montanari's explanation about Dea, Alessandra had tried hard to hide her attraction to him. But once she knew he and her sister were not involved and never had been, the news had thrilled her so much, she might have given herself away if she'd gone to dinner with him.

"I'm sorry we missed you, darling. I want to hear all about your scuba-diving trip, but it will have to wait another day." Alessandra had already forgotten about that. "Your aunt is really distressed."

"The poor thing. Give her my love and tell her I'll visit her soon."

"She'll love that. By the way, your father wants to know if you would be willing to show Signor Montanari around again? Today he wants to explore the coast by boat. Would you take him out on the cruiser?"

She sucked in her breath. "First let me ask you a question, Mom. What do you think about his idea to lease the property for drilling?"

"To be honest, I don't like the idea at all."

"I didn't think so."

"It seems a travesty to change anything about the land or what lies beneath it. Your father knows how I feel. Though your father believes Signor Montanari's ideas have merit, I'm not persuaded. There's a great deal to discuss before anything is decided."

"It sounds like Papà doesn't feel as strongly as you."

"Let's put it this way. He likes Signor Montanari's vision and is willing to hear more. What's your opinion?"

"He talked a lot about bolstering the economy by providing more jobs. My suspicion is that he's hoping to run for a high-level government position and this could be the feather in his cap."

"He's a brilliant man. That's what brilliant men do." *But not with Caracciolo land.* That's what her mother was really saying. The time Alessandra had spent with him yesterday had persuaded her he was worth listening to, but these were early days. "Alessandra? What's wrong? You don't sound yourself."

"I just wish I hadn't brought Dea into the conversation when I was talking with Papà. He ended up phoning her."

"Your father told me what happened. But when he learned that Signor Montanari had been a guest of Leonides Rossano on his yacht the other night and happened to get introduced to Dea, your father realized he'd made something out of nothing and overreacted. It certainly didn't have anything to do with you."

"But I didn't know the truth until Signor Montanari told me as much while I was driving him around."

"I'm sorry. It's understandable you thought he and your sister were involved."

"I didn't know. When I saw Dea at breakfast yesterday, she didn't explain anything."

"Well he made it clear to your father that meeting Dea was like ships passing in the night."

"But maybe Dea had hopes it could be more." Already Alessandra knew a man like Rinieri Montanari only came along once in a lifetime. She and Dea weren't twins for nothing.

"Why do you say that?"

"If their chance meeting had been so insignificant, how come she flew home last night?"

"Because your father was worried."

"He was," she conceded. "But she didn't even come in my room to talk to me."

"Alessandra—during dinner I got the impression that the CEO of Montanari Engineering is a force to contend with. If he'd been interested in your sister, he would have made future plans to let her know how he felt."

"You're right, but what if she finds out I'm showing him around?"

"What if she does?" After a silence, she asked, "You're attracted to him, aren't you? Otherwise you wouldn't think twice about this. There's nothing wrong with that! I'll admit my heart skipped several beats when I met him at dinner last night."

Her mother's instincts were never wrong.

"He said he truly enjoyed being shown around by you. I could tell he meant it. Don't blow up a simple misunderstanding your father has apologized for into something major."

"You're right. I'm being foolish."

"You are. Go ahead and show Signor Montanari around until we get back from Taranto. I'll call you tonight."

"Okay. Love you. Give Zia Fulvia a hug from me."

Alessandra hung up, realizing she was transparent to her mother, who understood the situation completely. She felt better after their talk. The longing to be with Signor Montanari again was all she could think about.

She pulled on a pair of pleated khaki pants and a blouse with a small tan-on-white geometric print. Once dressed, she went downstairs to the kitchen for coffee and a roll. The cook made her some eggs. While she ate, Liona poked her head in the door. "Alessandra? Did you see Alfredo when you came down the stairs?"

"No."

"He ate his food, but now I can't find him. He usually stays on the main floor while I'm working around. Maybe he's gone off sick somewhere."

"I'll look for him." She ate a last bite, thanked the cook, then began a search, wondering if Signor Montanari was around. "Alfredo—" She called his name several times. When she reached the front foyer, she worried that he'd slipped past some visitor at the entrance.

She opened the door and almost ran into the gorgeous man who'd haunted her dreams. He was just coming in. The sight of him made her heart leap. He held the big marmalade cat in his arms.

"*Buongiorno*, Alessandra," he said with a white smile. "I've been waiting for a limo and found him lying outside the door wanting to get back in."

"Liona will be so relieved. Here. I'll carry him to the kitchen."

"I'll be happy to do it."

"I don't mind."

She could tell he didn't want to give up the cat, who seemed perfectly happy to be held by him. It surprised her because Alfredo didn't like many people. "Then follow me." She opened the door and showed him the way.

Liona was thrilled to see them walk in the kitchen. The housekeeper reached for her cat.

"He found Alfredo outside the castle," Alessandra explained.

"The poor thing is getting confused. I'll take him back to my apartment. *Grazie, signor.*"

"*Prego, signora.*"

Alessandra trailed him out of the kitchen. "That was very nice of you. Her cat is getting old." She followed him to the entrance, but there was no sign of a limo yet, only three tour buses bringing tourists to tour the part of the castle open to the public. "I hope the driver didn't already come and leave."

"I'll call to find out." He reached in his jeans pocket.

Her eyes traveled over his rock-hard body. His blue crewneck shirt had the kind of short sleeves that only looked good on a man with a well-defined physique. In a minute he clicked off. "It'll be a while due to an accident near the causeway."

"What were your plans?"

His veiled gaze slid to hers. "To charter a boat."

"There's no need to do that," she said on impulse. "Since my father isn't here to take you, he suggested I drive you where you want to go in our cruiser."

"But that means interrupting your work."

"It's all right. As Papà reminded me, you're a busy man. Since you're here, you need to make the most of the time. I'll do my own work later." The talk with Alessandra's mother had taken away the guilt she'd been harboring over Dea. There was nothing she wanted more than to spend more time with him.

"Then I'll call off the limo."

"While you do that, I have to run in and get a few things. I'll meet you at the Land Rover in five minutes."

Alessandra hurried inside and up the staircase to her room. Her heart raced abnormally hard to think they were going out on the boat together. She filled her duffel bag with some necessary items, then rushed back down to the kitchen and stashed water and snacks in the top of it. She never knew how long she'd be gone, so she never left without being prepared.

When she walked out to the car beneath a semi-cloudy sky, she found him waiting for her with his own backpack. It had been years since she'd felt this alive around a man. This time when she unlocked the door with the remote, he opened her door and relieved her of her duffel bag so she could get in. He walked on around and put their things in the back before climbing inside.

"Our cruiser is docked on the other side of the island." She started the engine and drove them the short distance.

"It's right in your backyard!"

She smiled. "I know. Can you believe how convenient?"

Once she'd pulled up to the pier, they both got out. He obviously knew his way around a boat. After depositing their bags, he undid the ropes while she got on board and found them both life preservers. She put hers on first.

"Who's the scuba enthusiast?"

"You're looking at her."

His piercing dark brown eyes scrutinized her. "How long have you been a diver?"

"Since I was nineteen. Have you ever done it?"

"I learned at fourteen. It's probably my favorite activity."

His admission excited her no end. To scuba dive with him would be like a dream come true. "Mine, too," she admitted. "Excuse me for a minute."

She disappeared below and pulled out a special oceanography chart of the area for him to look at. When she came up on deck she discovered he'd climbed on board and had put on his preserver. "Here." She put the rolled-up chart on the banquette next to him. "You can look at this as we proceed." Alessandra started the engine at a wakeless speed and drove them toward open water.

"This cruiser is state of the art."

She nodded. "A huge change from our old boat I took everywhere until my father bought this for me so I could go on longer trips."

"For pleasure?"

"It's always a pleasure, but I'm part of a team working for the Institute of Archaeological and Monumental Heritage."

Her response seemed to surprise him. "Where did you go to college?"

"I received my master's degree from the University of Catania. Our job is to identify and retrieve buried structures of archaeological interest."

"Living on an archaeological wonder, you come by your interest naturally."

She nodded. "My area of academics is to study the advanced techniques for nondestructive testing and remote sensing. Hopefully our work will expand our knowledge and help restore the historical buildings above and below the water in this area of Italy."

He sat on the banquette across from her with his hands clasped between his knees. She felt his eyes probing her with new interest. "It's no wonder your father told me I would be in good hands with you. You're an archaeologist. I thought maybe you were an engineer.

"Your father knew that you're exactly the person I need to consult while I'm here. Like you, I'm anxious to identify where the drilling will cause the least amount of destruction to the environment, both on land and water."

"Tell you what. After I give you a tour of the coastline, we'll go to my office at the castle. Since you're an engineer, you can watch a series of videos we've produced that will open your eyes to the many roadblocks you'll have to consider in order to drill and transport oil."

"I'm indebted to you, Alessandra."

"You have no idea what kinds of snags you're up against, so don't get too excited, *signore*."

"Call me Rini," he urged for a second time in his deep male voice that affected her insides. "I like snags. They make life exciting."

Though she agreed with him, she needed to be careful not to let this man get under her skin. Alessandra had a hunch he wasn't just talking about the search for oil. He had a way of infiltrating her defenses no matter where she turned. She had a feeling that if she got involved with him, he had the power to hurt her in ways that she would never get over.

"Why don't you consult the map I brought up? It will explain a lot as we go."

As they cruised along the coast, she glimpsed a half smile that broke the corner of his compelling mouth before he did her bidding and unraveled it for his perusal. He was such a breathtaking man, she could hardly concentrate.

It was hard to believe he wanted to be with her and not Dea. For some reason Rini Montanari hadn't been interested in her sister. She couldn't comprehend it.

Probably Dea hadn't been able to comprehend it, either. But Alessandra didn't know what went on in her sister's mind and would be a fool to make any more assumptions about anything.

Just be excited that he wants to be with you, Alessandra.

CHAPTER THREE

BY FIVE IN the afternoon Rini had seen as much as he needed for a preliminary assessment. Alessandra had been a fountain of knowledge. Depending on Onorato's willingness to continue their talks, he wanted to bring out a team from the Naples office to begin an in-depth exploration.

But at this point business wasn't on his mind. During their outing he'd grown hungry. She'd brought along water and snacks, but he wanted a big dinner and intended to surprise her by taking her out for a meal. He'd seen a helipad at the side of the castle and went below deck to call for a helicopter.

With her expertise she guided the boat to the pier and shut off the engine. He discarded the life preserver and jumped to the dock to tie the ropes. In a moment the rotors of the helicopter sounded overhead.

Alessandra looked up. "I guess my parents are back. That's a surprise. Mother told me they could be gone for several days." She removed her preserver.

"I think that's *my* helicopter."

She blinked. "You sent for yours?" Did he see disappointment in her eyes?

"I chartered one to take us to dinner. Last night you turned me down. Tonight I decided not to take any chances on another rejection."

Her eyes slid away from his. "Where are we going?"

Good. She'd decided not to fight him. "That's my surprise. Bring what you need and leave the rest in the boat. We'll retrieve everything later."

"You don't want to change clothes?"

"There's no need."

She nodded. "I'll only be a moment." Before long she came back up on deck having applied a fresh coat of lipstick.

Avoiding his help, she climbed out of the boat and they made their way to the helicopter in the distance. But she couldn't refuse him when he opened the door to assist her into the back. Their arms brushed and he inhaled her light, flowery fragrance, which made him more aware of her.

Within seconds they lifted off and the pilot flew them due east. For the next little while her gaze fastened on the landscape below. When they started their descent to the city of a hundred thousand, she darted Rini an excited glance. "I love Lecce! It's a masterpiece of baroque architecture."

"I haven't been here in several years, but I remember a restaurant near the cathedral and hope it's still as good."

He'd arranged for a limo to drive them into the city nicknamed the Florence of the South. They got out and started walking along the narrow, shop-lined streets to the square for their dinner.

Lots of tourists, plus music from the many eating

places, put him in a holiday spirit, something he hadn't felt in years. Alessandra stopped in front of every shop and boutique, all of which were made from the soft local limestone. The facades were a mass of cherubs. She delighted in their faces as well as the displays. He hadn't felt this carefree in years.

"Oh, Rini. Look at that precious cat! It reminds me of Alfredo." They'd stopped in front of a souvenir shop selling the famous *Cartapesta* items of saints and animals made out of papier-mâché and painted.

"I think you're right. Let's buy it for your housekeeper." Without waiting for a response, he lifted the three-inch orange crouching cat from the shelf and walked inside to pay for it. The clerk put it in a sack. When he exited the shop, Alessandra stared up at him.

"She'll be thrilled."

He handed her the gift. "Will you keep it until we get back to the castle?"

"That was very kind of you," she said in a quiet voice. After sliding it in her purse, they walked out to the square.

"If my memory serves me correctly, our restaurant is on the right, halfway down the colonnade. We'll eat what they bring us. There's no menu." After the call to arrange for the helicopter, he made a reservation at the famous restaurant. When they reached it, the maître d' showed them inside to a table that looked out on the square.

Mugs of *caffé in ghiaccio con latte di mandorla* arrived. She smiled between sips. "I'm already addicted to that wonderful almond flavor."

"Agreed. How about the antipasto?"

She experimented. "These are fabulous. I could make a whole meal on the salmon-and-oyster bruschetta alone."

"I like the little tortillas with olives."

"There's nothing not to like, Rini." Soon they were served angel-hair pasta with sardines. If that wasn't enough, they were brought mouthwatering apple crostinos for dessert.

"I'm so full, I don't think I can move. Thank you for bringing us here. I haven't had a meal like this in years."

He loved it that she enjoyed her food. "It's the least I can do after everything you've done for me. I'm in awe of your knowledge. Not only that, you're a master sea woman." He put some bills on the table, then got up and escorted her out of the restaurant. Night had fallen, adding to the beauty of the square.

"A *sea woman*? Sounds like a new species." Her soft laughter charmed him.

"Until your father gets back, I'm hoping to spend a few more days on the water with you. It's true I'm here on business, but I've decided to take a few days to mix pleasure with it."

He led them through a street to find a taxi so they could head back to the helipad at the airport. Once on board they took off, then he turned to her. "Your scuba equipment has been calling to me. How about we pick up some gear for me tomorrow and you take us where you go diving. I'll charter us a boat."

"That would be ridiculous when we can use my boat."

"I wouldn't want you to think I'm taking advantage of you."

"Can we just not worry about that?"

"That's fine with me. What I'd like to do is camp out. I'll be your buddy. Could I tear you away from your work that long, or would it be asking too much?"

After they reached the island and got in the car, she eyed him speculatively. "After the exquisite meal, it pains me to have to turn you down. I'm afraid I'm behind on my project, but you're welcome to take the cruiser and go exploring on your own."

He didn't believe her excuse. She could be warm and engaging, but if he got too close, she'd retreat. After finally meeting a woman who thrilled him in so many ways, he couldn't take the disappointment that she put other plans first. It was driving him crazy.

"If you don't go with me, I won't have a buddy. You're so smart and know so much, a trip without you wouldn't be fun. What if we go out early after your work is over for the day? Say two o'clock?"

"I'm not sure I can be finished by then." She got out of the car and started walking to the entrance in an attempt to elude him.

He caught up to her. "Then we'll play it by ear."

"You never give up, do you?" But she said it with a smile. "All right."

Those two little words gave him hope, but the minute they went inside the castle, Liona and her cat were there to greet them. "You have a visitor, Alessandra. He insisted on waiting for you. I've put him in the small salon."

Him? Maybe Rini had been right and she was seeing someone.

"Thank you, Liona." She pulled the sack out of her purse. "This is for you. Signor Montanari bought it for you."

The older woman smiled. *"Veramente?"* She opened the sack and pulled out the cat. "This looks like *you*, Alfredo. You must have bought this in Lecce!"

Rini nodded. "It caught our eye."

"Mille grazie, signor. Come on, Alfredo. Let's look at this treasure together." She put the cat in her arms. *"Buona notte,"* she called over her shoulder.

Alessandra's eyes darted to him. "You've made her night."

He cocked his head. "But it appears yours isn't over yet, so I'll leave you to your guest and see you tomorrow. *Dormi bene.*"

After wishing her good-night he headed for the stairs, which he took two at a time to his room on the third floor. Full of adrenaline because she'd finally agreed to be with him tomorrow, he pulled out his phone and returned Guido's call. Though it was late, his friend would probably still be awake. On the third ring he answered.

"Rini? I'd given up and was headed for bed."

"Sorry. I just got back to my room."

"Where are you?"

"In a castle on the island of Posso."

Guido chuckled. "Sure you are. So what's happening? Are we still on for Saturday?"

"I'm not sure."

"Don't tell me it's work again."

"Not this time."

"That sounds serious."

"I am. Have you got a minute?"

"Since when do you have to ask me a question like that? Go ahead. I'm all ears."

For the next little while he unloaded on his friend, leaving nothing out. When he'd finished, Guido whistled in response.

"In my gut I know Alessandra likes me, but she's keeping me at a distance. I asked her to go scuba diving tomorrow and she finally gave in, but she's not easy to understand. She doesn't wear a ring, but tonight a man was waiting for her when we got back from dinner."

"Then the first thing you need to find out is if she's committed."

Rini's brows furrowed. "I don't think she is. The housekeeper referred to the man as a visitor."

"All's fair then. Are you thinking she's being hesitant because you met her sister first? You know, that kind of unwritten law thing."

"Maybe."

"The only way to find out is go after her and learn the truth for yourself."

"I'll do it. Thanks for the advice."

After a long silence, his friend said, "I've been wondering when this day would come."

Guido wasn't the only one...

"I'll call you later in the week to make final plans for Saturday. Ciao."

He rang off, but he was feeling restless and decided to go for a walk before trying to get some sleep.

* * *

Alessandra waited outside the castle entrance while Bruno drove to the dock to get his scuba gear. When he came back, she approached the driver's side of his van. "Did you find everything?"

He nodded. "I'm sorry to have bothered you so late. I have to leave on the diving trip for the institute in the morning. I wish you'd join us. We'll be out there for another three days at least."

"What spot this time?"

"The same one. We haven't begun to explore that area thoroughly."

"I agree."

"Will you come? I know you're busy on your book, but we need your expertise." His gray eyes urged her to say yes. "I'd rather buddy with you than anyone else."

I know. But she didn't feel the same. "Bruno? Please don't take this wrong, but I want to keep our friendship on a professional basis and won't be buddying with you again."

He looked surprised. "Does this mean there's someone else?"

Exasperated, she said, "It means I'd prefer to keep my work separate from my personal life. I hope you understand."

Tight-lipped, he accelerated faster than necessary and took off.

"Someone didn't seem very happy," a deep male voice said behind her.

She whirled around in shock. "Rini, I—I thought you'd gone to bed."

"It's a beautiful night. I was afraid I wouldn't be able to sleep, so I decided to go for a walk around the castle. Did the fact that my kidnapping you to Lecce upset certain plans you had with your visitor?"

"If I'd had plans, I wouldn't have gone with you. That man was Dr. Tozzi from the archaeological institute. He came to get his scuba gear out of the cruiser. Tomorrow he's going on another exploratory dive with the others for a few days."

"You two dive together a lot?"

"There's a whole group of us. Last week we went out on our boats from Metaponto. He happened to be my buddy that trip, so that's why his scuba gear ended up in the cruiser. Tonight I told him he'd have to find another buddy because I would like our relationship to stay completely professional. "

"He doesn't have his own boat?"

"Yes, but he forgot to transfer his equipment after we'd finished. The institute has a state-of-the-art oceanography boat, but he won't bring it out until we've made a positive find."

"I see. Are you supposed to go out with them again?"

"Yes, but I have to divide up my time."

His dark brows lifted. "You're a very important person, besieged on every side, so I have an idea for tomorrow. While you work on your book for part of the day, I'll run in to Metaponto to get me some gear. Then we'll join your group. En route you and I can talk over your father's business. That way you can please everyone, including me. What do you say?"

She let out a sigh. Already he was reducing her to

mush. "I'll get up early and work until lunch, then we'll leave for Metaponto. The dive shop will have the gear you need. From there we can head for the dive site and meet up with the others."

"I'd like to stay out overnight and camp."

"I would, too. It's one of my favorite things to do."

"Good." His eyes blazed. "I shall look forward to it. I'll see you at lunch."

He took off for another run around the tiny island without giving her a chance to say anything else. Alessandra hurried inside the castle, secretly excited to go diving with him. Thoughts of buddying with him left her breathless. The idea that they would protect each other was so appealing she couldn't wait.

At six the next morning she showered and dressed quickly before heading to the library to work on her book. While she was knee-deep in research, Liona entered the library.

"Alessandra? Signor Montanari is eating his lunch in the dining room."

Her head lifted. "It's that time already?"

"*Si*. One o'clock."

"I can't believe I lost track of time. Tell him I'll be right there."

She raced out of the room and up the stairs to freshen up, then hurried back down with her packed duffel bag. When she entered the dining room he stood up to greet her. The man looked amazing in white cargo pants and a dark brown crewneck shirt.

"Sorry I'm late."

His dark eyes traveled up her jean-clad legs to her

white pullover, then found her gaze. "We're in no hurry. Sit down and eat lunch."

"I'd rather not take the time now. While you rent scuba gear, I'll grab us some food and drinks at the nearby deli to hold us over until tomorrow."

"With the announcement of an overnight on the water, you've made my day, *signorina.*"

Everything he said and did made her pulse race. Her feelings for him were spilling all over the place. She didn't know how to stop them. *She didn't want to stop them.*

He followed her out of the room with his backpack and they left for Metaponto in the cruiser. At the dive shop they loaded up with extra tanks. Once they'd bought drinks and groceries, they gassed up the cruiser and headed west. She handed him the special ocean chart he'd looked at before.

"We'll be diving at the midway point between Metaponto and Crotone. Some of the finds date back to the Magna Graecia. We're looking for some columns from the sixth century before Christ reputed to be there.

"If we're really lucky, we'll see the remnants of a temple dedicated to the goddess Hera. This area of the Ionian is a treasure trove, but as you realize, all the artifacts are buried, making them almost impossible to discover."

Rini looked up from the chart to flash her an intriguing smile. "It's the *almost* impossible that fires your blood, *non è vero?*"

She nodded. But artifacts weren't the only thing that fired her blood. The flesh-and-blood male who was a living Adonis had made her come alive without even trying. She'd taken one look at him that first evening in the castle foyer and had fallen so hard, she feared she would never recover.

It was too late to wish he'd gone back to Naples. Already she hated the idea that he would have to leave at all. Her thoughts were crazy. This was the renowned Rinieri Montanari she was talking about, not just any man.

Alessandra imagined that every woman who met him couldn't get enough. Even her mother had been bowled over by him. But the fact that he was still a bachelor meant there was a big reason he didn't have a wife.

Maybe he'd lost a great love and could never bring himself to marry. Or he enjoyed women, but couldn't commit to one for fear of feeling trapped. So no matter how attentive he was being right now, Alessandra would be a fool to think *she* would be the one woman in Italy who could do what no other female had done and win his love.

She glanced at him. "How long has it been since you went diving?"

Rini folded up the chart. "A year, but don't worry. You can count on me." Deep down she knew she could trust him. He engendered a confidence she'd never felt around other men. It didn't bother her that he'd just said he wasn't concerned about the time that had passed since his last dive.

"How have you stayed away from it so long?"

"Too much work."

"But there are lots of marvelous diving sites in the

Naples area. Surely you could have taken some time off."

"True, but even though the office is there, I don't live in Naples and am always anxious to fly home at the end of the day."

That was a surprise. "Where is home?"

"Positano."

"Oh—such a glorious spot with fabulous diving opportunities."

"My friends and siblings did it with me for several years, but for most of the last year my sister Valentina lived with me while she was expecting her baby. That meant no diving for her. As I told you earlier, we'd just lost our mother in a car accident. I divided my time between visiting my father at our family home in Naples and staying around the villa for my sister in order to keep her company."

Alessandra hadn't realized he'd carried such a load. She was touched by the way he cared for his family. "Did she have her baby?"

"*Si*. My nephew, Vito, is thriving. The man Valentina married has adopted him. They live in Ravello with his son, Ric. Both babies were born the same day at the same hospital."

"You're kidding—"

"What's really amazing was that the babies got switched. Valentina brought the wrong baby home while the man she married took home Valentina's son."

"What?" She almost lost control of the wheel. "How awful! Where was the mother?"

"They were divorced. At birth she gave up her mother's rights to Giovanni. It was a nightmare after the babies were returned to their birth parents. By then Valentina and Giovanni had bonded with the children. At that point they began to see each other so they could be with both babies and they fell in love."

A smile lit up her face. "That's the greatest love story I ever heard. How hard to love the wrong baby, but how sweet they were able to make everything work out. The person I feel sorry for is the mother who gave her child away. I can't comprehend it. I love my mother so much, I don't want to think what it would have been like if she hadn't been there for me. In fact I can't wait until the day comes when I can have my own baby."

He seemed caught up in his own thoughts before he said, "Fortunately she came to her senses and has now worked out visitation so she can help raise her son."

"That's the way it should be!" But Alessandra couldn't help but wonder about the father of his sister's baby. Still, she didn't want to pry.

"I can read your mind, Alessandra. Vito's father was one of Valentina's engineering professors at the University in Naples, but he didn't want marriage or children. My sister suffered terribly, but today she's so happy, you would never know she'd been through so much trauma."

Alessandra could relate to the trauma. Her hands tightened on the controls. She was living proof you could get through a broken heart and survive the emotional pain, but not everyone could end up as happy as his sister.

"So she's an engineer, too."

"Yes. A brilliant one."

"What does her husband do for a living?"

"He's the CEO of the Laurito Corporation."

Alessandra smiled at him. "That's an amazing combination. Your sister was blessed to have a brother like you to watch over her." She was coming to find out Rini was an extraordinary man. He'd even bought that little gift for Liona.

"Our family is close."

Alessandra could say the same where her parents were concerned. Before long she could pick out the red-and-white scuba flags from two boats ahead. "There they are!" The group had already started diving in an area near the coast. "If anything of significance is found, Dr. Tozzi will bring out the institute's boat. Today we're still exploring."

Alessandra brought her boat to a stop and lowered the anchor. After she raised her flag, she looked back at Rini. He'd already slipped on his wet suit. By the gleam in his eyes she could tell he'd been anticipating this dive.

"I'll be right back." She took her wet suit below to change. Talk about excited. She could hardly keep her fingers from trembling before going back up on deck.

In a moment they'd put on their weight belts and buoyancy-control devices. He reminded her of the film phenomenon James Bond. She finished dressing and put her goggles in place. "We'll be going down eighty feet. Ready?"

"Si, bellissima."

He shouldn't have said that to her. The deep tone of his compliment curled to her insides, disturbing her concentration. She ended up jumping in the water after he did, almost forgetting to keep her goggles and regulator in place.

The air temperature registered eighty degrees, but the water was cooler. Once below the surface she pressed the button to let out some air. The weights carried her down, down. Rini stayed right with her, watching her as their ears adjusted to the pressure. She could tell by the way he moved that he was a pro. It made her feel perfectly safe.

Eight minutes later they reached the sea floor with its clumps of vegetation and only a smattering of tiny fish. He stayed with her as she moved toward the area where she could see the group working. They all waved to her. She motioned for Rini to swim with her beyond the circle and examine a nearby area. The ridge in the distance looked promising, but as she brushed some of the debris away, it turned out to be more debris instead of a column lying on its side.

Rini found some interesting spots and waved her over to him, but every investigation came up short. She got the feeling they were searching in the wrong area. After a half hour he tapped his watch. She'd been about to do the same thing because it was time to go up and it would take a while.

They started the ascent, listening to the rhythm of their breathing through their regulators. She felt like they were the only people alive and loved this dive that had been magical for her. The sheer pleasure of enjoying this experience with him, of depending on him, could never be equaled.

Once they broke the surface, he helped her onto the

transom before levering himself on board. Before she could sit down on a banquette, another boat approached them.

"Alessandra—"

"Ciao, Bruno." She waved to him and the three others from the institute who rode with him.

"I was hoping you'd make it. Who's your friend?"

"Bruno Tozzi, meet Signor Montanari." The two men nodded. She refused to tell him anything about Rini. "It's too bad we haven't turned up anything interesting yet."

"We'll have to keep searching tomorrow."

Another of the divers said, "Why don't you join us in Crotone for dinner?"

"Thank you, but I'm afraid we have other plans. We'll do another dive with you in the morning."

"Bene."

In a minute their boat drove off. Alessandra was glad he'd gone and hurried below deck to get out of her wet suit. When she came up on deck a few minutes, she found Rini already changed into his clothes. He'd organized their gear near the back of the boat and had taken down the flag.

His eyes played over her. "It's growing dark. Do you have a place in mind where we can camp?"

"Yes. A small, secluded cove five minutes from here. I'll raise the anchor." She turned on the boat lights and they headed for the coast. Her heart fluttered in her chest when she thought of spending the night out here with him. Because she knew this area so well, they arrived quickly. She cut the engine and the momentum swept them onto the sandy portion of the isolated beach.

Alessandra turned to him. "Do you want to eat on deck, or in the galley?"

"Since the food is already up here, let's stay put, shall we? I'll do the honors and serve you for a change."

"Well, thank you."

In a minute he had everything laid out on the opposite banquette and they could pick what they wanted— fruit, meat pastries, cheese rolls, drinks, chocolate and almonds.

He sat back in the chair opposite her and feasted. "After that dive, this is heaven," he admitted with satisfaction.

"I can tell you're a seasoned diver, Rini. It was a privilege to be with you today."

"Now you know how I feel to have joined you. I'm excited about tomorrow's dive. Maybe we'll find something, but even if we don't, it doesn't take away from the thrill of being with an expert like you."

His compliments sounded so sincere, she was in danger of believing them. "I loved it."

After a brief silence, he said, "Dr. Tozzi was upset to see you out here with me, so don't deny it."

"I wasn't going to." She reached for some more grapes. "I'm glad you were with me. I've told him I'm not interested in him. Now he's seen it for himself."

Rini's dark brows furrowed. "Is that the reason I was invited along?"

He couldn't really think that, could he? It would mean he felt vulnerable. She couldn't imagine him having a vulnerable bone in his body. She leaned forward. "Of course not!"

He bit into another plum. "Is there an important man in your life?"

Yes. I'm looking at him. "Not in years."

"Why not?"

"I could ask you the same thing," she blurted without thinking. "Why does Rinieri Montanari sail alone?"

"I asked you first," he returned. "A beautiful, fascinating woman like you has to have a history."

Alessandra wasn't used to hearing those adjectives attributed to herself. If he only knew it, she was totally enamored with him. "You don't really want to know."

"I wouldn't have asked otherwise." At this point he'd put the leftover food back in the sacks she would take down to the galley later.

"I fell in love with Francesco at twenty-two. He was a chef from Catania when I was in my last year of undergraduate school. He swore undying love for me and said he'd found his soul mate. I believed him. We talked about getting married.

"One weekend Dea came to visit. I was excited for her to meet him. She stayed in my apartment with me and the three of us spent time together. After she left for Rome, where she was pursuing a modeling career, everything seemed to change. He suddenly told me he had to go on vacation and would call me as soon as he got back. During those two weeks he didn't phone me once.

"I thought I'd lose my mind until I heard from him. I imagined every reason under the sun for his absence except the one he gave me. He didn't have the decency to tell me in person. Instead, he sent me a letter telling me he'd fallen in love with Dea and knew I couldn't forgive him."

Lines darkened Rini's features in the semidarkness.

"At the time it was terrible. Dea didn't come home for two months. When she did, she told me he'd followed her to Rome, but it was over between the two of them almost before it had begun. She thought he was a loser and told me I was better off without him.

"Though inwardly I agreed, my pain had reached its zenith because Dea always had this power to get the boys interested in her. But when it came to Francesco, who I thought was committed to me, something broke inside me. I suffered for a long time. But it happened over six years ago and is buried in the past." She took a drink of water. "Now it's your turn to tell me the secrets of your heart, dark or otherwise."

CHAPTER FOUR

RINI FELT LIKE he'd been stabbed in the chest. Too many emotions rocked him at once. There was someone he needed to talk to before he bared his soul to Alessandra.

"I'm afraid my story would take all night. Let's reserve it for tomorrow evening after another dive. If you don't mind, I'd like to sleep up here tonight."

"Then you'll need the quilt and pillow on the bed in the other cabin in order to be comfortable."

"I'll get them."

"You sound tired after that dive, Rini. I am too, so I'll say good night."

"Buona notte."

He waited an hour before going below to bring up the bedding. Once he'd made himself comfortable on the banquette at the rear of the cruiser, he pulled out his phone and called his sister. Rini knew it was too late to be phoning, but he had to talk to her.

After four rings he heard her voice. "Rini? What's wrong? Has something happened to Father?"

"No, no."

After a short silence she asked, "Are you ill?" He

could hear Giovanni's concerned voice in the background.

"Not physically. But I'm wrestling with a problem that needs your slant. Do you mind?"

"What a question! After all you've done for me, I'd give anything to help you if I can. Tell me what's going on."

He raised up on one elbow. "Let me give you a little background." Without wasting words, he explained his dilemma from beginning to end.

"Ooh" was all she said when he'd finished.

"Forgive me if this touches too close to home, but you're the one person in the world who would understand her pain after Francesco went after her sister."

"Rini? I got over Matteo's womanizing and it sounds like she has gotten over her pain, too, so forget her past. You only have one problem. Let this woman know how you feel about her and prove to her that your love for her is everlasting. If Mamma were still alive, she would tell you to follow your heart and not let anything get in the way."

He could hear his mother saying those very words. "Alessandra was really hurt."

"So was I. It passes when the right man comes along. Trust me."

He breathed deeply. "You make it sound so simple."

"Nothing worthwhile is simple, Rini. But look what happened when I followed my heart instead of letting go of Ric, the baby I thought was mine..."

"You mean instead of listening to me tell you not to

get involved with Giovanni," he groaned. "I was a fool to interfere."

"Of course you weren't! I know you were only trying to protect me. But it all worked out and I'm now an ecstatic wife and the mother of two angelic boys."

His eyes closed tightly. "But from the start Giovanni wanted you enough to defy convention, too. That's why it worked."

"Rini, tonight you're alone with her on her family's cruiser. Do you seriously think that would have happened if she weren't absolutely crazy about you?"

"Her father asked her to show me around."

"But to dive? Camp out over night? Have faith, dear brother. A little patience wouldn't hurt until she realizes she can trust you with her life."

A lump had lodged in his throat. "*Ti amo*, Valentina."

"*Ti amo. Buona notte.*"

Rini lay back down, thinking about what she'd said. Even if a miracle happened and her attraction grew into love, she didn't know about his infertility, an insurmountable hurdle in his mind.

The next thing he knew, the sound of gulls brought him fully awake. Clouds blotted out the sun. He sat up to check his watch. Seven thirty. Was Alessandra still asleep? He gathered the bedding and took it below to the other cabin. Her door was still closed.

One thing he could do was fix them his favorite prosciutto ham and eggs to go with their breakfast. As he was putting their plates and mugs on the table, she appeared in the doorway wearing jeans and a T-shirt that molded to her beautiful body.

"You've got color in your cheeks."

"I went for a walk."

He'd had no idea. What a wonderful bodyguard he'd made! "If you'd wakened me, I would have gone with you. Sit down and I'll serve you."

"Umm. Everything smells good."

He poured them coffee and sat opposite her.

She took a sip. "How did you sleep?"

Rini stared at her through shuttered eyes. "There's nothing better than spending the night under the stars. What about you?"

"It's fabulous out here, but I confess diving makes me tired. I fell asleep once my head touched the pillow."

"That's good. How soon do we need to join the others?"

"They'll be out there by nine o'clock."

He swallowed the last of his eggs. "Just for the fun of it, what would you think if we enlarged the search area by traveling a quarter of a mile farther east from them to dive at the same distance from the coast?" He wasn't ready to share her with the others yet. "I consulted the chart. The depth of the sea floor isn't quite as great there. Maybe seventy feet. Who knows? We might make a discovery."

Her lips turned up at the corners. "Your mother must have gone crazy to have a son who went around with such an excited gleam for adventure in his eyes."

Rini liked the idea that she'd noticed. "Is that what I have?"

"Oh, yes. It probably got you into a ton of trouble." He chuckled. "So what do you say?"

"I like your idea. Later on this afternoon we can join the others for another dive."

"Sounds like a plan." Pleased she was willing to go along with him so they could be alone a little longer, he got to his feet to clean up the kitchen. She cleared the dishes and they made quick work of it. He'd never experienced this kind of togetherness with a woman before. Rini couldn't imagine letting her go.

"Thanks for fixing the delicious breakfast. I'll change into my wet suit and meet you on deck."

He bounded up the stairs to put on his own gear. To spend a whole day with her doing something they both loved couldn't have excited him more.

In fifteen minutes they'd arrived at the spot he'd suggested for a dive. They had the whole sea to themselves for the moment. She lowered the anchor and erected the flag. Together they put on all their equipment. "Ready?" he called to her.

Her brandy eyes clung to his, pulling at his heart strings. "Let's go!"

They jumped in the water. He experienced delight as they sank lower past more tiny fish. Once they reached the bottom, they explored around all the vegetation that grew taller and was more plentiful than at the other spot. He saw traces of some deep-sea-fishing tackle caught by the undergrowth. It was like playing hide-and-seek as they swam here and there like little children let out to play.

His eyes followed her as they moved through a new chute. He was so mesmerized by the fun he was having, he almost ran into her because she'd suddenly stopped.

When he looked beyond her, he saw a large round-ish shape like a big boulder covered in debris ahead of them.

The hairs lifted on the back of his neck and knew she was feeling the same electricity. Something was here that didn't belong. He swam to one side of it and waited for her to approach the other side. She was the expert.

Her hands began to brush away the layers of silt. He helped her. After five minutes of hard work, they uncovered part of what looked like a sculpted mouth. Alessandra's eyes stared at him with a glow through her goggles. This was a fantastic find and they both knew it.

While he marveled, she tapped her watch. He'd been too engrossed and forgot the time. They needed to go up to the surface now! It was hard to leave after what they'd just discovered, but they would be back later.

Rini knew the rules by heart. Keep his breathing steady as they rose, but it was hard when his adrena-line was gushing. He could only imagine Alessandra's joy. This was her life!

They broke the top of the water and swam toward the boat. Like déjà vu he helped her on board the cruiser, then climbed in himself.

"Oh, Rini," she cried, having removed the belt and breathing apparatus. "We found something that could have belonged to the Temple of Hera. We've got to find Dr. Tozzi and bring the others here!"

Without conscious thought he grasped her upper arms, bringing her close to his body. "Congratulations!"

Her eyes, the color of dark vintage brandy, searched his. "It was your inspiration that brought us here."

For a moment he was caught up in the wonder of her beauty that went soul deep. "I'll never forget the experience of winding through that undersea garden with you."

"Neither will I," she whispered.

He pulled her closer and closed his mouth close over hers. The unexpectedness of it must have caught her off guard because she began kissing him back with a fervency he could only have dreamed about.

Hungry for her, Rini drove their kiss deeper, marveling over her response to him. Sensation after sensation of desire caused him to kiss her senseless. Only the wake from a passing boat that bounced the cruiser reminded him how far gone he was.

Alessandra seemed to feel it, too. She tore her lips from his and moved out of his arms. "If—if you'll mark this spot on the chart, I'll drive," she stuttered.

He didn't like it that she'd headed for the controls, leaving him bereft. So much for him practicing the patience Valentina had talked about. Rini hadn't been able to keep himself from crushing her in his arms. He'd wanted that divine fusion to go on and on.

While Alessandra raised the anchor and started the engine, he reached in his backpack for a pen. He found the rolled-up chart on the banquette and sat down to fill in the information, but it was difficult. To his surprise the wind had kicked up. He looked overhead and noticed that more clouds had been amassing. Three hours ago it had only been overcast and there hadn't been this breeze.

She drove as fast as the elements would allow. Finally

in the distance he saw the flags of the three boats. They drew closer and waved to several groups of divers in two of the boats. Soon Alessandra drew alongside one of them. "How long has Dr. Tozzi been down?"

"He and Gino should be coming up any minute."

"Did you find anything?"

They shook their heads.

"Well, all is not lost. We have some amazing news." She cut the engine and lowered the anchor while they waited in the rocking crafts for the head of the institute to appear. Rini shared a private glance with her. He could feel her eagerness to impart their finding.

Rini watched until he saw two heads pop out of the water. The divers reached their boat and climbed in. The second the good doctor removed his headgear, his gaze shot to Alessandra.

"You missed this morning's dive."

"We did our own dive farther east and raced here to tell you what we found." In the next breath she told everyone about the head.

"You uncovered a mouth?" The doctor sounded incredulous.

"I wish we could show it to you now, but the weather is acting up. Maybe by early evening we can do another dive. In the meantime, why don't you follow us to the cove where we spent the night on the beach? The site is right off the coast from there and a little east where we can eat before you leave for the port."

Everyone agreed it was a good idea. Alessandra raised the anchor and started the engine. Once again they took off for the cove. While he stayed on the cruiser, Alessandra climbed out to chat with the others. They decided the storm wouldn't hit until evening, but it would be better not to go out diving again today.

"Are you staying here again tonight?"

"I'm not sure what our plans are, Gino, but we'll definitely be here tomorrow at nine to show you the dive site, unless the weather is worse."

Rini had checked ahead. There'd be a storm later. On impulse he picked up the chart and got out of the boat to show it to them. "In case we don't get together, I've marked the coordinates on here if you want to write them down."

Dr. Tozzi glanced at it and made notes on the pad in his pocket before handing it back to Rini. "Thanks."

"You're welcome."

The group prepared to leave. Nothing could have made Rini happier. So happy, in fact, that he handed Alessandra the chart, then helped push the other boats back in the water and waved everyone off.

Alessandra had to suppress a smile. Rini couldn't have been more helpful. How could any man measure up to the famous CEO who could scuba dive and read ocean charts with the best of them?

In a few more days, when he'd finished up business with her father, he'd fly off to Naples and his busy life that sent him all over the country. She had to remember he was only here in the south of Italy for a few more days. To think of him leaving was killing her.

If it turned out her parents agreed to let his company do some drilling, Rini would send out their experts.

From time to time she'd see him coming and going from the castle. But for today and tomorrow, they would be together and it thrilled her heart.

She turned to him. "How would you like to do something fun?"

He cocked his dark head. "What kind of a ridiculous question is that to ask a man alone with a beautiful woman?"

"Just checking," she teased and got back in the boat with her heart thudding in her chest. "If you're game for a bumpy ride, I know a place where the food is divine. By boat it will take us about an hour and a half. When we get there we'll enjoy an early dinner and stay overnight."

"That good, hmm?"

"Yes."

"Only if you'll let me drive us. So far *you've* done all the work."

"I don't mind, but if that's what you want."

"It'll relieve my guilt."

"Over what?"

"I like to feel useful."

"You were amazingly useful when you pushed all the boats off the sand. You reminded me of Hercules."

His deep laughter resounded in the air.

"I'm not kidding. They would have had a terrible time in this wind without your help."

"If I impressed you, then it was worth the pain."

Her eyes scrutinized him from head to toe. "You did it so effortlessly, I doubt there's a sore muscle in your body."

He returned her gaze, sending the color flooding into her cheeks. "I guess it comes from both of us living in and out of the water."

She looked down. "Would you believe I still need to get out of my wet suit?"

"Do you need help?"

She felt the blush break out on her face. "I think I can handle it."

"While you do that I'll push us off and we'll get going."

Her chest fluttered as she hurried below deck to change and freshen up. After ascertaining that her parents had left her aunt's and had gone back to the castle, she joined Rini. He'd changed clothes and was seated in the captain's chair wearing his life preserver. "Tell me where to go."

Alessandra reached in the cubbyhole for her regular map and opened it, but the wind made it difficult to keep steady. "We're here. Keep following the coast past Metaponto, then we'll cut a diagonal and head straight for Taranto."

"That's where your aunt lives?"

"Yes. Our mother's titled family descends from the Duca di Taranto, although the title is now defunct, like my father's."

"Ah. It's all making sense." He put the map back and handed her a life preserver. "Sit across from me so we can talk."

She grinned. "Aye, aye, sir, but I don't think we'll be able to hear each other."

"As long as we're together, I don't care."

The man could read her mind. She sat on the banquette and stared out at a sea full of white caps. The moderate swells slowed them down, but she was having the time of her life. Since he hadn't vacationed in a year, Alessandra suspected he was happy, too, especially after he was the one to have picked the area where they'd made an underwater find. Every time he looked at her, his dark eyes burned with charged energy, melting her to the spot.

Outside Metaponto he stopped long enough to switch gas tanks. "I remember seeing Taranto's naval base and shipyards from the air."

"Then you know it's a big commercial city and port. Our Taranto relatives live in one of the eighteenth-century palazzi in the old town center. I've let my aunt know we're coming to see her. She broke her hip and has a nurse around the clock, but she loves visitors. Be warned she'll insist we eat dinner with her before we leave."

"I don't want to impose."

"She'll love it, Rini. Since you're a seafood lover, get ready to enjoy the most luscious roasted oysters you've ever eaten in your life. The cook prepares them in a special sauce followed by sea-bream-and-mussel soup. It's out of this world. Mother would steal her if she could."

He eyed her speculatively. "What's the other reason you're taking me there?"

You could never fool a man like Rini.

"She's mother's brilliant older sister by nine years and was married to a general who died two years ago. When Mamma was thirty, she almost died giving birth to me and Dea. Fulvia couldn't have children and was there to do everything. She won my father's devotion. As I told you earlier, her opinion goes a long way with both of them. I'd like you to tell her your business ideas for developing the property."

His features sobered. "Are you saying your mother doesn't approve?"

"I'm afraid not. Both of them were raised to be purists and believe that the former papal legacy should remain untouched."

"What about *your* opinion, Alessandra?"

She took a deep breath. "I've listened to my father and think your idea is an important one. If a lot of oil is found, it *will* help the economy. But what's important is what Zia Fulvia has to say."

Those dark eyes searched hers. "Why are you trying to help me?"

A good question. "I believe in you *and* an even playing field."

"I'm humbled by your faith in me." He rubbed his jaw where the shadow of his beard was showing. She thought him irresistible. "Will I find her difficult?"

"Yes."

She loved the bark of laughter that came out of him.

"But you told me you like snags because they make life more exciting."

When he smiled, she felt herself falling toward him. "I did say that, didn't I? Let's go and get this over with. It couldn't be worse than a visit to the dentist."

Alessandra kept chuckling as the cruiser pounded the white water on its way to Taranto. She'd never met anyone with a sense of humor like his. He was getting to her with every minute they spent together.

Due to the wind they made slow progress. It was after five when they passed through the outer and inner sea to pull into the private dock reserved for her aunt's family. Alessandra called for the limo that drove them to the Taranto palazzo in the old town.

"Tarantos have lived here for over four hundred years," she explained as they turned into the court-yard with its fountain supported by Taras, the son of Poseidon from Greek mythology. "You'll think you've entered a fabulous museum. Fulvia and Mamma were raised princesses and Fulvia still lives like one."

"She won't shudder at the sight of us fresh off the boat?"

At seventy-seven Fulvia was still all woman and would probably faint when she saw the gorgeous male Alessandra had brought with her. "No. She's used to my showing up a mess after a day at sea."

Rini helped her out of the limo. "Lippo," she called to the older man who opened the ornate front door at the same time. *"Come stai?"*

"Bene, grazie, Alessandra."

"Please meet Signor Montanari."

"Piacere di conoscerla."

She looked at Rini. "Lippo and Liona are cousins. Our families couldn't live without them."

"Your families are close-knit in many ways," Rini murmured. "Does he have a cat, too?"

Alessandra chuckled. "He would, but my aunt has allergies."

"Signora Fulvia is in the drawing room, but she's tired since your parents left and is still off her food."

"We won't stay long."

"After you've spoken with her, dinner will be served in the small dining room."

"*Grazie*, Lippo."

Alessandra led Rini through hallways of marble floors and walls lined with gilt-framed portraits to her aunt's favorite room. Still a beauty, she sat in a wheel chair surrounded by the mementos of her deceased husband, who'd enjoyed a distinguished military career.

"*Buonasera*, Zia. I've missed you." She hugged her aunt. "I'm so sorry about your hip."

"A hazard of old age. Don't let it happen to you, *cara*." Her brown eyes flicked to Rini, assessing him with uncommon interest. No woman could help it. "Your fame as an engineer precedes you, Signor Montanari. Alessandra, why don't you see if your dinner is ready while I have a chat with him? Then I'll ask the nurse to take me to my room."

Her aunt had to be more miserable than she looked in order to get down to business this fast. "You poor thing. Please don't overdo it. I'll be right back." She shared a private glance with Rini before leaving the room. Though she felt the slightest bit apprehensive, he seemed perfectly at ease.

She didn't think anything could throw him. If he couldn't achieve his goal with her father, Alessandra knew he'd look elsewhere for oil because he was a man on a mission.

* * *

By nine thirty the bad weather had turned ugly. Rini felt the rain as he helped Alessandra into the limo and gave the driver instructions to return them to the private dock. Though she'd told him they could stay the night at the palazzo, the illuminating conversation with her aunt had turned him inside out and he'd wanted to leave.

Her aunt had told him something that had nothing to do with his business meetings with the count. She'd brought up an alarming personal issue that had a direct bearing on Alessandra and her sister. He needed to think long and hard about it for the good of the Caracciolo family before he shared it with Alessandra, *if he ever did*. The only solution was to kill his feelings for her. In order to do that, he needed to leave the castello and search for hydrocarbons elsewhere in the south.

"I'd rather get back to the cruiser. It will do fine while we wait out the storm." He imagined it would last all night.

"Well?" she asked with a smile after they'd gone below deck to the small room she used as an office. The rain pounded down outside. He stretched out in one of the chairs and extended his legs, crossing them at the ankles. Across from him sat the woman he considered the greatest beauty of the Taranto family bar none.

The humidity had curled the tips of her delightful hair. With her pink cheeks, she reminded him of one of the adorable cherub faces from Lecce. Her physical looks were a given. But what he found truly exquisite was her spirit—she had decided to give him a fighting chance to carry through with an idea, although it would never see the light of day now.

"I loved the tour of the palazzo and the meal was superb."

"It always is, but I'm talking about your chat with my aunt. How did it go? She was too tired to talk to me before she went to bed."

None of it was meant for Alessandra's ears. "I thought I was talking to a strong minded woman."

Laughter bubbled out of her. "She's tough all right."

Choosing his words carefully he said, "We talked pro and con. Her knowledge and directness impressed me before she asked to be excused to go to bed."

She eyed him curiously. "That's all you can tell me?"

Tight bands constricted his chest. "There isn't anything else."

"Oh, dear. It doesn't sound like it went well."

"I have no idea. But be assured I enjoyed meeting her and I'm indebted for your help. Since it's getting late, why don't you go on to bed? I've got business calls to make. Sleep well."

After they'd left her aunt's palazzo the night before, Alessandra couldn't believe the change in Rini. He seemed to have turned into a different man, and was aloof, preoccupied. What on earth had they talked about that made him so unapproachable?

She went down to her cabin and cried herself to sleep over the way he'd just shut her out. She'd been waiting for him to kiss her again, but it never happened. What he and her aunt had talked about had changed him in some way.

When Alessandra woke up the next morning, Rini was already at the wheel. The weather had to be better, otherwise the cruiser wouldn't be skimming across the water with such speed.

Why hadn't he knocked on her door to waken her? Anything to let her know he was aware of her.

She couldn't understand it and got out of bed to dress. After making coffee in the galley, she went up on deck with her duffel bag in the hope he would be in a better frame of mind to talk to her.

But the second she saw the set jaw of that handsome face, she knew instinctively that now wasn't the right time. He was in no mood to confide in her. She walked over him. "I thought you might like this."

He eyed her briefly before taking the cup. "Thank you. You're an angel. As you can see, the storm has passed over. We'll have you home soon."

Home?

Her fear that something terrible was wrong had come to fruition. She frowned. "I thought we were going to dive. It's a great morning for it."

"I'd like to, but I'm afraid something came up while I made some business calls last night. I need to discuss them with your father. Please don't let that stop you from joining your group once you drop me off."

Diving was the last thing on her mind. She moved around and straightened the scuba equipment. They were almost to the island. Soon he eased the cruiser to the dock. When it was safe, she jumped out with her duffel bag and tied the ropes, leaving him to shut down the engine.

He joined her at the Land Rover. Their silent drive to the castle only took a minute, proof he was surprised she hadn't stayed in the boat before taking off again. Alessandra had the impression he couldn't wait to get away from her.

Sure enough, as soon as she'd parked the car, he reached for his backpack and got out. Alessandra followed him inside the foyer of the castle. He looked back at her. "I phoned your father earlier. He's waiting for me. Thank you for showing me your world. I loved every second of it."

So did I. Why are you acting like it's over? Rini— what's going on?

But he kept her in the dark. Without lingering, he walked toward her father's office.

With a heart that had fallen to the floor, she went up the staircase to shower and change into clean clothes. Her mother was probably in the day room so she hurried downstairs to talk to her. She would know what was going on with her father and Rini. This was a nightmare.

When she wasn't there, Alessandra went to the dining room and found it empty. "Hey, Alfredo. Are you looking for Liona?" She picked up the cat. On her way to the kitchen she heard the rotors of the helicopter. Someone must be arriving from the mainland. She kept on walking to the kitchen. No one was in there.

She lowered the cat to his food and water dishes, then she took off for her father's office. Maybe her mother was in there and she would find the three of them deep in conversation. After hesitating, she knocked on the door, unwilling to stay away any longer. "*Scusi*, Papà."

"Come in, *piccola*."

She found her father alone. "Where is everyone?"

"Your mother drove Liona to Metaponto for her dentist appointment." That explained why Alfredo looked lost.

"I—I thought Rini Montanari was still with you," she stammered.

He sat back in his leather chair. "He was here earlier to tell me that after thinking everything over, he decided that erecting oil derricks on our property would be a scab on the legacy Queen Joanna left to the family."

Those were the very words Alessandra had used. To hear her father say them brought inexpressible pain.

"He says he's off to search for another area to drill. After thanking both you and me profusely for our time and hospitality, he called for a helicopter and left."

Her legs started to buckle. She grabbed the first chair before she fell. "That's it? No other explanation?"

Her father smiled warmly. "Only to say that you discovered a large head while you were diving yesterday and he presumes it'll make you famous."

Except that Rini was the one with the inspiration to know where to dive.

"Oh—one more thing. He told me you're the most charming, lovely, intelligent woman he ever met and he understood why I wanted you to show him around. I could have told him that about you, but it's nice he discovered it for himself. As for the oil-drilling proposal,

I have to admit I'm glad he withdrew it. Neither your mother or Fulvia were in favor of it."

"I know." A boulder had lodged in her throat.

"Fulvia phoned your mother early this morning. We were surprised to learn you'd taken him to see her. It made her very happy to see you while she's recovering."

But the visit had turned out to be devastating for Alessandra. Once again her world had been destroyed. This time she knew she'd never be able to put it back together.

Alessandra took a quick breath. "Since the weather kept us from making another dive, I decided to pay her a visit. She was tired, but seems to be getting along fine."

"She was very impressed with Rinieri's honesty."

Honesty? What on earth did that mean?

Feeling ill, she got up from the chair. "I've been away from my work too long, so I'd better get busy or my editor will lose his patience. I'll be in the library if you need me." She hurried over to give him a kiss on the cheek before leaving the office.

When she reached her desk, she buried her face in her hands and sobbed. Several messages came in on her phone, all from Gino wanting to know if she would be joining them for the afternoon dive. None were from Rini.

Alessandra texted him that she couldn't make it, then left the castle in the Land Rover and drove to the mainland. After grabbing some food, she drove to the ridge where she'd taken Rini on that first day. The recent downpour had greened up the fields. She walked around, playing back their conversation in her head.

Alessandra was convinced that the excuse he'd given her father not to drill wasn't the real reason he'd backed off.

Deeply troubled, she returned to the castle and got busy on the historical biography she was writing on Queen Joanna. But by Saturday morning she couldn't stand it any longer. Rini had been cruel not to have contacted her, if only to say goodbye. After what they'd shared scuba diving, she wasn't about to let him walk away until he'd listened to a few things she had to say.

If this was how he ended every relationship with a woman, no wonder he was still a bachelor. He'd been clever to abort their growing attraction before it burned out of control. Rini had been every bit as hungry for her as she'd been for him when they'd kissed. So why had he done this?

He'd been the one to pursue her, to want to scuba dive with her. There'd been no stopping him getting his way because she'd wanted to be with him so badly, too, and still did. So what had changed everything? Alessandra needed answers and she wasn't going to let him get away with it.

After telling her parents she'd be home late, she drove the Land Rover to Metaponto and took a commercial flight to Positano. Without her father's knowledge she'd looked up Rini's home address on his computer.

She could have gone to the Montanari office in Naples, but figured he'd be home on the weekend. If she walked in on him entertaining another woman, that was too bad. She needed answers.

Three hours later the limo she'd hired wound around

the lush vegetation of his property. It stopped in front of a magnificent two-storied, ochre-colored villa, probably built at the turn of the century. Good heavens, the hilltop town above the Amalfi Coast was gorgeous beyond belief!

Alessandra marveled to know that Rini lived in this flower-filled paradise. The exterior was drenched in purple and red bougainvillea, robbing her of breath. So did the view of the sea from such a dizzying height.

A warm midafternoon sun shone down on her as she got out of the back. "Stay here, please," she said to the driver. She walked past several cars in the courtyard on her way to the front entrance. Alessandra hoped that meant Rini was home.

After using the bell pull, she waited for someone to answer and heard female voices inside. One said, "I'll get it, Bianca."

The moment the door opened, Alessandra knew she was looking at Rini's sister, who was a real blond beauty. Even though their coloring was different, the extraordinary family resemblance brought Rini to mind with a pang.

"Buon pomeriggio, signorina. Can I help you?" She'd answered the door in a bathing suit covered by a short lacy wrap.

Her heart was pounding too hard. "I hope so. I'm here to see Rini."

She studied Alessandra for a moment. "Aren't you the famous Diorucci model?"

CHAPTER FIVE

THIS WAS DÉJÀ VU all over again.

"That's my sister, Dea. I'm Alessandra Caracciolo."

"Well, you're both absolutely stunning."

"Thank you."

"I'm afraid my brother isn't here. I'm Valentina Laurito. Was he expecting you?"

"No." She swallowed hard. "I wanted to surprise him."

A mischievous smile broke the corners of his sister's mouth. "So did I. Bianca informed me he went fishing this morning and hasn't come back yet, but she's expecting him soon so I stayed."

Fishing…

While she took in the disappointing news, an older woman appeared in the foyer carrying a darling blond baby boy, the image of his mother. She made the introductions. "Have you come far?"

"I flew in from Metaponto."

"That's quite a ways. Won't you come in and wait with me while I give my son a bottle? We're out by the swimming pool. Vito loves his Zio Rini and keeps waiting for him to walk out."

Alessandra knew the feeling well. "If you don't mind, I'd love to."

"Tell your driver to come back for you later."

She did the other woman's bidding, then walked through Rini's elegant villa. The patio furniture included tables, chairs and a large swing. Alessandra saw plastic toys in the water. Valentina took the baby from the housekeeper and settled him in his baby swing with a cover to shield his eyes.

"We have extra bathing suits if you'd like to change and take a dip."

"Thank you, but no."

"You might like it after your flight."

"It didn't take that long. Besides I get in plenty of swimming." Valentina was so easy to talk to, Alessandra needed to be careful what she said to her. Rini was a private person who wouldn't appreciate her getting too familiar with his family. Especially not after he'd left the castle permanently.

She found a lounge chair close to the swing to watch the darling baby. In a minute she heard rotors overhead and her pulse leaped. What would Rini think when he found her out here with his family? Maybe she shouldn't have come, but it was too late now because moments later her gaze darted to the tall, dark figure striding toward them from the other end of the pool wearing jeans and a T-shirt.

"There's your *zio*!" Valentina cried.

"Vito—" Rini called to him. The baby turned his head toward his uncle and lifted his arms.

That's when Rini saw her and his eyes narrowed. "Alessandra," he murmured.

Without missing a beat he came close and picked up the baby in his arms, kissing him. "What a surprise. Two visitors in one afternoon."

"Alessandra has flown here from Metaponto, but I can't persuade her to take a swim."

"That's because she scuba dives for the archaeological institute from Catania and probably enjoys a break from swimming."

Valentina's head swung toward her. "Rini's a master diver, too!"

"I know. Your brother was instrumental in helping me make a find the other day. I'm indebted to him."

"Rini," his sister virtually blurted with excitement. "You didn't tell me about that." Her eyes took in the two of them.

With enviable calm he explained, "While I was looking for new oil fields, I tagged along with Alessandra. She lives on an archaeological treasure."

"Zio Salvatore called me when he couldn't find you at the office. You know how upset he gets."

He played with Vito, avoiding Alessandra's eyes. "I'm back from Calabria now and got in touch with him."

"That's a relief. So how was fishing?"

"Good. Guido caught two trout with the lure I gave him. We ate them for lunch."

"Lucky you. I'm glad you came home when you did. Vito and I waited as long as we could, and now we've got to get back to Ravello. Giovanni will be wondering where we are." She turned to Alessandra. "It was so nice to meet you."

"You, too. Your little boy is wonderful."

"Thank you. I think so, too. I have another son, Ric, but he's with his birth mother today." She took the baby from her brother's arms and disappeared into the villa.

Alessandra was left alone with Rini. Her pulse raced at the way his eyes ignited as he studied her for a moment without saying anything. She was glad she'd worn her white dress with the blue-and-green print, a favorite of hers. For once she'd knocked herself out trying to look beautiful for him. She'd even worn some eye makeup and had spent time on her hair.

"I think you know why I'm here," she said, answering the question he hadn't asked. "You didn't say goodbye." Her accusation hung in the air.

His hands went to his hips in a male gesture. "If you'll excuse me for a minute, I'll be right back."

"Promise?" she responded. He'd arrived dressed in outdoor gear with a navy crewneck shirt. With that hint of a dark beard on his jaw, she was almost overcome by his male virility. Alessandra had missed him so terribly, it hurt to look at him.

A nerve throbbed at the corner of his compelling mouth. "I swear it."

He left the patio on a run. She found a chair under the umbrella table and took in the sight of his own private Garden of Eden. So many species of flowers and trees astounded her, as everything looked perfect. All her life she'd lived in a castle surrounded by sand and water.

Alessandra loved the isolation, but being here in Rini's home made her appreciate what she'd been missing.

The fragrance from the roses intoxicated her. She got up and walked around to smell the various varieties. Soon she heard footsteps behind her. When she turned, she discovered that the woman Valentina had introduced her to had come out on the terrace. She pushed a cart of food and drinks to the table. "Rinieri will be right out, *signorina*."

"*Grazie*, Bianca."

From the corner of her eye she saw a baby sandal left on one of the chairs. She started to retrieve it when Rini came out on the patio dressed in tan trousers and a silky black sport shirt. Freshly shaved, he looked and smelled fabulous.

Alessandra held up the sandal. "Your sister left this in her wake. I'm afraid her fast exit was my fault."

"You're wrong." He took the little sandal and put it on the table. "She couldn't wait to join her husband. They're crazy about each other." Rini held out a chair for her. "Sit down and we'll eat. One trout apiece wasn't enough for the appetite I've developed."

"I'm hungry, too. They only served snacks on the plane."

In a minute they filled up on shrimp salad with penne, dried tomatoes and slices of grilled eggplant that melted in her mouth. Rolls and lemonade with mint leaves made their meal a feast, but clearly Rini was a fish man.

Filled to the brim, she sat back in the chair. "I'm waiting for an explanation."

He wiped the corner of his mouth with a napkin before his gaze fell on her. "All along there's been something I should have told you about myself, but I never seemed to find the right time."

"What? That you lead a secret life? That you have a wife hidden somewhere?"

"Nothing like that. After the visit to your aunt's, I decided that I'd wasted enough of your family's time and thought it best to leave so you could get on with your dive."

She shook her head. "You're a man who was raised with good manners, so your excuse doesn't wash. Something happened during your private talk with my aunt that put you off your desire to drill on my family's property. I deserve to know the truth. It's only fair after providing you the opportunity to talk to her."

His eyes glittered. "You're treading on dangerous ground to ask for the truth."

Her hands gripped the sides of her chair. "Now I know I'm right. As you can see, I'm a grown woman and can take whatever you have to tell me."

Lines darkened his striking face. "I'm not so sure."

"Are you afraid I'm too fragile if you tell me a secret about yourself I don't want to hear?"

He eyed her somberly. "I have no desire to bring hurt to you."

Bring? Such a cryptic comment brought a pain to her stomach. "What do you mean? In what way?"

"You need to leave it alone, Alessandra."

Anger sparked her emotions. "I don't accept that."

"I'm afraid you're going to have to." He sounded so remote, her insides froze.

"In other words you really meant it to be goodbye the other day."

Rini leaned forward. "I'd hoped I'd made that clear when I left the island the other morning without letting you know my intentions."

The forbidding CEO of Montanari's had spoken. *Don't you dare break down in front of him.*

She struggled for breath. "Don't worry. You've made me see the light. You and Francesco aren't that different after all. After he disappeared from my life, he sent his goodbye in a letter rather than face me. You flew off and left it to my father to do the honors. What is it about some attractive men? They seem to possess every quality except the one most vital."

A white ring appeared around his lips. She was pleased to see he wasn't completely impervious to her judgment of him. "Don't worry. Keep all your secrets! I'm leaving." She started to get up.

"No, Alessandra—you want the truth of everything, so I'll tell you. I never planned to, but since you've come all this way, I can't handle seeing you in this kind of pain. No one deserves an explanation more than you do."

"Go on."

"Where your aunt is concerned, we only talked business for a moment. The main thrust dealt with you."

"Me?"

Rini nodded slowly. "She loves you."

"I love her, too, but what does that have to do with anything?"

"She wanted clarification and asked to know what happened when I met Dea."

The moment he'd spoken, she stirred in the chair and averted her eyes. "I—I can't believe she brought up something that was none of her business." Her voice faltered. "Mother must have said something." After a long pause she said, "How uncomfortable that had to be for you."

"Not uncomfortable. I found it refreshing. You're a lot like her, you know. If I didn't know better, I'd think she was your mother."

Alessandra's head lifted. She blinked. "You're kidding—"

"Not at all. You and your aunt have a sense of fair play I admire very much. It's clear you both want the best for everyone. I told her nothing happened. Guido's father asked us to dance with the models he'd introduced us to. I had one dance with Dea, then she left. That was it. After my explanation, your aunt wanted to know my intentions toward you."

Alessandra shot out of the chair. "She had no right! I don't see how she could have asked you that when we hardly know each other!"

He stared up at her. "That's not true, Alessandra. Your aunt told me you've never taken a man to meet her before and what we had was something special. Naturally she's aware you've been showing me around for your father."

"So?"

"She realizes we would have learned a great deal about each other already."

"Well yes, but—"

"Her concern for both you and Dea is commendable," he interrupted. "So I had to be brutally honest and tell her that I didn't feel a connection to her. Since you and I met under the most innocent and extraordinary circumstances, she demanded to know if I felt a connection to you."

Alessandra paled.

"Don't you want to know what I said?"

"It's none of my business," she whispered.

"That's not an answer and you know it."

She turned away.

"I told her that my attraction to you was immediate and has been growing out of control." Her groan resounded in the air. "You feel it, too. I know you do. Out of loyalty to both her nieces, your aunt vetted me to make sure I wasn't using *you* to gain access to the legacy."

"That's absurd. I would never have thought that about you."

"But it's a mercenary world. She knew how hurt you were years ago and wanted to protect you."

"So you withdrew the proposal to prove to my family you had no ulterior motive? That's why you walked away from me?" Her voice rang out.

Instead of answering her, he reached for her and drew her over to the swing, pulling her down on his lap. "Look at me, Alessandra."

She shook her head. "I'm afraid to."

"Because you know I want to kiss you. The other morning while we were on the sea floor uncovering the mouth on that head, I was reminded of you. When I kissed you on the boat, I was half out of my mind with desire. My motives *are* ulterior, but intensely personal."

"No, Rini. We mustn't. Not out here where Bianca can see us."

"*I* must, *bellissima*."

He curved his hand against the side of her face and turned it toward him. Obeying blind need, he covered her trembling mouth with his own. She tried to elude him, but he drove his kisses deeper and deeper until her little cry allowed him the access he craved. Maybe he was dreaming because she slowly began returning his kisses with a heart-stopping hunger that caused him to forget everything except the heavenly woman in his arms.

His hands roved over her back and shoulders while they gave and took pleasure from each other's mouths. He felt her fingers slide up his neck into his hair. Every touch fed the fire enveloping him.

"Alessandra," he moaned. "I can't get enough of you. Do you have any idea how much I want you?"

"I want you, too," she confessed, covering his face with kisses.

"During the dive I was dying to grasp your hips and pull you into a secret cave where we could make love for months on end."

"Our wet suits would have presented a problem."

"But not now." He eased her down on the swing, where he had the freedom to look at her to his heart's content while he kissed the living daylights out of her.

Rini had never known this kind of all-consuming

desire before. The way she responded to him let him know something earthshaking had happened to her, too. She'd already had one love affair in her life, but it had been a long time ago. He was thankful it hadn't worked out because he was convinced she'd been reserved for him.

But what if she couldn't handle what he needed to tell her? He kissed her nose and eyelids. Before things went any further, she deserved to know the whole truth about him. Though terrified of her reaction, he couldn't stop now.

"You're the most divine creature this man has ever met. Since your aunt wanted to know my intentions toward you, it's only fair I tell you something about me first."

"You don't have to do this, Rini. You don't owe me anything. Please. I never dreamed my aunt would get personal with you like that."

"I'm glad she did. It woke me up to something I've been unwilling to face for years."

Her anxious eyes searched his. "What do you mean?"

"I've remained a bachelor for a reason."

"If you're allergic to marriage, you're not the only man. Until my father met Mother, he decided he'd always be single."

"That hasn't been my problem. In truth I've never gotten to the point in my adult life when I needed to state my intentions. But with you, it has become necessary."

She lifted a hand to caress his jaw. "Why?"

He kissed her succulent lips. "You're not just any

female I happen to have met. I'm not talking about the fact that you were born titled from both sides of your illustrious families. This is something that affects you as a woman. Don't you know you're head and shoulders above any woman I've ever known? Your pure honesty demands the same from me."

"Papà said my aunt was impressed with *your* honesty." She shivered. "What honesty is that? If your intention is to frighten me, you're doing a good job."

"*Frighten* might not be the best word." He sat up and got off the swing. "What I tell you will change the way you view me, but this has to come from me. I'll understand if you say it's been nice knowing you before you go your own way."

"For heaven sakes just tell me!"

Rini had angered her. This was going wrong. "From the time I could remember, I played soccer. By seventeen I was playing on a winning team with my friend Guido. On the day of the championship game, I got injured. At the hospital tests were done and I was told I was infertile. Over the years I've undergone tests, but the diagnosis is always the same..."

Her haunted eyes had fastened on him. She didn't move or cry out, but he saw pain break out on her face.

"Like anyone, I grew up thinking that one day I'd get married and have children. It was something I took for granted. Even after my first diagnosis, I didn't really believe it. I thought that surely in time the problem would go away and I'd be normal like everyone else. But every year I was tested, I was told that nothing had changed."

"I'm so sorry," she whispered, sounding agonized.

"So am I, Alessandra, because the diagnosis has impacted my life."

"So *that's* why you left me without saying goodbye? You thought I wouldn't be able to handle it?"

His lips thinned.

"Of course a woman wants babies with the man she marries. But there are other ways to have children."

"It's not the same. The other day when I was telling you about Valentina, you said you couldn't wait until you could have your own baby. It's a natural urge to want to procreate."

"Yes, but—"

"But nothing. I can't give any woman a baby, so I've been living my life with the reputation of being a dedicated bachelor. No one but my doctor, and now *you*, know I'm infertile."

"It happens to people, Rini. How tragic that you've let it rob you of the joy of life! It kills me that your fear has prevented you from settling down with a woman because you can't give her what you think she wants.

"I know you'd make a marvelous father, Rini. That's why there's adoption. Thousands of couples do it. For you to have lived your life since seventeen with such a dark cloud hanging over your head doesn't bear thinking about."

"You're very sweet, Alessandra, but you're not in my shoes." Her incredible reaction was all he could have hoped for and let him know her support would never be in question. His doctor had told him the right woman would be able to handle it.

But there was still something else to keep them apart.

All of it stemmed from his conversation with her aunt and her implied warning. Even now he held back, thinking it was better that she believe his infertility presented the biggest problem for them.

Alessandra stared at him. "What you're saying is that you're going to let this stand in the way of our having a relationship. If you really mean that, then you need counseling before you deny yourself the greatest joy in life."

"Therapy won't help me," he responded bleakly. He rubbed the back of his neck. "Combined with the conversation I had with your aunt, a relationship with you won't work."

"We're back to my aunt again?"

"She told me some things in confidence I can't share. Don't be upset with her. It's because she loves you."

"Rini—" she cried out, aghast. But she'd felt him withdraw emotionally from her. It had been a huge mistake to fly here after all.

Alessandra pulled out her cell and called for the limo to return to his house. Once off the phone she got up and walked over to the table to drink the rest of her lemonade. "Please tell the cook the food was delicious. Now if you'll excuse me, I'm going outside to wait for my ride."

Rini moved faster than she did and caught up to her outside the front door of the villa. "Alessandra—"

"It's all right, Rini. Though your explanation wasn't the one I expected, I got my answer, so thank you. Please forgive me for barging in here uninvited. I give you my promise it will never happen again."

When the limo turned into the courtyard, she rushed

to get in the backseat on her own. Rini was right there, but she refused to give him the satisfaction of meeting his eyes and closed the door herself. As the limo drove off, Rini's heart plummeted to his feet.

"Where do you wish to go, *signorina*?"

"The airport, *per favore*."

Alessandra didn't look back as they turned away. *No more looking back.*

Just now she'd wanted to comfort him over his infertility, but she sensed he wouldn't have been willing to listen to her. For him to have revealed his agony to her had been huge for him. Now that he'd told her the truth, he'd backed away, certain that she—like any other woman—wouldn't see him as a complete man.

Was that image of being incomplete the reason for his meteoric rise in the business world? Had he worked day and night to compensate for what he saw as an inadequacy? She'd detected the love in his voice when he'd talked about his sister and her babies. Pain pierced her heart to realize that every time Rini eyed his nephew, he was reminded that he could never give a woman a child from his own body.

She'd seen the way he'd kissed and loved Valentina's baby. The man had been there for her throughout her pregnancy. Yet all that time, he'd been gutted by the knowledge that he'd never be able to look forward to having a baby from his own body. Her heart ached for him.

As for his conversation with her aunt, that was something else again. If he'd been sworn to secrecy, then she wouldn't be getting an explanation out of him. Alessandra could go to her aunt and demand to know the truth, but it wasn't her right.

On the flight back to Metaponto, she stared out the window of the plane. Rini Montanari had been an earth-shaking interlude. But interlude was all he'd prepared for their association to be and became the operative word in her romance-less life.

Sunday evening the helicopter dipped lower over Ravello. Rini was late for his brother Carlo's birthday party, which Valentina and Giovanni were hosting.

For the last three weeks Rini had traveled to four areas of Calabria in Southern Italy, exploring the pos-sibility of developing more oil sites. But he'd been in agony since Alessandra had left his villa and couldn't concentrate.

Nothing he'd visited turned out to be as promising as the land owned by the Caracciolo family. But he'd writ-ten that off. Unfortunately, blotting Alessandra from his heart was another matter entirely. With love in her eyes, she'd reacted to the news that he was infertile as if it was of no consequence to her. She'd assured him it didn't matter. The way she'd kissed him, as if he was her whole life, he'd believed her.

But her aunt's fear that a relationship with Alessan-dra might cause a permanent rift between the twins had prompted him to back away. Fulvia had told him how close the girls had been growing up, how much fun they'd had as children. But everything changed when Alessandra fell in love and then was betrayed by her sister and the man she'd thought she would marry.

The girls had finally gotten past it, but now they'd reached another impasse because Dea had met Rini first. Apparently she'd been devastated when he didn't want to date her. Hearing that Alessandra had been showing him around the property had upset her.

Though the situation was totally unfair, Fulvia had looked him in the eye and asked him if he wanted to be responsible for bringing on more pain between the two of them that might last. It was his decision to make.

In the end, Rini couldn't do it, so he'd had to let Alessandra go. All he could do was watch news clips on television about the discovery of the Temple of Hera beneath the waters off Basilicata in the Ionian.

Dr. Bruno Tozzi and his team had been given credit for the find and Alessandra's name had been mentioned. Every few days more information was being fed to the media about more discoveries of a courtyard and temple walls.

Rini was proud of Alessandra and the amazing work she was doing. Thanks to the coverage, he was able to keep track of her without having to make contact with her father. But having said goodbye to her had thrown him into a black void.

Once Rini arrived at the Laurito villa, he was besieged by family. He played with Carlo's daughter, then took turns enjoying the two baby boys. Giovanni chatted with him for a while, but it was Valentina who sequestered him in the sunroom just off the terrace. He couldn't get out of it.

"I thought you'd be bringing Alessandra with you. She's fabulous!"

"That's over."

"Why? I know you're in love with her."

His eyes closed tightly. "It can't work."

"Rini—are you saying she doesn't love you?"

He inhaled sharply. "She's never said the words."

"Have you?"

"It doesn't matter."

"Yes it *does*! Alessandra came to your house unannounced. I saw the look in her eyes when you walked out on the patio. If ever a woman had it bad…"

"There are things you don't know and I can't tell you. Don't make this any harder on me."

"Okay." She patted his arm. "I'll leave it alone. Keep your secrets and come on back out. Papà wants to talk to you and find out what new areas you've found for drilling."

"I wish I had better results to report."

Together they joined the others. Near midnight he flew back to his villa and did some laps in the swimming pool before going to bed. To his chagrin, sleep wouldn't come. He spent most of the night outside on a lounger.

Three weeks… If he didn't see Alessandra again soon, he'd go mad. But he had certain knowledge that bound him to stay away from her. Early Monday morning he put his emotional needs in the deep freeze and left for his office, prepared to announce some new sites for drilling that would please the board. He worked steadily until Thursday, when his secretary put through a call from his sister.

"Valentina?"

"Have you heard the news?" She sounded frantic.
His gut clenched. "What is it?"

"The seismic research facility in Malta registered
a six-point-nine quake in the Ionian. The impact was
felt all along the coast. It affected the diving site where
Alessandra has been working with the institute."

Earthquake? He broke out in a cold sweat. *If anything happened to her, his life wouldn't be worth living.*
To hell with what her aunt had told him. He needed to
go to her and wouldn't let anything stop him.

"According to the news, apparently two or three divers were injured and transported to chambers at various
hospitals on the coast. I found out the institute's oceanography boat docks at Crotone, so I'm sure some of the
victims were taken there."

"I'm on my way. Bless you, Valentina."

He alerted his pilot and flew to the Naples airport,
where he took the company jet to Crotone. En route he
phoned to make certain a rental car was waiting. Following that he made calls to the three hospitals in the
town, but no one would give him information about the
injured because he wasn't a relative. Other injuries over
the southern area had been reported and hospitals all
along the coast were filling.

Emergency vehicles and fire trucks filled the parking area of the first hospital. He made it to the ER and
learned that one diver had been brought there. No one
would give him information, but one of the ambulance
crew helped him out by telling him they'd transported
a male diver here.

Thanking him, Rini drove to the next hospital. Again it was the wrong one. He made the rounds until he reached the last hospital. When he spotted Bruno Tozzi in the waiting room, he knew Alessandra had to be here. Avoiding conversation with him, Rini walked through the hospital to the director's office. He'd do whatever it took to be granted permission to see her.

"I'm fine," Alessandra assured her parents after she'd spent six hours in the chamber.

"Are you in pain?"

"No, not at all. The doctor told me I have a light case of the bends."

"Dr. Tozzi wants to see you."

"He worries about all the team, but I'm not up for visitors. Tell him I promise to call him tomorrow when I'm feeling better."

"All right. We'll find him out in the reception area and be back in two hours. The doctor said you'll be here overnight. We'll stay with you and drive you home in the morning. Try to rest in the meantime. Love you." They kissed her before slipping from the room.

No sooner had they gone than the door opened again. It was probably the nurse coming in to check her vital signs. When she saw who entered the room, her heart fluttered dangerously fast.

"*Rini*—what are you doing here?" After three weeks of not seeing him, the sight of his tall, well-honed body wearing a navy blue business suit was too much to handle in her weakened state.

"When I heard what happened, I couldn't stay away."

She turned on her side, trying to hide from him. "Did you talk to my parents?"

"They don't know I'm here."

Her breath caught. "You shouldn't have come. We've said all there is to say."

"I had to be sure you were going to recover," he said, his voice throbbing.

Tears stung her eyes, but she refused to let him see them. "I don't see how you found out where I was."

"A simple deduction after Valentina phoned me with the news about the epicenter of the quake."

She sighed. "How did you get past the desk? No one is allowed in here."

"I have my ways. Alessandra, you could have died out there. The doctor said you lost consciousness. It could have been fatal. Do you have any idea what I've been going through thinking I might have lost you?"

"Maybe now you know how I felt when you let me leave Positano and I knew it was over with you." A bitter little cry escaped her lips. "My parents will be taking me home in the morning. The only reason I can imagine you're being here is because of your guilt.

"What a surprise I'm going to survive! Surely it's a relief to you. That way you don't have to tell me what you've been holding back. It would only add to your guilt."

"Alessandra—" His mournful voice reached that vulnerable place inside her before he'd come around the side of the bed. She felt him cup her face with his hand. "*Grazie a dio* you're alive and safe."

She kept her eyes tightly closed. "I admit I'm happy about it, too."

His fingers toyed with her hair, sending fingers of delight through her exhausted body. "I once came down with a case of decompression sickness and know how it feels."

"One of the hazards when you're having fun."

"You don't need to pretend with me. I know you've had a fright and need sleep. Do you mind if I stay here with you for a little while?" He leaned down and kissed her lips. It felt like the touch of fire.

"The doctor won't like it, but that's up to you."

Peering at him through slits, she watched him draw a chair to the side of the bed next to her. He looked like a man with the weight of the world on his powerful shoulders. She needed him to go away and never come back, but she couldn't find the words.

In a minute a nurse came in to bring another bag for her IV. She checked Alessandra's vitals and left without saying a word to him. The man could get away with murder. "What did you do to get permission?"

"I told the administrator that Montanari Engineering would make a generous donation to the hospital if they'd let me in to see you."

There was no one like him, her heart cried out. "Rini Montanari. That was a naughty thing to do."

"It worked. That's all that mattered to me. To find you alive means everything. These last three weeks without you have been a hell I never want to live through again," he admitted, his voice breaking.

His pain was tangible. "Now you'll have to make

good on your offer and work all hours of the day and night to recoup the loss."

"It'll be worth it since the hospital helped save your life. You're the most precious thing in my world. I love you, *bellissima*," he said in the huskiest voice she'd ever heard. "Now go to sleep and don't worry about anything."

When Alessandra woke up in the middle of the night, she decided she'd been dreaming that Rini had come to visit her. Had he really said he loved her? There was no sign of him. The night nurse came in and helped her to the restroom, then walked her back to bed.

CHAPTER SIX

THE NEXT MORNING Alessandra awakened to find her parents in the room. They'd brought her a fresh change of jeans and a soft top, which she slipped into. At 11:00 a.m. the doctor discharged her with the proviso that she rest, stay hydrated and do no diving for at least fourteen days.

It felt good to be wheeled outside to her parents' limo. They made her comfortable before driving her back to the castle. Yet not at any time had they or the medical staff mentioned that Rini Montanari had been a visitor.

She'd really experienced a whopper of a dream to imagine he'd left his office to fly to Crotone in order to find out if she was all right. Alessandra was terrified it would take years, maybe a lifetime, to get over him. But what if she couldn't? The ache in her heart had grown acute.

Instead of going upstairs, she told her mom she wanted to stay in the day room and curled up on the couch under a quilt to watch television. Supplied with water and nuts, she didn't lack for the creature com-

forts. Alfredo wandered in and jumped up on her lap.
He supplied the love she craved.

"Alessandra?" She lifted her head to her mother. "Are
you up for company?"

"If it's anyone from the diving group, could you tell
them I need a few days?"

"It's Rinieri Montanari."

She reeled in place.

"He said he visited you at the hospital, but the nurse
put something in your IV and you fell asleep. He's anxious to know how you are."

Rini *had* been there!

She hadn't dreamed it after all and couldn't believe
it. Thrilled, yet tortured by what her mother had told
her, she couldn't concentrate on anything else. "I—I
look terrible."

"That would be impossible," her mother assured her,
"but if you want me to send him away, I will."

"No—but don't tell him to come in yet. Could you
hand me my purse? It's over on the credenza."

Her mother did her bidding. Alessandra's hand trembled as she brushed through her hair and applied a coat
of lipstick.

"Ready?"

Alessandra nodded. While she waited, she checked
her phone to find a dozen texts from friends, one of
them from Bruno, who wanted to know how soon she'd
be back. Fulvia had sent her love and condolences.
She wanted a good talk with her when she was feeling better.

Alessandra's editor was thankful she was all right

and told her not to feel pressured about delivering the book. He hadn't given her a deadline. But there was no message from Dea, the one person Alessandra wanted to talk to. The pit grew in her stomach as she realized her own sister hadn't tried to contact her. Why?

"You don't look like you've been sick," said the deep, familiar male voice she was dying to hear.

She looked up at the sinfully gorgeous man. "You're right. I'm a fraud."

Rini walked over to her. He'd dressed in jeans and a pullover sweater in slate blue. Combined with the soap he used in the shower to assail her, his presence had put her senses on overload. He reached down to scratch behind the cat's ears. "You have the right instincts, Alfredo. I'd trade places with you if I could."

In the next instant he leaned down and pressed a warm kiss to her mouth. "Welcome back to the land of the living. Your doctor told me you lost consciousness down there."

"Only for a moment. My buddy Gino knew exactly what to do. It all happened so fast."

"We can be thankful the divers with the institute are experts." He stood there looking down at her with an intense expression.

She squirmed. "Rini?" Her voice shook. "Why are you here?"

"Though I had my reasons, I treated you badly when I left here the first time without saying goodbye. My behavior was worse when you flew to Positano to see me and I wouldn't explain myself. I thought I was doing the right thing both times, but your accident has changed the way I feel about everything.

"I love you and I've never said that to another woman in my life. Almost losing you has made me realize I could no longer let my reason stand in the way of being with you, so I'm back to find out if you'd be willing to start over again with me."

While she sat there in shock, Liona wheeled in a tea cart laden with a meal for them. "If Alfredo is bothering you, I'll take him out."

"Oh, no. I love him right here. Thanks, Liona."

After she left, Rini got up and served both of them a plate of food and her favorite iced tea. His gaze found hers. While they ate he said, "Life has given both of us a second chance. What I'd like to do is invite you to my villa for a week where we can spend real time together."

Alessandra couldn't believe what she was hearing. She said the first thing that came into her head. "Can you take a vacation?"

"Of course. I want to get to know you without work or interruptions getting in the way. The nice thing about being CEO is that I can arrange it when I want. The doctor told me you shouldn't dive for at least two more weeks. You've shown me your world. Now it's time I showed you mine."

She smiled. "Like fishing?"

"Only if you'd want to."

"Rini, I adore the outdoors. Hiking, camping, all of it."

"The mountains are beautiful this time of year.

Could you talk to your editor and ask for an extension to turn in your book?"

"He already told me to take all the time I need."

If only Rini knew she loved him so much she felt like she could move mountains for him, but she was afraid. "When the week is over, *then* what? Will you consider you've done everything possible to obtain my forgiveness?

"Will we say goodbye like sensible people who've enjoyed their interlude together but knew it had to come to an end? You'll go your way because you can't offer me any more than what you've already done? I'll go mine?"

His jaw hardened. "Why don't we stop worrying about the future and just take things one day at a time? I need help because I've never done anything like this before."

She took a deep breath, surprised to hear the vulnerability in his voice. "Like what?"

"Invite a woman I care about to stay at my house."

"I've never done anything like it, either." Talk about needing help...

"The doctor told me you need rest and that you shouldn't fly until tomorrow. So if I leave you now, will you think about my invitation? I'll call you in the morning. If you decide you want to come, I'll arrange to pick you up in the limo and we'll fly in the company jet to Positano." He stood up.

"Where will you be in the meantime?"

"At the airport in Metaponto. I'm working in my office on the jet and will stay in the bedroom overnight.

I'll give you until ten a.m. to get in touch with me. If I don't hear from you by then, I'll be flying back to Naples."

She knew he meant it. This was it.

"If you'll give me your phone, I'll program my number for you."

Alessandra handed it to him. "Rini, whatever my answer is, I promise to call you."

Lines marred his arresting features. "I can't ask for more than that." He put the phone on the table. "You need rest now. Take care of yourself, *adorata.*"

The second he disappeared from the day room she wanted to call him back and tell him she'd go with him right now. But she needed to keep her wits about her. The decision to spend a week with him would change her life forever.

She kissed the cat's head. "Who am I kidding, Alfredo? My life changed beyond recognition the day he approached me in the foyer."

He said they'd take things a day at a time. She had no choice but to do what he wanted because at this point she knew she couldn't live without him. If it was only for a week, so be it. The man was so complicated it was driving her crazy. Somewhere in the mix, Rini's inability to give a woman a child had stunted his vision of life. She wanted to help him explore the world of adoption so he'd realize he could know total fulfillment.

With her heart ready to burst from the joy his invitation had brought her, she lay down and didn't awaken until hours later, when she heard her parents' muffled voices talking about her sleeping her life away.

Alessandra sat up, disturbing Alfredo, who jumped to the floor. "What time is it?"

"Time for you to be in bed. Let's get you upstairs."

Later when her mother tucked her in bed she told her about Rini's invitation. "I want to accept it, but I'm afraid."

"Don't let what Francesco did keep you from reaching out for your own happiness."

If her mother only knew this had nothing to do with Francesco. But at least she had her parents' blessing.

Liona brought her breakfast at eight, after which Alessandra pressed the button programmed to phone Rini.

"Am I going to hear what I want to hear?" he answered in that deep voice. She thought she heard a trace of nervousness and loved him for it.

"Maybe, unless you've had a change of heart during the night."

"Alessandra—don't keep me in suspense."

Her mouth had gone dry. "I want to come, but I need time to pack."

"How much?"

She chuckled. "Do we have to leave by ten?"

"I don't care when we leave today as long as you're with me."

"Then can we say noon?"

"I'll be at the castle at twelve and we'll eat on the plane during the flight."

"It sounds wonderful. Ciao, Rini."

After ringing off, she hurried around her room to get ready for her trip. She needed to pack everything under the sun. Normally she traveled light, but not this time. Besides sportswear for their outdoor activities, her plan was to bring a few new bikinis and evening dresses that would knock his socks off.

She turned on her radio to some light rock music. The cat wandered in her room and probably thought she was out of her mind as she danced around filling her two suitcases.

"Alfredo? You should see his gorgeous villa."

"Whose villa would that be?" asked a familiar female voice.

Alessandra spun around. "Dea!" After being caught off guard, she hurried over to her sister and hugged her. "I didn't know you were coming." With Rini coming for her, she couldn't believe the bad timing.

"Evidently not. Papà told me about your accident so I came home to see how you are. I thought you'd still be in bed recovering. I never expected to find you flying around your room having a conversation with the cat. What's all the packing for?"

"I—I'm going on a trip," she said, her voice faltering.

"I gathered as much." Dea's eyes looked at the bags on the bed. "I do believe you've emptied your drawers and closets. Are you finally giving Bruno Tozzi a chance? He's been after you for over a year."

"Not Bruno. I've never been interested in him that way. Actually I'm going to be a guest at Rini Montanari's villa." She'd had no choice but to tell her sister the truth.

At the mention of his name, any goodwill Alessandra had hoped could be resurrected between her and Dea on this visit had vanished. Her sister paled. Rini really had hurt her by not asking her out again. "Are you talking about the one in Naples or Positano?"

Of course her sister would know all about Rini. She'd danced with him on his friend's yacht. "I assume Positano."

"Is this because you showed him around the property for Papà?"

"Dea? Please sit down so we can talk." Alessandra closed the lids on her bags. "He'd been scuba diving with me. It's a sport we have in common. When he heard about the earthquake, he flew down. Yesterday he came by the castle to invite me to stay with him for a week."

"You mean he hasn't been here all month?"

"No. He's been gone for weeks on business. I was surprised to see him again." So surprised she'd thought she'd been dreaming when he came to her hospital room.

Dea's eyes followed her around while she packed her cosmetics. "I was shocked to learn he had business with Papà in the first place."

"Let's agree it was a shock all the way around." Alessandra was so uncomfortable she could hardly bear it.

Her sister studied her for a minute. "Be honest with me. Are you going with him because of what happened with Francesco?"

"No, Dea—not at all! How can you even think that?" Alessandra cried. "Whatever happened is long since buried in the past." She sank down on the end of the bed. "What do you want me to say?"

"Have you fallen for him?"

"I care for him very much."

"As much as you did Francesco?"

"You can't compare relationships. Francesco was my first boyfriend. I was young. As you reminded me, he ended up being a loser."

"Don't you know why I told you that?"

Alessandra frowned. "What do you mean?"

"He wasn't interested in me. Within a day of his arriving in Rome, he was chatting up another model."

"Oh, Dea—I didn't know that."

"I thought Mother would have said something. I'm telling you this to warn you about Rinicri Montanari."

Alessandra didn't want to hear it.

"On the yacht, his best friend's father, Leonides Rossano, confided in me that Rinieri was Italy's most eligible bachelor—as if my best friend, Daphne, and I didn't already know it. I read between the lines and deduced he'd been a player for years. Alessandra—he might end up breaking your heart after he gets what he wants from Papà."

"You're wrong about that, Dea. He doesn't want anything from him," she replied, defending Rini. "He withdrew his proposal weeks ago and has been looking elsewhere for oil in the southern part of Italy."

"I didn't know that. Sorry." Dea stood up, but Alessandra could tell the revelation had shaken her. "How soon is he coming for you?"

"At noon."

She looked at her watch. "It's almost that time now. I don't want to be around when he arrives, so I'll join the parents while you get the rest of your packing done. I'm glad you're recovered. Even gladder that I wasn't the one under the water when the quake struck."

A rush of warmth propelled Alessandra toward her sister. She put her arms around her again. "Thank you for coming. You don't know how much it means to me."

Dea hugged her back. "You've always been the brave one." She kissed her cheek before disappearing from the bedroom. Alfredo followed her out the door.

The brave one?

An hour later those words were still chasing around in Alessandra's psyche as Rini helped her out of the limo to board the Montanari jet.

Once they'd attained cruising speed, his steward served them an incredible lunch of lobster pasta with *sfogliatelle* for dessert. The shell shaped pastry had a divine ricotta filling with cinnamon. The wonderful flavor was beyond description.

They sat in the club area by the windows. His dark eyes never left hers. "I'm glad to see a smile. When I picked you up, you seemed preoccupied. For a moment I was afraid you still didn't feel well enough to come. We could have left tomorrow."

"I'm fine, Rini, but I have to admit I'm still a little tired."

"After what you experienced, that's understandable. When we get to the villa, you can rest all you want."

She looked out the window, wishing she felt the same excitement he'd engendered in her when she'd told him she would accept his invitation. But Dea's unannounced arrival had taken her by surprise. Though touched that she'd come to see her after her scuba-diving accident, her sister's questions about Rini had put a damper on this trip.

He was doing everything in his power to make her comfortable and had no idea Dea had been at the castle when he'd picked her up. She didn't want him to know, let alone tell him what her sister had said. Dea hadn't been unkind. Alessandra had been grateful for that, but she couldn't help feeling that her sister was suffering in some way.

Alessandra remembered how she'd felt when she'd first talked to Rini in the castle foyer. The immediate, overpowering attraction she'd felt for him had to be swallowed in the knowledge that he'd already been with Dea. She'd wondered then if she'd ever be able to get over him.

Yet today, her sister had to handle the news that Rini wanted to be with Alessandra enough to invite her to his home. If Dea had felt the same overwhelming attraction to him that night on the yacht, then who knew how long it would take her to get over Rini, especially if he ended up being in Alessandra's future. The thought haunted her.

"I think you really are tired." Rini got out of his seat and adjusted hers so she could lie back. "Our flight won't last long, then we'll put you to bed in the guest bedroom until you're feeling your old self."

"Thank you." But she no longer knew who her old self was. Life had taken on new meaning since she'd met him.

* * *

Something was wrong beyond Alessandra's fatigue. Rini had sensed it the moment she'd met him outside the castle doors with her suitcases. He'd expected to be invited in to speak to her parents, but she'd whisked them away as if she was in a great hurry. Rini hadn't questioned her about it. In time he'd get answers. They had a whole week. Today was only the beginning.

Once the jet touched down, the helicopter flew them to the villa. He carried her luggage while she made her way along the path that led to the back patio. She looked over her shoulder at him. "You truly do live in a garden. At home I smell the sea air. Here, I'm assailed by the most heavenly scents."

"After living in Naples with the occasional scent of sulfur from Vesuvius in the air, I chose this flower-filled mountaintop on purpose. Follow me through the house. Your room faces on the pool. You can walk out the French doors at any time and take a swim. Come on. Let's get you in bed."

He saw her eyes widen in appreciation when they entered the bedroom off the hallway. "It's a lovely room. Those blue hydrangeas on the coffee table take my breath."

"I'm glad you like them. Go ahead and freshen up. I'll be back in a minute." He put her cases down and left to get her a bottle of water from the kitchen. Rini had given Bianca the next three days off so he could be alone with Alessandra and wait on her himself.

When he returned, he found her sitting on the side of the bed still dressed in white culottes with a sharp front crease. She'd layered them with a multicolored blue silk top and looked so sensational, he couldn't take his eyes off her.

"I thought I'd find you under the covers. This is for you." He put the water on the bedside table before opening the shutters to let in the early evening light from the pool area.

She smiled up at him, but it lacked the joie de vivre he'd seen while they'd been out diving. "I'll sleep tonight. Now that I'm in your world again—but only because you invited me this time—I want to talk to you. Please sit down."

He sat in one of the upholstered chairs by the coffee table.

"Where's Bianca?"

"On a short holiday."

"So it's just you and me?" He heard a slight tremor in her voice.

He frowned. "Are you worried about being here alone with me?"

"Of course not." She got up from the bed and walked over to smell the flowers. "Can we have a frank talk? You said you wanted to start over again. I want that, too, but I need to understand you better."

Rini sat forward with his hands clasped between his legs. "Would I have brought you here if I didn't want the same thing? We've got all the time in the world. Go ahead. Ask me anything."

She darted him a curious glance. "You say that, but I wonder if you really mean it."

"Where's this doubt coming from?"

"I don't know exactly. Tell me about what happened when you first met Dea. Being twins, she and I have shared a unique past. Sometimes it has been eerie."

"In what way?"

"It's hard to explain, but there are times when even though we're two people, we think as one."

Rini got to his feet. "I've heard that happens to twins. But what does that have to do with me?"

"I'm not sure and am only feeling my way," she cried softly before turning away from him.

He put his hands on her shoulders and pulled her against him. "You sound frightened," he whispered into her fragrant hair.

"I am."

"Of what? Of me? Tell me." He shook her gently.

"I've been going over the conversation that my aunt had with you about me and Dea. You told her that you felt no connection with Dea, but it was different with me." Alessandra turned around in his arms. "But it doesn't provide all the answers."

"What more do you want?"

Her eyes searched his. "Will you bear with me a little longer and tell me your feelings when you realized I wasn't Dea?"

His hands slid to her face. "After I left your father's office and went back to my hotel in Metaponto that first night, I couldn't get you off my mind. Make no mistake. It was *you* I was thinking about. From a distance you had Dea's superficial features, the same features that had drawn me on the yacht. But the second you said you weren't Dea, I realized my mistake.

"You looked so adorable standing there in your shorter hair and man's shirt that didn't cover up your bikini. Tanned, no makeup, bare-legged, full of energy, duffel bag in hand. I thought, I've got to get to know this exciting woman! I told your aunt I felt a connection so powerful with you, I couldn't wait to get back to the castle the next morning to see you again."

He felt Alessandra's anxiety before she eased out of his arms. "Thank you for being so honest with me." She was shivering.

"Now that I have, do you want to tell me what's going on in your mind?"

"After I entered the castle, I heard a voice call out *signorina*. You'll think I'm out of my mind, but when I saw you walk toward me, it was like seeing the prince who'd haunted my dreams come to life before my very eyes. I felt your imprint on me before you said a word.

"But the second you started talking, I realized you thought I was Dea and my dream was crushed to grist. She'd had a history with you. She'd been there first. I'd never experienced such envy in my life. I've heard of love at first sight, but I never imagined it would happen to me. My pain that she'd met you first was too excruciating to bear."

Her eyes glistened with unshed tears. "Until I learned the truth of your relationship with Dea during our drive, I'd been forced to keep my feelings bottled up and pretend nothing was wrong in front of my father."

Her words shook Rini. *"Adorata."* He reached for her, but she took another step back. "I haven't finished. There's something else you need to hear."

Rini couldn't take much more and attempted to get his emotions under control. "What is it?"

"When Dea and I were little girls, we had many of the same likes and dislikes that in some cases baffled everyone. One of the things we had in common was to talk about the princes we would marry one day. We played our own form of house with a miniature castle and all the characters Papà had made for us.

"Our mother and aunt gave us beautiful clothes to dress our dolls. Dea always had the most glamorous and stupendous outfits because they knew how much she loved fashion. I was given a fabulous boat that would sail me and my prince around the castle and the world."

The lump was growing in Rini's throat.

"We played for hours about living in the castle all our lives and being happy forever with our princely husbands and children. In our case it wasn't pure fiction considering the lives of our titled parents and heritage."

"Alessandra—"

"Let me finish," she interrupted. "You were there when she first laid eyes on you. You saw what I can't see. Rini, I'm convinced that when Dea met you on the yacht, she had the same experience I did. She saw you sitting there and knew you were the prince of her dreams. It was one of those times we were both the same person. By the expression on your face, I can tell I'm right."

He closed his eyes tightly for a minute. *Incredibile!* This talk with Alessandra answered the questions that had lingered in his mind about Dea. In view of what he'd just learned, the way she'd linked her arms behind his head and the ardent kiss she'd given him when they'd stopped dancing as if she'd been claiming him for her own made a strange kind of sense. Her actions had borne out Alessandra's theory.

Guido had acted nonchalant about it, but Rini had seen the glint of envy in his friend's eyes. That was the only time he'd ever known him to show a side of emotion that surprised him. But Rini couldn't be that cruel to Dea or Alessandra by telling her what Dea had done that night to show her attraction to him. It had to be a secret he would take to the grave.

His head reared. "What you're saying is, Dea is now the one devastated."

"Maybe."

"Then we're back to where we were before. If your guilt is going to keep you from enjoying this vacation with me, then I'll fly you back home in the morning."

"No, Rini—that isn't what I want. I just needed to have this conversation with you."

"But it doesn't solve anything, does it?"

"I guess I want you to tell me what we should do."

"If you mean that, then I suggest we table our concerns and enjoy our vacation. We'll just have to hope that time and work will help Dea get over whatever disappointment she's feeling." But that wasn't going to be easy since he still hadn't forgotten the conversation with her aunt. He'd been burdened by it. "As for you and me, I'd hoped to take us on an overnight hike tomorrow."

"You know I'd love that."

"Then we'll pick you up a lightweight backpack and

sleeping bag in the morning." She nodded with a smile. "How are you feeling now?"

"Much better. I'm getting hungry and know you are. Why don't we go out to dinner someplace in Positano."

"I've been anxious to show it to you. If you're ready, we can go now."

CHAPTER SEVEN

As RINI HELPED Alessandra into the black BMW parked in front, he squeezed her waist and kissed the side of her neck. When he reached for her hand and held on, her heart pounded with anticipation of the night to come. He started the car and they wound through the lush greenery toward the town center. She could see the twinkle of lights from the fabulous villas half hidden behind cypress trees and palms.

The interior of the car smelled of the soap he used in the shower. She was so in love with him it was impossible to hide it from him. If she didn't put Dea out of her mind, she could ruin this incredible time for them.

"Whoa. We're right on the edge of the cliff."

Rini flashed her a smile and parked the car along the side of the narrow road. "We've arrived at my favorite place. You'll love the view from here." She could hear soft rock music as he helped her out. They walked up the rock steps lined with flowers growing out of the vegetation to the little restaurant perched high up. The view from the terrace, where a band was playing, opened to the sea below between two mountain sides.

She gasped and clung to him. "That's a steep drop."

"Kind of like dropping eighty feet with you in our own private world." Trust him to remind her. "Come on, *bellissima*."

He put his arm around her shoulders and guided her to an empty, candlelit table. The romantic ambience made her feel feverish. Rini seated her and asked for wine from the waiter who recognized him. "Will you trust me to order for you?"

"If you'll trust my cooking when we eat along the trail tomorrow evening."

"I can hardly wait." After the waiter walked away, Rini reached for her hand and pulled her onto the small dance floor, where another couple was dancing.

"There's no room for anyone else."

"That's the whole idea," he whispered before biting her earlobe gently. They danced in place, sending her body temperature skyrocketing. "If you knew the dreams I've had about holding you like this. Tonight there's no wet suit to separate us."

She chuckled. "I noticed."

"I never want to be separated from you," he admitted in a husky voice and crushed her to him. Alessandra closed her eyes and rocked in place with him. Never sounded like forever. Was it really possible? But that question led to the troubling question about Dea still hanging over her head, shooting more pain to her heart. So it was better not to think, just relish this night under the stars with Rini.

"I could stay this way indefinitely," she murmured, "but I can see our food has arrived. Let's get you fed."

"How lucky am I to be with a woman who understands me." He walked her back to their table and they plunged into an exquisite meal of octopus on creamed potatoes and prawns, followed by vegetables and *carpaccio* of swordfish with a dessert of *salame de chocolat*.

"If we keep eating like this, I'll have to buy me a larger wet suit," she quipped.

His dark eyes glinted with amusement. "We'll hike it off tomorrow. For now you need to get home to bed. It's been a long day for you."

"I have to admit bed will feel good tonight."

"I knew it." He paid the bill and ushered her out of the restaurant. "Careful as we go down the stairs. Hold on to me."

She didn't need his urging as she clung to him. He walked her to the car, keeping her hugged against his side. Before he opened the door, he lowered his head to kiss her. She'd been dying for it. The passion he aroused in her was so powerful, she almost fainted. Someone in a car driving by let out a wolf whistle, causing her to blush in embarrassment. Rini only chuckled and opened the door so she could hide inside.

"Sorry about that," he murmured as they drove back to his villa.

"No, you're not."

"Would you believe me if I told you I couldn't help myself?"

Yes, if his desire for her was half as great as hers for him. She rested her head against the back of the seat. "This has been a wonderful night. I rarely drink wine and am afraid I drank too much."

His hand reached out to give her thigh a squeeze, sending rivulets of desire through her body. "One glass?"

"Already you're a corrupting influence on me."

Male laughter rang inside the confines of the car. "Didn't you know you've become my addiction? You'd better lock your door tonight."

She rolled her head in his direction. "I trust you, Rini."

"Maybe you shouldn't."

"If I didn't, I wouldn't be going camping with you. Where are you going to take me?"

"Along the footpath of the gods."

"Did you just make that up?"

"No. It's the name of a trail formed by man years ago along the Amalfi Coast. In my opinion it's one of the most striking panoramas of this world. You'll know what I mean when we get going. We'll follow it part of the way through gorges and precipices, then veer inland into the mountains."

"You've given me goose bumps."

"When you uncovered the mouth on that head, it raised the hairs on the back of my neck."

She eyed him with longing. "I can't believe how you just happened to know where to dive."

"Pure selfishness. I wanted you to myself." He pulled into the courtyard and escorted her inside the villa to her bedroom. Putting his hands on her shoulders he said, "Tonight was the perfect way to start our vacation. I'll see you in the morning and we'll get going whenever you're ready. Sleep well."

He gave her a brief kiss before exiting the room. It was a good thing. If he'd lingered, she wouldn't have let him leave.

Before she went to bed, she hung up a few things in the closet, then checked her phone. Her mother had texted her to find out how she was feeling since her hospital stay. There was no mention of Dea, who was probably still there. Alessandra texted her back, telling her she felt fine and that they were going hiking tomorrow. She sent her love to her parents. But when she climbed under the covers, her heart ached for Dea, whom she knew was in deep pain.

The ringing of the house phone at the side of the bed awakened Alessandra the next morning. She checked her watch. Seven thirty a.m. He was a morning man who loved fish. Little by little she was learning those precious things about him. With a smile she reached for the phone. "*Buongiorno*, Rini."

"Hot coffee is waiting for you in the kitchen when you're ready, but there's no hurry."

The excitement in his voice was contagious. She swung her legs over the side of the bed. "If I told you I couldn't make it until noon, you know you'd have a heart attack."

"Please don't tell me that."

"You'll have to be patient with me," she teased. "Ciao."

She hung up the receiver and raced around the room getting ready, once she'd taken a shower. After diving into her suitcases, she pulled on jeans, a T-shirt and hiking boots. She packed a cloth bag she'd brought in her suitcase. Quickly she filled it with extra clothes, socks, a hoodie, a flashlight, matches, cosmetics and a brush—all the little things needed for their hike. She'd attach it to the backpack they were going to buy her.

When she hurried through his elegant home to the kitchen, she discovered she'd only taken eight minutes to get ready. Not bad considering the gorgeous male drinking coffee had assumed she would keep him waiting for hours.

The look of surprise on his handsome face was so comical, she thought he would drop his mug. Alessandra grinned. "Got ya."

His eyes blazed with intensity. In the next breath he wrapped her in his arms and whirled her around. "I figured five more minutes and I was charging in to get you."

"Now I wish I'd waited."

A bark of laughter escaped his throat before he kissed her fiercely. He didn't let her go until she struggled for breath. "I've made breakfast. Go ahead and eat while I take your bag out to the car with the food I've packed."

"You made food for our hike? I could have helped."

"Bianca always has my favorite meat and cheese pies on hand. We'll pack some to take with us."

"I'm salivating already."

She reached for a ham roll and grapes. After swallowing coffee, she hurried out to the car. Rini locked up the house and they left for the town to pick her up a backpacking frame. He knew exactly what he wanted for her and soon they were on their way to the outskirts of Positano, where he parked the car in an area reserved for hikers.

Rini was a master at assembling all the gear, which included a tent, fishing gear plus all the other things they'd brought. "How does that feel?" he asked after helping her adjust the straps. "Is it lopsided?"

"It's perfect and the day is absolutely glorious."

Through her sunglasses she stared at the striking male specimen standing before her wearing his own pack. He carried the bulk of their equipment as if it was nothing and smiled back at her through his sunglasses. "Get ready to be astounded by the sights."

"After you, Captain."

They were off. She followed him along a well-worn path for about a mile. Before she knew it they'd come to a section with a thousand-foot dropoff and no railing. "Rini," she squealed in awe.

"We're at the top of the cliff. You'll notice that people live up here and use this path coming and going."

"It's a miracle. Unbelievable." They continued walking and ran into farms and terraces that grew fruits and vegetables.

"Some people come here for a hike and decide to live here in one of the little houses on these mountains."

"I can see why. It's so peaceful up here, unconnected to anything else."

"You should be here during a storm. The clouds drift in from the sea and literally collide with the cliffs."

"The view from this spot is breathtaking. That water is so blue, I have to take a picture." She pulled the phone out of her pocket and insisted he get in it. They took turns so he could capture her, then they trudged on.

Alessandra really did feel she was walking on the footpath of the gods. One of them was right in front of her. He took such wonderful care of her every step of the way, she felt cherished.

They stopped at noon to eat lunch under a tree, then made a turn into the interior. Rini was an encyclopedia on the flora and fauna, let alone the history of the region governed by Byzantine rule from the third century when Amalfi was a trading post.

He took her past gorges and caves until they came to a mountain stream. "How are you at fly fishing?"

"I've only trolled for fish in the sea. You'll have to teach me."

"You're going to love it. Let's have a snack, then I'll set up our fishing poles and I'll show you how to cast."

It felt good to sit down and relax for a little while. He told her to look in his tackle box and see what kind of fly she'd like to use.

"Do they all work here?"

"Most of them. Look for a gray spider fly."

Alessandra rummaged around until she found one of that color. "This?" She held it up.

"That's it. I'll attach it and we'll walk down to the edge of the water to catch our dinner."

She watched him put her fly on the line before he chose a spot. "Show me how to cast."

He demonstrated five or six times so she could get the hang of it. "Okay. I think I'm ready to try." But it wasn't as easy as he made a look. She hit too low, too

high and was too jerky. On her last cast she put the fly
rod too far back and her line was snagged by a shrub.
"Oh, no!"

Rini didn't laugh outright, but she knew he had to be
chuckling as she scrambled up the side of the ravine to
retrieve the fly. She made several attempts to no avail.
"Help! I can't get it out!" He joined her and carefully
extricated it from the prickly bush. "You're so good at
this I bet you've never done that."

"You have no idea the mistakes I've made," he confessed after pressing a hungry kiss to her mouth. "Come
on. Let's try it again."

"I'm embarrassed and want to watch you fish for a
while."

He reached for his pole and aimed for a spot near a
rock where the water pooled in the stream. On his third
attempt to catch something at the same place, she saw
a little fish grab his fly and he reeled it in.

"That was poetry in motion, Rini. I'll never be able
to do that."

"Keep at it and you'll become an expert like you
are at everything else." He got out his fish knife and
removed the hook before throwing the fish back in the
stream.

"Why did you do that?"

His eyes lit on her. "It was too small. Maybe he has
a big brother or sister swimming around. Now it's your
turn to try again."

She reached for her pole. "I'll aim for the same place
you did." This time she threw it so hard, her pole landed
in the water. *"Diavolo!"* she cried and jumped into the

fast moving stream to catch it. But her boot tripped on a rock and she felt flat on her face. Her pole was carried farther downstream and got stuck around a bunch of rocks.

Like lightning Rini was there to help her up. By now they were knee-deep in the water. She lifted her head, not knowing whether to laugh or cry. His body was shaking with laughter, but being polite, he held it back. She loved him so much, she couldn't stay angry and started to laugh.

"Apologies for the slip."

His smile enveloped her. "Which one?"

"Both!" She broke free of his arms and made her way carefully downstream to recover her pole. "Ooh—a big trout just swam past me. I wish I could have grabbed it!"

Rini's deep male laughter poured out of him in waves. He moved toward her.

"No, no. I can make it back to shore myself. You're probably thinking, is this the scuba diver?" To her horror, the moment she said the words she slipped on a moss-covered rock and fell on her face, making another big splash.

When she stood up sputtering, there was Rini taking a picture of her. "That's not fair." Alessandra made a face. "This is ridiculous." She raised her rod and stomped out of the water, flinging herself down on a grassy spot. "Don't you dare laugh again."

Rini raised his hands. "I wouldn't dream of it. I was hoping we could hike farther to a small lake, but under the circumstances we'll camp here. I'll set up the tent so you can change out of your wet clothes."

"I'm all right. Let's keep going. Maybe I'll have better luck at the lake. I'll just troll for a fish by walking through the water and trailing my line."

One dark brow lifted above eyes that were dancing in amusement. "You're sure?"

"Let's go." She put on her backpack, deciding to carry her pole as is.

Rini started out first. All along the way she heard him chuckling, but he never turned around. A half hour later they dropped into a dark green gorge. With night falling fast, she was reminded of a primeval forest. The water from the stream emptied into a silvery narrow lake maybe a soccer field long. "It's shaped like a fat eel!"

"Spoken like a scuba diver. My father always thought it looked like a cigar."

"What about your brother?"

"A long blimp."

She laughed. "And you?"

"The Veil Nebula."

Alessandra blinked. "You love astronomy?" He nodded. "Did you ever consider becoming an astronomer?"

"No. The universe is too far away. With engineering I can get my hands on something once I design it."

"You like the tactile."

He nodded. "We'll set up camp here."

"I love this spot."

"Tomorrow we'll explore the other end of the lake. The water trickles down to become a waterfall and cascades to the sea."

"I wish we didn't have to wait."

His gaze trapped hers. "You know the old saying. All good things come to those who wait."

"But I don't want to. Aren't I awful?"

"Later tonight I'll tell you what I think."

His words filled with promise almost caused her legs to buckle. In seconds he'd found them a grassy area and pulled out the blue-and-white two-man tent. She helped him erect it. They worked along in harmony. Finally she was able to go inside and change into warm gray sweats and tennis shoes. All her clothes needed to be dried outside, including her boots.

While he built a small campfire, she laid their sleeping bags side by side. The whole time Alessandra worked, she feared he could hear her heart thudding through the walls of the tent. Tonight they'd be sleeping together. This was the kind of heaven she never imagined could happen to her.

The light from the flames flickered, revealing his tantalizing male features. He'd thrown on a tan crewneck sweater over his jeans. His beautiful olive skin and dark coloring had been bequeathed by his Neapolitan ancestry. She could feast her eyes on him all night.

He watched her approach. "Come and sit down. I've made coffee to go with our pies."

"You're wonderful." She kissed his jaw before making a place next to him. "I'm sorry I couldn't contribute anything for our dinner. I'll do better another time."

"I'm counting on it," he murmured.

Her pulse raced as she sipped her coffee from the plastic mug. "Did your mother camp with you when you came out here?"

"Many times. Valentina, too. It's dark in this part of the mountains. She would bring her hand telescope and pass it around. I remember the hours she taught us about the constellations. Then she and Papà would slip into their tent and leave the three of us to enjoy the wonders of the universe. When I grew old enough, I understood they sneaked away to enjoy the wonder of each other."

"Oh, I know all about that." Alessandra chuckled. "Our family went on expeditions to Sicily. One time at the Valley of the Temples, we'd set up our camp. I thought we'd explore that first night while there was still light. But our parents told us to run along and enjoy ourselves.

"My sister and I eyed each other. We could always amuse each other. But it was another one of those times when we were both thinking exactly the same thing. You could say that night contributed to our enlightenment. I never looked at my parents the same way again."

Rini ate another pie. "I can relate." He let the fire burn down.

She sat cross-legged in front of it. "You've never told me where you went to school."

"University of Naples, then MIT in Cambridge, Massachusetts."

"You didn't meet a special woman during those years?"

He swallowed the rest of his coffee. "Yes, but I had a goal to finish my education and didn't let anything get in the way."

"Still, you know what I mean."

"She didn't matter enough to distract me from my agenda since I knew I couldn't give her a baby."

"I'm glad it didn't work out. Otherwise I wouldn't be with you now."

Rini stirred and got to his feet. "I want to continue this conversation, but would rather do it in the tent. Give me a minute to put out the fire." While he went over to the stream half a dozen times for water to douse the flames, Alessandra put the food away, then found her flashlight and took a trip behind a fat bush.

She kept the light on for Rini. Once she'd removed her tennis shoes, she entered the tent and lay down inside one of bags. Before long he joined her having exchanged his sweater and jeans for a dark blue sweatshirt and pants. His dashing smile took her breath. "I'm having the most fun I've ever had in my life."

"So am I."

He zipped up the tent flaps and opened the little screened window for air. Then he stretched out on top of his sleeping bag and turned toward her. "Do you mind if we keep the light on for a little while? I want to look at you while we talk."

She rolled on her side to face him. "I love looking at you, but you already know that."

"Alessandra?" He reached for her hand and kissed the palm. "Though I want to make love to you and never stop, I can't wait any longer to tell you what's on my mind first."

"What is it?"

"I'm helplessly in love with you, *adorata*, and want to marry you."

A cry escaped her throat. "Rini—"

"That couldn't be news to you." He sat up to face her. "I fell in love with you that first day. You weren't the only one who had a surreal experience."

Joy permeated her body. "I hoped you felt that way, but I hardly dared to dream I would ever hear those words."

"I've been afraid to say them because of the burden it puts on you."

She raised up on one elbow. "What burden? If you're talking about the fact that you can't give me babies, we've already had this conversation. It doesn't matter."

He shook his head. "Of course it does. But putting the reality of adoption aside, I'm talking about something else that I should have discussed with you weeks ago."

Weeks?

With that word Alessandra got a sinking feeling in the pit of her stomach and sat up. "This has to do with my aunt, doesn't it?"

Lines marred his features, letting her know she was right, and her frustration grew. "Instead of going diving that morning, you drove us back to the castle because you said you had business with Papà."

"I did," he muttered.

"That's interesting. When I came down to the office later to find you, he told me you'd gone. I heard the helicopter. According to him you were no longer interested in drilling for oil on our property. As a footnote he said you thanked both of us profusely for our time."

Her voice quivered, but she couldn't stop it. "I thought I was in the middle of a nightmare."

Rini was quiet so long, she couldn't stand it. "What went on with my aunt behind closed doors that caused you to leave without even having the decency to say goodbye to me in person? If what happened was so terrible, why didn't you tell me immediately?"

"I held back because I didn't want to betray a confidence that could bring pain."

"You've said that before. To whom?" she demanded.

He stared her down. "Everyone involved."

"I don't understand." Her tears had started. He brushed them away with his thumbs.

"My feelings for you ran so deep, I was afraid to spend another moment with you. The only thing to do was get away and never see you again."

She shuddered. "Don't you know how cruel that was to me? I'd fallen hopelessly in love with you and you knew it."

"Listen to me." He grasped both her hands. "I slipped away because I thought it was the best thing to do considering that I never intended to see you again."

Alessandra couldn't take much more. "Then why did you come back?"

"You know the answer to that. When I heard about the earthquake and knew your diving team had been affected, I came close to having a coronary. Nothing could have kept me away, not even my reason for leaving you the way I did in the first place."

"The accident didn't turn out to be that serious."

"It could have been deadly," he argued. "Don't you

know *you* were the most important person in my life? To think of losing you was so terrifying, I flew out of my office and left for Crotone. I had to search for you at two other hospitals before I found you. The moment I saw you again and your doctor told me you would recover, I realized I couldn't walk away from you a second time."

"Even if what you're about to tell me will hurt everyone?" Her question rang inside the tent.

"Yes. I have to risk it because I've just asked you to be my wife. But I was premature and don't want your answer until you've heard the whole truth from me."

A groan came out of her. "How long are you going to make me wait? Please just tell me what it is and let it be the end of all the secrets."

The sick look on her face devastated Rini, but she needed to hear everything. He drank part of his bottle of water first, then screwed the top back on. "Did you know that Dea flew to Taranto to see your aunt the morning after being on the yacht?"

A delicate frown marred her features. "That's news to me. I thought she told you she had some fashion shows that kept her in Naples."

Rini nodded. "That's what she told me. Does your sister have a special bond with your aunt?"

"Yes. Many times over the years she's gone to stay with her. My aunt took care of her after she was born so Mamma could have a break from two children at once. I usually spent time with our mother. I adore my aunt, but I'm pretty sure Dea developed a deep attachment to Zia Fulvia that has lasted. Our aunt is very glamorous and exciting. Naturally it meant the world to her since she couldn't have children.

"I've always appreciated that Dea and I were raised to be individuals. Neither Mamma or Fulvia played up our twin status. We were never dressed alike or put in the same classes at school. They wanted us to be able to express ourselves in our own way and have our own friends. Dea gravitated to Fulvia."

"Yet interestingly enough, in some ways you're more like your aunt than she is."

"You told me that before." She took a ragged breath. "You still haven't told me why Dea went to see her."

After listening to the explanation of Alessandra's background, Rini was beginning to understand a great deal. "Your sister wanted to talk to her about me."

A haunted look crept into her lovely face. "I'm surprised my aunt would reveal something that private to you."

"So was I, until she explained herself. I'm convinced that what she told me was motivated out of pure love for both you and Dea."

Alessandra lowered her head. "What did she do? Ask you to stop seeing me?"

"No. That's exactly what she didn't do. For the first few minutes she told me a story about a wonderful, brilliant girl who fell in love with a chef from Catania named Francesco and got her heart broken. Fulvia feared this girl would never get over it and never be able to forgive her sister, whom she'd always felt was more beautiful and loveable than herself. To Fulvia's great surprise and joy, this girl *did* get over her heartache. She seized life to the fullest without blaming her sister for anything."

"What?" Alessandra's head flew back in shock.

"That's right," Rini murmured. "Then she told me a story about another exciting, bright girl who fell for an engineer named Rinieri Montanari. He represented her prince incarnate, but she discovered he didn't feel the same way about her and she wanted to die."

Alessandra's chin trembled. "Oh, Rini…"

"*Oh, Rini* is right. Your aunt asked me to think carefully before I took another step. She feared Dea might not be as strong and courageous in battling her heartache as was the scholarly twin she'd always envied."

"Dea envied me?"

The shock on her face was priceless and told him this was a woman without guile. "She left me with a question and a warning before she went up to bed. Her exact words were, 'Is the recent love you feel for Alessandra greater than the lifetime love between twin sisters? Whatever you decide, you'll have to live with the consequences forever.'"

Rini didn't know how she'd respond after telling her the truth, but he hadn't expected her to turn away from him and sob into her pillow. *"Cara—"* He lay down next to her with his arm around her shoulders. She convulsed so much, all he could do was hold her and kiss her cheeks and hair until the tears eventually subsided. "Talk to me, *bellissima.*"

After a long time she turned over, her face blotchy from crying. "The warning she gave you felt like someone just walked over my grave."

"Why do you say that?"

"Because when I found out you'd met Dea first, I determined to put you out of my mind. Nothing was worth coming between my twin and me since we'll be sisters forever. I was taken by surprise when Papà asked me to drive you around the property. Much as I wanted to be with you, I knew it would be taking a great risk. Fulvia's words have just confirmed my worst fears."

Gutted by her response, Rini shut off the flashlight and lay down on his back. "I'm sure your aunt didn't want me to reveal our conversation to you, but my world changed after your accident and I had to tell you."

"I'm thankful you did. I know she spoke to you out of love for Dea and me." He heard Alessandra's heavy sigh. "It took a lot of courage on your part to tell me and I admire you for keeping quiet about it for as long as you have in order to protect Dea."

"What worries me now is where you want to go from here."

"I don't know, Rini. In the morning I'll have an answer. Thank you for the greatest day I've ever known. *Buonanotte.*"

He heard the rustle of her sleeping bag. She'd turned away from him physically and emotionally. Unable to lie this close to her without reaching for her, he stood up and went outside to walk around. A three-quarter moon lit up the night sky. He didn't need a flashlight or a fire to see the forested landscape. The lake shone a mystic silver.

She's not going to marry you, Montanari. I can feel it in my bones.

Rini felt like he was burning up with fever. The cool night air brought some relief. He eventually planted himself beneath the trunk of a pine tree close to the tent so he could keep an eye on her. Several times he nodded off, but was wide awake at six craving coffee.

After making it, he heated it on the ultralight stove. Once he'd downed a cup, he walked over to the stream. Though he cast his line half a dozen times, nothing was biting yet. Maybe it was an omen to prepare him for what was to come.

He could have kept the secret he'd shared with her aunt, but wouldn't have been able to live with it long. Alessandra's tearful breakdown proved to him he'd done the right thing telling her. But it was possible he'd written the death sentence on a future life together with her.

Near eight o'clock she stepped outside the tent with a false smile, dressed in another pair of jeans and a white pullover. One by one she produced their sleeping bags, all rolled up and snug in their cases. He didn't have to hear a word from her to know their vacation had come to an end.

Her eyes darted to his. "*Buongiorno*, Rini. I detected coffee. It smells so much better out in the forest, don't you think?"

Without saying anything he poured her a cup and handed it to her.

"*Grazie.*" She eyed his pole. "I heard your line snaking in the air. Evidently you didn't have any luck fishing this morning or you'd be cooking our breakfast."

Rini had all the chitchat he could take. "Why don't you just tell me what I already know," he groaned.

This morning she was dry-eyed. "Papà once said that Zia Fulvia was the wisest woman he'd ever known. After what we talked about last night, I'm convinced of it. I'm honored by your marriage proposal, Rini. No thrill will ever equal it. But even if I'll love you to my dying breath, I don't want to see you again. I'm ready to hike back to the car whenever you say."

CHAPTER EIGHT

A WEEK AFTER returning to the castle, Alessandra realized she couldn't go on in this state of limbo. Even if
she could dive again, she didn't want to. The thought
of working on her book was out of the question. She
unpacked all the gorgeous clothes she hadn't worn and
put them away. Rini was on her mind night and day.

Though her parents didn't question her when she returned home having cut her vacation short, she knew
they wanted to. But her father didn't probe and she was
thankful for that. Her aunt came to stay for a few days
to enjoy a change of scene. Soon she'd be able to get
around without the wheelchair.

Fulvia was as warm and loving as always, giving nothing away about her private conversation with
Rini. They did some puzzles as a family and Alessandra learned that Dea was back in Rome after another
sensational show in Florence attended by some VIPs
in the television industry.

But talking about Dea had been like pressing on a
thorn until she was bleeding all over the place. The day
after her aunt flew back to Taranto, Alessandra told her

parents she was taking the Land Rover to visit friends in Metaponto and wouldn't be back until evening.

She gave Alfredo a kiss on the head before leaving the castle. "I don't like lying, but this is one time no one can know where I'm really going."

Once she reached the airport, she boarded a flight for Rome. The plane landed at noon. After hailing a taxi, she asked the driver to take her to the elegant apartment complex in the heart of the city where Dea had been living for the last year. The five-hundred-year-old street where it was located was a warren of fabulous shops near the Pantheon and the Piazza Navona.

When Alessandra approached the desk manager, he called her Signorina Loti. "You've mistaken me for her. Would you please ring her room? I'm her twin sister and have flown a long way to see her."

The middle-aged man did a double take. "*Scusi, signorina.* It's astonishing how much you two look alike. Except for the hair… I suppose in this case it will be all right to let you in."

"Thank you, *signor.* You're very kind."

Dea had a fabulous apartment on the third floor. Fulvia had come to Rome to help her furnish it in a lavish style. After she'd been let in and freshened up, she went out again and left a note for the manager to give Dea when she came in from work.

Four hours later she returned to the apartment building having eaten and done a little book shopping while she thought about what she was going to say to her sister.

"*Signorina?* Your sister came in ten minutes ago."

"Grazie."

Her heart pounding with anxiety, Alessandra took the lift and knocked on her apartment door. Dea opened it looking gorgeous in harem pants and a filmy short-sleeved top of aqua. "This is a surprise."

"For me, too."

"Come in."

They hugged before she walked into the living room. She put down her sacks and turned to her sister. "Forgive me for not letting you know I was coming. I didn't decide until this morning."

"No problem. I thought you were still on vacation in Positano."

She shook her head. "I returned early."

Dea eyed her critically. "What happened to change things?"

"That's what I want to talk to you about. Do you have time, or do you have other plans?"

"Not tonight. If you want juice or fruit, it's in the fridge."

"Thanks, but I've already eaten.

Her sister sank down on the sofa. "Go ahead. What's on your mind that has brought you all the way here?"

"The last time we saw each other, you asked me if I was seeing Rini because of what happened with Francesco."

"And you told me no. Why are we talking about this?"

She sucked in her breath. "Because I'm tired of ignoring the elephant in the room and I have a feeling you're sick of it, too."

Dea averted her eyes. It told Alessandra her sister knew exactly what she was driving at.

Tears sprang into Alessandra's eyes. "I'm going to tell you something I've never admitted to you before. From the time we were little, I looked up to you as my big sister."

"Three minutes hardly qualifies me for that title."

"It did for me because you came out first and no one let me forget it. You were beautiful and made friends easily. Everything you did was elegant and perfect. As I grew older, I felt more gawky and insecure around you. By our teens guys flocked around you. I'm ashamed to admit I was so jealous of you."

She had to be getting through to her sister because Dea lifted her head and stared at her in disbelief. "You... were jealous of me?"

"Oh, yes. When Francesco followed you to Rome, I didn't want to believe it, but deep down I wasn't surprised. I'd seen the way he'd looked at you. He never looked at me like that."

"I'm sorry, Alessandra," she cried.

"No, no. Don't be. You didn't do anything to attract him. You don't have to. It always happens because you're you. For a long time after that I lived in denial about it. Finally I realized I needed to grow up and face the fact that I could never be like you. It meant I had to work on myself."

"But you're perfect just the way you are!"

It was Alessandra's turn to stare at her sister in wonder.

"It's true. All my life I've been the one jealous of

you. You're beautiful without even trying and you're smart. You write books and do all these amazing things with the underwater archaeological society. I've envied your love of adventure and hated it that I have so many stupid fears."

Alessandra shook her head. "I had no idea."

"We're a mess," Dea muttered. "Since it's truth time, want to tell me why you're not still with Rinieri? He's the most gorgeous hunk of manliness I ever saw."

"I agree," she said quietly. "But I wish I hadn't met him."

"That's the biggest whopper of a lie you've ever told."

"Dea—"

"It's true. You're mad about him. So what are you doing here with me?"

"Y-you know why," she stuttered.

"Because I had a giant-sized crush on him first? That's true, but he wasn't enamored of me no matter how hard I tried to entice him. It killed me that he didn't want to see me again. I even told Zia Fulvia."

Alessandra swallowed hard to hear the admission she already knew about.

"She laughed and said, 'Dea Caracciolo—do you want to conquer every man you meet? What would you do with all of them? It's not natural!'"

Alessandra's laughter joined Dea's.

"She gave me a simple piece of advice that made sense. 'When the true prince of your dreams comes along, it'll work. Until then, dry your tears and do your thing you do better than anyone other woman in the country.'"

"Fulvia's wonderful."

"She is. So are you, and Rini Montanari is absolutely smitten with you. Otherwise he wouldn't have invited you to his villa for a whole week. The famous bachelor has fallen to his knees. If you don't snap him up, then you're a fool."

"You mean it?"

"Oh, come here." Dea reached out and hugged her hard. "I have something else to tell you that should make you happy."

"What?"

"I made a play for him. He didn't bite."

"What kind?"

"On the yacht, I kissed *him* good-night right on the mouth."

"Good grief!"

"Don't worry. He didn't kiss me back and turned me down when I asked him to go out to dinner with me the next night. Only an honorable man would do that. You're a very lucky woman and I'll welcome him into our family with open arms."

"I love you, Dea, and want only the best for you."

"I know that, and I love you, too."

"Let's never let anything come between us again."

"Never."

"We're sisters forever."

Forever.

"Now let's go on a shopping spree and find you an outfit that will deliver the coup de grâce the moment Rini sees you. Why not show up at his office and dazzle everyone in sight?"

"I only want to dazzle *him*."

"Then let's do it!"

The Montanari office complex dominated a portion of a city block in the downtown business center of Naples. At four in the afternoon, Alessandra was met by whistles and stares as she stepped out of the limo in her Jimmy Choo heels. She was wearing the designer dress Dea had picked out for her. It cost a fortune but she didn't care because she felt transformed in it.

The solid off-white pullover dress with long sleeves had a row of trendy buttons up the side from the tulip-styled hem to the neck. Around her shoulders she wore a flowing ivory-and-tan print scarf that matched the tan-and-ivory lace of her shoes.

Her hair glinted with streaks of gold among the brunette. She wore new lipstick in a deep pink with a soft blush on her high cheek-bones and a touch of eye shadow Dea said brought out her eyes. She'd never been so decked out. Her sister said she'd never looked more beautiful. Alessandra felt like she was moving in a fantastic dream.

His office building was like a small city, forcing her to pass through security before she could approach the bank of elevators. Her pride in his accomplishments made her throat swell with emotion as she rode one of them to the thirty-sixth floor, where his headquarters was located. She approached the secretary in the main reception area.

"I'm here to see Signor Montanari."

The attractive, thirtyish-looking woman looked up, then blinked. "You're Dea!"

Alessandra smiled, not minding it at all. "No, but you're close. I'm her sister."

"Do you model, too?"

"No. I scuba dive."

"Oh." Her blue eyes rounded. "Which Montanari did you wish to see?"

"Rinieri."

"I'm sorry, but the CEO is in a board meeting and can't be disturbed. If you'd like, I'll make an appointment for you."

At least he was here and not out of town. "Thank you, but no. I'll wait until he comes out."

"It might be several hours."

"I don't mind." *I'd wait forever for him.*

She sat down on one of the love seats with her ivory clutch bag in hand. Twenty minutes later she saw an attractive, dark-haired man who bore a superficial resemblance to Rini walk into the reception area and hand something to the secretary. His brother? A cousin?

The secretary must have said something to him because he turned in Alessandra's direction. Their eyes met before he walked over to her. "I understand you're here to see Rinieri?"

"Yes, but he didn't know I was coming. I wanted to surprise him."

The flattering male admiration in his eyes made her efforts to look beautiful worth it. "He's going to be surprised all right. I'm going back in to the meeting. I'll let him know someone is out here waiting for him, but I won't give you away."

Her heart fluttered in her chest. *"Grazie."*

"Prego."

Twelve men sat at the oblong conference table. Rini's Zio Salvatore scowled at him from a few seats down on the right. "I think we're moving too fast. Look what's happened in Greece!"

"If we don't strike now, someone else will." Rini was tired of the deadlock. Tonight he'd reached the end of his rope. He was ready to take off for places unknown to forget his pain. Guido had tried to talk to him, but Rini was in such a dark place, he wasn't fit company for anyone. Something had to change or his life wasn't worth living.

"My son's right," Rini's father said. "With this uncertain economy, we have to take advantage of these opportunities while we can."

While everyone offered an opinion, Carlo came back in the room. His brother's brows lifted, a signal that he wanted to talk to him about something. It would have to wait until they'd resolved the issue before the board.

"Let's take a vote," his cousin Piero said.

"We're not ready yet!" This from Rini's great uncle Niccolo.

The arguing went on another fifteen minutes. Rini received a text on his phone. Just so you know, Octavia said you have one more appointment before you leave tonight. The person is waiting in reception.

Since when? Rini didn't have the time or inclination

to do any more business once he left this room, but he nodded in acknowledgement to Carlo, who sat at the other end of the table. When five more minutes hadn't yielded a consensus, Rini brought the meeting to a close.

"It's late. We'll reconvene on Monday and take a vote then." Salvatore couldn't have been more pleased that no action had been taken yet. He came from the old school, unable to abide the kind of progress Rini felt the company should be making.

After slipping out a side door into his private office, Rini rang Octavia. "Send in the person who's been waiting. Since they're infringing on my weekend, tell them I can only give them one minute. My helicopter is waiting."

"Yes, sir."

While he leaned over his desk long enough to sign a pile of letters ready to be mailed, he heard a knock on the door.

"Come in."

"Signor Montanari? Please forgive me for barging in without an appointment, but this is a matter of life and death."

He knew that voice and spun around, convinced he was dreaming.

"Cat got your tongue?"

The vision before him left him breathless. He *had* to be dreaming!

"The last time we were together, you asked me an important question. I couldn't give you an answer then, but I'm prepared to give you one now. But maybe too much time has passed and you'd like to unask it."

He could hardly breathe. "Remind me of the question."

"You asked me to be your wife." The tremor in her voice made its way to his heart.

"I remember. But you had an irreconcilable conflict that prevented you from answering."

Her eyes filled with tears. "Since then I've *un*-conflicted it."

His breath caught in his lungs. "How was that possible?"

"Two days ago I flew to Rome and had the conversation with Dea we've needed to have since she visited me in Catania. It was the heart-to-heart kind that immersed two sisters in tears. It was a time of love and forgiveness for all past hurts and misunderstandings. In the end she told me something I needed desperately to hear. So do you.

"She said, 'I wanted Rini Montanari to want me, so I made a play for him and kissed him good-night right on the mouth. He didn't bite.'"

Rini's head reared. "She admitted that to you?"

"Oh, yes. There's more. She said she invited you to dinner but you turned her down flat."

He shook his head. "I don't believe what I'm hearing."

"I do. That's because you're an honorable man, my darling. Not only for turning her down because you didn't have those kinds of feelings for her, but for keeping that secret to yourself in order not to hurt her or me. She thinks I'm the luckiest woman alive. I am! She said to tell you that she welcomes you to the Caracciolo family with open arms. That's a good thing because I plan to be your wife. I can't live without you!"

She ran into his arms, almost knocking him over while she covered his face and mouth with kisses. "*Ti amo*, Rini. *Ti amo*."

"Hey, bro?"

Rini's eyes swerved to the door. Carlo had just walked in on them, but he came to an abrupt standstill and a huge smile broke out on his face. "Well, look what my *fratello* snagged on his last fishing trip! I wouldn't have missed this for the world. Looks like Guido's the only living bachelor left in Naples. I'll make sure you're not disturbed."

He closed the door. By now Rini had sat down in his chair with Alessandra in his lap. They kissed long and hard until he started to believe this was really happening. She looked and smelled divine.

"How soon can we get married, *bellissima*?"

"Whenever you want. I think the chapel in the castle would be the perfect place. Dea and I had a chapel in our play castle. We always planned elaborate weddings with our dolls. We even had a doll priest. Did you know Queen Joanna married one of her husbands there?"

Rini hugged her hard. "I can't think of a place more fitting for you."

"And you, because you're my prince. We'll invite all our friends and family. We have room for everyone. The cook will plan a wedding feast with all the fish you can eat." He started chuckling. "Dea will help me find the perfect wedding dress and Fulvia will help Mamma do everything else. We'll ask your sister to bring her babies and we'll dress them up like little princes. Alfredo will walk around excited because there's going to be food. And Papà will play the host with a twinkle in his eye."

By now his chuckling had turned to deep laughter. "There's one thing *I* want to do. Plan the honeymoon," he whispered against the side of her neck.

"I was hoping you'd say that. Can we leave now and go somewhere private where I can kiss you as long and wickedly as I want?"

"What a ridiculous question to ask the man who's headlong in love with the most gorgeous woman alive."

"I hope you'll always feel that way."

It took them a while to stop kissing long enough to make it to the roof. Rini told his pilot to fly them to Positano. "We're getting married, Lucca."

He grinned. "Tonight?"

"Don't I wish. It'll be soon."

With a background of Vesuvius, the helicopter rose into the evening sky. Rini was so full of emotion, he couldn't talk. While they were in the air, he pulled a ring out of his breast pocket. He'd bought it a month ago and had been carrying it around, keeping it close to him like a talisman.

"Give me your left hand, *adorata*."

Her whole countenance beamed as she did his bidding. He slid the ring on her finger. "It's fabulous, Rini!" She held it up close to inspect it. "The diamond and setting—this is like the one on Queen Joanna's hand in the foyer of the castle!"

"The foyer was the place I fell in love with you. She's

the reason you and I met. In a way I owe her my life. I'm glad you noticed."

Her beautiful eyes rounded. "You silly man. How could I not notice? Just wait till you see the ring I have planned for you."

Joy was a new emotion for him. So new, he clung to her hand, unable to find words.

CHAPTER NINE

ALESSANDRA STOOD OUTSIDE the closed chapel doors with her father, where they could hear the organ playing. After waiting a month for her wedding day, she was so anxious to be Rini's wife, she'd started to feel feverish in anticipation.

"Papà? Why are we waiting?" Everyone was inside including her husband-to-be, whom she knew was equally impatient to be married at this point.

Her distinguished-looking father, outfitted in wedding finery and a blue sash befitting the Count of Caracciolo, turned to her with a gleam in his eyes. "Your aunt has worked her magic."

"What do you mean?"

"As you are a princess of the Houses of Taranto and Caraciolla, the Archbishop of Taranto is going to preside. We're giving him time to enter the nave through the side entrance."

A quiet gasp escaped her. "Rini's not going to believe it."

"He's going to have to get used to a lot of surprises being married to my darling *piccola.*"

She smiled at him. "You're loving this, aren't you?"

He leaned over and kissed her forehead. "Almost as much as you. After all the weddings performed in your playhouse castle, you're going to be the star in your very own. You look like an angel in all that white fluff and lace."

"Dea found it for me."

"Of course. That explains the long train."

"It's spectacular."

"So are you. I see your mother gave you her tiara to wear."

"Something old and borrowed. Papà? Do you like Rini? I mean really like him?"

"I think he's an exceptional man who has met his match in you."

While they stood there, Dea came around the corner toward them. She looked a vision in pale lavender carrying two bouquets. She handed the one made of white roses to Alessandra. "I outdid myself when I picked out this wedding dress for you."

"I love it. I love you."

"Do you know where you're going on your honeymoon yet?"

"Rini's lips are sealed."

"Lucky you." Dea kissed her. "It's time."

The doors suddenly opened and Dea took her place behind Alessandra and her father. Together they entered the ornate chapel with its stained glass windows, where a lot of history had been made. Every single person she loved was assembled. The archbishop added a solemnity to the occasion in his ceremonial robes. But she only had eyes for the tall, dark-haired man turned out in dove-gray wedding clothes standing near the altar.

The dazzling white of his dress shirt set off his olive skin coloring to perfection. He was her prince in every sense of the word. She prayed her heart wouldn't give out before she reached his side. His dark eyes seemed to leap to hers as she reached his side. While the archbishop addressed the congregation, Rini didn't remove his gaze from her.

"Surely heaven is shining down on these two people this day while they are joined together in the most holy ordinance of the church," the archbishop began.

Rini's hand held hers. He rubbed his thumb over her palm and wrist. She was trying to concentrate on the sacredness of the occasion, but his touch sent fire through her entire body. By the time they came to exchanging vows, he'd reduced her to a weakened state. Thank heaven the words were finally pronounced.

"I now pronounce you, Rinieri di Brazzano Montanari, and you, Alessandra Taranto Caracciolo, man and wife in front of God and this congregation. What God has joined together, let no man put asunder."

Her clear conscience over Dea had freed her from bondage. They both kissed with restrained passion, forcing themselves to hold back. But she was bursting inside with love for him. When she turned to face her family, her joy was so great she could hardly contain it.

"It won't be long now," Rini whispered in an aside. He squeezed her hand as he led them down the aisle and out the doors to the great dining hall that had once seen the courtiers of kings and queens. He reached around her waist and pressed her against his hip while they greeted their parents and guests. She saw her father hand something to Rini before they took their places at the head table.

Guido and his parents sat together before he took over the emcee job. "One good thing about this marriage. Alessandra has taken him off the market. Now *I'm* the most famous bachelor of Naples." He ended with a wonderful trail of anecdotes about Rini that had people bursting with laughter.

Dea took her turn. "Alessandra and I were joined at the hip in the womb. It feels strange to be on my own at last, but I couldn't be happier for her." She shared more nuggets of personal moments with Alessandra to delight their audience. Alessandra turned beet-red.

One by one, the members of both families paid tribute. Valentina brought tears to everyone's eyes in her tribute to Rini, who'd been so wonderful to her after their mother had died. Carlo reminisced over his own touching memories of Rini when their mother was alive.

There were more speeches, but she could tell Rini was restless. In a move that appeared to surprise him, she rose to her feet with some difficulty considering the length of her train. "Rini and I want to thank everyone for making our wedding day unforgettable. Zia Fulvia? What would we do without you? In fact, what would we do without our marvelous staff, my darling Liona and her cat Alfredo and the families we cherish."

Rini got to his feet. "I couldn't have said it better, but I hope you'll understand that we need to leave."

"Sure you do," Guido quipped loud enough for everyone to hear. Dea laughed at his remark. Alessandra hid her head against Rini's shoulder as they left the hall on a run. He led her through the hallway to the foyer. They raced out the doors to the Land Rover. He stuffed her inside and ran around to drive them to the helipad.

Their pilot was all smiles as he helped her on board. Once they were strapped in, they took off with Rini seated in the copilot's seat. "*Complimenti*, Signora Montanari."

"*Grazie*, Lucca. My husband won't tell me where we're going."

"We'll be there soon, *bellissima*."

"It was a beautiful wedding, don't you think?"

"Yes, but I thought it would never be over."

"Mamma said the wedding is for the bride. She was right."

The pilot flew east to the Adriatic, then dropped to a luxury yacht making its way through the water. Her eyes darted to Rini's in question.

"Guido's parents insisted on providing their yacht for our honeymoon. We can stop anywhere we want and scuba dive in Croatian waters. There are caves you'll love to explore."

"It sounds wonderful, but as you once told me, I don't care where we go as long as we're together."

Lucca set them down on the yacht's helipad with remarkable expertise. Rini jumped out and reached for her, carrying her across the deck to a stairway with the master bedroom on the next level down. She could see everything had been prepared for them ahead of time.

Flowers overflowed the living area of the suite, creating a heavenly perfume.

"At last." The way he was looking at her caused her limbs to quiver. He wrapped his arms around her and undid the buttons of her wedding dress, while he gave her a husband's kiss that never ended.

Somehow they gravitated to the bedroom, leaving a trail of wedding clothes and a tiara. The covers had been turned down. He followed her on to the mattress, burying his face in her throat. "Alessandra, I can't believe you're my wife. I've been lonely for you for years."

"You don't know the half of it. I love you so terribly. Make love to me, darling, and never ever stop," she murmured feverishly until they were devouring each other and conversation ceased.

For the rest of the night they communicated with their bodies, trying to show each other how they felt in ways that words couldn't. Rini took her to another world, where she felt transformed. When morning came she couldn't bear for the night to be over. Even though he'd finally fallen asleep, she started kissing him again to wake him up. His eyes opened.

"You've married a wanton. Forgive me."

In a surprise move he rolled her over so he was looking down at her. "I wouldn't have you any other way. You're perfect." Another long, deep kiss ensued.

"But was it…good for you?"

He moaned. "What a question to ask me? Can't you tell what you've done? I'll never want to go to work again."

"I don't know if I'll be able to let you go."

"Then our problem is solved. *Buongiorno, moglie mia.* Welcome to my world."

She pressed another avid kiss to his compelling mouth. "We're not dreaming this, are we? This is real. You really are my husband."

"You'd better believe it, but in case you're in any doubt, let me prove it."

To her joy he proved it over and over. Except for taking the time to eat, she drowned in her husband's love. They didn't surface for three days.

At the end of that time they planned to go up on deck. But before they left their room, Alessandra rushed around in her robe to pick up their wedding attire still all over the room. It would be too embarrassing for any of the ship's staff to see the hurry they'd been in after arriving in the helicopter after the ceremony.

"Darling? I found this in the pocket of your suit." He'd just come out of the bathroom with a towel hitched around his hips. She handed him an envelope.

"Your father slipped this to me at the castle."

"I wondered what it was."

Rini opened it and pulled out a letter.

"What does it say?

"'Alessandra's mother and I wanted to give you a wedding present, but it's for selfish reasons on our part. If you want to drill on our land, you have our permission. That way we know we'll see you part of the time when you have to be at the castle to supervise everything.'"

He looked shocked. Alessandra slid her arms up his chest and around his neck. "Now you know how much they love and trust you."

"I never expected this."

"That's one of the reasons why they did it. But my guess is, Fulvia helped Mother see that your vision can help our country."

"Is that what you think, too? Your opinion is the one that matters to me."

"You know I do. Otherwise I would never have taken you to see my aunt."

"We can thank providence you did. She proved to be the catalyst that helped you and your sister put away your demons."

She nodded. "One problem solved and one to go."

He kissed her with almost primitive desire. "We don't have another one."

"You're almost thirty-three and not getting any younger. Neither am I. If we're going to adopt children, we need to do something about it soon. These things can take time."

His brow dipped. "Are you desperate for a child already? Or tired of me already?"

"Rini... I'm not going to dignify either of those questions with a response. I'm simply looking ahead to our future. When I saw you playing with Ric and Vito a couple of days ago, I could picture you playing with our own children.

"I'm not saying we're ready now. Maybe the day will come when you'll want to consult one of the attorneys who work for you and we'll make an application to begin the process. But if it upsets you, I promise I'll never bring it up again."

He let out a ragged sigh and crushed her in his arms.

"I'm sorry I got so defensive. It's different when you know you can't have your own baby. I don't know if I could be a good father."

"No one knows if they're going to be able to handle it. I bet if you ask Carlo, he'll tell you he was nervous before their daughter was born."

"But he knew it was his."

"But he didn't see the baby until she was born. If we adopt, we won't see the baby until it's born. What difference will it make?"

He smiled. "You're right. It won't."

"Come on. Let's go on deck and soak up a little sun."

"I have a better idea. How would you like to fly to Montenegro for dinner? We've been away from the ship for three days. Wear that gorgeous outfit you showed up in at my office."

"You liked that one? I'll start getting ready right now."

"I like you in anything when you have to wear clothes, but if I had my way…"

"That works for me where you're concerned too." She giggled and ran into the bathroom, but he caught up to her before she could lock the door.

EPILOGUE

Eight months later

RINI WAS AT the drilling site when his cell rang. Hopefully it was Alessandra telling him she was back at the castle after her visit to her editor in Rome. Her book on Queen Joanna would be coming out shortly and the publisher wanted to set up some book signings.

But when he checked the caller ID, he saw that it was Maso Vanni, the attorney who'd helped him and Alessandra make application for adoption. The unmarried mother from Naples who'd been the right match for them was expecting her baby in a month. Rini hoped everything was all right. The last thing he wanted was to give his wife bad news.

He clicked on. "Maso? What's going on?"

"Lauretta Conti is in labor."

"What?"

"The doctor is trying to slow things down, but my advice is for you and your wife to get to the hospital as soon as you can."

"We'll be there!" He rang off and phoned Alessandra, but her voice mail was on. He left her the message that he was on his way to the hospital in Naples because Lauretta Conti might be having her baby in the next little while.

After leaving instructions with the crew, he drove to Metaponto for his helicopter flight to the hospital in Naples. There was no time to shower or change out of his khaki work clothes. En route he tried several times to reach Alessandra. "Please answer as soon as you can, *cara.*"

Once at the hospital he was shown to Lauretta's private room. The doctor said they couldn't stop the baby from coming. "My patient needs a Caesarean. You're about to become a father."

Rini had never felt so helpless in his life.

"The nurse will show you where to scrub."

The situation was surreal as he washed and put on a gown. He was given a mask and gloves. Before long he returned to the room and stood by the head of the bed. He and Alessandra had met with Lauretta several times in preparation for the baby's arrival. Where was his wife?

Suddenly things began to happen. The anesthesiologist administered a spinal and a team came in while the doctor performed surgery. Everyone seemed so calm. When he heard a gurgling sound, a thrill shot through him. A second later the newborn cry of the baby filled the room.

The pediatrician took over and Rini was told to follow him to the room next door. "I understand you're going to be the father of this baby."

"Yes." But fear held him in its grip.

"Where's your wife?"

"She's on her way." She would be when she got the message.

"He's strong for a preemie. Six pounds, twenty-one inches long. Seems to be breathing on his own. As soon as we clean him up, you can hold him."

The baby had a dusting of dark hair. Rini watched in fascination as the doctor checked him out. One of the nurses came in and put the baby in a little shirt and diaper, then wrapped him in a receiving blanket.

"Sit down, *signore*, so you can hold your son."

Nothing had seemed real until she placed the baby in Rini's arms and he was able to look at him. The sight of the beautiful boy caused his heart to melt. He didn't make a peep. Rini couldn't tell the color of his eyes yet. His little mouth made an *O*.

"You've got a cute *bambino* there," the nurse said. "Don't be afraid of him. He won't break. I'll get a bottle ready for him."

Taking her advice, he put the baby on his shoulder and patted his back. The warmth of his tiny body was a revelation. Emotion swamped him as he realized this baby would look to him forever as his father. Rini removed the mask and kissed his little head, wanting to be all things to him. A longing to protect him and give him everything possible filled his soul.

"Here you go." The nurse handed him the bottle. "He'll be hungry soon. Tease his mouth with the nipple and he'll start to suck."

He followed her advice. Like magic the baby responded and started to drink with gusto. "Hey, you like this, don't you? I like food, too. I'm a big eater. Always have been."

"Like father, like son." His wife's voice.

He turned his head. "Alessandra… How long have you been standing there?"

"Long enough to watch you bond with him. I knew it would happen."

Tears filled his eyes. "It did. I was terrified when I got here, but when the nurse put him in my arms…"

She smiled down at both of them. "Fatherhood took over."

"You need to hold him."

"I will in a minute. It's enough to watch the two of you. What did the pediatrician say?"

"He seems fine and his lungs are functioning even though he came early."

"We're so blessed." Her eyes glistened with moisture. "Can you believe we're parents now? I'm a new mom and didn't even have to go through labor."

"You're the most gorgeous mother in the world."

"And you're already a natural father. I can tell he's so happy to be there with you. He has almost finished his bottle."

She put her arms around his shoulders and stared down at the baby with her cheek against Rini's. "We're going to learn how to do this minute by minute. I love you for being willing to adopt. I know it wasn't an easy decision to make."

Rini was close to being overcome by his deepest feelings. "I never dreamed I would see this day."

"I know. It's a surprise since you're a true man of vision."

He cleared his throat. "I don't think you have any idea how much I love you for marrying me when you knew I couldn't give you a baby."

"But you *have* given me one, darling. He's in your arms and you're both in mine. What more could a woman ask for in this life?"

* * * * *

MEET THE FORTUNES

Fortune of the Month: Zoe (Fortune?) Robinson

Age: 25

Vital statistics: She is the beautiful, sheltered daughter of computer guru Gerald Robinson— who just might be Jerome Fortune.

Claim to Fame: Zoe handles marketing for Robinson Tech. She is also a pro at "handling" some challenging family members, including her dear old dad.

Romantic prospects: She's the boss's daughter, which some might find highly appealing. For Joaquin Mendoza, it means she's wearing a big sign that says Keep Off.

"They say women of my generation don't believe in fairy tales. We are not sitting around waiting to be rescued by a handsome prince—we take care of ourselves.

"That may be true, but I still believe in love at first sight. And in recognizing your One True Love when he comes along. For me, that's Joaquin Mendoza. He's gorgeous and sexy, but he's so much more. I feel as if I can see straight into his soul. He wants me, too—I just know it—and I want him to be my first. My first, my last, my only. But my strong, silent hero is holding back. Joaquin has no idea how alike we really are..."

* * *

The Fortunes of Texas:
All Fortune's Children—
Money. Family. Cowboys.
Meet the Austin Fortunes!

FORTUNE'S PRINCE CHARMING

BY
NANCY ROBARDS THOMPSON

First Published in Great Britain 2016
By Mills & Boon, an imprint of HarperCollins*Publishers*
1 London Bridge Street, London, SE1 9GF

© 2016 Harlequin Books S.A.

Special thanks and acknowledgement to Nancy Robards Thompson for her contribution to the Fortunes of Texas: All Fortune's Children continuity.

ISBN: 978-0-263-91983-7

23-0516

Our policy is to use papers that are natural, renewable and recyclable products and made from wood grown in sustainable forests. The logging and manufacturing processes conform to the legal environmental regulations of the country of origin.

Printed and bound in Spain
by CPI, Barcelona

National bestselling author **Nancy Robards Thompson** holds a degree in journalism. She worked as a newspaper reporter until she realized reporting "just the facts" bored her silly. Much more content to report to her muse, Nancy loves writing women's fiction and romance full-time. Critics have deemed her work "funny, smart and observant." She resides in Florida with her husband and daughter. You can reach her at www.nancyrobardsthompson.com and Facebook.com/nancyrobardsthompsonbooks

This book is dedicated to Jennifer.
Never forget you're a princess. All my love, always.

Chapter One

"Zoe Robinson, you could have your choice of any man in this restaurant. Why must you fixate on the one guy you can't have?"

Zoe pursed her lips and tested her friend Veronica's theory, letting her gaze do a quick sweep of the people in the Gilded Pig's dining room. The rustic joint was jam-packed with its usual lunchtime clientele. Strains of a heartfelt country tune set the backdrop for the scene—mostly businessmen of varying ages, shapes and sizes who pushed up their shirtsleeves and tucked paper napkins into their collars to protect their white button-downs from what was arguably Austin's finest barbecue. Even though the room contained an appetizing smorgasbord of men, not a single one in the large barn-turned-restaurant piqued her interest. Each and every one of them probably had fine qualities and was certainly worthy of *someone's* love, but not a single one did anything for Zoe. Not even the cute guy who was grinning at her over his pulled pork sandwich.

As the music—Tim McGraw maybe?—asserted something about being a *real bad boy* who at the same time was a real good man—she flashed a noncommittal smile at the guy and turned back to Ronnie.

"Why fixate on Joaquin Mendoza? Because I can't get him out of my mind. That's why."

Ronnie scrunched up her face the way she always did before she stuck a big fat reality-check pin in Zoe's balloon of possibility. "That would be very romantic, Zoe, if only he would ask you out. Or even better, if he would talk to you about something other than business."

Okay. So, maybe Ronnie had a point.

Still, Joaquin Mendoza had swept her off her feet from the moment he'd first walked into Robinson Tech several months ago. Actually he'd captivated her the first time she'd met him when her sister Rachel married his brother Matteo, last year. They'd been paired as maid of honor and best man, but the focus of the weekend had been on the bride and groom and, at the time, Zoe had no idea her father would end up hiring him as a programmer at Robinson Tech to work on a special project.

It wasn't simply that he was older and tall and good-looking—no, scratch that—the guy was *gorgeous*. There was something about the cool way he held himself, and he had the strangest ability to put all of her senses on high alert the minute he ventured within five yards of her. It was like his superpower. Zoe had been ruined for other men since Joaquin Mendoza had walked back into her life three months ago. It was too bad he seemed more interested in work than in getting to know her better.

He hadn't messed with her equilibrium on purpose, of course. In fact, even after all this time, he didn't seem to recognize she was a woman who was interested in a man.

A very specific man.

"Okay, if you're going to be stubborn, maybe you need to take things into your own hands. Who says you have to wait for him to ask you out?" Ronnie continued, straining so that her voice was heard above the music. "I mean, if you like him, maybe you're the one who needs to break the ice—make sure he knows you're interested in him. In the past, you've never had a problem with making your intentions known."

Zoe sucked in a long, calming breath, blew it out in a measured gust and took in the Gilded Pig's decor. A decade ago the space had housed an antiques market. Keeping true to its roots, the Pig was decorated with vintage pieces such as the ornately carved church pews that served as seats for the booths, mirrors with light-reflecting mercury glass that seemed to double the already expansive space, and old wooden chests of drawers and sideboards that held napkins, silverware, condiments, steaming coffeemakers and sweating pitchers of iced tea.

"I don't know, Ronnie. This feels different."

"How so?" Ronnie asked.

Zoe thought about it for a moment, but she couldn't really put it into words. She knew Ronnie thought it was because Joaquin hadn't pursued her like the other guys. But putting that aside, he wasn't like anyone else she'd ever known. This was different. Even if she couldn't define it, she could feel it in her bones.

"Trust me. With him, I think the old-fashioned approach will work better than coming on like gangbusters. He's a little older than I am and I get the vibe that he likes to be the pursuer. So that's the new preamble to my Husband List. Let the guy be the hunter and stake his claim."

"You have a new preamble to the list?" Ronnie asked flatly.

Zoe lifted her chin. "Yes."

For as far back as Zoe could remember she'd had a list of deal-breaker qualities she wanted in a boyfriend. Over the years the Boyfriend List had morphed into the Husband List. It included things such as *must love animals; must make me laugh; must be passionate about his work but must not let work come before me.*

"Girl, you are no wallflower. You've never had any qualms about making the first move. I would so not sit at home and wait around for a man who can't seem to catch a clue."

"Who says I'm sitting around at home?"

"Didn't you just say you're waiting for Prince Charming to make the first move?"

"Just because I'm holding out for *Prince Charming* to ask me out doesn't mean I'm sitting around."

"All I'm saying is even Cinderella had to put herself out there to get what she wanted."

Zoe smiled and sat a little straighter. "I do feel like Cinderella. Only in reverse. Because I'm the one searching for the perfect fit. I'm the new-millennium Cinderella."

Yeah. She liked that.

Ronnie took a long sip of her sweet tea and then set it down and gave Zoe one of her *looks*.

"In my book, the new-millennium Cinderella doesn't even need a prince. She's her own woman and all she wants is a fun night out and a great outfit."

The two girlfriends laughed. But Zoe found nothing funny about the way Joaquin looked right past her unless she spoke first. When she spoke, he was always charming and amiable. So at least he didn't *hate* her. But there had to be a way to get through to him. Because these dead ends made her feel as though she was losing her mojo. She wasn't about to toss in the towel without a good try. Well, a try that involved getting him to make the first move.

The server refilled their iced tea and set a mountain of red-velvet cake and ice cream between them. The dessert was so big it could've easily fed four hungry adults. But in anticipation of a treat, Zoe had kept lunch light, ordering a salad with grilled chicken. She fully intended to do her fair share of damage to the Pig's signature dessert.

"Is there anything else I can get for you girls?" the server asked.

Yes, please. One surefire plan for how to get the guy?

"We're fine, thanks," said Zoe.

The server smiled. "Just holler if you need me."

She left them and went to a table across the way where a man was flagging her down.

Zoe settled back into the red-checked cushion that lined the booth's stark, hard wood.

"Okay, we are not leaving this restaurant until we

come up with a foolproof plan to get Joaquin Mendoza to ask me out."

Veronica sighed and propped her elbow on the table, resting her chin on her left hand and forking up a healthy bite of the cake with her other hand. "Why are you asking me? This is so not my department, Zoe. You've always been the one who gets the guys."

"You're only as good as your last victory," Zoe said. "Joaquin is always working, rarely looks up from his computer."

"Isn't that why your dad hired him?"

Yes, but…wait a minute…

"I think you're on to something, Ronnie."

"I am? Okay."

"I don't know why I didn't think of this myself."

"Um. You lost me somewhere between the first bite and the bit about Joaquin's computer obsession?"

"My dad. He mentioned that he loves Joaquin's work ethic, but he also said he wished he would get more involved around the office."

"Did he really say that?"

Zoe nodded.

"In so many words." She shrugged. "Actually, it was more like he thought Joaquin was sharp and hoped he could find a permanent position for him after he finished the consulting job. So you could interpret that to mean he should *get involved*."

Zoe shrugged again as she scooped up a forkful of cake. "Well, he *should* get involved. *With me*." She nodded resolutely and put the bite into her mouth.

"I don't know, Zoe. Don't you think you should be careful?"

Zoe swallowed. "What do you mean?"

"I mean, is this going to turn out like all the others?"

Zoe poked at the cake's white icing with her fork, leaving tine marks that looked like tiny bird footprints on a snowy lawn.

"The others?"

"Come on, Zoe, don't be coy. You know you love the thrill of the chase. Once you get the guy, you lose interest, you move on."

That was partially true, but not simply because she had a short attention span. She believed in happily-ever-after. She knew exactly what she was looking for in a man and she didn't intend to settle. What was the use of hanging on to a guy who was wrong for her? If she knew the relationship wasn't going anywhere, wasn't it better to not lead on a guy? So, when the relationship had run its course, it was time to move on. It wouldn't do anyone any favors, prolonging the inevitable.

"It may seem that way, but it's not what it seems like. I have my reasons."

Ronnie arched an eyebrow over a knowing smile.

It wasn't as everyone thought. She had her reasons for moving on. Reasons she didn't care to discuss with anyone—not even Ronnie—because it was a little too personal.

Why did everyone have to be so judgmental, anyway? Especially when they didn't know the full story. Even if she did like to flirt, she was young and free and she had high standards.

She wasn't sorry about that.

How would she ever meet her prince if she didn't do a little kissing? She was down with meeting her fair share of frogs to find Prince Charming.

And speaking of kissing— "I have a plan. I'm going to ask Joaquin to help me put together a new website for the launch of the new FX350 Tablet."

Ronnie frowned. "Doesn't Phil in design handle things like that?"

"Maybe, but not this time. Plus, Phil is swamped with other projects. He will probably welcome the help. Since Joaquin is such a computer geek, he has to know how to do a simple website. He can help out a damsel in distress."

She batted her eyes and fanned herself with her napkin. "What gentleman doesn't like coming to a lady's rescue?"

The project meeting lasted much longer than Joaquin expected, and he was behind schedule with his report. That meant he'd have to burn the midnight oil. But what was new? Late nights in the office had become a way of life since he'd come to Austin. In the three months since he'd moved from Miami, he'd traded dinners at South Beach restaurants for microwaved frozen meals eaten at his desk.

The sound of a knock on his open office door jolted him from memories of the Miami club scene back to his office at Robinson Tech.

Joaquin looked up at the sound of a knock on his open office door.

Zoe Robinson stood there like a vision in black and pink. Damn, she was a stunning woman.

"Are you busy?" she asked.

"I'm always busy." He minimized his computer screen, more out of habit than for privacy. "But come on in."

He could've set his watch by her visit. She seemed to find her way by his office most afternoons around this time. He really didn't mind, even if her reasons for stopping by were usually thinly veiled. He'd been around the block enough to know when a woman was flirting with him.

He had to admit he was flattered by her attention, but that was as far as it would go. She was a nice kid. And she was exceptionally easy on the eyes. Hell, she was innocently sexy with that long, honey-brown hair that hung midway down her back. Don't even get him started on those big gold-flecked chocolate eyes of hers that seemed to change colors with her moods and tempted him to stare a little too long.

Nope. She was strictly off-limits because, hypnotic eyes and short, flirty skirts aside, she was way too young for him. When he'd been hired on at Robinson Tech back in February, the entire office had celebrated her twenty-fifth birthday. That meant he was nine years her senior.

If the age gap wasn't enough reason to steer clear, all he had to do was remind himself that she was the boss's daughter. He knew better than to go there. Been there, done that back when he'd lived in Miami. He'd learned his lesson and he certainly didn't intend to make the same mistake again. Especially given that his brother was married to Zoe's sister Rachel. That could get very messy.

"What can I do for you, Zoe?" he asked as she entered his office. Today she looked even cuter than usual. Her skirt did a great job showing off her toned legs. Not that he noticed, because he kept his gaze glued to her eyes so that it didn't slip into forbidden territory.

"It's your lucky day, Joaquin," she said as she planted herself in the chair across from his desk. Her eyes sparkled and her broad smile was contagious.

"Is that so?" he asked. "Enlighten me."

She sat forward on the chair and leaned in conspiratorially.

"Out of all the people in the office, I've chosen you to help me with a project."

Her smile showcased perfect white teeth. She cocked a brow as though she was about to present him an offer he couldn't refuse.

The phrase "he who speaks first loses" came to mind. So, Joaquin arched a brow right back at her, leaned back in his chair and waited for her to give him the lowdown.

"So, you know the FX350, that new tablet that my father talked about at the staff meeting last week?"

Joaquin nodded.

"We are pushing up the launch date and I need someone to build a brand-new website for it."

He waited for her to laugh or at least crack a smile to indicate she was joking, but she didn't.

Okay. Well. This was interesting. He certainly wasn't above helping out with the project, but his pay grade didn't make that a very good use of his time for the company. Not to mention, Robinson Tech had a design department and he didn't want to step on anyone's toes.

He was trying to think of a way to say that without sounding pompous, but before he could find the words another big smile slowly spread over Zoe's face.

"Gotcha," she said. "I'm just kidding. I wish you could've seen your expression, though. It was priceless. I know that's not your department. Though you're more than welcome to be part of the web-site design project, if you'd like."

"You're quite the practical joker, aren't you?" he said.

Zoe shrugged. "As I said, you're welcome to join us. If you do, then it wasn't a joke at all. However, I did come to ask for your advice on something."

She was adorable and outgoing and sometimes she flitted from subject to subject so fast, he almost got whiplash. Like right now. But he really didn't mind.

"About what?"

Out in the hall the faint hum and purr of the copy machine provided the soundtrack to two coworkers discussing a sports match—sounded as if it might've been soccer, but Joaquin wasn't familiar enough with the local team to be sure.

"Do you mind if I close the door?" Zoe asked.

That probably wasn't a good idea, but Zoe was already on her feet. The door clicked shut, blocking out the extraneous office noise, and they were alone.

They'd be fine for a few minutes.

He had a meeting with Zoe's dad, Gerald, at three. No one was late to a meeting with the boss. He'd have to go soon, anyway. On his best days Gerald Robinson was gruff. Joaquin didn't want to know what he'd be like if someone kept him waiting because he was flirting with his daughter.

So that meant he could give Zoe fifteen minutes max.

Ten actually. He'd need a few minutes to gather his

thoughts and notes before he made his way to Gerald's office.

"What's on your mind?" he asked.

Zoe stared at her hands for a moment. Suddenly uncharacteristically somber.

"You've been here…what, three months now?"

"Something like that. I started in February."

Last December he'd moved from Miami to Horseback Hollow, Texas, a quaint little town just outside Lubbock. All but one of his brothers and his sister had moved there to be close to their father, who had relocated to work at the Redman Flight School. His dad had been mourning the loss of his wife, Joaquin's mother, and thought the change of scenery would be good for him. Horseback Hollow had agreed with his father so well that Joaquin had decided to leave Miami and give small-town living a try, as well.

Sometimes the grind of South Florida was just too much. Plus, he had accumulated too much excess baggage living there for so long. All he wanted to do was to lighten his load. But even though Horseback Hollow had been a good fit for his father and siblings—his dad was in love again, and his brothers and sister had met and married their future spouses there—the laid-back pace was way too slow for him.

He'd wanted to make a new start, but after being there only a couple of weeks he'd felt as if he was stuck in a different kind of rut in the small Texas town. When his brother Matteo's wife, Rachel, offered to put in a good word for him at Robinson Tech, Joaquin had jumped at the chance to move to Austin when Gerald Robinson, the man himself, had offered to bring him on to consult on a temporary project.

"Since you've been here," Zoe said, "you've worked pretty closely with my dad and you've had a chance to get to know him." Her words trailed off.

"I haven't worked directly with him that much. But your dad is a computer genius and I consider myself fortunate to have had the opportunity to work for Robinson."

Zoe raised a finger. "That's precisely my point. He is so smart. Sometimes too smart for his own good. How can I put this delicately? Because I adore my father, I just want what's best for him."

"Right," Joaquin said. "Everyone knows you and your father are close."

"Joaquin, will you please help me help my father improve his image? He's not exactly a diplomat or even a people person for that matter, and it's really starting to take its toll."

Oh, hell, no. That was a recipe for disaster if he'd ever heard one. He was a computer geek, for God's sake. Gerald probably knew more about diplomacy than he did. Well, that was stretching it, but not by much.

"Just the other day," Zoe continued, "I called a Robinson client who works with the South by Southwest Festival to see if I could interview him for that lifestyle blog I do for Robinson Tech. I was going to tie it into the calendar software program we have and, you know, have the event on the calendar. But you know what happened?"

Joaquin shook his head. "What happened?"

"The guy hung up on me. Before he did, he asked if this was Gerald Robinson's company and when I said it was, he called my dad a bunch of names I won't repeat and said he didn't want anything to do with anything that Gerald Robinson was involved with and he would be taking his business elsewhere. The he hung up on me. I mean, my dad has even started offending clients. So someone needs to stage an intervention. And quick."

"You want me to help you stage an intervention for your father?"

Gerald Robinson was a gruff, cranky old genius who certainly wouldn't appreciate a temporarily contracted employee butting in where he didn't belong. That was the quickest way to get him a first-class ticket out of there. Do not pass Go. Do not collect two hundred dollars.

Yet one look at Zoe's earnest face and he knew this time she was not kidding. He'd have to find a way to let her down easily.

He smiled and shook his head. "You must have me confused with someone else, Zoe. I'm the guy who's good with computers, not people. In fact, I could probably borrow some of those tips you're trying to gather up for your father. This is a delicate issue. You, his daughter, might be able to go there, but the rest of us need to tread carefully. If I got involved, I guarantee you it wouldn't be pretty."

She didn't say anything. Just stared at her hands in her lap. He hated disappointing her, but this was way out of his league.

"That website you were talking about a minute ago?" he said. "I'd rather do that. It's more my speed than making over your father's image."

She looked up and blinked as if her mind was changing gears.

"Are you saying you'll help me with the website?"

"Wait. What? No."

"But you just said you'd rather do that, and I was only half joking when I brought up the new site a minute ago. Phil in design is swamped and I could really use some help. Otherwise, I'll have to outsource the job. I can write the content, but all that technical HTML stuff is like a foreign language to me. Will you help me, Joaquin? *Please?*"

She wrinkled her nose and gave him a tentative smile that almost seemed as if she was holding her breath waiting for his answer.

The woman was a force of nature. He wasn't quite sure what she'd just done there, and he obviously didn't know what he was doing when he heard himself saying, "Sure, I'll help you with the website. Why don't we schedule a meeting?"

He thought he saw a flicker of surprise in Zoe's eyes. "Oh, thank you. Does tomorrow at three o'clock work for you?"

He called up the calendar on his phone. "I can spare a half hour."

"Well, we will just have to make the most of that time, then."

She smiled at him as she stood and smoothed her skirt. Before he could stop himself, his gaze followed the path her hands were tracing. When he realized what he was doing, his gaze skidded back up to her face so fast, if there'd been a music to accompany the moment it would've sounded like a needle scratching across a vinyl record.

Had she just played him? The treacherous waters of possibly hosting an intervention to teach Gerald Robinson manners had certainly made the thought of designing a website for the FX350 seem like a child's birthday party in comparison.

The victorious glint in her eyes tempted him to backpedal, but he didn't. And when the unspoken window of opportunity to back out closed, he knew he'd need to be careful.

He had to admit he was attracted to her. He'd have to be dead or barely breathing not to be. She was a stunningly beautiful woman, but he was not going to cross that line. He could exercise some self-control for the duration of their thirty-minute meeting.

"So, your place or mine?" The flirtatious note was back in her voice.

But before he could answer, someone knocked and opened the door. "Sorry to bother you— *Oh!*" Steffi-Anne Bunting, the office manager, stuck her blond head in but stopped midsentence when she saw Zoe standing there.

Her eyes narrowed as she looked back and forth between Zoe and him.

"Do you need something, Steffi-Anne?" Joaquin asked.

"I was just, uh—" She pointed at a clipboard in her hand. "I just noticed that we don't have your RSVP for the executive office trip to Cowboy Country. We leave this Thursday afternoon and we need a final head count. May I put you down as a yes?"

Steffi-Anne was another one who tended to pop into his office regularly. She could've emailed him about this. But since she was here now… "Actually, I sent my regrets last week. Didn't you get it?"

"Yes," Steffi-Anne said, "I got it, but—"

"You're not going?" Zoe cried. "You have to go."

Joaquin shook his head. "This is a team-building thing. I'm a temporary employee. I didn't think it was appropriate."

"It's completely appropriate," Steffi-Anne countered with a slightly condescending tone. "That's why you were invited. That's why I'm following up."

The truth was he just wasn't good at this rah-rah, team-building bull. It made him uncomfortable. No, *uncomfortable* wasn't a strong enough word. It made him feel like a caged animal. And all he wanted to do when he felt backed into a corner was get the hell out.

He looked at the two attractive women standing in his office and knew that he should've loved the fact that they both seemed to take extra interest in him. There was a time not so long ago when he would've dated both of them. At the same time, as a matter of fact. He would've reveled in the game of juggling them both, along with various other women he might've kept up in the air right along with them.

Not anymore, though.

He'd learned the hard way that office romances usually led to disaster, and he knew damn good and well that toying with emotions was the fastest way to earn an express ticket to hell.

"I'm sure you'll have a great time at Cowboy Country, but I have a lot of work to get done and a very short amount of time to accomplish it. So, thanks, but I'll have to decline."

"We'll see about that." Steffi-Anne's smile was out of context with the edge in her voice.

"Stop pushing him," Zoe said. "If he doesn't want to go, he doesn't have to."

Clutching the clipboard to her chest, Steffi-Anne

put her free hand on her thin hip. "Look, Mr. Robinson wants every employee in the executive office to go on this Cowboy Country retreat. If it makes you feel any better, Joaquin, it's for work. It's not for fun. Heaven forbid anyone ever force you to have fun. I think you'll want to clear your schedule."

His gaze snared Zoe's. Despite the way she'd defended him, there seemed to be something hopeful in her eyes. She'd be there, of course. Suddenly, the thought of attending the retreat seemed a lot more palatable.

Chapter Two

The next afternoon Zoe positioned two cappuccinos, red plastic stirrers and various packets of sugar and artificial sweetener on the corner of her desk. She turned the cups just so, then walked over to her office door and looked at them from the angle of someone just entering the room.

"That looks too posed," she murmured under her breath as she walked back to her desk.

Well, of course it did. "It *is* posed. Just be cool and casual about it."

She picked up one of the paper cups and took a sip, making sure to leave a bright red lipstick imprint before setting it closer to her computer keyboard. That way it would look less formal. Not as if she was waiting for Joaquin to drink her coffee.

For good measure she returned the other cup and

the condiments to the beverage carrier on the credenza behind her desk.

What if he didn't like cappuccino? What if it looked too presumptuous that she'd bought him a coffee? What if she drove herself crazy with all this second-guessing?

She placed her hand on her breastbone. Her heart was thudding. She took in a steadying deep breath—going in through her nose, releasing it through her mouth.

This wasn't a date, and it wasn't as if she was delivering a coffee to his office out of the blue. He was helping her with the website. It was a nice gesture. Of course it didn't seem presumptuous.

If he didn't like coffee, she would simply give it to someone else.

"What are you looking at?" The sound of Joaquin's deep voice made her jump. He was standing behind her, following her gaze with his own.

She turned to him with a sudden feeling of clarity. "You want to know the truth?"

"Of course."

"I got you a cappuccino when I went out to get myself one, and I just realized I have no idea if you even like coffee. Do you?"

"I love it," he said. "And, actually, I could use a shot of caffeine right now."

Zoe gestured toward the credenza. "Well, there you go. At your service."

As Joaquin helped himself to the lone cup in the holder, Zoe made a mental note that he didn't add any sweeteners to his coffee.

Good to know. For future reference.

"Thanks for this."

Joaquin took a long sip of his drink, set it on her desk and then proceeded to move one of her office chairs around to the other side of the desk so the two of them would be sitting side by side. She couldn't help but notice how his biceps flexed and bunched under the short sleeve of his white polo shirt. The light color showcased the deep, bronzy tan of his skin and she had a sudden mental picture of him on South Beach in Miami in a pair of board shorts and nothing else. She'd gone there for spring break when she was in college. Too bad she hadn't known him then.

It made her wonder about his life before coming to Robinson Tech. Had he dated a lot of women or did he have someone special?

"Shall we get started?" Joaquin gestured for her to sit. After she slid into her seat, he settled in next to her. He was close enough that she could smell the soap he'd used and the subtle herbal scent of his aftershave. She propped her elbow on the chair's armrest and leaned closer, breathing in a little deeper, savoring the scent of him as he pulled the wireless keyboard toward him.

Obviously he was oblivious because he was all business. With a few keystrokes he'd called up the page they needed and had signed in to a screen that looked utterly foreign to Zoe.

She centered herself in her chair, prepared to act like the consummate professional and not some love-sick puppy fawning all over him. That was the opposite of the tactics Steffi-Anne used. Zoe knew the woman had it bad for Joaquin. She and every other female in the office. But where Zoe tended to go all starry and wistful around him, Steffi-Anne became a dominatrix.

It was interesting how Joaquin didn't seem to be partial to either of them.

Professionalism was Zoe's safety net, her comfort zone. She'd gotten her job because of her ability and not simply because her father owned the company.

Steffi-Anne had made a few passive-aggressive digs about nepotism and, if Zoe were completely honest, it used to bother her, but she'd learned to let her job performance speak for itself.

That's why she needed this website to be top-notch. That's why she'd asked for Joaquin to lend his expertise.

She'd emailed him the specs and design ideas for the new site, as well as some images she'd procured for the project. Since she'd already turned in her homework and had no idea what all the numbers, letters and symbols he was keying in meant, she knew she would be no help right now.

What was the harm in making a little small talk?

"So, you like coffee," Zoe said. "What else don't I know about you?"

"What do you mean?" He kept his gaze trained on the computer monitor as his fingers tapped on the keyboard.

"I mean, I realized that we've been working together for three months and I barely know anything about you."

"I'm a private person," he said.

"So, does that mean that you won't even share basics with me? You know, the niceties that people share when they're getting to know each other? Even if it's just to make conversation?"

"Is that what we're doing? Getting to know each other? Or making conversation?"

"I'd like to get to know you."

When he didn't protest, she took it a step further.

"How about if I ask you one question and then you can ask me one after you answer mine?"

"Why do you get to go first?" he asked drily.

"If you feel strongly about it, you can go first. By all means. Please."

His hands stopped typing and he slanted a glance in her direction. So, he was going to humor her, after all. For the first time since Joaquin had walked through the Robinson Tech doors Zoe felt a glimmer of hope where he was concerned.

Casually, she shifted her weight to her right elbow and discreetly inhaled another deep breath.

"Ladies first. By all means."

"You're such a gentleman."

There were a million things she wanted to ask him, but she knew if she went right for the juicy, personal stuff, it might send him back into his shell.

So she opted for something that stayed on neutral territory to warm up the conversation.

"What did you decide about the Cowboy Country trip?" she asked. "Are you going?"

"Actually, I think I will."

"Really? Are you just trying to get Steffi-Anne off your back? The woman doesn't like to take no for an answer, does she? You'd think it was her own personal party."

"I don't know about that," he said. "But I have family in Horseback Hollow and I figured it would be a good chance to visit. But instead of riding the bus with everyone and staying with the group on Thursday, I think I'll drive down on my own and stay with my dad. I'll miss the dinner Thursday evening, but I'll catch up with everyone Friday."

"That's right. You lived in Horseback Hollow before you moved here, didn't you?"

"I'm from Miami, originally. I only lived there for a few months to be with my family before I moved here. Horseback Hollow was a little too sleepy for me."

He had a point. It probably was dull when compared to Miami. Even Austin had a different feel than South Florida. Granted, there was a lot more going on in Austin than in Horseback Hollow; Austin was edgy while Miami had more of a sultry, sexy feel.

Yes, sexy, sultry, like Joaquin Mendoza. With those brown bedroom eyes, he could've been the poster boy for everything that was exciting about Miami. She was certainly glad he'd brought that excitement into her world.

Her stomach fluttered.

Yes, she was very glad he was here now. Maybe if he continued to help with projects like this website, her father would find a permanent position for him after Joaquin had completed his temporary assignment. Then he could move here full-time.

"How do you like Austin?" she asked.

He shrugged, but just barely because his full concentration seemed to be focused on the computer screen.

"So far, so good."

Okay, that was a little noncommittal. His expression and body language were a little aloof. And he'd given a closed answer.

Maybe she should move on to another topic?

Horseback Hollow was too sleepy for him. He'd gone there to be closer to his family. She liked that. Family was everything to her, even if her siblings could be a little overbearing sometimes.

Like the way her older brother Ben had been harping on the fact that several members of the illustrious Fortune family lived in Horseback Hollow. He was obsessed with the Fortunes and the absurd notion that their own father was related to them. Between Ben and her sister Rachel who lived in Horseback Hollow, they'd managed to get their sisters and brothers on the bandwagon, too. It was causing a lot of strain with their father, who insisted there wasn't a drop of Fortune blood in his veins.

Even though Zoe was firmly on her father's side and respected his word that he wasn't related to the distinguished clan, she still thought it would be interesting to see what Joaquin had to say about them.

"So you know the Fortune family, don't you?" Zoe asked. "I mean you have a connection to them, right?"

He looked at her for a moment as if he were trying to read her.

"It's a huge clan, but I do know some of them since my brother Cisco is married to Delaney Fortune Jones, and my sister, Gabriella, is married to Jude Fortune Jones. But, honestly, I haven't spent much time around them. Why do you ask?"

Her stomach clenched and she suddenly regretted bringing up the subject. Still, she had, so she felt as if she owed him some sort of explanation.

"The Fortune name has been bandied about quite a bit these days among my family."

"Really? How come?"

Zoe sighed. "It's a long, complicated story."

Joaquin turned his attention back to the computer. "If you'd rather not say, that's fine. I really don't know them that well. If you think about it, my brother is married to your sister. So, really, there's as much of a connection between us as there is between the Fortunes and me."

She might have taken offense to that remark if he hadn't raised his brows and smiled at her in a way that sent ribbons of awareness fluttering in her stomach.

Zoe remembered the first time she'd met Joaquin. It was last year at Rachel's wedding. She'd been the maid of honor and Joaquin had been Matteo's best man. She guessed the special honor had been bestowed upon him because he was the oldest of his siblings. She wondered how he felt being the eldest and having three of his four younger siblings married before him. She knew about his family because she'd pumped her own sister for information. Then again, the order in which siblings married didn't seem to bother guys.

All she knew was that she was glad she was one of the youngest of her clan because there seemed to be something in the water in Austin, too. In addition to Rachel getting married last year, her brothers Ben and Wes had meet their soul mates this year and were living their very own happily-ever-afters.

At the rate she was going she might end up being the spinster sister, or at least the last one married. Her gaze swept over Joaquin's perfect profile and her stomach performed that somersault that was becoming all too familiar when she saw him.

"Were there any Fortunes in Miami?"

He shook his head.

"Not to my knowledge. It seems like this is bothering you a bit more than you're admitting. Sure you don't want to talk about it?"

As she looked into his eyes all she could think of was how much she'd love to talk to him about anything. Shoot, she'd even be happy sitting there discussing the complicated gibberish on the computer screen. Then again, she'd do more listening than talking since she knew so little about it.

"Can you keep a secret?" she asked.

He looked at her warily. "If this is something you shouldn't be telling me, then maybe you shouldn't."

"No, it's not really a *secret*. I mean, not one that shouldn't be told. If it was, I wouldn't talk about it. I guess what I was trying to ask is that you keep it between you and me. Of course, it's not as if you'd tell anyone here. You don't seem the type to engage in office gossip."

He chuckled. "No, gossip isn't really my thing."

He had turned his full attention on her now. As he sipped his coffee, watching her over the cup, her mouth went a little dry.

She followed suit and took a sip of her coffee before speaking. "All right. So, get this. My siblings have latched on to the absurd notion that my father is somehow related to the Fortunes."

Joaquin squinted at her, looking as confused as Zoe had felt when she'd first heard the news.

"Is he?" Joaquin asked. "It's a huge family. There are branches all over the place. It wouldn't surprise me if there were Fortunes in Austin."

"There aren't. I mean, at least there aren't any Fortune bloodlines tied to the Robinson family. My father has made that perfectly clear. I don't completely understand where my brothers and sisters got this notion, but I think they should drop the issue since our father has asked them to."

"But they keep pushing?"

"Right. My brother Ben went as far as tracking down a woman named Jacqueline Fortune. He's convinced that she is our long-lost grandmother. But get this. She had one son named Jerome—*Jerome*, not Gerald, mind you—and when Ben asked her about him, she told him that her son, Jerome, was dead. She said he died decades ago. But do you think that stopped Ben from moving ahead with this weird crusade? No, he just keeps pushing and pushing and hitting dead end after dead end. He thinks Jacqueline Fortune is mistaken."

Not only did Joaquin knit his gorgeous brows, he flinched at the notion.

"What?" he said. "Wouldn't a mother know if her son died?"

"I know, right? Apparently, Ben located Jacqueline in a memory-care unit of a nursing home. I think she is suffering from some form of dementia."

Joaquin was a good listener and Zoe appreciated it. He drew in a breath the way people do when they're weighing whether or not to say something.

When he didn't speak, Zoe asked, "What?"

"I can see that you are one hundred percent convinced that your father is telling the truth. But I still don't understand why you are asking me about the Fortunes."

"I'm not trying to dig up more evidence, if that's what you're getting at."

"No, of course not."

Zoe shrugged. "I guess I'm just curious. But, you know, let's just say even on the very far-flung chance my father was related to the Fortunes and for some reason he wanted to keep it from us… A—why would he hire you with your connection to that family? And, B—I mean, he's clearly made a new life for himself and he's asked his kids to drop it. I don't see why they're going against his wishes, continuing to doubt him and trying to dig up new evidence that proves he's lying. If he says he's not a Fortune, I think the family should respect that and leave the past in the past. What difference does it make who he used to be?"

As Joaquin sat back in his chair, his eyes darkened a shade.

"Are you asking my opinion or are those rhetorical questions?" he said.

"I'd love to hear your opinion," Zoe said.

Joaquin took in a breath and let it out slowly, as if weighing his words. "Personally, I believe a family has a right to know their roots and where they came from, even if one person thinks he has a good reason for hiding the information. I think it's better to get everything out into the open."

Now there was a faraway look in Joaquin's eyes. His expression and his words hinted that there might be something personal going on there.

"You sound like you're speaking from experience," she ventured.

"Me?" He shook his head. "We're not talking about

me. I'm just saying I believe it's not right to withhold important information like that."

For a moment he looked as if he was going to add something, but the moment came and went. Instead he said, "I also think it's nice the way you look out for your father. Everything else aside, your dad must have done something very right to raise a daughter like you."

Her heart did a strange little cha-cha-cha in her chest. Had Joaquin just complimented her? Maybe this *thing* she felt for him wasn't hopeless, after all.

Friday morning Joaquin arrived at Cowboy Country USA, a Western-themed amusement park that had opened a year ago in Horseback Hollow, ready to meet his coworkers at the Sagebrush Pavilion inside the park.

He'd made the six-hour trip from Austin to Horseback Hollow after work yesterday evening. He'd arrived at his father, Orlando Mendoza's, house around eleven o'clock, spent the night and had made it to the team-building retreat as everyone was finishing breakfast.

His coworkers had boarded a bus at the office just after noon the day before and had spent the night in Cowboy Country's Cowboy Condos. Joaquin had been relieved when Steffi-Anne hadn't hassled him about skipping the overnight portion of the trip. Sometimes the woman could be bossy and just this side of relentless, but at least she seemed to know when to back off and recognize that he was meeting her in the middle.

Inside the park's gates, he made his way down Cowboy Country's Main Street, past the old-fashioned restaurants and themed refreshment stands and gift shops. As he approached a rough-hewn wooden gate indicated on the map that Steffi-Anne had provided with the invitation, he heard gunshots and a loud round of whooping and hollering. About twenty yards down Main Street, a couple of cowboys, one dressed in white from his hat to his boots, the other clad in all black, tumbled out of the saloon, the doors swinging behind them.

"That's the Main Street Shootout show," said a park attendant who was dressed like a cowgirl and standing at the gates. "Right on schedule. Feel free to get closer if you'd like, but I must warn you, partner, they take innocent bystanders hostage from time to time."

He wondered if everyone who worked here had to stay in character day in and day out.

"Actually, I'm here for the Robinson Tech event. According to this map, I'm supposed to meet someone here who will point me in the direction of the Sagebrush Pavilion. Am I in the right place? Are you the person?"

"You certainly are and I certainly am. May I see your invitation, please? And I will direct you the rest of the way."

He scrolled up on his smartphone to the invite page and handed it to the woman. Finding it satisfactory, she handed him a map of the park that had his route sketched out with arrows. She opened the gate and ushered him through.

"Just follow the map and it will take you where you need to go. The Sagebrush Pavilion is right behind the executive office buildings. You can't miss it."

She shut the gate behind him and he was transported from the nineteenth-century cowboy town to the more modern backstage area. There, people not in costume went in and out of flat-roofed white buildings that looked like the portables that had served as extra classrooms when he was in elementary school.

In the distance he could still see the top of a huge roller coaster and hear the delighted screams of revelers as it turned a cart full of people upside down on a loop-de-loop.

Better them than me, he thought.

Then again, even though he hated roller coasters, maybe he would rather be upended on a theme-park ride than jump through the hoops of team-building exercises.

He hated rah-rah sessions like this. The forced proximity to coworkers with whom he had nothing in common had him grinding his teeth. Did retreats like this really work? Did people really grow closer after being strong-armed into mandatory fun and games?

Steffi-Anne had organized a full day of obligatory amusement for the Robinson Tech crew. She'd provided him with a schedule when he'd changed his RSVP to yes on the condition that he was released from the bus ride and overnight portion of the program. Actually, she'd thrown him a bonus when she'd told him he could arrive after breakfast because it was only provided to those who were staying in the Cowboy Condos. He certainly hadn't argued.

His dad had been glad to see him, even if it had been late when Joaquin had rolled in. They'd chatted for a few minutes before making plans to meet for dinner tonight at the Coyote Steak House just outside the Cowboy Country main gates. By that time, his coworkers would be on the bus and headed for home.

Cowboy Country was probably a fun place, but it

was quite a haul from Austin. He wondered why Gerald had chosen it for the retreat.

He thought about what Zoe had told him about her father's possible Fortune connection. Since Horseback Hollow was full of Fortune family members, it really didn't make sense that Gerald would agree to have the event here if he had anything to hide. Then again, the boss probably hadn't coordinated the event, and if the Fortune connection bothered Gerald, he probably wouldn't have hired him, either, given his own ties to the family. In addition to Cisco marrying into the family, his father was involved with Josephine Fortune Chesterfield. In fact, she would be joining them for dinner this evening. She was a wonderful woman and since his father seemed pretty serious about her, Joaquin was eager to get to know her.

However he also had some things he wanted to discuss with his father. Matters he had pushed under the rug for far too long. Funny, Zoe's confiding in him had actually brought his own family issues to the forefront.

What was behind his father's decades-long estrangement with his brother Esteban? Joaquin had a sneaking suspicion he knew. And it was high time everything was brought out into the open. Because if Joaquin was right, his father's alienation from Uncle Esteban was an issue that stretched further than a simple disagreement between the two of them.

Joaquin passed a group of modern-looking buildings and took a left at the last one. As he headed to the secluded area where the theme park hosted large groups for private events, he caught a glimpse of Gerald Robinson walking alongside one of the white buildings. It was odd that a CEO would attend a function like this, but Zoe had mentioned that her dad had meetings with Cowboy Country executives. Joaquin quickened his pace in an effort to catch up with him. It wouldn't hurt to say hello to the man who signed his paycheck and to let him see that he could be a team player.

Austin was growing on him. He liked how progressive the city was and he loved the creative freedom that Robinson Tech afforded him. If they had a permanent place for him, he wouldn't mind considering one once he completed the temporary project.

Gerald was just far enough ahead of him that he ducked into a building with a sign that read Guest Kitchen before Joaquin could catch up with him.

Joaquin veered from his path to stick his head in the door for a quick "good morning." It was a rare opportunity to get Gerald Robinson alone and probably in a good mood since he was away from the office at an amusement park, strengthening his team. Although Joaquin wanted to believe the boss hated events like this as much as he did.

That's why it paid to be the boss. You didn't necessarily have to practice what you preached. This might be a good time to ask him about specifics about the software he was writing for Robinson.

Joaquin pulled open the door and was hit by a blast of cool air. He blinked. First, to allow his eyes to adjust to the dimmer light, then out of surprise, because at the far end of the room he saw Gerald Robinson kissing a woman who was not his wife, Charlotte.

Chapter Three

*T*alk about being in the wrong place at the wrong time, Joaquin silently groused as he walked away. He didn't get a good look at the petite redhead in Gerald's arms because she was engulfed by his boss's large body, and Joaquin certainly didn't stay around long enough to see if he could identify her.

He quickly and quietly let himself out the same way he'd entered, hoping like hell that the sound of the door closing didn't break the couple's spell and alert them he'd witnessed their tryst.

Actually, scratch that. On second thought, part of him did hope Robinson had seen him so he would know he wasn't as sly as he thought he was. Because who brought his mistress to a team-building retreat?

Joaquin shook his head as he retraced his steps and returned to the path toward the Sagebrush Pavilion, a path from which he should've never strayed. As he turned the corner, Zoe was the first person he saw. His gaze had automatically zeroed in on her shiny dark hair and picked her out of the crowd of one hundred or so Robinson Tech employees who had gathered to become a stronger team. At the sight of her, his disgust for what he had just witnessed gave way to compassion for her. She was such a naturally kind, happy person who seemed to think only the best of people and especially saw only the good in her father.

Based on the conversation he and Zoe had had in her office the other day, she thought her father could do no wrong. The prospect of telling her what he'd seen made Joaquin's heart feel as if it would split in two.

Really, why would he tell her?

Zoe, I just saw your dad kissing a woman that wasn't your mom.

Yeah. No.

Actually he wasn't going to tell anyone. Because what good would it do? It certainly wouldn't fix anything or teach Gerald a lesson in morality. He'd only met Charlotte Robinson once in passing. For all he knew Gerald and his wife had an open marriage. Though why a woman would want to tie herself to a cheater like that baffled him.

He simply didn't get it. The whole point of marriage was to pledge your loyalty to one person. If that caused a hardship, stay single; play the field and be forthright about it. Just don't be a damn cheater.

He knew how it felt to be cheated on and it wasn't fun. He also knew playing the field was good in theory. Sometimes when you were open and honest about your intentions people still only heard what they wanted to hear.

He knew that from experience. He'd been on both sides of that relationship coin. It didn't make him eager to be in either place again.

He didn't see himself settling down and he didn't want to get back in the rat race of juggling multiple women—or making false promises to one woman, for that matter.

An image of Zoe with her beautiful, trusting smile popped into his head. Sure, he could date her. But he knew that was not what she wanted. Women like Zoe didn't take things casually.

There were too many odds stacked against them. Add in the fact that she was the boss's daughter and the tidbit about his not wanting to get serious right now—hell, he didn't even know where he'd be after this project wrapped up—and garnish it with the huge secret he knew about her father. A relationship with Zoe would never work.

He detested cheating and cheaters.

Not that he was such a do-gooder. Before he'd proposed to Selena, he'd done some things he wasn't proud of. He knew the damage deception like that could cause, and he didn't want to cause anyone that pain.

As he approached his colleagues, he shook his head to clear his thoughts. Because why was he even thinking about such ridiculous things as dating Zoe Robinson? Things like getting to know her better. Spending time with her. Kissing her—not to mention going to the places that kisses usually led.

She was the first person who saw him as he entered the pavilion. Her eyes flashed as she smiled and waved at him.

She looked adorable and bright and stylish in her pink shorts and orange top. Her dark hair was pulled back from her face with a pink-and-orange headband.

No matter the occasion, Zoe always looked as though she'd stepped out of a magazine. Not in a high-fashion sense, but in a fresh, cute, girl-next-door way.

He couldn't help but smile back at her, but he stopped short of going over and standing with her.

Yep, the only thing telling her what he'd witnessed would accomplish was heartbreak. He looked away.

Forget dating; this was precisely why Joaquin hated getting involved with his colleagues on a personal level. Knowing things about them. Now, every time he looked at Zoe, he would remember he was keeping a secret from her.

"Good morning, Joaquin," Steffi-Anne said. "Your timing is perfect. We are just getting ready to break into pairs and begin our first game. So, if you'll join group B over there under the pavilion, we'll get started."

Steffi-Anne called everyone to order.

"We're going to have a scavenger hunt," she said. "Each person in group A will draw a name out of this bag."

She held up a small brown bag with handles, the kind that you got when you purchased something in one of those fancy department stores.

"This will match you with your partner in group B. Zoe, how about if you start us off by drawing the first name?" Steffi-Anne smiled at Zoe, but the sentiment didn't seem to make it all the way to her eyes.

Joaquin had the sinking feeling she was up to something. The woman always had an agenda.

As Zoe reached into the bag to pull out a name, her gaze drifted over to Joaquin. He looked so darn good in those jeans and that white T-shirt. The color of the shirt showed off his tan, and the jeans weren't tight, but they hugged his butt in the most perfect way. It made her want to squeeze his buns to see if they really were as firm as they looked.

The naughty thought made her smile. How wonderful it would be if she pulled his name. Since she was the first to draw, she had a chance of being paired with him. However, since there were so many names to choose from, the odds were stacked against her.

She reached in and let her hand sift through the dozens of names handwritten on small slips of paper, willing her fingers to pull the golden ticket that read Joaquin Mendoza.

When Joaquin's gorgeous brown gaze connected with hers, it was like a lightning strike and she grabbed a piece of paper, sure it was the right choice.

She held her breath as she pulled it into the daylight and read, "Sissy Hanson."

Ugh. Sissy from accounting? No! Couldn't she have a do-over? No disrespect to Sissy. She was nice enough, but she wasn't Joaquin.

As Sissy came over to stand with her, Zoe did her best not to act disappointed. It would be fine. As long as Steffi-Anne didn't end up with him.

It took about five minutes before everyone had chosen a partner. Each time Joaquin's name wasn't called, putting him one step closer to Steffi-Anne, the tension in Zoe's chest wound a notch tighter.

Joaquin still hadn't been paired up by the time there were just two people left: Steffi-Anne and Jill Winski, who was the second-to-last person to draw.

After Jill drew a name, she knit her brows and looked into the bag. "I think we may be short a name. It felt like I pulled the last slip of paper."

"We should be fine," Steffi-Anne said a bit too fast.

The only people left standing in Group B were Homer Martin from IT and Joaquin.

Of course.

Zoe was willing to wager that the paper caught between Jill's forefinger and thumb read Homer Martin.

A slow burn began to simmer in Zoe's stomach.

Jill started to turn the bag upside down, but Steffi-Anne reached out and snatched it away from her before she could, poking her pointed nose into the sack.

"No, no. Look. Right here. Here it is. There's still one slip of paper left."

A vaguely victorious smile curled her lips. "Joaquin, you and I are partners for the scavenger hunt."

Oh. Well, will you look at that? What a surprise.

Before anyone could challenge the outcome, Steffi-Anne was barking orders about how they would execute the scavenger hunt, how it was important to work as a team and that there would be a nice prize for the team that won: lunch at the Copper Kettle.

As the scavenger hunt played out, Zoe noticed that the vast majority of her female coworkers were playing hard to win.

When Jill and Homer were the first to cross the finish line with their list completed, Zoe's partner, Sissy, quipped, "You know Jill didn't work that hard to have lunch with Homer. She did it to keep Steffi-Anne from winning the lunch with Joaquin."

Keep-away. Was that how this retreat had digressed? It had become one big game of keep-away. Well, in the name of team-building, Zoe intended to do her part.

Pretending not to be a sore loser, Steffi-Anne herded the group right into the next activity: the three-legged race. It would be cozy to have a legit reason to stand that close to Joaquin, arms around each other, their bodies becoming one as they reached climax—er— the *finish line*.

The *finish line*.

Good grief! Where had *that* come from?

Okay, she knew what had inspired the inappropriate thought, but she needed to get her head under control. It said a lot about the state of her love life when a three-legged race inspired thoughts of dancing the horizontal tango.

She risked a glance at Joaquin.

Then again, who wouldn't be inspired by him?

Heat began at the base of her neck and worked its way up to the tips of her ears. She took a deep breath to cool herself down before anyone noticed.

Yes, she had it bad for Joaquin Mendoza. So was she just going to stand around blushing over the predicament or was she going to do something about it?

"Zoe, would you please start us off again by pulling the name of your partner for the race?"

"You know what, Steffi-Anne? Since Jill and Homer won the last round, it's only fair that we let her draw first. Since they're such a power team, we need to make sure they don't get paired up again. Right?"

Steffi-Anne clapped her hands. "May I please have everyone's attention? We have just a few more teamwork exercises before we break for lunch and then we will have some free time in the park. Since it takes so long to draw names, why don't we make this round of pairings permanent partners for the duration of our drills? That will make things easier and give us more free time in the park."

As the bag made its way clockwise around the circle, Zoe drifted over to a picnic table a few paces behind the action. Keeping her back to the group and her ears open for the names each person announced as they drew, she took a pen out of her wristlet and retrieved the scrap of paper she'd drawn from the previous scavenger hunt round. Since she hadn't been near a trash can, she'd tucked it into the pocket of her shorts. Now, she was happy she'd done that.

Quickly and discreetly, she folded the paper, creased it and tore off the part with Sissy's name. She wrote Joaquin Mendoza on the small scrap.

If perchance he was called by one of the last few remaining people, Zoe would admit to herself that she'd been barking up the wrong tree and draw a new name from the bag. But her gut instinct told her this was rigged. She intended to draw right before Steffi-Anne and if her hunch was right, there would only be one slip of paper in that bag—and it wouldn't have Joaquin's name on it.

So she stayed back at the picnic table until the bag had made it all the way around the circle—and, oh, how interesting, no one had called Joaquin's name yet.

Zoe knew she was taking a chance by calling Steffi-

Anne's bluff. But what were the odds that out of fifty names his name was among the last two *twice in a row*?

Nah, something was definitely rotten in Cowboy Country.

Zoe held the brown bag with her left hand and, careful to hold the doctored slip of paper tight with her thumb against the palm of her right hand, she reached in and pretended to pull a name.

"Joaquin Mendoza," she said, reading the paper she'd forged. "Come on down."

"What?" Steffi-Anne pierced her with the look of death, confirming Zoe's hunch. She hadn't included Joaquin's name with the others. Since she'd gone last, she had pretended to pull his name. Did she really believe that no one would think it was odd that she drew Joaquin as a partner every single time? Worse yet, did she not think Joaquin might find it a little creepy that she'd rigged the pairings to throw them together?

It didn't matter now because Zoe would be the one getting up close and personal with Joaquin in the three-legged race and the remaining team-building exercises.

Now, he was walking toward her.

As Zoe turned to meet him halfway, she felt a hand on her shoulder.

"Well played, Zoe." Steffi-Anne's voice was low and venomous, completely at odds with that sickening smile that didn't reach her eyes. "Well played."

"What do you mean?" Zoe asked, all sugar with just enough spice mixed in to warn Steffi-Anne that she wasn't playing.

"You know exactly what I'm talking about. I know what you did."

"Oh, are you talking about how the pairings were rigged?"

Before she could answer, Joaquin walked up to them.

"Is everything all right?"

He looked back and forth between them, obviously sensing that something was off. But Steffi-Anne sprang into action.

"Everything is great. Are you having fun, Joaquin?" She reached out and touched his arm. "Aren't you glad you came?"

Zoe could tell by his expression that he wasn't buying her nicey-nicey act.

"Yeah. Sure. It's nice to spend a day outside. I don't get to do that often enough."

"Right. You know I was just telling Zoe that Cowboy Country's Main Street Shootouts are so realistic." She locked eyes with Zoe. "Almost makes you want to watch your back."

She laughed. "And, Joaquin, be sure to save me a ride on the roller coaster, okay?"

"Roller coasters?" He shook his head. "Sorry, I'm not a fan." He smiled at Zoe. "But I am looking forward to the three-legged race."

Chapter Four

"What was that about?" Joaquin asked Zoe as soon as Steffi-Anne was out of earshot.

Zoe looked as if she wanted to say something but instead opted for the high road.

"Nothing. She was just telling me about Cowboy Country. This is the first time I've been here. How about you? Did you spend any time here when you lived in Horseback Hollow?"

"No. It's my first time, too."

Zoe arched a brow. "Well, I'm glad we can share each other's *first time*. You know, make it special."

Phew! Did she realize the double entendre she was bandying about?

Of course she did. She could be a first-class flirt sometimes. When she was, it caught him off guard. He didn't quite know what to say. He didn't want to encourage her. But on the other hand, encouraging her—adding fuel to the fire—was exactly what he wanted to do.

And that latter won out handily.

"Please be gentle with me," he quipped. "I don't ride roller coasters. I'm not that kind of guy."

She locked gazes with him, her eyes sparkling.

"So, you don't like it rough and fast, huh?"

Damn, how far was she going to take this? She was killing him.

"No, I'm more of a smooth and easy kind of a guy."

"Really? Do tell."

A rush of awareness coursed through him.

Her smile was nothing short of wicked. Obviously she knew she was getting to him, but that seemed only to fuel her fire. And his, for that matter. For a moment he fought the urge to close the distance between them and show her exactly how easy things between them could be, but somewhere in the fog of his lust-hazy brain, he knew that would only muddy the waters between them.

Especially since he was already keeping a secret from her. If things became intimate between them— and God knew it was taking every ounce of restraint he could muster to not cross that line—he would have to tell her about what he'd witnessed as he'd arrived.

Or would he?

Hell, his brain was so fried with want right now, he didn't even know. The only way around it was to get out now.

He took a symbolic step back from her.

"I have a feeling Steffi-Anne is not going to go very easy on us if we hold up her race," he said. "She seems to have us on a tight schedule. Why don't we get over there now?"

Just as he'd predicted, Steffi-Anne was in a mood and she looked disheveled and frazzled, as if she was just about at her wit's end. She'd pulled her straight blond hair back into a haphazard ponytail and her yellow blouse had a dirty smudge on it. From this angle, the harsh daylight and the scowl on her face aged her about ten years.

"Yes. Let's go."

Zoe moved closer to him and pressed her pretty, tanned leg flush against his so that they were hip to hip. Well, they were in a sense. She was so petite that her hip hit his body in the upper thigh region. He loved how utterly un-self-conscious she was about invading his personal space. But the other good thing that came out of it was that he now knew for a fact that she seemed to fit perfectly under his arm. Just as if she belonged there.

And what her nicely tanned legs lacked in length they more than made up for in supple shapeliness. They looked strong and quite lovely, he thought as he bound the two of them together.

Being this close to her brought back the rush of awareness he'd felt earlier. He could smell her shampoo, something light and floral, and he could smell her soap—or maybe it was her perfume? Whatever it was, it was intoxicating and he wanted to lean down and bury his face in that sweet, delicate spot where her neck curved into her shoulder.

Being here with her like this, feeling how well she fit in his arms, was an unexpected surprise. Suddenly this team-building nonsense seemed a little more palatable.

Even though he knew getting involved with the boss's daughter was not a wise idea, it didn't mean he couldn't enjoy every single thing about being all tied up with Zoe Robinson. Win or lose.

It had been said the way a person danced revealed a lot about what kind of lover they would be. Zoe couldn't help but wonder if the same rule applied to the way a couple's bodies moved together and adapted to tests like the three-legged race and the water balloon toss. Because, if so, she and Joaquin were destined for greatness between the sheets.

They'd been beasts at the challenges that required them working together physically. Of course, it didn't hurt at all that they had permission—no, they were required—to get into each other's personal spaces and violate boundaries that were usually off-limits.

Could they please do team-building exercises every day?

Then again, if they did, Steffi-Anne would surely find some way to ensure she ended up paired with Joaquin.

Now that they were breaking for the barbecue lunch Cowboy Country was providing, Steffi-Anne was already weaseling her way back in to Joaquin's company.

It had only been natural for Zoe and Joaquin to fall into the buffet line together since they'd been partners. After they got their food—pulled chicken and barbecued brisket with baked beans, coleslaw, potato salad and ice-cold glasses of sweet tea—they'd found two spots at a table.

Steffi-Anne filled her plate and brought her lunch over to the full table where Joaquin and Zoe were sitting with six other coworkers. Zoe was sitting next to Joaquin, who was on the end.

"Scooch, please," she said, gently nudging Tracy from accounts receivable, on the opposite side of the table.

"There are plenty of places at the other tables," said Tracy.

"Yes, but this is the only table in the shade." Steffi-Anne had given the entire table the big, poor-me eyes and it had worked. Well, it had sent Tracy grumbling to another table where she could have more elbow room.

After Tracy left, Steffi-Anne zeroed in on Joaquin like a homing device.

"Aren't you glad you came today?" Steffi-Anne said.

Joaquin smiled at Zoe. "Actually, I am. I'm having a lot of fun."

The way he looked at her made Zoe's heart perform a quickstep.

"I've been dying to go ride the Twin Rattlers Roller Coaster," Steffi-Anne said. "I've been waiting for that all day."

"I've been looking forward to the funnel cakes," Zoe said. "I love them so much."

Steffi-Anne looked at her as if she'd just said she was going to go eat a bucket of fish heads.

"God, Zoe, funnel cakes are pure fat. Fat, carbs and sugar," she said. "You're young now, sweetheart, but if you keep eating things like that, you'll regret it sooner than you think."

Since when had eating a funnel cake become a capital offense?

"I enjoy the occasional one," she said. "One every five years won't hurt anything."

"Suit yourself." Steffi-Anne shrugged, her gaze scanning the picnic area. "Oh, Zoe, look. There's Ron Lowell. Didn't the two of you used to date? He's kind of cute in a bookish sort of way."

"We went out a couple of times," Zoe said, thrown by the non sequitur. "He's a nice guy, but it was nothing serious."

"Who are you dating now?" Steffi-Anne pressed.

"No one."

"I thought you had a boyfriend," she said.

"No, I'm completely free."

The way Steffi-Anne was moving the food around on her plate instead of eating it made Zoe think of a witch at her cauldron. At any moment she might pull out a poison apple and lob it at her because it was much healthier than a funnel cake.

"I'm surprised you don't have someone special by now," she continued. "You've dated a lot of really nice guys. Like Jake over there and George Simpson from marketing."

She pointed with her fork.

"And why didn't things work out with Frank? I thought you two looked especially cute together." Steffi-Anne turned her attention back to Joaquin. "I'm not saying this girl gets around. She's just very popular in the office. Joaquin, if you're interested, you'd better take a number."

Okay, so that was her game. Zoe had always known that Steffi-Anne was the queen of the backhanded compliments, but she'd never pegged her as a mean girl. Then again, she'd never gone head-to-head with her over a man.

"That's what dating is for," Zoe said, "trying out potential relationships, seeing how they fit. If they don't, there's no use in prolonging them."

Since the day Zoe had started working for her father at Robinson Tech, she'd made a point of not playing the daddy's-girl card. She realized, by virtue of birth, she'd been born with some privileges. She was deeply grateful for her blessings, and she didn't want to get the reputation that the only reason she'd gotten ahead at work was because she was the founder's daughter. It was important that she got her jobs and any promotions on the merit of her knowledge and expertise, because she was the best person for the job. Not through nepotism. She never wanted to come across as entitled. That's why she worked hard and went out of her way to be extra nice to people.

But sometimes when people like Steffi-Anne knew she wouldn't fight back, they tended to push her more than they would someone who would put them in their place.

Today, Steffi-Anne was hitting extra hard and low. Zoe wasn't about to get into a catfight with her, and she seemed to be spoiling for exactly that. Zoe really thought the woman was more professional than that. But she was dishing it out, and the others at the table looked eager to feast on a huge helping of juicy drama.

Zoe hadn't finished her lunch, but she'd lost her appetite. Maybe the best thing she could do would be to go get that funnel cake and enjoy every fat-laden bite. Part of her hated to leave Joaquin in Steffi-Anne's clutches, but if he sat back and allowed himself to be clutched, then maybe he wasn't the guy for her, after all. Better to find out now. Her heart sank at the thought.

Zoe tossed her napkin on her plate, stood and gathered the rest of her garbage. "I think I'm going to go get that funnel cake now."

To her surprise Joaquin stood, too. "I'm not surprised Zoe's popular. She's got a lot going for her. A guy would be lucky to get a date with her."

He turned to Zoe. "I'd love a funnel cake. May I join you?"

Zoe stopped at the garbage can to dispose of her trash. She took a deep breath and tried to shake off the sting of Steffi-Anne's words. Swallowing the urge to fight back when someone came at her swinging wasn't easy. It was human nature to want to defend oneself, but the perverse part was that doing so would've made her look just as bad as Steffi-Anne.

Joaquin must have read her mind because he tossed away his trash and said, "Come on, let's get out of here."

They walked in silence as they made their way toward the exit of the backstage area. But before they made it to the park, Zoe caught sight of her father and waved.

"Where are you two off to?" Gerald asked. He always came across so gruff, but Zoe knew he was a big softy on the inside. She wished more people knew him the way she did.

"We are going in search of funnel cakes." Zoe planted a kiss on his cheek. "When did you get here?"

"I drove down last night," Gerald said. "Had business to tend to."

"Joaquin." Gerald stuck out his hand and Joaquin gave it a firm shake.

"Hello, sir."

Her father liked him. That scored Joaquin huge points in Zoe's book. As if he needed extra ones.

It was another quality she could check off her potential Husband List. Suddenly things were looking a lot brighter than they had a moment ago.

"Is lunch over?" Gerald asked. "I wanted to say a few words to the staff."

"No, the group is still over there," Zoe said. "We're just sneaking away a little early to get some dessert."

"Good," Gerald said. "I'm glad I didn't miss it. I've been busy all morning. This is the soonest I could get away. I'll let you two go and get on with your business. Joaquin, you take good care of her. She is my little girl."

He sounded stern but Zoe knew he meant well. She liked the way Joaquin held up under his scrutiny.

Check.

"Yes, sir," Joaquin said.

Her father gave a curt nod and walked away.

Once they'd stepped out from behind the fence and onto Main Street, Joaquin said, "Your dad is pretty protective."

She wanted to say, *Yes, but don't let him scare you off.*

"You know how fathers can be. Don't you? Are you close to your family?"

Shrieks and whoops filled the air as log-shaped cars splashed down the final drop of the Gulch Holler Rapids water flume ride. The waterlogged merriment was set against the *pow-pow-pow* of pistols from the Main Street Shooting Gallery, which was located next door.

"We are pretty tight," he said as they strolled past Gus's General Store where a cute straw cowgirl hat caught Zoe's eye. She decided to look at it later so as not to interrupt what Joaquin was saying. "I stayed with my dad last night and I will again tonight. After we're finished here, I'm meeting him for dinner at the Coyote Steak House just outside the main gates."

So, not only was the guy smart and gorgeous, but he was family oriented, too. Could he be any more perfect?

Check. Check. Check.

She had to resist closing her eyes to revel in the thought and the smell of funnel cakes cooking somewhere nearby.

"May I ask you a personal question?" Joaquin said.

Zoe's heart leaped into her throat. She had to wait for it to settle back into her chest again before she could answer. Even then it beat a thrilling staccato.

"Sure. Ask me anything." And she meant it.

He could ask her out.

He could ask her to marry him.

He could ask her to—

"Why do you let Steffi-Anne get away with acting like that?"

Oh. Except for that.

She had hoped that they'd left Steffi-Anne back at the pavilion. But here she was again, virtually elbowing her way between them like a ghost they couldn't exorcize.

"I'm not letting her get away with anything," Zoe

said, making sure her voice was steady and matter-of-fact but not defensive. "I choose to not respond. Because when you react to a bully like her, you're playing right into her hands. Don't you see it? What she wants most is a reaction from me, and I'm not going to give it to her."

Joaquin watched her intently as she spoke, nodding his head as though he agreed with her.

"Actually, getting a reaction out of me probably falls second to getting one out of you," Zoe said. "Just sayin'. Because you know she wants you to ask her out."

She was happy when he flinched, as if the suggestion was the furthest thing from his mind. And her heart nearly leaped out of her chest when he frowned and said, "That's not going to happen. I'm not interested in Steffi-Anne."

She wished she could've paused the moment—that perfect moment when she knew exactly where her nemesis stood with the man of her dreams—but he ruined the moment when he said, "I don't date women I work with."

Well, why the heck are you sending me mixed signals? Why did you sit with me at lunch, defend me to Steffi-Anne, make me want you in the worst way, when it was all for nothing?

But before she could respond or even mask her expression to make sure it didn't expose the utter disappointment that had eclipsed all the joy she had been feeling a moment ago, a street performer dressed in period costume planted his feet in front of them. His big voice boomed, "Gather 'round, all ye good people. I do believe I have found the happy couple who will be the next victims—er—the next bride and groom I will unite in connubial bliss in the Cowboy Country Matrimonial *Extraaaavaganza*."

Somehow the man, whom Zoe now realized was wearing a sash that read Honorable Justice D. Peace, managed to hook his arms through Zoe's on the right and Joaquin's on the left and herd them toward a small stage raised about ten inches off the ground.

"What in the world—?" Zoe asked.

"Does our beautiful, blushing bride have cold feet? Please tell me I am mistaken. Honey, your groom looks bucking ready to go. I think he has the wedding night on his mind."

As he made a couple more jokes, a player–pipe organ started churning out a dramatic version of the "Wedding March." A woman dressed in period costume with a sash that read Matchmaker made an overblown show of fawning over Zoe and Joaquin. She shoved a wispy tulle veil onto Zoe's head, placed a bouquet of tattered-looking flowers in her hands and thrust a tall top hat at Joaquin.

The music and the fuss the performers were making over them drew a crowd.

"Oh, my gosh," Zoe said. "Like it or not, I guess we're part of the show."

"You only live once." Joaquin shrugged and placed the top hat on his head at a cocky angle, playing the good sport. "I said I don't date coworkers. I didn't say anything about not marrying them."

Chapter Five

The best souvenir that Zoe was taking home from Cowboy Country was being pronounced Joaquin's pretend wife. Even though the marriage wasn't real—obviously— for a few fabulous hours, it was fun to pretend she was his wife and they were on their honeymoon in Cowboy Country.

She even had the gaudy plastic ring on her left hand to prove it.

It was so romantic, in a kitschy-fun sort of way. Joaquin had been a great sport, playing along and even hamming it up a little bit. It was a side of him she'd never seen before.

As she waited in line to get on the charter bus that would take everyone back to Austin, her thumb found the back of the band. Joaquin had seemed pretty firm about not dating someone he worked with. But he had said that marriage was not out of the question. Okay, so that statement was as pretend as the plastic ring on her finger. It didn't change her feelings for him; if anything, it made her desire him more. It was evident to everyone else who was paying attention that Steffi-Anne was his for the taking. And there were also a dozen or so other women in the office interested in him. At least they'd had the good grace not to be so obvious.

But he didn't seem to be out for what he could get. That was a very attractive quality in a man. So was him having the good sense to know that office romances could get sticky. That's why Zoe was willing to take things slowly. As Steffi-Anne had so gleefully pointed out, Zoe had had her share of office romances that fizzled out for one reason or the other. She'd loved what Joaquin had said at lunch about it being okay to have dated a lot of guys. He was right. How would she ever find her prince if she didn't kiss a few toads along the way?

"Did you have fun, Zoe?" Steffi-Ann asked through her Cheshire cat grin as she checked in Zoe, ticking her name off the passenger roster.

"I had a great time, thank you," Zoe said, infusing a smile into her voice, determined to kill her with kindness. "Look at this cute cowgirl hat I bought."

As Zoe reached for the package, she realized her wristlet that held her phone, her credit cards and all her money wasn't on her arm. She looked in her bags and patted herself down, but it wasn't there.

Panic seared through her.

"Steffi-Anne, I don't have my purse," Zoe said as she excused herself past the others who were waiting in line to get on the bus. "I have to go find it. I'll be right back."

Mentally, she retraced her steps. She'd probably set it down during the wedding show. But no, she'd purchased the cute little straw hat with a pink gingham band at Gus's General Store. After that, she and Joaquin had ridden a couple of rides. Next they'd gone to the Patty's Cakes Funnel Cake stand and stopped by Foaming Barrel Root Beer to get something to drink before he said goodbye to go meet his dad. That meant she'd left it at either Patty's Cakes or the Foaming Barrel. But Joaquin had paid for the cakes and the root beer.

Her purse could be anywhere.

She jogged as fast as she could back to Patty's Cakes. It was almost at the farthest corner of the park, away from the entrance.

"Excuse me, I was here earlier and I think I may have left my purse and phone. It's small, pink, has a loop so I can wear it over my wrist." Zoe pointed to her arm. "Please tell me someone turned it in."

The kid shook his head. "Sorry, no one has turned in anything like that. You might want to try Lost and Found."

The woman behind her made a sympathetic noise.

Zoe's heart sank. It was getting late and she knew she was holding up the bus. Maybe she'd have to give up the search for now. She didn't want to keep everyone waiting. She would've called Steffi-Anne to let her know she'd be right there, but she didn't even have a phone.

"Where is Lost and Found?" she asked, just in case it was nearby.

"Up front," said the guy. "Right by the exit."

Well, that was good, but it didn't do much to calm the panic festering inside her at the thought of losing her phone. It contained all of her contacts—phone numbers, addresses, her schedule, her life. Without it, she wouldn't know her next move.

She swallowed the mounting hysteria.

She thanked the guy and jogged toward the main gates. She would tell her coworkers what she was doing and then run and check Lost and Found. If it wasn't there, perhaps they could assist her with calling the other locations in the park.

It had been a long time since she'd run this far this fast, and her lungs were about to burst when she finally made it to the front. She breathed in great gulps of air as she walked to where the bus was parked.

Or—where it was supposed to be parked?

It wasn't there.

Frantically, Zoe looked around, trying in vain to locate it. Cowboy Country wasn't that large. Not like Disney World. There was only one place for buses, and this was it.

But the bus wasn't there. Had they left without her?

Her heart pounded in her chest like a caged bird thrashing against its pen. As horror slowly morphed into fury, she realized that the bus had indeed taken off without her.

She had no money, no phone and no way to get in touch with anyone. Then her gaze found the Coyote Steak House, where Joaquin was dining with his father.

As much as she had wanted to spend more time with him, she didn't want to do it like this—barging in on his family time, prevailing upon him to be her knight in shining armor whether he wanted to be or not.

She would look so stupid—worse yet, this would look so contrived. So planned. Steffi-Anne-level manipulation. But she had no choice, unless she wanted to start walking back to Austin.

Instead she took a deep breath and prepared herself to take the interloper's walk of shame.

"The new job sounds like it's agreeing with you, son," said Orlando Mendoza as he helped himself to a dinner roll out of the basket and smeared a slab of butter on his bread plate.

"It is," said Joaquin. "I like it very much. Although it doesn't seem like a new job anymore. It's already been three months."

The aroma of grilled steak filled the dimly lit restaurant and Joaquin's stomach growled in anticipation. The place was decorated in upscale cowboy chic. The walls were painted a deep green color, which set off the various cow heads and longhorn trophies intermixed with framed photos of famous country singers and rodeo champions.

"Has it been that long already?" asked Josephine Fortune Chesterfield. Her proper British accent sounded crisp and neat. "Where does the time go? Don't get me wrong, we've missed you living in Horseback Hollow. But time does fly."

His father had been seeing Josephine for a while now—since Orlando had moved to Texas from Miami a couple of years ago. Not only did they seem happy, they seemed to be getting serious. Although, Joaquin didn't know what *serious* actually entailed for someone like his father. He couldn't imagine him married to anyone else but his mother, but he did want Orlando to be happy and he couldn't have handpicked a better woman for him than Josephine.

He felt that old familiar tug of apprehension. He had things he needed to discuss with his father. Questions that he'd kept buried for far too long that needed to be brought out into the daylight and have the truth shone on them.

His mother had been gone for four years now and it had been so long since he'd seen his father smile. He'd taken her death hard. It hadn't seemed right to add to his suffering by opening a can of worms.

He was holding Josephine's hand and they were exchanging a look that belonged to lovers who had made it through the uncertainty of a new relationship and were firmly grounded in a confidence of where they wanted to be, where they belonged.

Orlando had finally remembered how to smile again.

Now it didn't seem right to mess that up by telling him Joaquin knew he wasn't his birth father. Maybe Orlando knew the truth. If he didn't, it meant his mother—the love of Orlando's life—had cheated on him. Joaquin had a pretty good idea whom she'd slept with.

The issue was too important not to get some answers. But not tonight, of course. Not with Josephine here. Maybe this weekend. He'd have to gauge it.

"Have you given any thought to what you're going to do once this project is over?" Orlando asked.

Joaquin took a long pull of his beer. It tasted good after spending the day outdoors and it took the edge off his appetite. Even though he and Zoe had eaten their fill of funnel cakes and drunk a good amount of root beer, he was hungry for some real food.

Spending the afternoon walking and talking with Zoe had given him an appetite. And not for food. If he were completely honest with himself, he was hungry to see her again. He'd have to give that some thought this weekend, too. Given the way things had turned out back in Miami, he should've learned his lesson about messing with the boss's daughter, but Zoe Robinson was a far cry from Selena Marks.

Selena was another type of daddy's girl, a different brand than Zoe, who seemed much too sweet to sleep with her fiancé's best friend the way Selena had done. Selena took what she wanted when she wanted it, no matter whom she hurt. But Zoe seemed like a breath of fresh air compared to the suffocating pitch-black of Selena's darkness. That was probably why he was tempted to break his number-one rule: no inter-office romance.

"Funny you should ask," Joaquin said in response to his father's question. "I have been thinking about the future. I wouldn't mind taking a permanent position with Robinson if they had something for me. Gerald Robinson is an interesting guy."

He glanced at Josephine to see if she had any reaction to the mention of Gerald Robinson's name, but she didn't. She simply smiled at him and looked as if she were waiting for Joaquin to expound.

"Josephine, I heard something interesting about Gerald Robinson. Do you remember him from Matteo and Rachel's wedding? He's Matteo's father-in-law."

"Yes, of course," Josephine said.

"There's a rumor that Gerald is related to the Fortunes. Have you heard anything about that?"

Josephine cocked her pretty gray head to the right.
"I haven't heard a thing about that. But the Fortunes
are a large and ever-expanding clan. I wouldn't rule
out anything. Look at my story, how I ended up finding out I was related to them."

She had a point. It was an interesting saga, like
something out of a novel. After more than half a century spent growing up in England, she'd learned she
was adopted. Not only that, but that she was part of a
set of triplets—two girls and a boy. She and her sister,
Jeanne Marie, had been put up for adoption when they
were babies. All these years later their brother, James
Fortune, had learned of the existence and stopped at
nothing until he'd found his long-lost sisters.

When Josephine, a widow, had learned of her new
family connections, she'd moved to Horseback Hollow
to be closer to her family. That was when she'd met
Orlando. From what Joaquin had heard, it had been
love at first sight but a relationship slow to take root.

Could Gerald Robinson have a similar connection
to the Fortunes that he didn't know about, the same
way Josephine and her sister hadn't known all those
years? Zoe was adamant that wasn't the case. He probably shouldn't even have brought it up to Josephine. It
was best to let the subject drop.

"Robinson stays out of my way for the most part,"
Joaquin said. "He lets me do my own thing. Of course,
I get my work done. So he has no reason to crowd me.
But it's a good atmosphere. It's stimulating and I like
my coworkers."

Zoe's face came to mind. Actually he hadn't been

able to get her out of his head. Those big brown eyes. That smile. The sound of her laugh. The way he'd wanted to kiss her when they had ridden the Ferris wheel today. And how, for a crazy second, he had thought about asking her to ditch the bus ride back and stay with him here in Horseback Hollow for the weekend. But just as fast, he'd come to his senses. He'd blamed it on the altitude of the Ferris wheel, which was a lame excuse, of course. Almost as lame as the idea of her spending the weekend with him.

Maybe not lame, exactly.

Unwise. Reckless.

Tempting as hell.

His reckless days of buckling under temptation were over. If he knew what was good for him and her—for both of them—he'd stop thinking about her right now, look at the menu and figure out what he wanted to eat. Then he would focus his mental energies on how he would broach the subject of his paternity and his father's estrangement with Esteban once they'd said goodnight to Josephine.

As he lowered his gaze to study the menu, he caught a glimpse of a woman across the dimly lit steak house that reminded him of Zoe.

Now he was imagining her. Hell, he was conjuring her—the woman could be her twin. Her identical twin. Dressed in an orange blouse and pink shorts—

Oh, for God's sake, that *was* Zoe. She looked a little frantic.

Joaquin stood and waved at her, and relief seemed to wash over her as she headed in their direction.

"Who are you waving at?" Orlando asked, looking in the direction Joaquin was facing.

"It's Zoe Robinson. Gerald Robinson's daughter. Hey, please don't mention anything about the rumors about his Fortune connection."

"I remember Zoe from Matteo and Rachel's wedding," Orlando said. "I won't mention anything."

Josephine nodded in agreement and Orlando stood as Zoe reached the table.

"Hi, I'm so sorry to barge in like this," Zoe said. She looked at Josephine and Orlando. "Hello, I'm Zoe. I work with Joaquin. I'm so sorry to interrupt your dinner. But I have a minor emergency. I need to borrow Joaquin's phone."

"Hi. Uh, no, it's fine," Joaquin said. "You're not interrupting. We haven't even ordered yet. What's wrong?"

Orlando cleared his throat.

"Zoe, this is my father, Orlando Mendoza, and Josephine Fortune Chesterfield. I believe you met briefly at Rachel and Matteo's wedding."

Zoe's eyes flashed at the mention of the Fortune name and her gaze swept over Josephine. It was so subtle that no one else probably caught it. Especially because she smiled sweetly and greeted them both.

"Yes. Of course, I remember you. Please, carry on with ordering. Don't let me interrupt. Joaquin, if I could borrow your phone, I'll just take it into the lobby and make my call."

He handed it to her. "Sure, but what happened to yours?"

She always seemed to have it with her. He knew she'd had it today in the park because she'd been afraid it would get wet when they rode the Gulch Holler Rapids log flume ride.

"I don't know." Her voice sounded shaky. "And—"
She covered her face with her free hand for a quick moment. "This is so embarrassing. I must've lost it in the
park. I realized it after I'd checked in to get on the bus.
Before I went to look for it, I told Steffi-Anne that I'd
be right back, but she must not have heard me because
the bus left without me. Now, here I am stranded with
no phone and no money and I'm just thanking God that
you are here because I don't know what I would do if
you weren't. Well, actually, Rachel lives in Horseback
Hollow and before I bothered you I used the restaurant's house phone to call her, but she's not picking up."

"You are not bothering us," Orlando interjected.
"The reason you can't get hold of Matteo and Rachel
is that they're out of town for the night. But you have
nothing to worry about. We will take care of you.
Please join us for dinner."

Orlando gestured to the empty seat next to Joaquin.

"Oh, thank you. That's so kind of you to offer, but
I can't impose like that."

"Looks like you don't have many other options,"
Joaquin joked. "So you might as well."

He gestured to the empty chair next to him. Zoe's
face clouded and he realized his words might not have
sounded as humorous as he'd meant them.

"Thank you," she said. "But I'll call Steffi-Anne
and ask if they can come back and get me."

She squeezed her eyes shut for a moment and Joaquin knew even the thought was humiliating to her.
What the hell was wrong with Steffi-Anne to go off
and leave her stranded like that?

"Do you really want to do that?" he asked.

"No, of course not. But as you said, I'm sort of short on options."

"Do you know her phone number, because I certainly don't have it?" Joaquin said.

Zoe frowned. "No, I don't. Okay, time for plan C. Will you lend me some money for a place to stay tonight? I will pay you back as soon as Rachel gets home and she can take me back to Austin."

"Nonsense," said Orlando. "The closest hotel is the bed-and-breakfast in Vicker's Corners. There is no need for you to stay there when I have plenty of room at my house. I insist that not only you stay with us tonight but that also you join us for dinner."

Orlando flashed his trademark winning smile and it seemed to work on Zoe because she heaved a full-bodied sigh and her entire demeanor changed. She glanced at Joaquin as if to make sure he was amenable to his father's suggestion.

They would be sleeping under the same roof tonight. A frisson of awareness sparked inside him. What would her body feel like pressed against his? What would it be like to wake up with her in his arms? He blinked away the thoughts because he wouldn't find out tonight. She was in a vulnerable position right now. She was depending on him. He would never take advantage of her. The thoughts brought out a protectiveness he didn't know he possessed. "Please, join us," Joaquin tried again. "There's an empty place right here next to me, just waiting for you."

Chapter Six

What a way to meet the parents—or *parent*, in this case—Zoe thought as she bid Orlando good-night from the couch in front of the fireplace in the expansive living room of his ranch-style home. He was such a nice man. He'd made her feel so welcome. Not as though she was an idiot who had lost her purse, missed the bus and barged in on their dinner, which was all true.

Or worse yet, he had not suggested that she might be a manipulator who had manufactured the excuse simply to spend time with his son, which was 100 percent untrue, but still made her cringe thinking about how it looked.

No, both Orlando and Joaquin had been nothing but gracious, right down to opening an after-dinner bottle of wine and building a fire in the fireplace.

Even though it had been a pretty day with temperatures in the low seventies, the thermometer had dropped into the forties tonight. It was downright chilly.

Now that Orlando was retiring for the night, she and Joaquin would be left alone to finish the bottle of merlot. The realization left her nearly breathless. So, she turned her thoughts on expressing her appreciation to Orlando.

"Thanks, again, for the dinner and your generous hospitality, Orlando. I really don't know what I would've done without you and Joaquin."

After dinner the four of them had gone to the lost and found to see if anyone had turned in her wristlet and phone, but no one had. The manager on duty had taken her name and contact information and had promised to call her if they turned up.

"It was my honor and pleasure to welcome such a lovely guest," Orlando said. "I hope you will be very comfortable tonight. If you need anything, please don't hesitate to ask. Either Joaquin or I will be happy to get it for you."

He smiled warmly and gave a quick parting salute as he left the room. She knew instantly where Joaquin had gotten his good looks and gentlemanly manners.

Josephine had been wonderful, too. Kind, engaging and interesting to talk to. If she was representative of what the Fortune family was like as a whole, being related to them might not be such a bad thing, after all. But Zoe hadn't brought up the subject of her father's possible connection to the clan.

Given the way Gerald had so vehemently denied it, broaching it felt like a betrayal. Besides, who knew how Josephine felt about the rumors—if she'd even heard them. Why risk ruining what had turned out to be a perfectly lovely dinner with potentially upsetting talk of hearsay and speculation?

Zoe had been stranded and they had rescued her. She was touched by how warmly they'd included her and offered her a place to stay until she could reach Rachel, who, according to Orlando, was supposed to return tomorrow morning.

But that seemed light-years away.

Right now she and Joaquin were alone. Soft music played on the stereo and something electric vibrated between them. Was this really happening? Was she really *spending the night* with Joaquin?

The thought made her a little light-headed and it also scared her more than a wee bit. They hadn't even been on a date. In fact, until today, she hadn't even been sure Joaquin wanted to be her friend. He was a puzzle. Gruff and silent one minute, but then he showed up when it really mattered.

And now here they were. Alone, sharing a bottle of wine and conversation that, for once, wasn't about work.

She'd seen a different side of Joaquin today. A more human and personal side of him. She'd loved how relaxed he'd been. How natural things had felt between them.

But despite their easy-going good time at Cowboy Country, she realized that there was still so much about him that she didn't know.

Nothing else would happen between them tonight, as much as her body begged to differ. There wasn't going to be any hanky-panky, but she fully intended to leave here knowing him better.

"Would you like some more wine?" he asked, picking up the bottle and pouring more into her glass even before she had a chance to answer.

"Are you trying to get me drunk?" she joked. "Because I usually don't drink much."

One side of his mouth kicked up, just the hint of a smile. He refilled his own glass and sat back against the sofa cushions.

That was a good sign. It meant he was in no hurry to call it a night and head to their separate bedrooms, which were at opposite ends of the hall from each other.

When they'd gotten back to the house, Orlando had showed her to her room, which had an en suite bathroom. He had set out fresh towels and a new toothbrush. He'd asked Joaquin to get her a blanket from the closet in the room where he was staying. Joaquin said he would and also agreed to lend her one of his T-shirts to sleep in. But for now they sat on the couch in front of the fire, not so close that it might suggest crossing that line, but certainly close enough to edge right up to that line. Whether his interest was strictly platonic or more personal and much more exciting remained to be seen.

Now that they were alone, though, she felt as if she owed him some sort of explanation.

"I'm so sorry for this," she said.

He sipped his wine. "For what?"

"For barging in on your dinner and putting you in the position to have to take me in. My sister should be home tomorrow. I'll get out of your hair once she gets back."

"No worries," he said. "In fact, if you want, you can

hang out until Sunday. That's when I'm returning to Austin. You can ride back with me."

Another day in paradise and then a six-hour car ride back? It was so tempting.

"Rachel was planning on going to Austin tomorrow for some family business," she said. "We've been having regular meetings on that issue involving my father that I told you about. But thanks, anyway. I just want to make sure you didn't think I did this on purpose."

The second the words escaped her lips, the phrase "the lady doth protest too much" sprang to mind.

"You didn't?" he said.

She wanted to die until his mouth quirked up again and she realized he was kidding. Joaquin Mendoza had a sense of humor. Another checkmark in the sexy-as-hell column on the Husband List.

"For the record, *no*, I did not do it on purpose. I'm sure it might look that way. Especially after Steffi-Anne took such pleasure in pointing out all the guys I've dated."

"To put your mind at ease, I figured you wouldn't intentionally ditch your purse and cell phone just to spend the night with me."

"Another item for the record, I haven't spent the night with all the guys I've dated. Even though she made it sound like that, it's not true."

"Good to know."

"Well, personally, I was surprised you didn't have Steffi-Anne's phone number in your phone."

"I have no reason to call her. Why would I have her number in my phone?"

"I thought she would've at least punched in the digits herself. To make sure you could get in touch with her. You know, in case of an emergency. I guess she's falling down on the job."

"Guess so."

The two drank their wine as the fire blazed and music played in the background. Zoe recognized the song from a Ray Lamontagne CD she loved, but she couldn't remember the name of the track. She wanted to commit the melody to memory because it fit the mood so perfectly.

She had no idea where this was going, if it was even going anywhere. That's why she wanted to sip the moment slowly, savor it so it would last. Because this—being with him, just the two of them here with their defenses down—was something she could get used to.

"Do you need to call anyone to let them know you're here? Because once they realize you weren't on the bus, don't you think they'll worry? Especially if they try your phone and you don't answer."

"When I was at the restaurant, before I found you, I called my brother Ben. I left a message on his voice mail and told him I'd lost my purse, but I would catch a ride back to Austin with Rachel."

Joaquin frowned. "Won't he worry if he knows that Rachel isn't home and no one can get in touch with you?"

"Nah, it's just one night. It's fine."

Ah, this was a little tricky to explain. It dawned on her that while they were both close to their families, they were a *different* kind of close. His was obviously tightly knit. The kind of closeness she longed for one day. But her family—they were so busy going in opposite directions, racing toward their various goals and agendas, they probably wouldn't miss her if she was incommunicado for one night.

The thought was sobering. What did that say about the Robinsons? To outsiders looking in, they probably seemed like the family that had everything. And they really didn't want for much. But her parents were like two trains on different tracks. They shared the same station, but came and went on different schedules. The same could be said for her siblings. They worked together, yet maintained separate lives in the same city. Except for Rachel, who had made an enviable life for herself here in Horseback Hollow. Zoe had been completely unaware that Rachel and Matteo would be away tonight or even where they were going. Not that they needed to check in. It was just a different dynamic than Joaquin had with his family, and it made Zoe wish the Robinsons were a little more connected.

This "Fortune hunt" her siblings were on was turning out to be polarizing. Ben was at one end of the spectrum with his dogged determination and she was on the other end, the lone supporter of their father's wishes to leave well enough alone. The rest of her brothers and sisters were either on Ben's side or somewhere in the middle.

Maybe she could be the one to stop this nonsense and bring them all together at their family meeting on Monday.

"Where'd you go?" Joaquin's voice brought her back to the present. He was gazing at her intently and it unleashed a swarm of butterflies that performed a loop-de-loop in the pit of her stomach.

"I was just trying to think of how to say that even though my family is tight, we're *different*."

"What do you mean?"

Zoe shrugged. "It's hard to explain. They would certainly be concerned if they thought something had happened to me. But we're not the type to check in. But on the other hand, if I called my dad and told him that the bus left without me, he'd go ballistic. He would probably fire Steffi-Anne. I'm not kidding. He's superprotective of me. Maybe it's because I'm one of his youngest. Or maybe it's because, despite his gruff and bluster, we've always understood each other. Or maybe I should say, I understand him and he is protective of me. So, he can't know about the bus, okay?"

Joaquin cocked his head to the right. "Despite all the crap Steffi-Anne pulls on you, you're not going to put her in her place?"

"Don't get me wrong, I'm not afraid of her. I just don't ever want to contribute to someone losing her job. You never know what motivates people to act the way they do. Maybe it's insecurity. Maybe it's jealousy, though I'm not suggesting she's jealous of me. Although I can guarantee you she would be if she knew I was sitting here with you like this."

A lock of hair had fallen onto Joaquin's forehead and Zoe reached out and smoothed it back into place. Joaquin caught her hand and pulled her closer.

The next thing she knew, his lips were on hers. The kiss started whisper-soft, tentatively at first, as if he were testing the waters. When she leaned in and opened her mouth, inviting him in, he deepened the kiss. The world disappeared for a moment and the only thing Zoe was aware of was the feel of his lips on hers and that he tasted like something she'd been craving her entire life. She would've been perfectly content if the rest of the world had broken away, leaving the two of them to become one.

Time drifted and she had no idea how long the kiss lasted. It could've been a moment or a lifetime, but when it finally tapered off and they reclaimed their personal spaces, Zoe knew she was forever changed.

It was just a kiss, but it had been so much more than that. Because even as innocent as it had been, she'd given him a part of her she didn't want back. In fact, she wanted to give him more.

That was why it was probably a good thing when he stood, looking a little disoriented, and said, "We should probably call it a night. Let me get you that blanket and T-shirt."

He'd kissed Zoe. What the hell was wrong with him?

He couldn't shake the self-flagellation even three days later as he sat in his office on Monday morning. He was an idiot. He should've had more self-control than that. She deserved better. Certainly more than he could offer. But there was something about Zoe that rendered him stupid.

Her sister had called first thing Saturday morning. Before he and Zoe had been able to talk about what had happened and how they should move forward, Rachel and Matteo had arrived to say hello to Joaquin and whisk Zoe away.

He'd had the rest of the weekend to beat himself up and set himself straight. He hadn't seen her since she'd driven away with Rachel and Matteo, but he'd decided he'd gauge how she acted toward him and then see if they needed to talk and he needed to make things right. For all he knew, now that she'd had time to gain some distance and put everything into perspective, she might be just as sorry as he was that they had crossed that line. Yeah. It was unlikely, judging by her body language Saturday morning.

She had looked beautiful, all fresh-faced and natural. That's probably how she would look if they woke up together.

He leaned back in his desk chair, lacing his fingers behind his neck and looking up at the ceiling. *Sorry* was a strong word to describe how he was feeling. He *was* sorry he'd initiated the kiss and had put them in this situation, but he'd be lying to himself if he didn't concede that in the moment he had enjoyed every last second of it. But he'd been down this path before. He'd made the mistake of messing with the boss's daughter and if that experience had taught him one thing, it was that you don't play with people's emotions.

He should know. He'd been the biggest player in Miami until one spoiled, rich woman had played the player and taught him a lesson he couldn't forget. A lesson he'd be wise to remember now.

Zoe deserved someone who could offer her everything she wanted. He could not promise that right now. He didn't even know where he'd be when this project at Robinson ended. Knowing Gerald Robinson, if Joaquin hurt Zoe in any way, he'd have to deal with the big guy.

Joaquin had to figure out his own head before he'd be capable of knowing what he could offer anyone else. And, of course, there was the issue with his dad. He needed to get that out into the open and get to the heart of that matter before he could move on. If things turned out the way his hunch thought they would, it would be a game changer of unfathomable magnitude. He couldn't even wrap his mind around it yet. Because of that, he hadn't broached the subject with his dad after Zoe left. Josephine had come over and cooked a fabulous breakfast for them. And Orlando was smiling. Joaquin was pretty sure his dad was in love again. That was such a good thing since, when his mom died, it had seemed as if his father had lost his will to go on. Because Luz had been the love of Orlando's life.

The paternity bombshell Joaquin was about to drop was of nuclear proportions. Sometimes, such as when he saw the way Orlando had looked at Josephine, Joaquin wondered if exposing the truth was even worth it. Because if his mother had cheated, it might very well change Orlando's ability to love, similarly to how Selena had shattered the way Joaquin looked at just about everything.

But, he reminded himself, there was a lot more at stake than having a second chance at love or having the carpet yanked out from under him by a woman. The secret he harbored affected more people than Orlando and Josephine.

Even if they'd have a lot rebuilding to do after Joaquin dropped the bomb, it was something that couldn't be swept under the rug any longer.

He returned his attention to his computer, ready to get to down to business, when a message notification popped up in the bottom right corner of the screen.

It was from Zoe. His chest clenched as he clicked on it.

Are you still up for meeting about the website at 9:00?

The website?

That's right. Last week they had agreed to meet again today to work on it.

He knew darn good and well they'd have to talk about the weekend. He really didn't want to have this conversation here, because it was bound to make things awkward. But he couldn't put it off forever. The best thing he could do would be to show her that, as far as he was concerned, everything could still be normal.

My office or yours?

He waited for a response but it came in the form of a knock on the door.

"Come in," he said.

Zoe closed the door behind her and walked into his office looking bright and shiny and beautiful. Her long dark hair hung in loose waves down her back. She wore a red dress with a short black jacket. The outfit danced the fine line between professional and flirty. But if anyone could pull it off, she could. She had painted her lips bright red to match the dress.

His mouth went dry and his heart twisted a little. Because, though every bit as beautiful, this polished, professional Zoe was a sharp contrast to the freshly scrubbed, makeup-free beauty who'd greeted him Saturday morning.

That mental snapshot had his mind racing back to the kiss they'd shared, how those lush lips had tasted and how she'd fit so perfectly in his arms.

For a split second he longed to hold her again and his mind searched for something, anything, that would justify kissing her one more time.

Thank God, a moment later good sense took over and he gave himself a mental shake.

"Good morning." She flashed her usual warm smile and it made him feel a little more at ease.

"How was your weekend?"

"I had to spend a good chunk of time canceling my credit cards, but all that aside, it was great. It would've been even better if we would've had more time together."

His mind raced, trying to think of something to say that wouldn't hurt her feelings but wouldn't lead her on as he'd done on Friday night.

Before he could form the words, she said, "I got a new phone. I wanted to call you, but I didn't have your number."

She sat on the edge of one of the chairs in front of his desk.

"And you know what?" she said.

"What?" he asked because, well, why the hell not?

"Not knowing your number made me realize that that are a lot of things I don't know about you, and I figured out an easy way to remedy that."

He scowled as he picked up his cup of coffee and sipped it.

It burned his tongue.

That's what was wrong with him. He hadn't had enough coffee this morning. And along those same lines, he supposed he could blame his Friday-night weakness on the long day and the wine.

Lame. Yep. It was a lame excuse. But it was all he had. That, a cup of scalding coffee and woman right in front of him who was even hotter—too hot for him to handle.

"What I decided," she continued, undeterred by his silence, "is I'm starting a new column for the employee newsletter called 'Getting to Know You.' I'm going to interview a new employee every week, and guess who gets to go first? *You* do."

He winced before he could help it.

"Oh, come on. It's not that bad. In fact, it will be painless. I promise. It's five simple questions."

"Zoe," he said.

"Come on, Joaquin. This is me trying to show you that nothing has changed between us. So don't make it weird. Okay? I mean, unless you don't even want to be friends. Is that how you want it? Because that would make things very weird."

Their gazes locked across the expanse of the desk.

No. That wasn't how he wanted it. He still wanted to talk to her, joke around with her. She was fun and refreshing and optimistic. Exactly the type of person he needed in his life.

She was a million surprises. He had to admit, this take-charge, direct, professional attitude wasn't what he had expected from her this morning. Obviously he'd underestimated her.

"Of course, I want to be your friend," he said. "Since you brought up friendship, friends should be frank with each other. In that spirit, I owe you an apology."

"An apology? For what?"

"For kissing you."

She flinched. "Was it that bad?"

"No. It was fabulous, but it can't happen again."

Her face fell for a moment, but she recovered quickly. Held out her hand. "Okay. Friends, then?"

He nodded and shook her hand. "Friends. But I can't

do the interview right now. We have to make some
headway on this website and then I'm in meetings all
day. Tomorrow, too."

"Then meet me for a drink at Señor Iguana's tonight," she said.

He shook his head. "No. Zoe, that is not a good
idea."

"Joaquin, *friends* meet for drinks all the time. Besides, we will have chaperones. Plenty of them. My
brothers and sisters and I are having dinner there tonight. It's that family meeting I told you about."

"At Señor Iguana's? That doesn't seem very private."

Señor Iguana's had a cantina in the front where people could meet and order bar food, and a full-service
Tex-Mex restaurant in the back. The casual atmosphere
and good food made it a popular place, and it was busy
seven days a week.

"There's a private dining room in the back. Ben reserved it. He thought it might be nice to meet on neutral territory for a change."

She shook her head.

"I am not looking forward to this. I don't know how
many times my father will have to tell them he is not
a Fortune before they stop this nonsense."

"Why do you go to these meetings?" Joaquin asked.

"Because I seem to be the only one who brings a
voice of reason to this circus. It's not fun. So, will you
please be a *friend* and meet me there? If nothing else
it will give me a reason to escape the nonsense if they
get long-winded. I can tell them I have to go because
I'm meeting a friend."

She was right. *Friends* did meet for drinks, but he'd
already seen what happened when he was alone with

her. That line between friendship and *more* had gotten so blurry he'd lost his way. Even though his brain warned him against doing so with Zoe again, pure, primal need shoved him toward the outer edges of that boundary. And there didn't seem to be a thing his brain could do to stop the momentum.

Chapter Seven

"Zoe, Rachel tells me you had dinner with Josephine Fortune Chesterfield this weekend?" Ben Fortune Robinson set down his fork and looked at Zoe expectantly.

The private dining room at Señor Iguana's suddenly became so quiet she could almost hear the questions swirling around in Ben's mind as her siblings, Wes, Graham, Kieran, Olivia and Sophie, gazed at her eagerly.

The only one whose attention wasn't trained on Zoe was Rachel. Her head was down and she was focusing on her enchiladas as though they were the most fascinating special in the world.

Yeah, thanks, Rach. That's the last time I share anything like this with you.

She tried to catch Rachel's eye, but her sister wasn't looking.

"I did," Zoe said. "But that's not why you called us together, Ben. Why don't you tell us what's on your mind? I need to leave in a few minutes. So can we please get started?"

Ben pushed away his plate and leaned forward. "I'll get to my thing in a minute. How did it go with Josephine?"

Zoe frowned and tried to dam a wave of irritation that was cresting and threatening to break.

"It went fine, Ben. How else would it go? It was strictly a chance meeting because Joaquin Mendoza and his father, Orlando, were gracious enough to take me in after I missed the bus in Horseback Hollow. I certainly wasn't going to barge in on their dinner and dominate the conversation by quizzing her about her family tree. Classless, Ben. Even the thought is classless."

Ben didn't seem to hear her or maybe he simply didn't care because he clamped down on the topic like a bulldog with a meaty bone.

All this talk about her father having a secret identity and being part of the Fortune family had become boring. Their dad denied it and Zoe chose not to believe it because it was yet another example of secrets harming relationships. Only these secrets belonged to her siblings, who kept on digging into their father's past behind his back and against his wishes.

Her words rolled right off her brother.

"You all are aware that Josephine Fortune Chesterfield was adopted and only found out a few years ago that she was a Fortune, right? I believe the same could be true for Dad."

Zoe sighed loud enough that everyone turned to look

at her. Even Rachel, who was the one who'd started this whole mess last year when she'd discovered evidence that she thought suggested their dad's real name might be Jerome Fortune. That's all it had taken to get Ben started on this "Fortune hunt." Never mind the way their father had denied the allegations, and the fact that the rest of the Fortune family claimed it was impossible. Ben was determined to uncover this so-called truth.

Zoe wished he'd put as much effort into his job as chief operating officer at Robinson Tech. The way he'd been going against their dad's wishes, bird-dogging this issue, she was surprised their father didn't fire him, or at least demote him.

Each new lead seemed to turn into a stone wall at a dead end. Most recently, after much wasted time and energy, Ben had located a woman named Jacqueline Fortune, who was this Jerome's mother and, as Ben insisted, their grandmother.

Never mind that the poor woman, who was in her nineties and living in a memory-care unit of a nursing home, suffered from dementia. Ben just kept pushing.

He almost took this one too far because when he brought up Jerome's name, poor Jacqueline had completely freaked out and started yelling that Jerome Fortune was dead.

Wouldn't he think that would be a sign that it was time to close this ridiculous case? *Nooo.* Ben still wouldn't let it go. He had to keep raking up the muck.

His latest allegation was that their father might have illegitimate offspring scattered all over the world. This stemmed from a British guy named Keaton Whitfield whom Ben had come across on this odyssey to drag their father through the mud.

The wave of anger that Zoe had tried to contain finally crested and crashed.

Until this point she had tried to stay out of the fray and do what she could to be the peacemaker. She attended these monthly meetings Ben insisted on holding to be the voice of reason. As a general rule, she preferred to take the kind approach and focus on the positive things in life. But now Ben had gone too far.

Zoe stood, her chair scraping loudly across the wooden floorboards. "Okay, Ben, if we're just going to rehash false starts we already know have led to dead ends, then I'm going to say good-night."

She grabbed her purse and fished out her phone, looking at the time...and to see if Joaquin had texted her to say that he was there.

He hadn't. Probably because he wasn't due to meet her for another half hour. But she had to get out of there. She couldn't stand one more minute of hearing her brother's desperate attempt to turn their father into a liar and rehash the rumors of his infidelity.

Even on the far-flung chance that their dad was this Jerome Fortune in another life, what difference did it make? He had always been a good parent. He had provided for his family, making it possible for his kids to not only have every material possession a person could ask for but also careers for each and every one of them if they wanted to be a part of the family business. He also gave them the freedom to not be part of it—with no prejudice—if they so chose. Rachel was a good case in point.

"Sit down, Zoe. That's not why I've asked everyone

to be here tonight. I have a new lead, and it just might be the breakthrough we've been looking for."

Zoe rolled her eyes.

Here we go again.

The only reason she sat again was that she wanted to know what inane tree Ben was barking up now. Since he had gone so far as to produce someone who claimed to be a half brother—and was making noises that there might be more—she needed to stay to make sure her siblings hadn't done something stupid like invite him to move into the Robinson estate. At this point, nothing would surprise her.

"I have found an old friend of Jacqueline Fortune's. Her name is Marian Brandt. She was Jacqueline's neighbor. She and I talked at length."

Zoe glanced at Ben. He was holding up a small photograph. Zoe squinted, but she couldn't tell what the image was since he was at the head of the table and she was toward the other end.

If he went to the trouble of bringing props, he would certainly show and tell. Zoe took one last look in her compact mirror, snapped it shut and put away her cosmetics.

"Her late son, Eddie, and Jerome Fortune used to play when they were very young. She even shared this photo."

Ben gave it to Olivia, who sat to his right.

"Jacqueline and Marian have a lot in common. Both of them were widowed at a fairly young age and both lost their only sons. It's no wonder that they bonded over their tragic losses."

The picture had made its way around the table to Zoe. Of course, it was hard to tell if one of the boys was their father because they were so young in the picture. Zoe realized she couldn't recall ever seeing a picture of her father as a child. But that didn't mean anything.

As she passed it to Wes, she considered asking him if he'd ever seen pictures of their father as a kid, but quickly decided not to because if he hadn't, it might give Ben more fuel for his fire.

"Even now that Jacqueline is bedridden, Marian is still a good friend and goes to visit her several times a week. When she heard that I had been to visit Jacqueline, she got my number from the nurses and called me and agreed to meet me for lunch."

"Did she give you this picture?" Kieran asked.

"She brought the original and allowed me to snap a shot of it with my phone. I had it printed out."

Of course, he would. Zoe wondered if Ben had a big evidence board similar to ones the FBI used when they were trying to solve a crime. Because he certainly was trying his best to turn their father into a criminal.

"Was she able to tell you anything new?" Sophie asked.

Ben grimaced and gave a palms-up shrug. "Technically, no. She said Jerome mailed his mom a suicide note and that the boat that had washed ashore without him in it was registered to the Fortune family. But, remember, even though he was presumed dead, Jerome Fortune's body was never found."

"Really, Ben?" Zoe groaned. "The neighbor woman confirmed what the police have already told you—that Jerome Fortune took out his family's boat and committed suicide—and that's still not enough to convince you it's time to end this ludicrous obsession?"

He ignored her.

"I'm going to see if the police have a copy of the suicide note in the evidence file. I'll get a graphologist to compare it with a sample of dad's handwriting."

"Jerome Fortune has been dead for more than thirty years," Sophie challenged. "Do you really think they'll still have his file?"

Again, Ben shrugged. "I'll never know unless I check into it. My gut still believes Jerome Fortune is very much alive and that he is our father. I will keep looking until I find irrefutable evidence to prove it— one way or the other."

That's enough.

Zoe slid her purse onto her arm and stood. "I think you're ridiculous and you need to stop this nonsense right now. It's your business if you want to waste your time chasing the ghost of Jerome Fortune, but until you have that irrefutable evidence, this is the last meeting I will attend. You all should be ashamed of yourselves for dragging our father through the mud when he has been nothing but generous to each and every one of you."

This time she ignored her siblings' attempted justifications and explanations and walked out of the meeting. They each had their own reasons for doing this to their father, but she didn't want to hear it. It was hurtful and disrespectful.

Sure, some might have considered Gerald Robinson a tyrant, and, yes, she knew she had always been his favorite, but they were a family. Even though she was aware of her father's indiscretions, she didn't want to know the gory details. That was between him and her mother. She knew their parents' relationship was strained enough. If Ben kept it up, they would eventually hit the breaking point. If her brothers and sisters would stop looking for trouble, it would go a long way toward strengthening family relations. Families stuck together; they didn't try to tear each other apart, because when one went down, they all went down.

Zoe wasn't going to sit there and watch them destroy the people who had given them life.

She made her way to Señor Iguana's crowded cantina area. It buzzed with the noisy music and energy of a beloved night spot. She squinted as she scanned the dimly lit room, past its neon signs and perennial Christmas-tree lights strung in draping swags, to see if Joaquin was waiting, but it was still a little early. She was tempted to leave and come back, but a quick glance at her phone revealed they were due to meet in fifteen minutes. She couldn't go anywhere and get back in that short amount of time. So she might as well stay.

She needed to change gears so that the irritation her siblings had stoked up in her was not rolling off her in waves when Joaquin arrived. Normally she didn't drink much, but right now nothing sounded better than a great big frozen-lime margarita. It would surely take the edge off.

She marched up to the bar and ordered, "One Iguana-rita, please."

In less than a minute the bartender set something the size of a fishbowl in front of her.

"Oh! This is enough for four people," she said as she handed him the cash to pay for it. "I didn't realize it was so large."

The bartender, a good-looking guy despite his man-bun and tattoo sleeves, said, "You've been here before, haven't you?"

Or maybe his bohemian look was what made him attractive.

"I have. I love this place."

"I thought I'd seen you around." He lingered, leaning his elbows on the bar. The tat on his right forearm was a skull with a clock face in one of its eyes. The more she looked at it, the more she saw how the individual images played into the bigger picture. It was a mesmerizing in a freaky Where's Waldo sort of way.

She'd never dated a guy with a tattoo. She wondered if Joaquin had any hidden pictures on his gorgeous body. *Mmm.* She'd like to find out. It would be like a treasure hunt.

"Have you never ordered the Thirsty Iguana?" Man-Bun asked.

She shook her head. "I've never ordered one. I asked for an iguana-rita. I think that's the much smaller version of this fish tank."

"My mistake," said Man-Bun. "It's on the house since I screwed up your order."

"No, that's okay. I can pay for it." She took her first sip. It was cold and delicious, and went down way too easy. Probably way stronger than it tasted. She'd have to be careful or she might be picking herself up off the floor.

While she was no stranger to the club scene and she certainly enjoyed partying on the weekends, she was not a big drinker and never did drugs. Some might say she didn't like to be out of control. She liked to think of it as being high on life.

Someone at the other end of the bar flagged down the bartender. "Enjoy it—what did you say your name was?"

"I didn't," she said.

"We'll enjoy it, *I Didn't*. May I call you *I* for short?"

Zoe laughed and sipped her drink. "Suit yourself."

"After things slow down, maybe I can help you finish that iguana?" he said.

"She won't need your help," Joaquin said as he slid onto the vacant stool next to her. "But thanks."

Joaquin didn't like the looks of that guy, with his tattoo sleeves and his long hair piled on top of his head. What kind of a guy wore his hair like that? He had *player* written all over him. He'd probably helped a lot of women finish their drinks. Probably a different one every night.

"He won't bother you anymore," Joaquin said. "But, hey, how are you doing? How was the meeting?"

Zoe frowned at him. "What makes you think he was bothering me?"

Her words and sharp tone made Joaquin do a double-take. "He was hitting on you."

She pursed her lips and her right brow shot up. That expression was starting to become a familiar challenge, even though her tone was a lot more intense than the Zoe he knew.

"And it bothers you that he was hitting on me?" she asked.

"What? You like him?"

"Don't answer my question with a question." She took a long sip of her margarita.

"He doesn't seem like your type."

She put her hands on her hips. "What is my type, Joaquin?"

Their gazes locked and for a moment something

electric passed between them. It was all he could do to keep from saying, "I am. I'm your type." But that was such a bad idea.

When he didn't answer, she said. "It seems like *you're* the one who is bothered by his flirting with me."

True. It did bother him. He knew he had no right because he had made it perfectly clear where they stood. He was probably worse for her than the tattooed bartender.

He glanced down the bar. The dude was talking and laughing with another woman. Zoe deserved better than that.

Better than the flirting bartender or better than a guy who kissed her and backed the hell up?

Better than both of them.

That guy was a player. But Joaquin was nine years her senior. She needed someone young, someone who was not preoccupied with his own issues.

When he turned back to look at her, he saw that she was watching the bartender, too. He couldn't tell if she looked disappointed or resigned.

"I thought I was doing you a favor by rescuing you from that one," he said.

"Thank you, but just because I missed the bus in Horseback Hollow doesn't mean I need you to keep rescuing me."

He nodded.

"No, you don't. You're a strong, smart, capable woman."

He almost added *beautiful* to the list, but he bit back the word before it escaped.

"Thank you for that." She sighed and looked a little defeated. "Look, I'm sorry. I'm in a mood and I don't mean to take it out on you. The family meeting didn't go very well. Why don't we start over?" She took a deep breath and extended her hand. "Hi, Joaquin. I'm glad to see you."

This was a different disposition for her. She was usually so happy and full of good spirits that her kindness and effervescence were contagious. But no one was perfect. She was allowed an off night.

"Do you want to talk about it?"

She looked at him for a long, silent moment filled by the loud salsa music playing in the background. He thought she was going to decline.

"Actually, yes, I would. I think that would help."

A four-top in the corner was just opening up. "Why don't we go grab that table over there?"

As soon as they sat, a server approached and Joaquin ordered a beer.

"Would you like anything else?" he asked Zoe.

She toasted him with her large glass. "Thanks, I think I'm all set for tonight—and possibly into next week. This drink is huge. There's no way I'll be able to finish it. So, please, help yourself."

"Why don't you bring us an order of chips and salsa?" Joaquin said to the server. Then he turned back to Zoe. "It might come in handy to soak up some of that alcohol."

As she pushed the drink aside, Joaquin felt an irrational satisfaction that he would be the one sharing Zoe's beverage, not the bartender.

After the server walked away, Joaquin said, "What's going on with your family?"

Her pretty eyes darkened a shade and she lowered her lids as she traced a crack in the Formica tabletop.

"I don't understand why Ben is so determined to prove that our father is lying about his identity. Now he's alleging Dad has illegitimate children scattered all over the place. Can't he see how humiliating this is for our mother? Though I don't think she's aware of this allegation. It seems like Ben is determined to tear our family apart. He keeps trying to dig up a past for our dad. When he doesn't find anything, he invents something. Ben just needs to hop off.

"But let's say by some fluke my dad *is* this Jerome Fortune person. He obviously doesn't want anyone to know. He has asked Ben time and again to stop. Why does Ben keep digging? What difference does would it make if our father actually did have a past that he isn't proud of? What good is it going to do if Ben uncovers buried skeletons and drags them out for everyone to see? What difference is that going to make except to hurt everyone involved?"

Joaquin wore his best poker face. He knew that Ben was on a mission to prove a Fortune connection, but he hadn't realized until this very moment how closely Zoe's family issues overlapped with his own. It gave him pause.

"I don't know Ben very well, but I can't imagine he's purposely trying to tear apart your family."

Zoe looked at him as if he'd spit in her drink.

"So, you're saying he's right to do this, even though my dad has asked him to stop?"

Joaquin shook his head. "I'm not saying anyone is right or wrong. What I was getting at is that I think it's natural to want to know your roots and where you came from."

"Well, he *is* tearing us apart. Or at least he's headed in that direction."

When there were issues—tough issues—that needed to be discussed, someone was bound to get hurt. But it didn't do anyone any good to ignore it.

"Before it gets any later," Zoe said, "we better start the interview. Since that's why we came here in the first place."

Good idea. Since they seemed to have opposite opinions about a similar family issue, it was bound to cause hurt feelings. As if to second the motion to change subjects, the server approached the table with his beer.

Since Zoe didn't want anything else, he paid for his drink rather than run a tab. Once that was taken care of, he said, "What's the first question?"

She pulled a small tablet out of her purse. As she typed, pink nails clicking on the built-in keyboard, her earlier tension seemed to ease.

"What do you like best about working at Robinson Tech?"

"The project I'm working on is interesting. I love the creative freedom I have at Robinson."

She glanced up at him and nodded before recording his answer.

"Favorite color?"

"How is that work-related?"

"Favorite color," she repeated. "I didn't promise that this was strictly about the professional you. That's boring, Joaquin. We have to spice it up with a little bit of personality. So, favorite color?"

He smiled and shook his head. "Blue."

"Really?" Zoe said as she tap-tapped away, typing

up his answer. "I had you pegged for a green man, but blue works. Favorite food?"

"There's not much I don't like. Everything from steak to sushi to all ethnic cuisines. I love good food. It's something I'm passionate about."

She propped her elbow on the table and rested her chin on the heel of her hand. "I think it's very sexy when a man is adventurous."

He laughed. "Are you going to put that in your article?"

"Maybe. How would you describe your perfect day?"

It had been so long since he'd had a perfect day that he had to think about it for a minute.

"Spending it with someone special. Maybe exploring new places, or if there was a somewhere we both liked, we could go there."

He remembered days spent on the beach and in a boat out on the ocean in Florida. He remembered the cruel way Selena had let him know their relationship was over. Funny, it was a fading memory now. He had been humiliated at the time, cut to the quick, but the pain was gone. He hadn't realized it until now.

"I haven't made it to the Driskill Hotel yet," he said. "I hear it's a quite a place."

Zoe reached out and put a hand on his arm. "Oh, my gosh. It's one of my favorite places in Austin. Maybe we could meet there for drinks some time?"

"Yeah."

And there it was again, that energy that coursed between them. If he wasn't careful, he might mistake it for chemistry. Aw, hell, who was he kidding? This was chemistry and it was undeniable. Admitting it was the best safeguard against crossing that line. That damn line. It kept tempting him closer and closer.

"What are you most grateful for?" she asked.

He was grateful she'd changed the subject. "That's easy—my family."

"See, you do know that family is most important over everything. *Everything.*"

The episode with Selena had underscored that. A lot of women had come and gone in his life, but his family was the one constant.

"Have you ever been married?" she asked.

"I agreed to answer five questions. That's number six."

She closed the tablet's cover and slid it into her purse. "That one is for me. Not for the newsletter."

He took a swig of his beer, debating whether he wanted to talk about this or not. But one look at Zoe's pretty face and he was putty.

"I was engaged once."

"Was?" Zoe asked.

Joaquin nodded.

"What was her name?"

"Selena Marks."

Zoe's eyes widened. "As in Marks Telecom in Miami? That's where you worked, right?"

"How did you know that?" he asked.

"I have my ways. Does your broken engagement have anything to do with why you won't date people you work with?"

For all of her fun-loving ways, she was pretty astute. He drained the last of his beer and set the bottle on the table.

"It has everything to do with that. On that note, I

think it's time to call it a night. Do you want me to give you a ride home?"

"No, of course not. I have my car here."

"Are you okay to drive?"

"I've had maybe three sips. I'm a lightweight. It was way too strong for me. So, I'm fine to drive."

"Come on," he said. "I'll walk you out to your car."

They navigated their way to the front of the cantina and he held the door for her.

When they got to her car, a sporty little red BMW convertible, she turned to him, her voice soft and little shaky. "I don't know what happened that caused your engagement to end, but I hate that it caused you so much pain. And I'm sorry that it may be keeping you from potentially good relationships."

A moment passed between them. She looked vulnerable and angelic standing there backlit by the glow of the streetlight. She was right. He had been letting Selena keep him from moving forward, but tonight Zoe had helped him see that he'd moved further ahead than he'd realized.

"May I be perfectly honest with you?" he asked.

"Of course. I'd expect nothing less from you."

He nodded. "The thing is, I like working at Robinson. I didn't realize just how much until I realized that this project is almost finished and I'm not ready to go."

Her eyes widened. "Are you saying you want a permanent position?"

"I have a meeting with Gerald later this week and I was going to talk to him about it."

"I have an idea," she said. "What are you doing Thursday night?"

"I don't know. Why?"

"My dad is hosting a dinner for a handful of high-level employees. You should come."

Joaquin laughed. "You are something else. I cannot crash your father's party. He didn't invite me. Thanks, but I'll talk to him when we meet at the office."

"He's going to invite you. So, be prepared to clear your calendar on Thursday night."

Joaquin shook his head. It was more of a head-clearing gesture than a negative response to her promised invitation.

"Just like that, your father is going to invite me? Because you said so."

She shrugged and nodded, making a face as if he'd just asked the dumbest question ever.

Joaquin couldn't help but smile at her self-assurance. It was one of the things he loved about her. She wasn't arrogant or mean; there wasn't a cruel bone in her body. She simply knew what was what and she wasn't afraid to own it.

"You always get what you want, don't you?"

She cocked her head to the side. "You say that like it's a bad thing, Mr. Mendoza."

"No, actually, it's not. I was thinking that you're pretty amazing."

"Really? You think so?"

It took everything he had not to lean in and taste those lips again. But he knew better and he pulled himself back from the edge.

"You're a good friend, a good daughter, and you're great at what you do. I'd say all that adds up to *amazing*."

"I'm a good friend, huh?"

He tried to ignore the way the disappointment in

her eyes belied the smile curving up the edges of those tempting lips. "Well, Joaquin, you keeping me in the friend zone proves I don't get *everything* I want. You need to know I won't give up on you."

God, she was killing him.

"You also need to know that people have told me that I'm passionate and persistent." She let the words hang between them. "So I'm not letting you friend-zone me, Joaquin."

He bent down and kissed her on the forehead.

"Good night, Zoe."

"Seriously? Is that the best you can do?"

"Were you expecting something else?"

"Joaquin, that was like getting a kiss from my brother."

"Since your sister is married to my brother, doesn't that make us related in some way?"

She put her hands on her hips. "No, it does not. You're a hot Latino from Miami. I expected more from you than a kiss on the forehead. You have *no* game."

Joaquin laughed. "You think I just made a move on you? That shows just how innocent you are. Because when I make a move on a woman, she knows it."

Chapter Eight

As an independent contractor who'd only had a minimal amount of one-on-one time with Gerald Robinson, Joaquin had mixed emotions when the big boss stopped by his office on Tuesday to invite him to the Thursday-night dinner party.

He knew Gerald wouldn't have done it if not for Zoe's prompting. But on the other hand, despite how much Gerald loved his daughter, Joaquin was certain the man wouldn't have been goaded into inviting anyone to something like this simply for his daughter's amusement.

There was a time for pride and then there was a time when someone didn't refuse a bona fide invitation that could change his career. Robinson Tech was the premier technology company. It was the wave of the future. It was the only place for anyone interested in designing cutting-edge software.

When Thursday night rolled around and Joaquin arrived at the Robinson estate with its stone walls and iron gates, he felt like a fish out of water the minute he started up the long, winding driveway. When the house, a Mediterranean number that looked like a castle, came into view in, it knocked him back into his seat. He'd led a perfectly comfortable life in Miami. He'd never wanted for anything, but he had never been exposed to quite this level of wealth.

Not even with Selena.

Not that it mattered. The last thing he was looking for was to get tangled up with another spoiled little rich girl. But giving credit where credit was due, the more he got to know Zoe, the more he realized she wasn't spoiled. Even though she usually got what she wanted, she was pretty damn down to earth. It sounded like a contradiction, but it wasn't. It was the truth. She was fresh and fun and bubbly, and everyone would be better off if they borrowed a page from her outlook on life. Even when she was down, as she had been the other night, she didn't wallow and she kept other people's best interests at heart.

As Joaquin got closer, he saw a couple of guys standing out in front of the house. Of course there would be valets. He had a feeling everything would be first-class tonight.

After he got out of the car and handed over the keys, he started to tip the guy, but the kid held up his hand.

"Thanks, but Mr. Robinson has taken care of us. Have a nice evening, sir."

Sir? The guy wasn't *that* much younger than he was. Then again, he was probably closer to Zoe's age than Joaquin, and it was probably just a show of re-

spect for anyone fortunate enough to be invited to the
Robinson estate.

The guy jumped into the car and carefully drove
away, leaving Joaquin to contemplate the huge wooden
front doors. He wondered if Zoe was somewhere inside.
Then he realized he didn't even know if she lived here
or if she had a place of her own. From the looks of this
house, she could have an entire wing and it would be
more space than most middle-class houses.

Joaquin ignored the knot in his gut. He squared his
shoulders and rang the bell. A middle-aged man in a
black suit answered, greeting him formally.

"Good evening, sir." Ha! *Sir.* There it was again.
"Mr. Robinson would like everyone to gather in the
living room for cocktails before dinner."

Joaquin followed the directions the butler gave
him—down the polished wooden hallway, first door
on the left—and joined a handful of men and women,
none of whom he recognized. Robinson Tech was
a huge business and Joaquin mostly kept to himself, keeping his head down, focusing on his work.
They were all mixing and mingling and seemed to
know each other. It wasn't any wonder that he was the
stranger here, since he hadn't made much of an effort
to get to know his coworkers socially.

His gaze took in the room from its hardwood floors
covered with Persian rugs to its high, arched ceilings.
The fine antique furniture and artwork, which looked
like an art lover's dream, gave the place an air of old-
world elegance that he'd only encountered in the finest hotels and the couple of mansion museums he'd
toured over the years.

But one important element was missing: Zoe hadn't

arrived yet. Earlier today she'd stopped by his office and said she'd see him tonight. He hoped something else hadn't come up. Until now, he hadn't realized how much he missed her. But as quickly as the thought registered, he shook it off. Tonight was about business, not about exploring odd feelings he didn't know how to process.

He needed a beer. That's what was wrong. He found his way to the open bar and ordered his drink, which the bartender poured from a tap into a frosted pilsner glass. When Joaquin turned around, Zoe was just walking into the room. She looked like something from his dreams in a short black dress and strappy sandals. She wore bright red lipstick and had swept her hair back from her face into a fancy ponytail. Somehow she always managed to look as though she'd just stepped out of the salon. The rush of emotion that hit him nearly knocked him to the floor.

Her face lit up when she saw him. He couldn't take his eyes off her as she crossed the room. It hit him that this beautiful woman, who could have any man she chose, wanted to spend time with *him*. *With him*. He'd be lying if he didn't admit that he wanted spend time with her, too. He'd spent so much time denying it, all for the sake of not dating the boss's daughter— but why?

It wasn't because of her family or because Gerald was her father. It wasn't this castle of a house or the fact that she had the power to connect him to the man who could define his future. All of those things were great, but what smacked him so hard that it forced his eyes wide-open was the way she looked at him, the way she lit up just for him. It shifted something inside him, tantamount to rolling aside a boulder that had sealed off a cold, dark cave that had trapped his soul.

Seeing her was like stepping out into the sunshine again.

After his broken engagement, after the hell Selena had put him through, tonight he realized he could still feel. It came like a lightning bolt because it had been a couple of years since he'd been able to feel anything remotely like this. That could only mean one thing: the past was behind him now. He'd left it inside that cave that had held him prisoner and rolled that rock back into place, so those difficult times could wither and die inside and never plague him again. He wasn't sure where this was going or if it would even go anywhere, but for the first time in a long time, he was ready to move forward.

"Hi, Joaquin." She leaned in and kissed him on the cheek and he kissed her back. She smelled good, like roses and honey and sunshine. He breathed in deeply, wanting to commit her scent to memory.

"You look handsome," she said after she pulled away, making no bones about giving him the slow, sexy once-over.

"You're not so bad yourself," he said. "May I get you a drink?"

"A glass of white wine would be lovely, thank you."

He made short order of fetching it, but by the time he returned to her side, Gerald had entered the room.

"Hello, everyone. Welcome and thank you for taking time out of your busy lives to join me for dinner tonight. I hope you all brought your appetites because the chef has prepared a delicious feast for us to enjoy. Without further delay, why don't we make our way into the dining room, because dinner is ready and I am starving."

The small crowd, about fifteen in all, made the appropriate adoring and convivial noises as they filed past Gerald. He took the time to greet everyone by name and express how happy he was to see him or her. The man seemed like a different person than the rough, gruff boss at work. Apparently he had different faces that ranged from dictatorial tyrant to beloved king of the castle. It was good to meet the more human side of him. Joaquin realized not everyone was privileged to glimpse the less gruff side of Gerald Robinson, whom one news magazine had named the Bully Genius and another had called the Attila the Hun of Technology.

Joaquin was beginning to understand why Zoe had come into his office that day and asked for help spinning her father's reputation in a more positive direction. It made sense after glimpsing the more benevolent side of Gerald Robinson. Zoe knew and loved this side of her dad and wanted everyone to see how great he could be. Still, Joaquin would wager that Gerald Robinson didn't give a rat's ass what people thought of him.

"Joaquin, good to see you." Gerald extended his hand and Joaquin gave it a firm shake. "It was short notice. I'm glad you could make it."

"Thanks for inviting me," he said, taking care to express his appreciation without gushing.

"Are we still on for that sit-down tomorrow? I'm looking forward to talking about what you want to do after you after you finish your current project." Gerald turned his attention to his daughter and Joaquin was dismissed. "Hello, princess. It's always a good night when we get to have dinner together."

"Hi, Dad." Zoe threw both of her arms around Gerald's neck. It was the first time Joaquin had ever seen Gerald's face go completely soft. But it only lasted a moment before he reclaimed his tough armor.

"Get in there to dinner," he said to Joaquin. "It's rude to keep everyone waiting."

Zoe looked at Joaquin and rolled her eyes good-naturedly, but her father didn't see it. Joaquin wasn't sure if Gerald missed it by accident or design.

There were no place cards. The guests were free to sit where they wanted. By the time he and Zoe made it into the dining room, the places near Gerald were taken. Joaquin wished he'd gotten in there earlier. It would have been fun watching the others jockey for the prime real estate. The two seats available were at the opposite end of the sprawling table.

At each place setting there was a menu detailing the five-course feast: Oysters Rockefeller, cream of roasted walnut soup, surf and turf, salad of baby greens with vinaigrette, and flourless chocolate cake with raspberry coulis. Each course had its own wine pairing.

During dinner, everyone made small talk, but Gerald was quiet, hunching over his meal, paying more attention to the food than to his guests. While everyone except for Joaquin and Zoe tried to be the centers of attention, entertaining with their best anecdotes and worldly stories, they seemed to know better than to interrupt Gerald's rapturous dinner.

By the time dessert was served, Joaquin thought they'd have to roll him out of the dining room. But the after-dinner Calvados was the perfect ending to the delicious meal.

When he was done, Gerald commanded the stage and regaled his guests with a bit of his own history.

"As most of you know, I'm a self-made man," he said. "I built Robinson Tech from the ground up with my own two hands, starting with only the shirt on my back and the cash in my pockets. No one ever gave me anything, and I never asked them to."

There was an edge to Gerald's tone that bordered on bitter and Joaquin wondered if it had anything to do with the rumored Fortune connection. Joaquin glanced around the table, watching the others smiling and nodding and shaking their heads in solidarity. He wondered if they could hear the undercurrent in Gerald's words. It sounded a lot like hurt.

If the man really was a Fortune, as Zoe's siblings kept insisting, what must it have been like to walk away from that dynasty and start over? Or had he walked away? Maybe he'd been pushed. Or, as Zoe maintained, maybe it was all a moot point.

Zoe was facing questions about her family, questions about truth and lies and whom to believe, what was important and what didn't matter. Yet she still managed to see the good in life and give those she loved the benefit of the doubt.

She had questions very similar to the ones he was facing. For a moment Joaquin wondered if exposing the truth really mattered. Would it change anything for the better?

He cast a glance at Zoe, who was listening intently. In Gerald's case, exposing his past might not make things better. Of course, it would hurt Zoe and that in itself colored Joaquin's opinion on Fortune-gate. Because when he thought of his own situation, the devastating questions he needed to ask his father, it still seemed necessary.

"I respect hard work and dedication," Gerald continued. "It's what's gotten me where I am today. I want Robinson Tech to reflect that ethos of perseverance and independence. That's why I've asked each of you here tonight. Because I recognize a similar drive and determination in your work. I want this company to forge new paths. You don't get ahead in this business by regurgitating what your competitors have already created. So that's where you come in. You bring the fresh and the original to Robinson Tech. Over the next few weeks I'm going to meet with each of you one-on-one and we are going to map out your future with the company."

Gerald stood suddenly, tossing the linen napkin onto his dessert plate with the flick of his wrist. "But right now, it's time for you all to leave. Good night, everyone."

Zoe had never been so happy for a dinner to end. And even happier, since it was still early.

Stanley, who had been the Robinson's butler for as far back as Zoe could remember, herded the guests to the door, and it gave her a chance to grab Joaquin's hand and pull him toward the opposite door that led to the butler's pantry.

"Where are we going?" he asked.

"Away from here," she said, happy that he hadn't let go of her hand. Their fingers were laced and his palm felt big and warm against hers.

She led him through the butler's pantry and took a sharp left down a hall that led to the family room.

"Let's go outside," she said. "It's such a nice night."

Joaquin smiled. "That sounds like a great idea."

They walked hand in hand across the travertine porch, down the steps that led to the pool area and to a wooden bench that overlooked Lake Austin.

"This view is my favorite thing about this house," Zoe said. "Sometimes when I just need to think, I come out here and sit."

"It's a great view," Joaquin said. "What do you think about when you're out here?"

His thigh had drifted over into her space and was resting against her leg. She liked the feel of him next to her.

"Whatever's on my mind. Right now, I'm hoping to get a promotion. That's one of the reasons I was at the dinner tonight. Just because I'm the boss's daughter doesn't mean he automatically promotes me. I have to earn advancement like everyone else. And that's the way it should be. Why should I get special privileges? Shouldn't I have to earn my way just like everyone else does?"

Joaquin raised his brows and nodded.

"What?" she said. "Did you think I was here tonight just to see you?"

"I was hoping," he said.

She couldn't believe he'd said that. It made her stomach jump and her heart race, but she tried to play it cool, even though what she wanted to do was to wrap her arms around him and show him exactly how happy she was to be there with him.

"But you live here," he said. "Of course I'd expect you to be here."

"I don't anymore. I grew up here, but I have a place

of my own now. This is a great house, though, isn't it? It was fun growing up here. So, did you have fun tonight?"

Joaquin nodded. "It was interesting. I saw a side of your father I'd never seen before. I have acquired a brand-new appreciation for him."

"That makes me so happy, you don't even know. I wish everyone could see him the way you do."

"Thanks for having him invite me."

Zoe held up her hand. "Actually, all I did was ask him if you were coming tonight, and he's the one who decided to invite you. I didn't ask him to. He really likes you, Joaquin. And so do I."

She saw Joaquin's throat work. He was silent for a moment, just looking at her in way that she couldn't read. For a second she was afraid he was going to friend-zone her again.

"I like you, too, Zoe. You know what I like best about you?"

She shook her head.

"You always see the best in everyone, even in me. I know I haven't been the easiest person to get to know."

Zoe laughed. Even if he was hard to get to know, Joaquin obviously had no idea what a great guy he was.

"I wish I could claim that as a heroic quality," she said. "But it's not hard to see the good in you. I mean, good grief, half the women in the office are in love with you."

He made a face that said he didn't believe her.

"Or at least Steffi-Anne is," she said. "If you don't know that, then you're clueless. And if you are clueless, that's okay, because then I can tell you that it's true, but—"

She stopped, biting back her words before she said the wrong thing. But, really, what was the point of censoring herself now?

"Joaquin, I don't want to share you. Not with Steffi-Anne. With no one."

He answered her by lowering his head and covering her mouth with his. It was a kiss that she felt all the way down to her curled toes.

When they finally came up for air, he said, "In case you're wondering, I just made a move on you."

Chapter Nine

After the Robinson dinner, Zoe and Joaquin were inseparable outside of the office. The more time he spent with her, the more he wondered why it had taken him so long to get his head on straight. She made him so damn happy, he couldn't imagine a day, or a night, going by without seeing her.

That was why, when Zoe decided to show Joaquin some of her favorite places around Austin, he was psyched to let her be his tour guide. Once, they went to dinner at Botticelli's South Congress. Another night they headed to the SoCo area to hear a band that Zoe loved. They went for drinks at the Driskill Hotel. And that night after work, they'd visited the Harry Ransom Center, a museum on the edge of the University of Texas campus. The place was open until seven on Thursday nights. Afterward, they grabbed a quick bite to eat.

In the past, when Joaquin started dating someone new, this much togetherness would have made him itchy for his own space. But after dinner, when he took Zoe to get her car, which she'd left in the Robinson office parking lot, he didn't even hesitate when she asked him to come over.

In fact, the thought of saying good-night left him with an emptiness he didn't quite understand. So he followed her back to her place, a nice town home located about fifteen minutes from the office.

Once inside, he followed her past the small foyer and into the living room. She turned to him. The sensual way she looked at him made him crazy. He closed the distance between them and pulled her into his arms, weaving his fingers into her hair and kissing her deeply and soundly with all the pent-up passion that had been building in him since the first time he'd set eyes on her.

When they came up for air, she took a step back, looking a little disoriented. A piece of hair had fallen across one eye and he brushed it back, resisting the urge to pull her to him again.

"Have a seat," she said, gesturing toward a teal blue sofa. "I'll get us some wine."

The living area was an open design. He could see her in the kitchen, taking two wineglasses down from the cupboard.

"Do you need any help?" he asked.

"Nope. I'm good," she called. "I'll be right there."

He looked around, taking in everything. The high ceilings and the crown molding. The walls were painted light blue and the furniture was a perfect mix of formal and quirky, like Zoe herself. It was a nice place, tastefully decorated with feminine floral patterns and lots of color.

It was the first time he had been to her place. It was good to get a glimpse of Zoe's world. He hadn't had a mental picture of where she lived, but now that he was here, it was so her, somehow he couldn't imagine her anywhere else.

She came into the living room, carrying two wine-glasses and an open bottle of red, and set them on the coffee table so she could pour some into each glass. She handed him one, kicked off her sandals and curled up next to him on the couch.

They clinked glasses. The crystal pinged a melodic note and they each took a sip.

"I remember the first time I saw you," she said. "It was at Rachel and Matteo's wedding. You were late because your flight had been delayed—remember that?"

Joaquin nodded. He'd thought she was the most beautiful woman he had ever seen, with those large dark eyes and long brown hair.

"I guess it turns out that you really were the *best man*," she said.

They laughed and clinked glasses again.

"I just keep thinking how I had no idea at the wedding that things would turn out like this. But I'm glad it did. Little did we know."

He'd had no idea that Zoe had noticed him. It had been his own fault. He'd been so blindsided by the breakup with Selena that he'd turned inward, living inside his head and protecting his fractured heart. At that point, he had only been free a couple months. Thinking back to that time in his life, it had been sort of a blur. He was still reeling from the breakup, but he'd wanted to do right by his brother and be the best best man possible. Matteo was obviously so much in love with Rachel. What was it about these Robinson women that mesmerized Mendoza men?

"You're so quiet tonight," she said. "Are you okay?"

"I couldn't be better. I'm just enjoying being here with you like this."

She leaned in and rested her head on his shoulder. He put his arm around her, loving the feel of her next to him.

"So, if you count the wedding as when we first met," she said, looking up at him, "technically we've known each other for more than a year. Unless... You weren't engaged then, were you?"

He shook his head. "No, by that point we'd called it off."

"If it was that fresh, it must have been hard for you to be thrown into wedding festivities."

"It doesn't matter now. I was happy for my brother and Rachel. They're family. You do what you have to do."

"That's one of the things I like best about you. Your family seems so important to you."

Zoe reached out and trailed her thumb over Joaquin's bottom lip. He gently caught it with his teeth and drew it into his mouth, suckling it before he let it go.

"So... We've known each other a whole year. And this the first time we've been alone. I mean really *alone*."

Joaquin's hands locked on her waist and he pulled her close. "It's about time."

He inhaled in her scent and wanted to melt with the heat of her body. His finger traced the neckline of her blouse, teasing the valley between her breasts. She took a sharp breath, which he captured when his lips closed over hers.

She tasted like the most delicious delicacy and he couldn't help but want more.

As they kissed, his palm brushed over her breasts. Even through the fabric, he felt her nipples stiffen under his touch. Instinctively he ventured down and slipped his hand under her blouse, skimming her stomach until his thumb brushed the underside of one breast.

He ached for her with his entire being. The need quickly morphed into a ravenous hunger.

"I want you," he whispered against her mouth.

When he pulled back to look at her, he saw the dark desire in her eyes. That desire was for him. To realize she wanted him as much as he wanted her was a rush and it fueled his fire for her.

In a delirious rush, he claimed her mouth and she commandeered his sanity. He held her so close that he could feel their hearts beat in sync. Or maybe it was simply the rush of desire coursing through them, creating their very own rhythm. She slipped her fingers into his hair, and the need between them became so feverish it threatened to consume them both.

Without breaking the spell, he eased her back on the couch and made short order of ridding himself of his shirt. He wanted to feel her skin against his.

He undid the first two buttons on her blouse but then grabbed the hem and pulled it up and over her head. He was too impatient to work the rest of the damn things. At least he had enough of his wits about him to know better than to give it a firm yank and rip it off of her.

As he tossed her blouse aside, he felt her demeanor shift.

"Are you okay?" he asked. He probably needed to slow down. He wanted her so badly, but this was not a race. He wanted to savor every moment of the first time he made love to her. Most of all, he wanted her to enjoy it, too.

"I need to tell you something." Her voice was small.
Birth control.

Damn it. Why hadn't he thought of that before now? Probably because he hadn't counted on this happening just yet. But it felt so right.

"If you don't have anything, I can go out and get something."

Her face was a question mark.

"Condoms?" he said.

"Oh. No, that's not it. Well, yeah, we would need those." Her voice was a little shaky. Joaquin lifted himself off her to give her some room. She wriggled out from under him and sat up, crossing her arms over the front of her.

"If we're moving too fast, we can slow down," he said.

"I know this might sound corny and old-fashioned, but for a long time I wanted to save it for my wedding night."

It?

Oh—

"So you've never—"

She shook her head. "Don't look at me like I'm some sort of unicorn."

"No. I'm not. Or if you thought I was, I'm sorry. I'm just surprised, that's all."

"Why?" she asked.

He probably needed to shut the hell up because everything he said was just making the situation worse.

She shrugged. "Actually, I'm sorry. I probably sounded a little defensive. I didn't mean to. All of Steffi-Anne's innuendos and her pointing out all the guys I dated probably gave you the wrong idea."

God, was that what she thought? "Do you think I'm here just because I think you're easy?"

A nervous hiccup escaped her beautiful lips. "That sounds so high school–ish. Are you trying to make it with the *fast girl*, Joaquin?"

"Zoe. Be serious."

"I'm just kidding. Please don't make this any weirder than it already is. And I'll stop making it weird on my end. So, I'll just say it. I have dated a lot of guys, but I've never slept with any of them. In fact, in the past when things have gotten to this point, I usually don't see them anymore."

Joaquin sat back against the couch. "Are you breaking up with me?"

"Am I your girlfriend?"

"Aren't you? I just assumed. But if we're reliving high school, do you want me to ask you to go steady? I know it took me a while to get here." He gestured between them. "But I'd like to see where this goes. We can take things slowly. That doesn't bother me at all. I just want you to be okay with…us."

Zoe looked uncertain and a little uncomfortable.

Joaquin reached down and picked her blouse off the floor and handed it to her.

"Thank you." But she held it in her lap. Sitting there

in her lacy bra, she didn't get dressed or try to hide herself.

"I hope you don't think I'm some kind of a weirdo," she finally said.

"No." He reached out and took her hand. "Of course not."

"When I was in college, one of my friends got burned by a guy who promised to love her forever. So, she gave herself to him body and soul. It lasted maybe three months. He broke her. I know people get hurt every day and lots of relationships don't last, but she was so devastated and I couldn't help but think that if everything was going to end, I didn't want to give myself to a guy who really didn't care that he was taking the most special gift I could give him. He'd just move on like it was nothing. If you think that's weird, it's okay, but it's who I am and I can't be anyone else."

He reached out and lifted her chin so that she was looking him in the eye.

"I don't take it lightly. As long as you'll have me, I'd like to keep exploring this thing between you and me. I want to spend time with you, but let's take it slow."

She smiled at him. "You really are a prince, aren't you?"

He bent down and kissed her, soft and tender.

After he said good-night with a plan for them to cook dinner together tomorrow night, the slow realization washed over him that they *didn't* need to rush things. Women like Zoe didn't fool around for fun. Before anything could happen, he needed to make sure he was ready for the type of serious commitment she was expecting.

* * *

The next day Zoe was relieved when Joaquin acted perfectly normal. She might not be ready to give him that ultimate part of herself just yet, but after he'd left she knew down to her bones that she didn't want to lose him.

She hadn't been kidding when she'd called him a prince. After kissing as many frogs as she had in her life, she would know.

She'd stopped by the coffee shop and picked up two cappuccinos. It was a peace offering, or at least a gesture that meant she truly wanted things to be okay between them.

She'd worried for a moment when she'd gone to his office and he had asked her to shut the door. She was afraid that he'd had time to think about things and change his mind. Because in her experience when guys discovered she was a virgin, they took it one of two ways: they either beat a hasty retreat or they took it as a challenge that they were going to be the one who would convince her she didn't want to save it for marriage.

But after she closed the door, Joaquin had taken the coffees from her and set them on the desk. Then he'd pulled her into his arms and kissed her until she was questioning whether waiting was what she really wanted.

That's how good they were together.

Crazy good.

Fireworks good.

I-want-to-wake-up-to-a-kiss-like-that-every-morning-for-the-rest-of-my-life good.

Zoe wasn't sure if the knocking she heard was her heart pounding or—

"Excuse me?"

Oh, God. It was Steffi-Anne.

After they broke the kiss, Joaquin kept his arm around Zoe.

"Good morning, Steffi-Anne," he said. "How can I help you?"

The woman looked as if she had been sucking on lemons.

"Elaine Baker from personnel and I need to see the two of you in her office right now."

That evening, Zoe sat at Joaquin's kitchen table, looking over the consensual relationship agreement that Elaine Baker and their good friend Steffi-Anne had insisted they sign.

Apparently if two employees were in a relationship, they had to declare it—even if one was an independent contractor and the other was the boss's daughter.

"It's policy set by Mr. Robinson's attorneys," said Steffi-Anne. "It's so people won't sue Robinson Tech for sexual harassment. Zoe, as Gerald's daughter, you of all people should understand how important this is."

"I'm not going to sue anyone," Joaquin said, clearly irritated.

Steffi-Anne pushed the document across the desk toward him. "Then you should have no problem signing this agreement."

"This is the first I've heard of this," Zoe said. "I've dated several Robinson employees, but why has this never come up before now?"

"That's not important," said Elaine. "But I do need both of you to sign these now."

"Neither of us is going to sign anything until we

have time to read through the document carefully," said Zoe. "I'm sure you will understand that we need to take the forms with us."

"Be my guest." Steffi-Anne sniffed. "In fact, take the weekend. But we need them signed and turned in first thing Monday morning."

Or what? Zoe wanted to say. *Are you going to fire us? I don't think so.*

Never in her life had she wanted to play the boss's daughter card so much. Never in the history of working for Robinson Tech had she been so tempted to tell both Elaine Baker and Steffi-Anne to back off or she'd have their jobs. And it had crossed her mind more than once to go to her father and sweet-talk him into letting her be an exception to the rule. And he probably would've done it. He liked Joaquin. He respected him.

Even though Zoe knew that the stunt was strictly fueled by jealousy, she refused to let it compromise her principles.

She had taken such pride in being like everyone else, in working her way up the ladder and proving her worth, that she wasn't going to buckle now. Even if Joaquin had seemed a little bothered by signing a statement that would essentially formalize their relationship. She didn't want to pressure him.

Could there be a case for sexual harassment when they hadn't even had sex? She almost made a joke about it but stopped. She couldn't quite tell if Joaquin was quiet because he was feeling boxed in by this agreement or if her lack of experience was finally sinking in. When she had tried to talk to him about it earlier, he had managed to put her off by changing the subject.

Since they were supposed to be cooking together tonight, it would probably be best to forget the form for now and spend time in the kitchen with him.

Zoe was glad she did because it seemed to be the right choice. Together they made one of Joaquin's favorite dishes: arroz con pollo, chicken and rice. But it was so much more than that. It had red bell peppers and peas cooked in a broth of wine, saffron and tomato paste. It was a little bit of Miami heaven on a plate.

Dinner was so delicious that it seemed to lighten the mood. She certainly didn't want to cause things to go south by pressing the darned consensual relationship agreement.

They had all weekend to deal with it. Right now, she was content to snuggle up next to Joaquin on the couch. While he watched some political show on TV, she read a magazine that she'd picked up on her lunch break because of the cover story about "Bonnie Lord Charlie" Fortune Chesterfield and his fiancée, Alice Meyers.

It was so cozy, she couldn't help but think, *This is what it would be like to be married to Joaquin.* It made her heart sing and the butterflies in her stomach fly in giddy formation.

Savoring the feeling, Zoe flipped the pages until she came to the article on Charles and Alice. Charles Fortune Chesterfield wasn't actually a prince, though that was what the media had dubbed him. But he did come from a long line of British nobility and was devastatingly handsome, if you liked the dark-haired, blue-eyed rakish type. Personally, Zoe preferred men who were tall, dark and Latin. Her appreciative gaze drifted to Joaquin and lingered for a moment before finding its way back to the article about Charles and Alice's whirl-

wind romance. Their story was enough to make a girl
believe in fairy tales. And, of course, she adored those.

The other thing Zoe found so compelling about
Charles was that he was actually the youngest son of
Josephine Fortune Chesterfield, the same Josephine
with whom she'd had dinner at Cowboy Country. Joaquin had cracked a joke about "Bonnie Lord Charlie"
when he'd seen the magazine cover, but he hadn't said
much else.

In fact, even though Joaquin had been gracious
about introducing her to his father when she'd been
stranded in Horseback Hollow, he'd told her so little about his family and his background that she had
the feeling he might be holding back. As crazy as it
seemed, reading about his potential stepbrother felt
as though she was getting a glimpse into one facet of
Joaquin's life.

Charles and Alice were so old-world chic it made her
wistful. She stared at a picture of the couple with their
baby boy, Flynn, who had Charles's dark hair and blue
eyes. They made an adorable family. Alice was beautiful with her wavy blond shoulder-length hair and blue
eyes; she was tall and thin, with long legs that went
on for miles. A perfect *lady* for Bonnie Lord Charlie.

She tried not to think of the great Fortune hunt and
how Ben kept pushing the issue against their father's
wishes. She hadn't talked to her brother since the family meeting last week. But they'd be okay, once he finally accepted the fact that Gerald Robinson was not
Jerome Fortune. She just needed to put some distance
between them for now.

Yes, it was crazy, she thought as she flipped the
pages in the magazine, looking at the photos, paus-

ing to read the captions. Yep. It was all crazy and far-fetched and— She paused at one of the pictures, a close-up of the heirloom ring Charles had given Alice when they got engaged. She held the magazine up to get better light so she could get a better look. The caption said it was a present passed down to Charles from the famous Kate Fortune.

In the light, she could see it was an emerald ring with the letter *F* on it.

Zoe gasped. *No. It can't be. This has to be some sort of* Twilight Zone *coincidence.*

"What's wrong?" Joaquin asked.

Zoe didn't answer because she didn't quite know how to explain. Because if she was remembering right— She suddenly felt a little light-headed.

Joaquin turned off the TV with the remote. "Are you okay? You look like you've seen a ghost."

Zoe gave herself a mental shake. Joaquin was so levelheaded. He could probably help her process this. Besides, if their relationship was going to grow, they needed to share. Just a moment ago she had been thinking about how he didn't seem very open about his own family. Maybe she should encourage communication by example.

"Look at this ring." She pointed to the picture. "I've seen it before. Or one almost exactly like it. I found it when I was a little girl, playing around in my father's office. I thought it was such a treasure. When I asked my dad if I could have it, he snatched it away from me and yelled at me, asking me where I found it. I told him it was in a box on his desk. He asked me how I opened the box because it was supposed to be locked."

Joaquin was listening attentively. She paused, think-ing about how to say this last part.

She took a deep breath.

"I remember what happened so vividly because it's the only time I can ever remember my father yelling at me. Even though he yells at everyone else on a daily basis."

She tried to laugh, but it turned into a sob and the tears began to meander down her face.

"Zoe, don't cry." Joaquin wiped her tears. "I want to help, but I'm not sure I understand."

It nearly broke her heart to explain. "This ring in the picture is exactly like my father's. I think I just found the proof that Ben has been looking for to prove—"

A sob caused her voice to break. She cleared her throat before she began again.

"Don't you see what the picture caption says?"

Joaquin picked up the magazine and read it silently.

Zoe found her voice again. "Kate Fortune gave Charles a family heirloom ring that is identical to the one I saw in my father's office that day. Are you doing the math with me, Joaquin?"

Joaquin's brow knit and he nodded as if the truth was slowly dawning on him. But what was he supposed to say? She knew he wasn't going to damn her father. Even after all of this, she didn't want him to.

"I think my father has been lying to us all this time. But why? I don't understand why."

He lowered his gaze, but not before Zoe saw the shadow that darkened his eyes. He was such a com-plex man that she didn't know what he was thinking. Maybe she shouldn't have told him.

"If it's true," he said, "the only one who can answer that question is your father. All I know is that all families have secrets. So this doesn't make your family any worse."

Zoe's mind was reeling.

"All families have secrets? What's yours, Joaquin?" she asked through her tears.

He frowned, shrugged, but he wouldn't look at her. She had to fight the urge to reach out and lift his chin, to force his eyes to meet hers.

The question seemed to catch him by surprise, but right before he spoke, he leaned in unexpectedly and dusted her lips with a kiss.

"My secret is...that I think I'm falling in love with you."

Chapter Ten

Joaquin was such a study in contradictions.

He claimed to be falling in love with her, yet when Sunday evening rolled 'round, he still hadn't signed the consensual relationship agreement. She'd mentioned it again later Saturday evening, thinking his declaration of love would make signing it a no-brainer. If they were a couple, didn't it stand to reason that they were in a consensual relationship? Then again, they hadn't had sex, so maybe his definition was different than hers. Because when she'd brought it up again, he'd hedged.

That was the last time she was going to mention it. She had other things to sort out right now. Questioning Joaquin's feelings wouldn't do anyone any good.

She had to figure out what she was going to do with the information she'd discovered about the ring Charles Fortune Chesterfield had given his fiancée. What were

the chances it was a coincidence that it was identical
to the one she'd found in that box that was supposed
to be locked in her father's study? If it didn't matter,
why had he gone off the rails the way he had? It was
the one and only time he'd ever yelled at her. His anger
had been so white-hot, it had burned the details of that
moment into her brain. She remembered that ring as
though she were looking at a photograph of it—and it
was the same one she had seen on Alice Meyers's left
hand in that magazine photograph.

The question remained, did Alice have his ring?
Had her father sold it or pawned it? Although that
wasn't his style. He certainly didn't need the money.
So had he given it away? But how would it end up in
the hands of a member of the Fortune family—the very
one Ben had been insisting their father was related to?

The thoughts sent a shiver rushing up Zoe's spine.

She thought about calling a family meeting but two
seconds later realized that if she told the others before
she talked to her father she would be opening Pan-
dora's box. She didn't want to be the one responsible
for that. It felt as though she were letting her father
down. No, worse than that. It felt as though she were
betraying him.

That's how she came to find herself standing in a
hallway in the Robinson estate, outside her father's
study. She'd come over to talk to him, but he wasn't
home, which she knew because his car wasn't in the
garage. She'd checked when she arrived. When the
stall had been empty, a great rush of relief had swept
through her.

She probably should've called and asked when he
would be at home, but she couldn't seem to make the

call. Instead she'd come over hoping for the best. She wanted to see his eyes when she told him what she'd found. That way, she would know if he was telling the truth—or not.

Despite his car being gone, Zoe rapped gently on the study door. As she expected, no one answered. However, her knock had pushed the door ajar just a little. Enough for her to see that the lights were off and there were no signs of life in the room, which was lit only by the diffused daylight streaming through the slats of the closed shutters. Still, there was enough light to make out the bookcases that lined the walls, the fine leather furniture and his desk, where she had originally discovered the ring all those years ago. The timeless room with its classic elegance hadn't changed a bit since then. It was like stepping back in time.

Maybe this wouldn't be a wasted trip, after all. If she looked at his ring again, maybe she'd discover that she was mistaken. Maybe it was similar, but different from the piece of jewelry in the magazine picture. In fact, just to be sure, it would be a good idea if she snapped a photo of it with her cell phone. That way she could put the ring away and compare her photo with the picture of Charles Fortune Chesterfield's. She'd torn it out of the magazine and put in her purse, but she would need better light to compare the details.

Yes. That's what she'd do. Just to be sure.

After all, there was no need to upset her father unless she was 100 percent certain that the rings were identical.

She stepped into the study and quietly closed the door behind her. She went to her father's desk and found the fine mahogany box—the one Zoe used to think was a treasure chest, especially when she'd opened it and discovered the ring.

It had been such an unexpected delight, finding jewelry, of all things, in her father's office. She'd been so mesmerized by the gorgeous green stone and the fine gold-filigree setting. She thought it was a magic ring like the one in E. Nesbit's novel *The Enchanted Castle*. She'd put it on her finger and made a wish. Then she'd run to her father, shown him the great treasure she'd discovered and asked him if she could keep it. Of course, the last thing she'd expected was for him to come unglued.

Even though it had happened a long time ago and it hadn't taken long for her father and her to move past it, the incident had scarred her.

Now she tried to lift the lid on the box, but it wouldn't budge. It was locked up tight. She opened the top desk drawer to see if she could find a key. When that search proved fruitless, she picked up a paperclip to see if she could pick the lock. She'd never done that before, but it was worth a try.

She closed the desk drawer, lowered herself into her father's chair and moved the box closer to her. She had the paperclip in the lock and was actively working it when the door to the study opened.

Her father turned on the lights and started when he saw her.

"What the hell, Zoe? What the hell are you doing in here?"

All of a sudden she was six years old again, caught red-handed doing something that this time she knew good and well displeased him.

But before she could come up with an excuse—she

never had been able to lie—she had a moment of clarity. She cupped the paperclip in her hand and stood to face him.

"Dad, we need to talk."

"The only thing we're going to talk about is why the hell you are in here, trying to jimmy open my private lockbox."

Only this time his anger didn't shred her the way it had the first time.

He walked over to the desk, reached across and grabbed the box, turning it around to inspect the front of it.

"What are you doing, Zoe?"

Maybe she should've talked to him before entering his study. Despite the sickening feeling that she knew the answer to the question, she still needed to ask him. Even so, it would've been nice to have irrefutable proof before she opened this can of worms. The only way to handle this was to be direct.

"I'm looking for that emerald ring. You know the one I'm talking about, don't you? The one with the filigree setting and the *F* monogram."

"I have no idea what you're talking about. I think you'd better leave and don't you ever let me catch you sneaking around and snooping through my possessions again."

"You can't tell me you don't know which ring I'm talking about. It was the one I discovered when I was six years old. It was right here in this box." She reached for her purse and pulled out the picture of Charles and Alice. "It's just like this one that Charles Fortune Chesterfield gave to his fiancée."

"I said I have no idea what you're talking about. Are you deaf? I also told you to get out."

Zoe grabbed her purse. "Fine. If you won't talk to me about it, I'll talk to Ben. I think this might be the missing piece he's been looking for in his search to prove that we are, in fact, related to the Fortunes."

She walked past her father and out the door, knowing full well that he knew she was calling his bluff. She also knew that if he let her leave without talking to her about this, she fully intended to go straight to Ben's house and show him the photo.

Gerald let her get down the hallway before he called to her.

"Zoe, get back here."

She didn't wait for him to ask her twice. She came back into his office and shut the door. But she waited for him to speak first.

"Look, I don't want you to go away mad," Gerald said. "You know we've always had a special bond." His tone was softer now, the anger that had flown off his tongue in sparks and flames a moment ago diffused. Of course he was being nice and playing the favorite-child card again. He didn't want her to spill the beans about the ring.

At heart, she'd always been the consummate daddy's girl, the one who'd loved him unconditionally. She'd wanted nothing more than to please him. But his time his ploys weren't going to work.

"I know it's the same ring, Dad. Do you want to explain?"

He couldn't look her in the eyes.

"Come on, Dad. It's me you're talking to. I'm not

going to run out and tell everyone. You can trust me to keep your secret. But you do owe me an explanation."

It was the first time she'd ever seen her father look defeated. But he did. He stood there, slack jawed and confused, staring at the floor.

She resolved not to say a word until he spoke. She'd let him break the silence.

A couple of uncomfortable minutes ticked by before he finally spoke.

"I was never accepted by the Fortune family."

So, it was true.

Even though she knew it was coming, his confession knocked the air out of Zoe. It took all of her willpower to keep from demanding to know why he'd lied. But she managed to hold it in, despite the way her heart ached and all the questions that flooded her mind: Was he Jerome Fortune? If so, why did everyone think Jerome was dead?

Gerald motioned toward the couch. They both sat down.

Her dad rested his forearms on his knees and stared at the ground as if arranging his thoughts.

"My father was a brutal man." Gerald's voice was shaky. "I was an only child and he was dead-set on me following in his footsteps and going into the family business. He wanted me to be his protégé. So he could control me. He owned a brokerage firm. I had absolutely no interest in following in my old man's footsteps. And he couldn't stand that.

"Computers fascinated me. People did not. I couldn't deal with the all the phoniness and small talk you had to do to con people into giving you their money to invest. But I tried. I actually went to work for the company, and I failed miserably. The clients didn't appreciate the way I spoke my mind. I didn't blow sunshine up their asses, and it cost my dad business. Every day of my life my father reminded me that I was a disappointment. That I was a loser. He had no idea what I was capable of. So, I decided to show him."

Gerald harrumphed.

Zoe sat rapt, afraid that if she made a sound she might jar him out of this almost trancelike state.

"I had discovered how to breach some pretty sophisticated mainframe firewalls," he said. "I figured if I could hack into systems and learn of pending deals, my dad could have the jump on the average Joe. That meant I could not only make up for the business I'd cost him, but I could make it possible for him to have unheard-of success. If I hacked my way to the information, could it really be considered insider trading? So, I did it and for a few months things were better. He couldn't believe I had made such a miraculous turnaround. I hated myself. I felt like I was living a lie. I decided to tell him the truth. When I did, the man went ballistic and gave me an ultimatum—give up computers or leave.

"So, I left."

Zoe had heard rumblings that her dad didn't always operate aboveboard, that no one made the kind of money he made by being on the up-and-up. She'd figured it was envy and sour grapes. Maybe she was naive, but having it confirmed that her father was just as bad as everyone claimed was devastating. He was supposed to be better than that. She'd always believed in him.

"My mother said that if I walked out, I could never come back. I would be dead to them."

As stunned as she was by her father's fall from grace, her heart also ached for him. Obviously he hadn't had an easy time of it growing up. Her father was gruff and usually a little too focused on business, but he'd never called his children losers or made them feel bad about using their God-given gifts and talents. He had offered all of them jobs at Robinson Tech, but he hadn't taken it personally when a couple of them had wanted to explore their own paths.

What's more, he had built this company from nothing. The man was a genius and the things he had done with Robinson Tech had made a difference in the world. He'd never really hurt anyone. Maybe the good that he'd done canceled out his transgressions.

Zoe knew she was kidding herself again.

"So is that what Jacqueline Fortune meant when she said her son was dead?" Zoe asked.

Gerald's head snapped up and his nostrils flared. "How do you know Jacqueline Fortune?"

"Ben found her and contacted her. I thought he would've told you. She's your mother, right?"

"No. He didn't tell me. What exactly did Ben say to you?"

It didn't escape her that he'd evaded her question about his mother. She'd come back to that.

Zoe took a deep breath as she processed everything. Her dad had always said that his parents were dead. Yet her grandmother had been alive all these years. Alive, and she'd never had the chance to get to know her.

"Ben said she's in a nursing home and is suffering from dementia. When he asked her about Jerome Fortune, Jacqueline got hysterical and insisted that her son was dead. You sent her a suicide note and let her live alone all these years?"

Gerald hung his head.

"Why would you let your own mother think that? It must've broken her heart."

Her tone was a little sharper than she'd intended, but, come on. "How could you do that, Dad? Let all these years go by with her thinking you were dead?"

For that matter, how had he pulled it off?

Her father stared at her for so long that it felt as if he was looking through her, not at her.

Finally he shrugged. "I told you this much, I might as well tell you everything. After they told me I was dead to them and kicked me out, I *borrowed* some money from them. I was going to pay them back, but I was on the street. I needed some money to tide me over until I could find a job. We're talking food and shelter here. I wasn't funding a lavish lifestyle. I figured it was the least they could do. They brought me into this world and they kicked me out. I was barely eighteen. When my father realized I'd taken the money, he confronted me. We got into an argument. He said he was going to call the cops and have me arrested. I told him if he did, I would alert the authorities about the insider trading. The words had no sooner left my mouth when my father had a heart attack and died right in front of me."

Zoe gasped. "How awful. I'm sorry you had to go through that."

Her father shrugged. "If I'm being completely candid, I wasn't sorry the man was gone. His self-righteous attitude was like the pot calling the kettle black because not all of his business deals were honest. My old man had his own set of values. He hated technology and computers because he didn't understand them and couldn't control them. What he couldn't control pissed him off.

"I think the worst part of it was that my mom blamed me for his death. She said I murdered my father and that she never wanted to see me again. She accused me of killing him so that I could get my inheritance. The guy was loaded, but I didn't want his money. Her accusations cut me so deeply that I decided I wanted to make her pay. The way I did that was by leaving town. I used my hacking skills to create a new identity and I staged my own death so no one would come looking for me. I sent my mother a note saying I couldn't live with myself for causing my father's death and she would be better off without me."

"Oh, my God. Are you making this up?"

He shook his head.

"I launched an unmanned boat that was registered to my family and when the empty vessel washed ashore, Jerome Fortune was presumed dead."

Zoe wiped at the horrified tears clouding her eyes. "This is the saddest thing I have ever heard." A sob swallowed the rest of her words.

"As far as I am concerned, Jerome Fortune is dead," her father said. "He died the day I became Gerald Robinson. But don't be sad for me, princess. Gerald Robinson has had a wonderful life. I am a self-made man. I am successful beyond my wildest dreams. I have raised a family and I wouldn't change a thing."

Zoe was trying her hardest to stop the sobbing, but it had gripped her like a spirit possessing her body. "You wouldn't change the fact that you lied to your children about who you are? About who *we* are? Not the fact that you let your own mother believe you were dead? What pain she must've suffered."

Gerald shook his head. "She accused me of murder, princess." His voice was so resigned that it was spooky. "She told me she didn't want to be the mother of a murderer. She made it perfectly clear. She disowned me."

Zoe stood and held up her hands in a signal for him to stop talking. "I have to go. This is all too much. I believed in you, Dad. I defended you when Ben went against your wishes and kept pushing the Fortune connection. But he was right all along."

Zoe remembered the rumor about the legions of illegitimate children her father might have sired. But she didn't ask him because she really didn't want to know. At this point, she couldn't bear that it might be true.

Who was this man who used to be her knight in shining armor? She didn't even know him anymore. She opened her purse, fished for a tissue and blotted her eyes before she blew her nose.

"Are you going to tell your siblings everything?"

The walls suddenly felt as if they were closing in on her.

"No, I'm not. But it's not because I'm protecting you. You're the one who owes them an explanation. They need to hear it from you. So, this all on you, Dad."

Chapter Eleven

Zoe drove around Austin for a good hour, trying to process everything her father had told her. Her mind was on overload, with a pileup of thoughts converging and screaming all at once. On the one hand, her dad had suffered a terrible upbringing. It sounded as if his father had been unspeakably cruel. But, on the other hand, he had not only lived a lie, he also had lied to his family all these years, robbing his children of their own history and possibly a relationship with their grandmother.

Now Zoe faced the monumental task of deciding what to do with the information. To tell her siblings or not to tell? She'd been in such shock when she'd left her parents' house that she'd told her father she'd keep his secret. Not because she was protecting him or slighting her siblings—and definitely not because she was afraid to admit she had been wrong not to support their crusade—but because it was not her story to tell. It belonged to her father—it was his confession and it needed to come from him.

Still, Zoe couldn't quite make peace with that, either.

She needed to talk to somebody. Somebody who was unbiased. Somebody whose judgment she trusted.

Even before she was aware of what she was doing, she was steering her car into the parking lot of Joaquin's apartment building.

She pulled out her phone and texted him.

Are you home?

I am.

Look out your window.

She saw the blinds open in the second-story window of his apartment.

I'm glad you're here. I need to talk to you about something. Come up.

She felt better already because of how welcome he made her feel. He always brightened her days, especially when they got tough. It warmed her from the inside out.

When she got upstairs to his place, he was waiting for her at the door. He was wearing jeans and a brown Life is Good T-shirt with a picture of a dog next to a campfire. It struck her as funny because she didn't think of him as rugged or outdoorsy. He was more of a suit-and-tie, office sort of guy. Or better yet, a tangled-bodies-in-the-bedroom type.

The last thought made her blush. It was pretty amazing that she would even think that way because her relationships never made it to the point where her subconscious was contemplating getting—no, longing to get—naked and tangled up with a man. But this wasn't just any man. This was Joaquin.

Joaquin, who had said he was falling in love with her, which had opened the flood gates and allowed so many emotions to start pouring out.

As she fell into his arms, inhaling the delicious scent of him, she felt as if she'd finally found the place where she belonged.

"Hey, what's going on?" Joaquin asked. "Are you okay?"

He held her at arm's length for a moment, studying her face. When she didn't answer he said, "Come in. Talk to me."

He ushered her inside. He was leasing the furnished apartment for six months while he was working on the project for Robinson. The place was clean and, while the furniture wasn't fancy, it looked new and functional. He had told her not too long ago that if he stayed in Austin, he would look to buy. He'd even asked her to recommend good areas. While he hadn't said anything about them moving in together, it seemed as if they had a future.

In the midst of the family maelstrom, he was her touchstone, her beacon in the stormy night.

She took a seat on the couch and was a little surprised when he chose the chair across from her rather than sitting next to her, but the concern on his face was real.

"Zoe? What's going on?"

For a moment she couldn't speak. She didn't know where to start or how to tell him that the one man in her life she had always trusted had been lying to her and her siblings their entire lives.

Finally she forced out the words. "I'm confiding in you. Please promise me what I tell you will remain in the strictest confidence. Because I trust you, Joaquin."

He nodded. His brows knit with obvious concern. "Of course."

"It turns out that my dad is Jerome Fortune, after all."

His eyes widened and, for a moment, he looked as though she had just told him she had had a personal encounter with the Sasquatch. In a sense, Jerome Fortune did feel like a mythical creature.

"What do you mean?" he asked.

"I mean exactly what I said. Gerald Robinson is Jerome Fortune."

He shook his head. "No, what I meant was, how do you know this, or what makes you think this? You were always so adamantly against your siblings pushing to establish this connection. Did they find some evidence that supports their theory?"

"No. I'm the one who found it. Actually, it's not just evidence. It's irrefutable proof."

His eyes widened again and all of a sudden a look of realization passed over his face. "Is it the ring? Did you talk to your father?"

She nodded, and she hated herself, but the tears started falling and she couldn't stop them.

"I went to see him this morning and we sort of had it out. He tried to deny it at first, but when I threatened to take the picture to Ben, he told me everything. The ring is only the tip of the iceberg."

She didn't know if she could tell him, because relaying the whole sordid tale to someone else underscored the terrible things her father was capable of, the things he'd done. But she needed his advice. She needed to sort it all out and the only way she could do that was to review everything her dad had told her, detail by dirty detail.

She took a deep breath and told Joaquin everything.

"Now I don't know what to do. I told him I wouldn't say anything to my brothers and sisters. And when I came over here, I wasn't sure if that was the right thing to do—"

"Of course it is. You have to tell them, Zoe. You owe it to them."

She flinched at his words. "What I *started to say* was, after telling you everything, I think I've decided that it's not my place to tell them. He needs to be the one to do that."

Joaquin shook his head resolutely. "I don't agree with you."

Irritation sparked in her veins. Why was he being like this? She may have thought she'd come over here for advice, but she hadn't asked him for any. And as it turned out, she didn't want it; she just needed a trusted sounding board.

"I don't mean to be mean," she said, "but I didn't ask you if you agreed or not."

She saw his walls go up and his gate slam shut.

"Then why did you come over here?"

His words connected like a punch to the gut. Wow. And it hurt.

"It certainly wasn't to make you mad. I came over here because I needed someone to listen. I had no idea this would make you so angry and judgmental."

Yeah, why was he so angry about this? It really didn't have anything to do with him. That was one of the reasons she'd decided to talk to him about it. Well, that, and if things were getting as serious between them as they seemed, she needed to be able to share things like this with him. But what she didn't need was stern disapproval.

He drummed his fingers on the arm of the chair. "Look, Zoe, you said yourself that one of the reasons you were upset was that he had kept your heritage from you all these years. Because of that, you'll never know your grandmother. You know firsthand that it's wrong to keep someone's heritage from him or her. Now, no matter how painful it is for you, you owe it to your siblings to tell them what you've discovered."

"Joaquin, it's not my secret to tell."

He shrugged. "Since we're talking about your father and I'm advocating full disclosure, there's something I need to tell you."

"Absolutely," she said. "You can tell me anything."

"You might not want to hear this. But that day that we were at Cowboy Country, I saw your father getting pretty cozy with a woman who wasn't your mother."

Zoe winced. Her father's indiscretions weren't a secret. Even though it hurt her heart and was embarrassing, the issue was between him and her mother. She certainly didn't want to discuss it with Joaquin. Not on top of what she'd come to tell him. "I appreciate you telling me, but that's nothing compared to what I learned today."

Joaquin squinted at her. "Cheating is nothing?"

Zoe rolled her eyes. "You're putting words in my mouth. Don't."

The two of them sat there in stalemate silence. He wasn't going to budge and neither was she. She did appreciate his honesty, but the last thing she needed right now was another issue heaped on top of the mess she was already carrying. She couldn't even look at Joaquin right now. She couldn't even look at him. Actually she wished she hadn't told him. She wished she hadn't even come over.

She stood. "I need to go. Please just forget I said anything about this."

As she started toward the door, she spied his copy of the consensual relationship agreement lying on the bar area that separated the kitchen from the living room. He still hadn't signed it. Great. She wasn't about to remind him about it. He was a big boy and God knew a fight wasn't the right moment to bring that up.

Were they having their first fight?

"Zoe, I don't mean to be unsupportive. Secrets are never a good idea. Your siblings had a feeling that your father was Jerome Fortune and it turns out to be the truth. You keeping your dad's confession from them doesn't change the facts. It also doesn't mean that you're spreading gossip and rumors. You are not going to hurt them by telling them the truth. You are going to give them a gift of knowing who they really are. If anything, you're hurting them by not telling them."

Obviously they weren't going to solve anything. Joaquin may have had a point that keeping this to herself wasn't going to change the truth, but she stood by the fact that it wasn't her place to tell her father's story. Her dad may have proved himself to be a liar, but he was still her dad. He had always been good to her. Basically, without saying it, she had promised him he could tell his kids the truth in his own way and in his own time. She couldn't see how Joaquin could think he was being supportive by badgering her to break a promise.

"I'll talk to you tomorrow, Joaquin."

"I'm speaking from a place of experience, Zoe."

Before she could think better of it, she whirled around. "How in the world could you have had a similar experience to this? Your family is wonderful. I met your dad. He's great. I'm sure he never faked his death, created a new identity and pretended to be someone he's not. So please don't say that you've been here, because you haven't."

"It's true, Orlando is a great man. But sometimes things are not always as they appear on the surface. So, even though I haven't experienced verbatim what you're going through, I am facing the challenge of someone dear to me not being who they *think* they are." He softened his tone. "But you wouldn't know that because I haven't told you."

What in the world?

"What are you talking about, Joaquin?"

Those lips that she loved so much were pressed into a thin line and she could see the wheels in his mind turning. He looked just as upset as she felt.

She walked back to the sofa and lowered herself onto the cushion.

"Please tell me what's going on," she said. "Help me understand."

He looked at her with such heartbreak in his eyes that she wanted to take him into her arms and assure him that, no matter what it was, together they could make it better. But she didn't. Instead she sat there, letting him tell her in his own time.

"In a nutshell, I have very good reason to believe that Orlando is not my father. Or not my biological father, anyway. I don't know if he knows. I do know that once upon a time my mother had a thing for my uncle Esteban and apparently he led her on quite a chase. I don't know if my dad stole my mother away from my uncle or what happened. But I found a person with Orlando's blood type can't father a child with mine."

"How did you find out?"

"When my mother was sick. She needed a blood transfusion and Orlando was not a match for her blood type. I was, though. Of course. The doctor had mentioned Orlando's blood type in passing and it floored me. I remembered some basic genetics from high school biology, and there was no way that his blood type and my mother's blood type would produce a baby with my blood type."

Zoe reached out and squeezed his hand. "Have you talked to your father about this?"

"Not yet."

"How long has your mom been gone?"

"She died four years ago."

Zoe tried not to frown. "That was a while ago. Why haven't you talked to your dad about it?"

"That's a good question. I don't know the whole story. But I have reason to believe that my mother may have been cheating on him. He may be aware of it, too. And that could be why he brushed me off when I initially questioned the discrepancy at the hospital. But my mother was dying and my dad was grief-stricken. She was his soul mate and if he does know, he obviously forgave her.

"For a long time I brushed it off because I thought if he could forgive her, then there was no reason to talk about it. But the more time that went by, the more it weighed on me. If he's not my biological father, who is? I mean, Orlando was the best dad anyone could ever want, but I finally came to the conclusion that knowing about my birth father didn't necessarily have to take anything away from the love and gratitude I feel for Orlando."

"So...why are you having a tough time talking to him about it?"

"How do you ask your father if your mother—his wife, his soul mate—was unfaithful? It's even trickier than that. I think I know who my birth father might be."

Zoe's eyes widened and she leaned forward. "Who?"

"I have very good reason to believe that my mother may have had an affair with my uncle Esteban, my father's brother. I put two and two together and it just made sense. My dad and my uncle have been estranged for years—all my life. Nobody talks about the reason they don't speak. I've wondered if anybody even knows. My dad and my uncle aren't prone to holding grudges with anyone else. But the bad blood between them seems to run deep. It's the only thing that makes sense. So, for the last year or so, I've been pondering whether my uncle actually is my father. And wondering if Orlando has been keeping it from me all this time."

Zoe's heart ached for him. That would be a huge burden to shoulder. She understood why he might hesitate to bring up the issue after it had been buried all these years. Even though it wasn't a carbon copy of her own situation, it was parallel and she understood the angst he must be feeling. She just wondered why he couldn't seem to cut her any slack, since he hadn't yet faced his own demons.

"I've contemplated talking to Esteban about it, but I feel duty bound to discuss it with Orlando first."

"I totally get that," said Zoe. "So, are you going to talk to your dad?"

Joaquin shrugged. "I don't know. I've been waiting for the right time. At first Orlando was so grief-stricken I thought he was never going to get over my mother's death. The last thing he needed was for me to ask, 'Oh, by the way, did you know your wife may have been having an affair, *and* did you know that I'm not your biological son?'"

Zoe nodded her understanding.

"My sister Gabi had some medical problems. Her health was still fragile when my mom died. He had just lost his wife and he was afraid he would lose his daughter, too. It wasn't the time. After he was sure Gabi was stable, he moved to Horseback Hollow. Since I was still in Miami, I barely got to see him as it was. I didn't want what little time we had together to be overshadowed by the revelation that I'm not his son. Then I moved to Horseback Hollow, fully intending to get to the bottom of the situation, but he had just started coming out of his grief. He's so happy with Josephine. I just couldn't pull him back into the shadows again. He's happy. I can't remember a time when he was so happy. I guess it was before my mom and Gabi got sick."

"You do understand that there never will be a perfect time, right?" Zoe's voice was gentle. "Since it's weighing so heavily on you, I think you need to just go visit your father and talk to him. He is happy now. If he takes it hard, he has Josephine to lean on."

She shook her head and gave him a sad smile. "Now it's my turn to be the bossy one. Take it from someone who knows. You think it's going to be painful to dig up the past, but the truth is, it's worse to keep it bottled up. Silence is so corrosive. It eats away at you and your relationships. Look at the wedges that my father's lies have driven between my brothers and sisters and me, and between them and him. I know the truth and I still maintain that my dad needs to be the one to tell them, but there's no getting around it. The truth is the only thing that will set you free, and the only way you're going to find that truth is to talk to Orlando yourself. Otherwise, this baggage you're carrying around will keep coming between you and the life you deserve. The past doesn't change how Orlando has loved you and it doesn't have to change your relationship with him going forward. Take it from someone who is speaking from experience."

She'd meant the part about speaking from experience to lighten the mood, since she was echoing what he'd said earlier. But Joaquin wasn't laughing. He was sitting there with a blank look on his face that bordered on annoyance.

"Look, I think we are going to have to agree to disagree on these issues," he said. "I think you need to tell your siblings and I think there will be a better time to talk to my dad about my issue."

"You think I'm wrong for not breaking my father's

confidence, but you are not willing to talk to your father about your paternity?"

"Right," Joaquin said. "They are similar situations, but they need to be handled differently. The only reason I brought up my situation was because I know how it feels to be lied to about your heritage. Nobody deserves that, Zoe. I'm not the one keeping this from anyone."

"You might be if your father doesn't know. You're just assuming that he does."

Joaquin shook his head. "It's still different. You know and you're perpetuating the lie if you don't expose it."

Who is this person?

Just last night he told her he thought he was falling in love with her. Now he was condemning her and casting her into the same liar's arena as her father.

"So, you're pinning this on me? You are not even willing to fix your own situation, and you are judging me for keeping my father's confidence? Oh, that's rich, Joaquin. Neither one of us seems to be in a good place to talk about this right now. I'll see you at work tomorrow."

Tears stung her eyes. She swiped at them before they could fall.

She had just put her hand on the doorknob when he said, "I don't think it's a good idea for us to sign that form."

She looked at him over her shoulder and her heart clenched when she saw his face. "The consensual relationship agreement?"

He nodded. "I'm sorry to bring it up now. I know you're dealing with a lot, but Steffi-Anne is bound to ask us about it tomorrow and I thought we needed to be on the same page or even be proactive and go talk to her in the morning."

"Talk to her about what?" Zoe didn't even try to hide the irritation in her voice. She was too busy trying to recover from the emotional whiplash. First, he did the two-step about their family situations, saying she should tell when he had no plans to fix his own. He said he was falling in love with her, then he objected to signing a simple form stating that they were in a consensual relationship.

This day was becoming her worst nightmare. Everything was falling apart.

"I've been thinking about it this morning," he said. "I'm still not sure where I'm going to be when this project ends in a couple of weeks. Actually, I've been doing some thinking since Steffi-Anne thrust that consensual relationship agreement on us. I think the world of you, Zoe. You are one of the most amazing women I've ever met in my life. You are just sweet and unjaded. You still believe in fairy tales and happy endings, and you deserve someone who can give that to you. I meant what I said last night about falling in love with you, but I just don't know if I can be the man you need. The man who deserves you."

Standing there with her hand on the doorknob, Zoe felt her heart shatter into a million irreparable pieces. This was the first time she had found someone who seemed so right, someone who actually did make her believe she could have her happily-ever-after, and now he wanted out.

Through the tears and the fog in her head, she heard herself telling him, "Please don't do this, Joaquin. I love you. Take some time if you need to figure out what you want, but I won't give up on you."

She heard him say something about doing this for her own good, about protecting her from worse heartache down the road. But she simply opened the door and let herself out. He didn't come after her.

He let her walk away.

Even though it was ridiculous to keep pursuing a man who had made it perfectly clear he didn't want her, the tiny shard of her heart that held the illogical belief that love would triumph over all was still hanging on by a thread.

She meant what she'd said. No matter how hopeless it seemed, she loved him and she wouldn't give up on him.

Chapter Twelve

If Joaquin thought his heart had ached when he had caught his fiancée, Selena, in bed with his best friend, it seemed like nothing compared to the black tar of despair he sank in to Sunday night after ending things with Zoe.

One of the conclusions he'd come to during his sleepless night was that he had made a big mistake by letting her go. The conundrum was, it was a mistake for him to not have her in his life, but reason reminded him she was better off without him. She was such a light in this world. She didn't need him and all his darkness snuffing out her flame.

He felt like such a jackass for being so hard on her yesterday. She hadn't deserved that and he would apologize once he got back to work. She had come to him looking for support, but he had let the stress of know-

ing he had to tell her he wasn't going to sign the relationship document, and the nerve that her situation
with her father had struck in him, turn him into a beast.

That in itself proved he didn't deserve her.

Who was he to tell her what to do—so arrogantly,
too—when he couldn't even figure out his own
screwed-up life?

Still that didn't mitigate the way he missed her. It
hadn't even been a full twenty-four hours and his heart
felt as if it would bleed out. He had plenty of time to
think about it as he drove to visit his father in Horseback Hollow.

After stewing on Zoe's words all night, he realized
she was right. There never would be a perfect time.
The only way he was going to lose his baggage was
by talking to his father.

Since Orlando was an early riser, Joaquin knew it
was okay to call at five o'clock on Monday morning. In
fact, it would probably be the best time to reach him,
because it would be before he got to work at the Redmond Flight School.

When he'd asked his dad if he had plans for lunch,
that he would like to drive up to see him, Orlando
had said even if he'd had plans, he would've canceled
them to have lunch with his oldest son. He sounded
so happy that Joaquin would take the time to come
visit him. As he got closer to Horseback Hollow, Joaquin started second-guessing his decision to finally
ask his dad about the paternity issue, but Zoe's words
echoed in his head.

There will never be a perfect time.

He may have already blown it with Zoe. The way
he'd acted yesterday, he was certain he had. But he

would never be at peace with himself if he didn't have this conversation with his father.

Rather than having everything unfold in a public place, Joaquin stopped at a gourmet sandwich shop in Vicker's Corners, a small, funky town located right next to Horseback Hollow. He picked up two roast beef, arugula and béarnaise sauce sandwiches, some red potato salad, a large bag of kettle chips and a gallon of freshly brewed peach iced tea.

He picked up his father from work and they went to Hanging Moss Park, a scenic little oasis not too far from Redmond Flight School. They sat at a picnic table and enjoyed their feast. Joaquin waited until they were both finished before he brought up the paternity question.

As Orlando gathered up his fork and the paper his sandwich had been wrapped in and stuffed them back into the empty sack the lunch had come in, he said, "Now, this was a treat and such a nice surprise. It isn't every day that I get to have lunch with my oldest son."

It seemed the perfect segue into what Joaquin had come to talk about.

"We don't get to spend enough time together, do we?" Joaquin said. "I was thinking the other day, I don't know that I've ever thanked you for the way you raised me."

Orlando looked slightly bemused. "You're welcome. But where is this coming from?"

It was now or never.

"You know, that no matter what, I love you and nothing can ever change that fact."

Now, Orlando was scrutinizing him through narrowed eyes.

"There's something I've needed to talk to you about for a few years now. I haven't, because the time simply never seemed right. And I finally realized that there never would be a perfect time. That's why I decided on a random Monday to drive six hours and have lunch and a heart-to-heart with my *father*."

He emphasized the word, wanting to see if Orlando would have a reaction, but his demeanor didn't change. He still sat there, watching Joaquin, as if he wasn't quite sure where the conversation was going.

"Remember at the hospital when Mom needed the blood transfusion? I gave her blood because mine was a match and yours wasn't."

He saw a flicker in his father's eyes.

"I'll cut to the chase, Dad. Simple genetics show that there is no way your and Mom's blood types could've produced a child with my blood type. Mine is consistent with hers. That means you're not my biological father. I'm not sure what this means. But I've worried for years it meant that Mom was having an affair when I was conceived."

Joaquin held his breath as he waited for a reaction from his father. Each second that ticked by was a dagger in Joaquin's heart as he anticipated Orlando's response.

Finally his father said, "I'm sorry you've shouldered this burden for so long, son. I wish you would've come to me sooner. Ah, hell, I should have opened the dialogue with you after you gave blood for your mother. There's really no excuse, except that I knew you were grieving. I was grieving. We lost her so soon after that and then it seemed like everything, life as we knew it, had been sucked into a black hole. I didn't know how you would take the truth and since you didn't bring it up again, I figured you didn't want to know. I used the excuse of all the change in our lives, of all the grief that we were suffering, to chicken out of leveling with you. But if you would like to know the truth, I'm willing to tell you everything."

Joaquin's heart beat so fast and furiously he could hear it in his ears.

"I do want to know, but I don't want it to change anything between us. Someone else may be my biological father, but you will always be my dad."

Orlando forced a smile as he nodded. Joaquin could see his dad's throat work as he swallowed.

"Nothing could ever change the love I have for you," Orlando said as he picked at a rough grain of wood on the picnic-table surface. He was quiet for a long, excruciating moment before he continued.

"Esteban is your father, but it's not what you think. Your mother was not cheating on me with him. Nor did she deceive me about your paternity. I've always known that you were Esteban's son."

Joaquin's mind whirled. "I knew that Mom briefly dated Esteban, but I never knew what happened or how the two of you ended up together. It seemed like a taboo subject. I mean, the two of you were soul mates. It seemed like there was nobody else for her before you. Will you tell me what happened? Because if she didn't cheat on you, I don't understand how she could conceive a child with him."

Orlando nodded. "That's a fair question. It's sort of complicated, but I'll do my best to explain."

His dad took a long swallow of iced tea, set the glass down and looked him in the eyes.

"I'd always, always had a crush on your mother. We'd known each other since we were children. I think my first memory is of falling in love with her. But Luz always carried a torch for Esteban. Your uncle, he was kind of a scoundrel and a rake. He led your mom on a merry chase. She used to confide in me about her feelings for Esteban. I loved Luz so much it was enough for me to be her confidante because it was the only way I could be with her. Esteban used to always take Luz for granted. He knew he could have her, but he was a popular guy. He had all kinds of girls after him. But Esteban and Luz did eventually date. It nearly killed me. Because he was not really in love with her and he still carried on with other women. In fact, he and I used to fight about that all the time, but he justified it by saying that that he and Luz were not exclusive.

"Well, your mama wound up pregnant, but she didn't discover it until after Esteban had run off and eloped with somebody else. When Luz told me about the pregnancy, I married her and vowed to raise the child as my own. I knew I had enough love for the two of us. Esteban was married. What good would it have done to tell him? Your mama and I promised each other we would never tell a soul that the baby wasn't mine. And as far as I'm concerned, you are as much mine as your brothers and sister."

Joaquin knew Orlando was a good guy. He had always thought so much of his father that he didn't think there was room to idolize him any more than he already did. But in the moment following his confession, Orlando Mendoza—his father—became a saint in his eyes.

"What about the bad blood between you and Esteban? Does he know the truth? Is that why you two don't speak?"

Orlando sighed. It was the sound of discontent, resignation.

"Because of Luz's pregnancy and premature delivery, Esteban believes that Luz and I were sleeping together while he was still dating her."

Joaquin balked. "That's ridiculous and pretty damn hypocritical. He was cheating on Mom left and right, according to what you say."

Orlando nodded. "Yes, he was. But all he could see was that I betrayed him. I was never interested in anyone beside your mother, so I didn't date very much. Oh, I tried here and there, but my heart belonged to your mama. Since Luz and I were close, he automatically assumed that I'd been sleeping with her when he was dating her.

"You know, for years, I felt justified in not telling Esteban that you were his son. I wanted to protect your mama from further pain, because you know it was bound to get sticky once anyone found out. Luz was the love of my life. I worshiped that woman and I would've given my life to spare hers. I didn't think I was ever going to survive losing her, but over the past few years that she's been gone I've realized that we were wrong to keep the paternity from both you and Esteban. I didn't know how to undo that mistake. So much time had passed, I didn't know if it would make things better or worse. I don't expect you to ever forgive me, but I hope someday you will understand why I did what I did. When you love someone the way I loved your mama—the way I love you—you'd do absolutely anything to protect them. Life is short, son.

Way too short not to do everything in your power to take care of those you love. But, son, I will do whatever you want. If you want to tell Esteban, we can. We'll handle it however you think we should."

The midday sun streamed through the branches of the live oak tree that shaded their picnic table. Rays of light, like beacons of hope, streamed down and a gentle breeze blew in like a comforting kiss from his mother.

"There's nothing to forgive," Joaquin said. "You did the best you could with the situation you found yourself in. If not for you, who knows what might've happened to Mom and me? There's no way I could ever be anything but grateful."

The look of absolute relief on his father's face nearly did him in.

Joaquin cleared his throat. "However, Esteban needs to know the truth. When do you think we could go to Miami to talk to him?"

Orlando nodded. "If you're available, we can go right now. We can take one of the Redman planes and be there in a couple of hours."

"Let's do it," said Joaquin.

Three hours later Joaquin and Orlando landed at Miami Executive Airport. They had called Esteban before they'd left to make sure he was around and willing to see them. Joaquin told him they had urgent family business to discuss, and Esteban agreed to see them.

In Miami they rented a car, checked into the hotel they had booked after confirming their visit with Esteban—Orlando didn't like to fly at night—and set out to mend some fences.

It was strange how Miami, with its electric-neon

lights, royal palm trees and colorful bougainvillea, was so familiar yet felt so strange. On the drive to his uncle's home, they passed many places that used to be Joaquin's local haunts, but now they felt unfamiliar, like acquaintances from another lifetime.

He hadn't expected Miami to feel so distant. It definitely wasn't home anymore. Funny, sometimes you had to leave your own backyard to discover how much it meant to you. In this case, Austin was now his backyard.

They arrived at Esteban's brick ranch-style house right on time. As Joaquin killed the rental car's engine, he glanced over at Orlando, who looked a little green and subdued.

"You all right?" Joaquin asked.

Orlando gave a resolute nod. "I should've done this a long time ago. Even if he tells me he doesn't want to see me again, at least I know I tried. At least he knows the truth."

Both Joaquin and Orlando had been surprised by how happy Esteban sounded when they told him they were coming for a visit. Actually, they had been amazed by Esteban's warm greeting, which had made it much easier to get down to business and tell him what they had come to say.

"When my mother was sick, she needed a blood transfusion," Joaquin said. "My mom and I both had O positive blood, which meant I was a perfect match for her, but Orlando couldn't be a donor because he had type AB blood, which is incompatible with ours."

Joaquin paused and saw the flicker of understanding dawning in Esteban's eyes.

"I'm not a genetics expert," Esteban said, "but if

I remember high school biology, it's impossible for types O and AB to produce a child with type O blood."

Joaquin nodded.

Esteban's brow knit, and he stared at a space somewhere over Joaquin's shoulder for a moment before a look of resolute acceptance softened his bewilderment.

"Just last month, I had blood work done for my annual physical. The tech told me I should consider donating blood since I'm type O positive, and there's always a high demand for that."

His lips flattened into a thin line, but his eyes looked sad, rather than angry.

Orlando cleared his throat. "I should've told you a long time ago, but—"

Esteban shook his head. "No. I was already married to Ginger by the time you and Luz got married. It would've only complicated matters."

His apologetic gaze swung back to Joaquin. "That doesn't mean I wouldn't have wanted to be your father. It's just—" Esteban's voice cracked.

"It's complicated," Joaquin finished. "I know that."

"I'm sorry," Orlando said.

"You did the right thing," Esteban said. "You stood by Luz and raised Joaquin as your own. I don't know if I would've had it in me back then."

They stood in silence for a moment until Esteban broke the silence. "You weren't sleeping with her when we were together, then?"

Orlando shook his head. "Not until our wedding night."

"I'm ashamed of myself for thinking she was fooling around with you while she was seeing me. I should've known that you would never betray me, and Luz had too much class to do something like that."

Tears misted Esteban's eyes. "I wanted to come to her funeral. I almost did, but in the end, I was afraid it might make it harder on you, brother. After the way I treated her, I didn't think I deserved to be there."

"I wish you would've come," Orlando said. "I would have welcomed you with open arms."

He closed the distance between his brother and himself and enfolded him in a hug.

"Now we both know that we could've saved ourselves a lot of angst if we had only spoken sooner," Esteban said. "I'm so tired of fighting with you, Orlando. I don't have any animosity left inside me. The simple act of you reaching out means a lot."

Joaquin knew that the brothers mending their relationship had to come before talk of Esteban's newfound paternity. Orlando and Esteban had been estranged for as long as Joaquin had been alive. Even though there had been bad blood between the brothers, Orlando had never begrudged Joaquin spending time with his cousins and uncle. Esteban had five sons; he'd probably needed a minute or two to digest the addition of the sixth. Joaquin was prepared to give him as much time as he needed. He was in the unique position to sit back and contemplate the fact that now he had not one but two fathers. Because Orlando, the good man who raised him, would always be his father.

As he glanced around Esteban's living room, at the well-worn upholstered furniture and the stacks of *National Geographic* magazines lined up neatly on the coffee table, along with the *Miami Herald* sports section and four remote controls for various electronic pieces, it dawned on him that the place looked exactly the same as it had all the years he'd been coming over to hang out with his cousins. Hearing Orlando and Esteban reminisce so fondly about Luz made Joaquin's heart fill to the point of nearly bursting.

Before too long the conversation drifted to Esteban's regrets of losing Luz's love.

"She ended up with the best man," Esteban said. "I was too wild. When I had her, I couldn't stand the thought of being tied down. That's why I didn't realize she was such a gem until after I married Ginger. I suppose she deserved better, too. In those days I didn't know how to treat a quality woman. I was too busy romancing the bottom of my highball glass. God knows that's what held my attention. That's why Ginger eventually left me. She put up with my crap for way too long. I didn't deserve the years she gave me and I certainly didn't deserve Luz, but you did, Orlando."

Esteban was silent for a moment. The ticking of the grandfather clock and the AC clicking on were the only sounds in the room.

"Although, I must admit that knowing Luz didn't cheat on me is a huge, healing comfort. She had every right, but she was a good woman."

He turned, almost shyly to Joaquin. "Discovering that you are my son is like having part of Luz back in my life." He gestured to Orlando. "Your father is an honorable man for so fiercely protecting your mother. The dumbest thing I even did was to let Luz get away. I guess deep down inside I always thought she deserved more than me. In life, you get what you expect. I expected that I was bad for her and I was."

As the sun set, Esteban excused himself because he

had a previous engagement—a date with a woman in the neighborhood. They were going to a potluck dinner. No, it wasn't anything serious; they were just spending time together.

It was comforting that things hadn't changed.

He told Orlando and Joaquin that they were welcome to stay, but the two thanked him and said they had to be going.

Even though Joaquin had had a while to sit with the reality that Esteban was his father, he was still a jumble of emotions: satisfied that the truth was finally out in the open, happy that Esteban had taken it so well, ecstatic that this rift between the brothers was on the mend. But he couldn't ignore the jangling uncertainty rattling his equilibrium.

"Let's definitely get the entire family together for Christmas," Orlando said as he hugged his brother again. "But let's not wait until then. That's more than six months away."

As Joaquin backed the car out of Esteban's driveway, he thought about what had just happened and how, even though nothing had changed, everything was different—in the best way possible, he reminded himself. He and Esteban knew the truth. Orlando was still and always would be his father. He only wished he had done this sooner. But who knew? Maybe if they'd done it sooner things wouldn't have turned out as well as they had today. Maybe he and Esteban wouldn't have been ready.

Everything happened for a reason and in its own time.

All he knew was that he had Zoe to thank for making this happen. He thought about calling her when he got back to the hotel, but before he could share his good news, he had some making up to do for the way he had treated her.

He'd learned two things today. When you were lucky enough to find a good woman, you treated her like a queen. And time waits for no one. If you don't act when you have chance, you just might lose the love of your life.

On Monday, Zoe didn't even look for Joaquin. In fact, she seriously contemplated not even going in to work because she didn't want to see him. Then she decided she didn't want to give him the satisfaction of thinking she was home pining for him. Okay, so in reality, he probably wouldn't be satisfied that their argument had kept her away, but it was still the principle of the matter. She was embarrassed by the way she'd sacrificed her dignity, telling him she wouldn't give up on him when clearly he just wanted her to go away.

So she'd come into the office, holding her head high, purposely immersing herself in a project to keep from wandering over to his side of the building.

On Tuesday at around two o'clock she couldn't avoid that side of the building because she had to pick up printed samples of the new company stationery. She walked by, pretending not to look, yet she couldn't help but notice that his door was open and the lights were off. He had either not come in or was taking an exceptionally long lunch. Or maybe he'd left early?

Why hadn't he at least texted her by now?

Okay, so maybe she hadn't given up on him, but that didn't mean she wouldn't wait for him to make the first move toward reconciliation. If this was how he fought, she wasn't sure he was the right guy for her. She'd have to think about this.

When she still hadn't heard from or seen him by Wednesday morning, Zoe's anger had faded and she was downright concerned. Where was he?

This had gone too far.

She hoped he was okay.

She swallowed her pride and called Steffi-Anne. She hated to do it, but what if he was sick or something had happened? He didn't have family in town. What if he'd slipped in the shower and hit his head and had amnesia and was wandering around the streets of Austin lost?

Okay, that was a little far-fetched, but still, if she'd been gone for three days—okay, technically it was two full days and this was the morning of the third—she would want people to check on her.

"Yes, Zoe." Steffi-Anne's usual mildly irritated monotone assaulted her ear.

"Good morning, Steffi-Anne." She infused as much sunshine as she could into her tone. "I hope your day is off to a good start."

"What do you want, Zoe? I'm sure you didn't call simply to inquire about my morning."

"You're so smart." Effervescence and sunshine this time. "I didn't call to ask about you. When will Joaquin be in?"

She squeezed her eyes shut and gritted her teeth. Being humbled like this would be worth it if she could find out when he was supposed to be back.

"What? Is there trouble in paradise? I would've thought that you, of all people, would be able to keep track of lover boy. And speaking of, I have not received a signed consensual relationship agreement form from either of you. Have things changed?"

Zoe wanted to slam down the phone. But first she wanted to tell her it was none of her stinking business and then she wanted to slam the phone. Instead she said, "You are so funny. Are you still running with that gag? It's getting a little old, don't you think?"

"It's not a gag, Zoe. Unless you get special treatment because you are the boss's daughter, I need those forms on my desk by the end of tomorrow."

Sunshine, effervescence and chirping bluebirds—she sounded like Snow White, Cinderella and Sleeping Beauty all rolled into one. "Oh, Steffi-Anne, you're so observant. I *am* the boss's daughter and it will behoove you to remember that. We will not be signing your silly form. So don't ask me again. Am I clear?"

"Perfectly."

Zoe hung up the phone, feeling queasy and giddy at the same time. She hadn't gotten the information about Joaquin she needed, but she was pretty certain it was the last time Steffi-Anne would bully her.

By four o'clock on Wednesday there was still no trace of Joaquin. Zoe swallowed her pride and texted him.

Hey, stranger. Do you still work here?

Her heart nearly jumped into her throat when he answered immediately.

I do. I've been in Miami. Got back late last night. Meeting your father for lunch. Talk to you later.

Her father? What was going on?

Why in the world had Joaquin been in Miami? She remembered him saying he wasn't sure what was going to happen after his project ended in a couple of weeks. Had he been there on a job interview?

And why in the world was Joaquin having lunch with her dad? She hadn't spoken to either of them since Sunday. God, she hoped Joaquin wasn't giving him his resignation.

For that matter, Joaquin had been so upset by Gerald's confession, she hoped and prayed he wasn't going straight to the source to tell him exactly what he thought of the situation.

For a moment Zoe couldn't breathe. If he was leaving, he certainly had nothing to lose by giving her dad a piece of his mind.

Chapter Thirteen

Wednesday evening, the last thing Zoe wanted to do was to go out and socialize. But Veronica had called her at quarter to five and insisted they go for drinks at the Driskill Hotel that night.

The Driskill? Of all places? Even thinking of it made her sad, because the last time she was there she'd been with Joaquin.

Was this what life was going to be like from now on? Thinking of him as she turned every corner? Avoiding her favorite places because they reminded her of him?

"Thanks, Ronnie, but I'll pass."

"I don't think so." She was particularly sassy tonight. "There's this bartender at the Driskill. I want him to ask me out. Come on, Zoe. You owe me. Be my wing woman tonight."

So that was the reason she was insisting on going

to the Driskill. Zoe should've known this urgent plan would involve a guy.

Zoe knew when Ronnie got that way, there was no escaping her will. So she might as well go and have one drink. Okay, maybe two. Lord knew that Ronnie had been her wing woman plenty of times.

After she'd relented, Ronnie said, "Why do you sound so glum? Trouble in paradise?"

"For God's sake, is that the theme of the day?"

"I have no idea," Ronnie said. "Is it?"

When Zoe didn't answer, Ronnie pressed on. "Is everything okay with Joaquin?"

As Zoe went through the paces of shutting down her computer, she said, "We will have plenty of time to talk at the Driskill. But if I don't get out of here now, it'll be eight o'clock before I can meet you."

"Actually, how about if I swing by your place and pick you up?" Ronnie said.

"Why would you want to do that? You have to pass the Driskill to get to my place. It's way out of your way. I'll just meet you there."

"No, I don't mind. Really, I don't. I will be there to get you at six thirty sharp. Oh, and I feel like dressing up tonight. So wear something nice."

By the time they got to the Driskill, Zoe was glad Ronnie had insisted on taking her car because that meant her friend was the designated driver. She probably hadn't thought of that when she'd insisted on picking her up. That's what she got for being bossy.

Zoe knew the reason her friend had gone out of her way was that she was afraid Zoe would cancel. While Zoe wasn't prone to flaking out on friends, tonight she might've been tempted. But when she'd gotten home

to her empty condo, all she could think about was the
night she and Joaquin had made out on the sofa.

Maybe she would go shopping for a new couch this
weekend. Her sister Sophie had coveted Zoe's teal sofa.
No doubt she would be delighted to have it.

She had seriously considered making love with Joaquin right there on that sofa. A wave of nearly unbear-
able sadness washed over her. She *loved* him. And she
had believed him when he'd said he was falling in love
with her.

If she hurt this bad now, she couldn't imagine how
she would've felt if she had slept with him.

That was when she knew that Ronnie was her life-
saver. This condo was the last place Zoe needed to
be tonight. If she stayed in, she would wallow in her
misery.

"So, drinks are on me tonight," Zoe said as they
settled into an overstuffed leather sofa in one of the
quiet nooks in the kitschy, ranch-themed Driskill bar.

"What? Why are you buying drinks?" As soon as
the words had escaped her mouth, Ronnie held up her
hand. "Never mind. Far be it from me to turn down free
booze. Ohhh, I gotcha. You're buying the drinks because I'm the designated driver. *Clever.* But seriously,
Zoe, what's going on with you tonight? You just don't
seem like yourself."

Zoe waved her off. "I don't want to be a buzzkill.
I'm your wing woman tonight. Speaking of, do you
think we could sit any farther away from the bar? How
can you work your magic a football field away from
the guy?"

Ronnie wiped her wavy blond hair out of her eyes

and looked at her cell phone again for about the fiftieth time tonight. This time she replied to a text.

"Here and now, Ronnie." Zoe snapped her fingers. "I'm talking to you. Do I have to take that thing away from you?"

"Huh? Sorry, that was important."

Ronnie was an artist who specialized in abstract acrylic paintings. Zoe understood that her friend's career was not the typical nine to five. Sometimes Ronnie had to interact with clients after hours. Though tonight she was wishing her friend wasn't quite so distracted.

"That had better be a client or better yet, a hot guy," Zoe joked. "Speaking of, where is this guy you're interested in? I want to see him."

Ronnie craned her neck, looking around the sparsely populated bar. "I don't know. It looks like he might not be working tonight."

Zoe was surprised Ronnie hadn't called to ask if— "What's his name? And when did you meet him?"

"Oh…" She was still looking around the bar, a little distracted. "His name? Uh…John?"

"You're not sure?"

"Of course I am. But enough about me. Tell me what is going on with you and Joaquin. Last I heard, you were in love. And that's why I haven't seen you in a couple of weeks."

Zoe knew if she didn't tell Ronnie what was going on, her friend would keep asking questions. And on the flipside of that, if she did tell her, she knew Ronnie would be a good friend and listen.

"I don't know what's going on with Joaquin. We had an argument on Sunday. It was a pretty bad one. But arguments happen in relationships. I wanted to believe that just because we disagreed on something, it wasn't over. But I haven't heard from him since then. Well, actually, that's not true. I broke down and texted him today."

Ronnie looked at her sympathetically. "Did he text you back?"

Zoe shrugged. "Yes, but it was a very short and to-the-point answer. He told me he's been in Miami for the past couple of days. That's where he is from. Then he told me he was having lunch with my dad. He said, 'Got to go.' And that was it. I thought he might have texted me back after lunch. But he didn't, and then you called and here we are."

"That's odd," said Ronnie.

"Ya think?"

"Why do you suppose he and your dad were having lunch?"

Zoe shrugged. "I don't know. Sunday, he was talking about not knowing what he was going to do or where he was going to be after his project here was finished. I know my dad wanted to talk to him about staying on in a permanent position at Robinson. So maybe that's what they were talking about today. But it's odd that he missed two days of work to go to Miami. That has 'job interview' written all over it. I hope he wasn't telling my dad he was going back to Miami."

Or worse.

Although, if Joaquin had said anything to her father about the Jerome Fortune stuff, her dad would've undoubtedly called and given her a piece of his mind about sharing personal issues with nonfamily members. So she felt a little better about that, and actually kind of silly that she had doubted him. That wasn't Joaquin's style and she knew it.

"Why would he want to go back to Miami when Robinson is the place where most software designers would give their firstborn to work? It doesn't make sense. Oh, God, Ronnie, I love him. I don't know what to do."

Nothing made sense anymore.

"Just give him space. I have a feeling he's crazy for you, too. Everything will work out. Mark my words, because you know my gut feelings are usually right. Where in the world is the server? Do we have to go to the bar and get our own drinks?"

"Why would you not want to go to the bar?"

"Yeah, I guess I could ask if Steve was working tonight," Ronnie said.

"Steve? I thought his name was John?"

Ronnie got another text. "Oh, crap. I have to go make a phone call. I'll be right back."

As she walked away Zoe called to her, "What do you want to drink? I'll order it while you're on the phone."

Ronnie pulled the phone away from her ear. "No, don't get up. We'll lose our seats."

Before Zoe could point out the fact that there were plenty of other places and most of them closer to the bar, Ronnie disappeared around the corner.

Ronnie was acting so weird tonight. She was distracted and now that they were here to see this John or Steve or whoever he was, she wasn't excited about it and they weren't even sitting near the bar.

Then Zoe sighed. She would admit she was a little hypersensitive right now. Maybe she was simply projecting her own antsy-ness onto her friend.

She thought about the adage that when the rest of the world felt like it was out of step, there was a pretty good chance the rest of the world wasn't the one with the problem.

Zoe needed to chill out. Ronnie was allowed to make a phone call. She would be back in a minute. Zoe didn't have to be anywhere and she certainly didn't want to go home to her teal couch.

She leaned her head against the back of the leather sofa. Looking up, she could see the stuffed head of a big steer. Not enjoying that view, she sat up and looked around the bar.

There was a couple getting cozy at a table across the way. She looked in the other direction and saw a group of six women clustered in another of the nooks. It looked as if they were either celebrating a birthday or out on the town for a bachelorette party. When she looked past them, she saw a guy sipping a beer and checking her out. When he realized she was looking, he flashed a seductive smile and waved her over.

Uh, no, thank you.

Since looking around appeared not to be a safe means of distraction, she took her phone out of her purse. Maybe there would be a text from Joaquin.

Nope.

She was just starting to check her email when a text from Ronnie popped up.

Come outside. I need you.

Zoe's heart lurched. What the heck was going on?

You okay? Be right there.

Zoe grabbed her purse and made her way out of the bar and into the Driskill's grand lobby with its splendid staircase and stained-glass ceiling. She rushed out the front doors, looking around for Ronnie. That's when she saw the horse and carriage and a guy who could've been Joaquin's identical twin standing next to it.

Oh! That is Joaquin.

Zoe stopped dead in her tracks, suddenly afraid that she had stumbled into something she wasn't supposed to see—like maybe he was here on a date. Had Ronnie seen him earlier and that's why she'd been acting so squirrely? But why would she call her outside?

Her gaze performed a quick check of the horse and carriage, but it was empty and Joaquin was walking toward her. And he was smiling and holding out his hand. And there was a single, long-stemmed red rose in his hand.

Her heart pounded so hard, she was afraid it might burst.

"Go to him." Ronnie was nudging her. "You can thank me later."

Zoe did a double-take because she hadn't realized her friend was standing next to her.

All of a sudden it hit her that this night had not been about being Ronnie's wing woman. Not at all. Ronnie telling her to dress nicely, insisting on picking her up, her being so distracted with her phone and then getting up and leaving.

This was a plan, and quite a well-orchestrated surprise.

Joaquin was standing in front of her now. He handed her the rose.

"Zoe, I'm so sorry for everything that happened on

Sunday. You have every right to not want to see me again, but I love you, and on Sunday you told me you loved me, too. If you can find it in your heart to forgive me, will you take a carriage ride with me? I have so much to tell you."

Zoe stood there paralyzed by emotion.

"This is where you say, 'Yes, Joaquin, I would love to take a carriage ride with you,'" Ronnie said in a stage whisper. "And this is where I leave. Have fun, kids."

As Joaquin thanked Ronnie, all Zoe could manage was a nod because she was still trying to process everything. Surely the things he wanted to talk to her about were good, because why would he have gone to the trouble to contact her best friend, whom he'd never even met, and get her to help him coordinate this surprise if they weren't good?

And then there was the horse and carriage. Had she told him how much she loved carriage rides? She couldn't remember.

But it didn't matter because here they were here and he was helping her into the carriage. That's when she noticed the silver ice bucket holding a bottle of champagne and the two crystal flutes in a special holder next to the bucket.

Joaquin signaled the driver and the carriage took off down the Driskill's driveway.

"Zoe, before I went to Miami, I went to Horseback Hollow to see my father. I did it because you made me realize I would never be able to unload all the baggage I was carrying until I had talked to him. You are absolutely right and I feel like a new person."

"That's great, Joaquin," she said, finally settling

back into her senses again. "So I take it that it went well?"

He nodded. "It couldn't have gone better."

"Tell me about it."

"I would love to, but before I do, I need to know, are we okay?"

All it took was one look at his gorgeous, anxious face and she knew that there was nowhere else she wanted to be. She felt whole again for the first time since she'd left his apartment on Sunday. Granted, the past three days had been hell, but if he'd needed that time to figure things out, it was all worth it. Obviously he had put it to good use.

"I told you I wouldn't give up on you, and I meant it. But if this is going to work, and I really want it to, you realize this isn't going to be our last fight, right? Even the best relationships have arguments."

He nodded.

"I need you to promise me this is the last time that we will go three days without talking."

Zoe saw his throat work beneath the white shirt and blue tie he wore with his black suit. "I promise you that and so much more, because I don't want to spend another day without you. I realized that over these last three days."

He told her about driving to Horseback Hollow on Monday and what his father had told him. He told her about Orlando flying them to Miami and how his father and his uncle had been estranged and how they had both loved his mother.

"But my uncle—my dad? Er, *Esteban* was too wrapped up in his own issues and too busy chasing skirts to realize he was losing the best thing that ever happened to him. However, my dad, Orlando, loved my mom so fiercely he was willing to sacrifice himself to protect her.

"If I learned one thing while we were apart, it's that you deserve to be loved just as fiercely as Orlando loved Luz, and I now know I can love you that way if you'll let me."

When he leaned in and kissed her, Zoe melted into him. His lips were a touchstone, grounding her in love.

"So, I saw your father today."

Zoe tensed for a second, but only for a second, because she somehow knew that he wasn't going to ask her if she'd talked to her siblings about the Jerome Fortune issue. And she was right.

"Were you talking about a permanent position at Robinson Tech?"

Joaquin smiled. "You might say that."

"What do you mean?"

"I asked his permission to propose to you."

Zoe's mouth fell open and she covered it with her hand. That's when she realized she was shaking. "What did he say?"

"He said it was fine with him, but it was up to you."

Joaquin reached into the pocket of his jacket and pulled out a small light blue box. The world moved in slow motion as he managed to position himself so that he could get down on one knee in the swaying carriage.

"Zoe Robinson, will you do me the honor of being my wife? If you say yes, I vow to bring you as much happiness as you have brought me."

Tears streamed down her face as she threw her arms around his neck. As the carriage rolled along, passersby realized what was happening and cheered and applauded.

When he sat next to her, he placed the gorgeous, traditional round diamond on her left ring finger and opened the bottle of champagne.

"I don't want to wait long to get married," Zoe said. "In fact, how would you feel about Memorial Day weekend? It's a long weekend. We should be able to gather all of our family. Do you think that will work?"

He put his arm around her. "It should, but as far as I'm concerned, we could elope."

She snuggled closer to him. "I want a wedding. I've always dreamed of that special day. In fact, I've been planning our wedding since I was about nine. So it will be no problem to get everything ready in a couple of weeks."

"I want you to have that wedding of your dreams," he said. "The only thing that matters to me is that you're happy."

If this was a dream, Zoe hoped she would never wake up.

Chapter Fourteen

When Zoe and Joaquin announced their big news, everybody was elated. Rachel and Matteo even decided to come up from Horseback Hollow to take them out for a celebratory dinner, which soon turned into a family meal at the Robinson estate.

For the first time in a long time the Robinson siblings had something else to focus on besides "the great Fortune hunt."

Not only was the pending wedding romantic and exciting, it had offered a much-needed breath of fresh air for a family on the brink of civil war.

It was as if they had hit the reset button.

At least for now.

If the engagement hadn't already made Zoe's heart so full it was overflowing, she might've been relieved that the secret her dad had saddled her with had been pushed into the background. But she wasn't even thinking about it.

Of course, that didn't mean the conundrum about whether to keep his secret was gone. She still didn't know what she was going to do. What had changed was that the problem simply wasn't the first thing she thought about when she opened her eyes in the morning and the last thing on her mind as she drifted off to sleep.

Now her mind was full of wedding dresses, flower arrangements, cakes and signature wedding cocktails, dinner menus and invitations, because there wasn't enough time to send out a save-the-date card.

While it was a lot of work, it wasn't as hard as it seemed. Because she really had been planning her dream wedding since she was nine.

Until recently, the only thing missing from her well-thought-out plan was the groom. Now that she'd met her prince, everything was complete.

As she and Rachel walked arm in arm up the front steps that led to their parents' front door, they talked about bridesmaids' dresses and upon whom, out of her three sisters and best friend, she would bestow the honor of serving as maid of honor.

As Joaquin and Matteo trailed along behind them, talking about Orlando's newly mended relationship with Esteban—Joaquin had told his brother about his paternity issue, and it had turned out to be a nonissue because nothing had changed except for Esteban and Orlando ending their feud—Rachel said, "I have the perfect solution to your problem. I can be the matron of honor since I'm married. Olivia, Sophie and Ronnie can duke it out for who will be the maid of honor.

Or if you want an easy way to settle it, since I am the oldest of the sisters, I should get special distinction and they can all be bridesmaids. Since I have already been through this, I have the most experience. I know what the perfect matron of honor needs to do."

Maybe Joaquin had been onto something when he'd suggested they elope.

Oh, who was she kidding? She loved every single second of agonizing over every single tough wedding decision she'd faced so far. She was only doing this once and she intended to do it right.

A cluster of nerves knotted in her stomach, catching Zoe by surprise. *This is really happening, isn't it?* She had dreamed of this time for so long, it was hard to believe it was finally here.

"We will figure something out," Zoe said. "I don't want to hurt anybody's feelings. So we will make it work."

She glanced over her shoulder at her fiancé, who was still laughing and talking with Matteo, oblivious to the wedding plans being discussed right in front of them. This time the butterflies swooped and circled in her belly for a completely different reason.

That handsome, incredible man was the one she would spend the rest of her life with, the man for whom she had waited her whole life.

He is the one.

The one.

Matteo was in the middle of saying something, but Zoe caught Joaquin's eye. The smoldering exchange made her ache for him.

Since he'd proposed, when Zoe wasn't thinking

about the wedding her thoughts were consumed with giving herself, body and soul, to Joaquin.

She had waited so long for everything to be just right, and he was being such a good sport about honoring her wish to wait for their wedding night to make love. But it hadn't been easy for her to resist him. There were times when she was with him that it took every ounce of willpower she possessed to not give in to her desire.

Rachel opened the door and motioned for Zoe and Joaquin to enter first. Zoe breathed in the aroma of something delicious and it suddenly occurred to her that they must be the first to arrive because the driveway had been oddly absent of cars.

As she made a mental note to talk to her siblings about punctuality, since they would all be part of the wedding party, she turned the corner into the living room, into the thunderous sound of a crowd yelling, "Surprise!"

This was no family dinner. Some very sneaky people had apparently invited every single person she and Joaquin had ever met—and then some—to a surprise engagement party/wedding shower.

Good grief, the wedding was right around the corner, but Zoe was touched and a little taken aback by the generous, loving gesture that their friends would come out on a Saturday night to celebrate Joaquin's and her love.

She truly felt like Cinderella as she received good wish upon good wish. She fully intended to talk to each and every guest in attendance and to tell each and every one of them how much she appreciated them being here tonight.

About an hour into her mission, the waitstaff began circulating with trays of champagne flutes, and her father, with her mother, Charlotte, standing at his side, called everyone to order.

"I love all my kids," Gerald said. "But it's no secret that Zoe and I share an extraspecial bond." Her father's gaze snagged hers and Zoe couldn't quite tell if he was simply nervous or if something else was going on, because something in his demeanor didn't quite match the tone of the father-of-the-bride-to-be speech he was giving.

No one else probably noticed because Gerald Robinson was not known for being an emotional, warm and fuzzy kind of guy. Maybe it was because the two of them hadn't spoken since the showdown in his study nearly a week ago. Maybe this was his way of sending her a message, like a male peacock who fans out his feathers in splendid glory when the gesture was really meant to serve as a warning.

Whatever the case, everything that had gone out of her mind elbowed its way back into the forefront. She'd resolved not to think about the situation until after her wedding, because it upset her. She still hadn't wrapped her mind around the fact that her father was, despite how vehemently he'd railed against it, Jerome Fortune. She hadn't come to terms with the fact that her knight in shining armor had lied to his family all these years.

No! She wasn't going to think about that now. Joaquin's arm was around her waist and when she looked up at him, his smile turned the butterflies loose again. Boy, they were really swarming tonight amid all the excitement. She took a deep breath and raised her glass to his, refusing to let Jerome Fortune spoil any part of

Joaquin's and her party. No, Jerome Fortune was not welcome at anything that had to do with their wedding. The next two weeks would be a Jerome Fortune–free zone.

She mustered the appropriate smile and made all of the coos and sighs expected of a consummate daddy's girl and bride-to-be.

As everyone raised their glass and said, "Cheers!" Zoe scanned the crowd of happy faces, letting the merriment of celebration wash through her.

That's when she noticed an unfamiliar face among the crowd. A nice-looking guy was standing in the back, holding a glass of champagne and engrossed in conversation with her brother Ben.

She hugged her father because that's what everyone expected and kissed her mother on the cheek. Then she said to Joaquin, "I'm going to say hello to Ben. I'll be back in a moment."

Resuming her mission to greet everyone, Zoe headed toward the two men. Her brother had kept a relatively low profile tonight, or maybe there were just so many people here this was the first she'd seen him.

As she approached, she heard the stranger's proper British accent. "Why don't I come to your next family meeting and we can tell everyone about the others?"

Zoe stopped in her tracks, trying to figure out what they were talking about. Because surely Ben wouldn't discuss their family's dirty laundry with a stranger and air it at her engagement party.

Zoe stood there, intending to listen to their conversation, hoping to hear something that proved this wasn't what it looked like, but Ben looked over and saw her.

"Zoe." He motioned for her to come closer. "I want to introduce you to Keaton Whitfield. Keaton, this is my sister Zoe."

Keaton Whitfield?

Was he kidding? He had better be kidding.

"Ah, yes, Zoe. It is lovely to meet you. Congratulations on your engagement. I am delighted to celebrate with you."

The British accent confirmed Zoe's nightmare.

This was *the* Keaton Whitfield. The guy Ben had found who claimed to be a half sibling and supposedly knew of *others*.

Was that what he meant a moment ago when he said he would come to the next family meeting and they could talk about *the others*?

"What are you doing, Ben?"

Her brother gave her an odd look. "I'm introducing you to Keaton?"

"Don't be a smartass," Zoe said. "You know what I mean. Why did you bring him here tonight? Tonight of all nights, Ben? Why would you do this?"

Keaton transferred his weight from foot to foot, looking uncomfortable. "I see that this is upsetting you, Zoe. I am terribly sorry. I will say good-night."

Zoe couldn't even look at Keaton as he walked away. Her angry gaze was glued to Ben's. Her brother stood there looking just as annoyed.

Zoe lowered her voice to a whispering growl. "Why would you pull a stunt like this at my engagement party? What are you trying to prove? Did you see this as your chance to rub your crusade in Dad's nose? What about Mom? How do you think she would feel about you bringing Keaton Whitfield into her home?

Did you ever think that maybe at least until after the wedding is over you could give it a rest? It's only two weeks, Ben. If you don't have enough empathy or common sense to know what's appropriate and what's not, then maybe you just need to stay away from me for a while. I'm going to leave for a bit. When I get back, I want you to be gone."

She didn't give him the chance to answer. Tears were welling in her eyes. She had to get out of there before anyone noticed.

She ducked her head so that her hair fell in her face, hiding her tears until she'd made it to the hallway and out the front door. She couldn't leave her own party, so she would walk around until she got her emotions under control and her brother had time to leave.

What was he thinking, bringing Keaton Whitfield to a family event? Their mother was there. Did he have no regard for her and the pain it would cause if she had discovered her husband's illegitimate son in her own house?

As Zoe stepped out into the humid night, she saw that the valets were there now. They must've had instructions to lie low until she and Joaquin were inside. The two young men stood as Zoe approached.

"Good evening," said the tall one. "May I get your car?"

She was grateful that the light was low and hoped he couldn't see her misty eyes. She mustered a smile to give the impression that everything was okay.

"No, thank you. I'm just out for a short walk."

Because everyone leaves a party to take a walk.

He nodded. "Have a nice evening."

Zoe walked toward the garden on the west side of

the property, where she knew she could have some privacy.

Try as she might, she couldn't find the strength of spirit to give her father the benefit of the doubt on the cheating accusations and proof of illegitimate children Ben had dug up.

She was still coming to grips with the fact that her father had lied about his past and had asked her to keep it a secret.

Lying and cheating went against everything Zoe believed in. She certainly didn't want it paraded around at her engagement party, or her wedding, for that matter. But the damage had already been done. And she could no longer ignore the stark reality that had burrowed into the pit of her stomach: because of her father's actions, she now doubted everything she'd ever believed to be true.

These sickening doubts were dredging up all sorts of unwelcome memories of incidents she'd rationalized in the past.

Such as that time with her father and their neighbor Mrs. Caldwell. Zoe hadn't thought about it since she was six or seven years old.

Her parents had hosted their annual New Year's Eve party. At least one hundred and fifty people dressed in their finest evening wear had converged on the Robinson estate. It was a party worthy of Jay Gatsby.

Zoe was supposed to be in bed, but she'd gotten up to get a drink of water and seen her dad embracing Mrs. Caldwell on the second-floor landing of the main staircase. Now it dawned on Zoe that they'd probably thought they were tucked out of sight. The woman had been crying and Zoe thought she'd heard her whimper something about a baby. When they'd seen Zoe, Mrs. Caldwell had gasped and descended the stairs like a weeping Cinderella racing against the strike of the clock.

"What's wrong with Mrs. Caldwell, Daddy?" Zoe had asked as her father filled her princess cup with water from the bathroom faucet.

"She's sad and I was comforting her." Her dad's voice had sounded so kind, Zoe hadn't imagined he could be telling her anything but the truth. Still, as he'd tucked her into bed, Zoe had persisted. "Did a baby upset Mrs. Caldwell?"

"Why would you think that, princess?"

"Because I heard her say something about a baby."

"Sweet girl, you must've misunderstood."

"Then what made her so sad, Daddy?"

Zoe remembered how he'd gently brushed her bangs off her forehead and smiled down at her with sad eyes. "I'm not allowed to tell, princess. It's Mrs. Caldwell's secret. She would be very upset if I betrayed her confidence. You understand, don't you?"

Zoe had nodded even though she hadn't understood. She *knew* she'd heard the word *baby*.

"I think Mrs. Caldwell was embarrassed that you saw her crying. Will you promise me that you won't say anything to anyone? Because that would make her cry even harder. I know you're too sweet and kind to make anyone feel sad. Besides, this can be our secret. Something that you and I share that no one else knows. Just like the fact that you are my favorite of all my children."

He'd planted a kiss on her forehead and then plucked at her nose, which had made her giggle.

"*You* know you're my favorite and *I* know it, but if you tell your brothers and sisters it would make them sad. So, that's our secret, too. Right?"

She'd loved having secrets with her father. It made her feel special. So they'd sealed her promise with a pinkie shake.

When Zoe was a little girl, a pinkie promise was sacred and her father's word meant everything. She'd been his princess and he'd been her steadfast knight. So, naturally, she'd believed him because heroes didn't lie.

She'd kept his secret all those years ago. Now, even when he'd admitted to telling a lie of staggering proportions, he had asked her to cast aside what was right and good and keep another one. Only this time his knight's armor was tarnished and she didn't believe in fairy tales anymore.

If, in fact, he had fathered children outside of his marriage, that meant the situation was worse than she'd originally thought. Even though her parents weren't prone to public displays of affection, she'd always thought their marriage was strong, that it was impenetrable, rock solid.

Given her father's confession and Keaton Whitfield's talk about "the others," Zoe couldn't help but wonder whether Mrs. Caldwell had been pregnant with her father's baby. Was yet another half sibling out there somewhere, too? Had every word her from father's mouth been a bald-faced lie?

She didn't know what to believe now. She wasn't sure what was real and what was an illusion built on naive dreams…or delusions.

All she knew was that she had to leave. She couldn't

stay and pretend that everything was fine when it felt as if her whole world was crumbling around her.

Apparently nothing was sacred anymore. Apparently her tendency to see the best in people amounted to nothing more than naïveté. How could she have been so stupid? So blind?

Was she rushing into things with Joaquin? How well did she really know him? For all the joking about knowing each other for more than a year, really, it had only been a few weeks. He hadn't even wanted to ask her out. She'd had to all but cajole him into it. And then he'd disappeared for three days and come back with a ring.

Zoe's head was spinning.

The proposal had been lovely and romantic and everything she'd ever dreamed a proposal would be, but it had happened so fast.

Maybe she needed to take a step back and think about what they were doing. The wedding was less than two weeks away. If they canceled everything tomorrow, they could still get partial refunds.

Zoe only intended to get married once. She wanted a life with one man who wanted to spend the rest of his life with one woman: her.

In the wake of all that had happened with her father, happily-ever-after suddenly felt like the biggest fairy tale a naive woman could buy into. It was high time she removed her rose-colored glasses and saw the world and people for who they really were.

Out of the corner of his eye Joaquin caught a flash of Zoe's long, golden-brown hair as she turned into the hallway. Something about the way she moved warned him something wasn't right.

After the toast she had said she was going to say hello to Ben. Now she looked as if she was leaving in a hurry.

"Please excuse me," he said to the small group of well-wishers who were clustered around him asking about his and Zoe's plans for the future. "My bride needs me."

By the time he made it to the hallway, Zoe was nowhere to be found. On instinct he went outside and saw the same valets who had been working the night of the Robinson Tech dinner, but Zoe was nowhere in sight.

"Did a beautiful woman come through here a few minutes ago?"

"Long brown hair, white dress?"

"That's the one," Joaquin said.

"She went that way." The guy pointed toward the far side of the grounds.

"Thanks," Joaquin said and took off in that direction.

Once he had cleared the driveway, he called, "Zoe? Are you out here?"

He heard something rustling near a vine-covered arbor and headed in that direction. As he passed through, he caught a glimpse of something white a few feet ahead.

"Zoe? It's me. Are you okay?"

He passed through another arbor, this one heavy with pink wisteria, and saw Zoe sitting on a stone bench, her head bent so that her hair shielded her face.

"Zoe? What's wrong?"

When she didn't look up, that was when he noticed her shoulders were shaking. Was she crying?

He walked over and put his arms around her. "Hey, what's wrong?"

When he tried to lift her chin, she shrugged away from him.

"What's wrong?" he repeated.

"I don't think I can do this," she said.

"What are you talking about?" he asked.

"The wedding." Her voice broke on a hiccupping sob. "I think we need to postpone everything."

"No," Joaquin insisted, his heart thudding at the thought.

"Okay, then we can call it off," Zoe said. "I can't marry you right now, Joaquin. It's all happening too fast."

"Can we talk about this?"

"What's there to talk about?"

"I love you. That's what there is to talk about. Did I do something to make you change your mind?"

She took in a shuddering breath. "You didn't do anything wrong. You've been nothing but wonderful."

"And that's why you want to call off the wedding? Because I've been wonderful?"

"No—" Her voice broke and she shuddered out a sob.

He hated to see her cry. It cut him down to the quick. "You don't want to be part of this family. I love you so much that I don't want you to have to deal with them. I'm stuck with them, but you're not. So, get out while you can."

"That's crazy. If you're going to call off the wedding, the least you can do is talk to me." He had driven the four of them to the Robinsons' house tonight. "My car is still in the driveway. Can we go somewhere and talk?"

With tears still rolling down her cheeks, she gave a faint nod. He took off his jacket and draped it over her shoulders and they made their way back to his car.

The valets had the decency to not stare and stayed on the other side of the driveway, giving them some privacy. Joaquin opened the passenger-side door and helped Zoe inside before sliding behind the wheel.

They drove in silence. The only sounds were the hum of the engine and an occasional sniff from Zoe. Finally, when they arrived at a spot overlooking Lake Austin where Joaquin could pull off onto the side of the road, he killed the engine and turned in his seat to look at her.

"I love you more than I've ever loved anyone in my life, Zoe. I don't want to lose you. I'm not afraid of your family."

"I just don't even know what I believe anymore," Zoe said.

She told him about the encounter with Ben and Keaton Whitfield.

"Every day something that had defined my life is shattered. I don't even know my own mind anymore. This relationship has happened so fast. I love you, but what if we're moving too fast? What if I wake up and discover this had all been a lie, too?"

"It's not a lie. I have never been so sure of anything in my life," Joaquin said. "But if you're not ready to get married, I'm not going to force you into anything. Just say the word and we can call the wedding off. It's the last thing I want to do, but if that's what you need, that's what we'll do. Whatever happens, I'm going to tell you what somebody wise once told me—take some time if you need to figure out what you want, but I won't give up on you."

Epilogue

Two Weeks Later

Joaquin hadn't given up on her.

When it came right down to it, she couldn't give up on him, either.

Now she knew she could never give up on *them*. They were too good together.

He'd taken her breath away the moment she'd first set eyes on him. She experienced the same reaction when she stood at the back of the chapel sanctuary, saw him standing at the altar, looking so handsome in his tux.

Her prince.

The love of her life.

They'd scaled some challenges through their whirlwind romance and had come out stronger on the other side of those thorn-covered walls.

Now here they were making the ultimate commitment in front of God, family and friends. Today they'd put aside their differences. She'd even told Ben he could invite Keaton Whitfield on the stipulation that Keaton would blend into the background and steer clear of her mother, Charlotte.

After giving the situation some time and space, she had realized that since Keaton probably was her brother, she'd eventually want to get to know him. Inviting him to the wedding was a way to test the waters. However she had made Ben promise that there would not be any surprises or family drama caused by his stirring the pot. She'd also asked him to relay the message to Keaton and tell him that she didn't want to hear a word about "the others" until after the wedding. The two of them could talk about things as soon as she returned from her honeymoon. But not before.

She wondered if the stipulation might inspire Keaton to turn down the invitation, but as she stood there, waiting for her sister Rachel, who had persevered in claiming the matron-of-honor job, to make her way down the aisle and take her place at the altar, Zoe spied Keaton sitting in the very back row, blending in, just as she had asked.

He smiled at her and nodded. Zoe offered a tentative smile before glancing at her father to see if he realized Keaton was there. Actually she didn't know if her father even knew about Keaton. Because just as she was keeping her dad's secret—at least until after her honeymoon—she hadn't said anything to her father about Ben locating Keaton Whitfield.

As the harpist transitioned from "Pachelbel's Canon" into the traditional "Wedding March," Zoe exiled all thoughts of family drama. She'd waited so long for this day and had almost let family issues cost her the love of her life. But with Joaquin's love and support and a little time, she was able to put everything into perspective.

And here she was.

And there was Joaquin waiting for her, just as he'd promised.

She floated down the aisle on her father's arm, feeling like Cinderella in her dream dress—a ball gown fit for a princess. The chapel was lit by hundreds of white candles and decorated to perfection with white and pale pink roses, peonies, lilies and cymbidium orchids interwoven with smilax garland and variegated ivy.

It looked like a wonderland.

When she and her father reached the altar, the minister asked, "Who gives this woman in marriage?"

Her father answered in a proud voice, "Her mother and I do."

As he lifted her veil, kissed her cheek and put her hand in Joaquin's, she realized she was no longer daddy's little girl, and that was okay. She was about to marry the love of her life and become his wife.

The ceremony went by in a romantic blur.

What she remembered best was when she and Joaquin had promised to love and protect each other for the rest of their lives.

And, of course, there was that kiss.

Oh, that toe-curling kiss.

When the minister pronounced them Mr. and Mrs. Joaquin Mendoza, their friends and family had broken into a round of applause that drowned out the harpist's recessional, but the sound of them clapping was the most beautiful music Zoe had ever heard.

A short while later, after taking pictures with family and the bridal party—they'd even gotten a picture of Orlando and Esteban with their arms around each other's shoulders, beaming at the camera—she and Joaquin made their way to the reception at the Robinson estate.

The wedding planner had erected a large white tent with dozens of linen-covered tables around the parquet dance floor. From its position on the lawn, the tent had a stunning view of Lake Austin.

As the bandleader introduced Zoe and Joaquin, they took to the floor and had their very first dance as man and wife. As Joaquin led her around the floor, Zoe saw her father talking to Keaton Whitfield. If she weren't so happy, she might have wondered what they were talking about, but the funny thing was, it really didn't bother her. It was just as well because the next time she looked, they were gone.

That was fine, too. Because she had more important things to focus on: her wedding night. No matter what her father said to Keaton or who her family turned out to be—Robinson or Fortune—she had just married her soul mate; she was Joaquin Mendoza's wife. They were a family now and that was all she needed to be happy.

Later that night, a Rolls-Royce whisked Joaquin and Zoe, who was still in her wedding gown, away from the reception to the Driskill for their wedding night.

They'd sent their luggage to the hotel ahead of their arrival, and early the next morning they would catch a flight to Paris, but right now, it was just the two of them. They had the entire glorious night ahead of them.

Giddy nervousness danced in Zoe's stomach as Joa-

quin unlocked the door to the Yellow Rose Bridal Suite.
He lifted her into his arms with a decisive sweep and
kissed her soundly, a preview of what was to come. It
was a good thing he finally carried her over the marble
threshold and nudged the door shut with his hip, because for a crazy moment, Zoe'd felt the urge to have
him right there in the hallway.

Well, not really, but that was how much she wanted
him.

With one last kiss, he set her down, but their bodies remained flush against one other, arms entangled,
as they stood in the middle of the suite's living room.
Everything about him—his touch, his taste, his scent—
was so familiar tonight. It was like a touchstone an-
choring her in the here and now; yet, at the same time,
everything seemed brand-new. It was invigorating and
it hit her soul in a way that rendered her weak in the
knees.

Joaquin pulled away just enough to murmur, "Hold
that thought. We need some champagne."

Zoe quirked a brow. "There's only one thing I
want right now." Playfully, she nipped at his bottom
lip. "Maybe we should save the champagne for later. I
have a feeling we're going to be extra thirsty."

His forehead was pressed against hers. The way he
looked at her with those dark, dark eyes melted her
insides. "Pace yourself, my love." He kissed her again
and the passion of it ran contrary to his suggestion to
take things slowly. "In a moment I'm going to love
you into incoherence. We should probably enjoy the
champagne now."

His promise had desire spiraling through her again.
As she watched her handsome husband open the cham-

pagne, his strong hands gently coaxing the cork from the bottle of Krug Grande Cuvée, she couldn't help but anticipate the feel of those hands on her body. Her skin prickled with intense longing, and heat pooled in her most intimate places.

She didn't quite know what to do with herself. So she walked over to the bedroom to have a look. It was decorated in cream and pale yellow. Tiffany lamps graced marble-topped nightstands. But it was the romantic canopy bed in the center of the magnificent room that made Zoe sigh. Draped in yards of sheer fabric swagged and tied to the bedposts by tassels that looked as if they were made of spun gold, her wedding bed was perfect.

Almost as perfect as her husband.

Joaquin Mendoza may have been her last first kiss, her prince who never had been a frog, but he would be her one and only love. She would give herself to him right here in this bed.

This was forever.

It was worth the wait. *He* was worth the wait. She knew without a doubt that he felt the same way, too. He'd proved it by his actions so they could have this… this first night together—this first time together. It would be heaven. She already knew.

She'd loved him from the depths of her soul the moment she'd first seen him. He'd been so patient, waiting for her so they could have this fairy-tale night. The wedding had been a dream come true. Now it was just the two of them, alone at last. To make their wedding night as magical as possible, she'd started birth control pills a few days after Joaquin proposed. The doctor had assured her that they would be protected after the first week. She was eager to start a family with Joaquin, but they wanted some time together as a couple first.

She sensed her husband behind her and turned. He handed her a flute of champagne. They clinked glasses, but only managed a couple sips before they were in each other's arms again.

Liquid spilled, glasses were forgotten and a moment later, they were tangled up again and he had taken possession of her body. That was good because nothing mattered but being joined together. "Make love to me, Joaquin."

They made short work of ridding themselves of fabric barriers. Finally, nothing stood between them. He eased her onto the bed. Smoothing a lock of hair off her forehead, he searched her eyes. Radiating love, he looked so earnest as he gazed deep into her eyes, asking the unspoken question.

Yes, I'm ready.

She answered him with a kiss.

They took their time exploring each other, getting to know each other's most intimate places. Joaquin's deft hands touched her with such love that she wanted to cry out from the ecstasy of it. Finally, when she was ready, he claimed her with one slow, gentle push. It didn't hurt. In fact, it was as if something that had been missing in her had finally clicked into place, making her whole for the first time in her life.

Joaquin feathered kisses over her lips and whispered gentle words of love as he slowly pulled out and tenderly thrust into her again. Instinctively, she matched his rhythm. Together, their bodies created magic. Finally, ecstasy, the likes of which she'd never dreamed possible, seized her body and rippled through her, lifting her to such an exquisite peak before they went over the edge together.

She was sure she would never be the same again.

Of course not. She was in love and forever changed in the best possible way.

As they lay there together, sweaty and spent, she relished the warmth of his solid body. He shifted to his left elbow and gazed at her with such reverence. "Zoe Mendoza, I love you."

As she reached up and brushed a wayward lock of dark hair off his forehead, a deep peace filled her entire being. "I love you, too."

In that perfect moment, she gave silent thanks to the heavens for leading her to her very own handsome prince.

* * * * *

MILLS & BOON®

Cherish™

EXPERIENCE THE ULTIMATE RUSH OF FALLING IN LOVE

A sneak peek at next month's titles...

In stores from 5th May 2016:

- **A Baby to Save Their Marriage** – Scarlet Wilson *and* **Wed by Fortune** – Judy Duarte
- **The Greek's Nine-Month Surprise** – Jennifer Faye *and* **Having the Rancher's Baby** – Cathy McDavid

In stores from 19th May 2016:

- **Stranded with Her Rescuer** – Nikki Logan *and* **His Destiny Bride** – Christyne Butler
- **Expecting the Fellani Heir** – Lucy Gordon *and* **High Country Baby** – Joanna Sims

---

Available at WHSmith, Tesco, Asda, Eason, Amazon and Apple

Just can't wait?
Buy our books online a month before they hit the shops!
visit www.millsandboon.co.uk

These books are also available in eBook format!

MILLS & BOON®

Mills & Boon have been at the heart of romance since 1908… and while the fashions may have changed, one thing remains the same: from pulse-pounding passion to the gentlest caress, we're always known how to bring romance alive.

Now, we're delighted to present you with these irresistible illustrations, inspired by the vintage glamour of our covers. So indulge your wildest dreams and unleash your imagination as we present the most iconic Mills & Boon moments of the last century.

Visit **www.millsandboon.co.uk/ArtofRomance** to order yours!

MILLS & BOON®

Why shop at millsandboon.co.uk?

Each year, thousands of romance readers find their perfect read at millsandboon.co.uk. That's because we're passionate about bringing you the very best romantic fiction. Here are some of the advantages of shopping at www.millsandboon.co.uk:

* **Get new books first**—you'll be able to buy your favourite books one month before they hit the shops

* **Get exclusive discounts**—you'll also be able to buy our specially created monthly collections, with up to 50% off the RRP

* **Find your favourite authors**—latest news, interviews and new releases for all your favourite authors and series on our website, plus ideas for what to try next

* **Join in**—once you've bought your favourite books, don't forget to register with us to rate, review and join in the discussions

Visit **www.millsandboon.co.uk**
for all this and more today!